Legion Surgeon – Beginner's Luck

Joseph LoCicero, III

To my wife for her perpetual support

Table of Contents

Prologue

It is the spring of 58 BCE or the year of the Consulship of Piso and Gabinius as they call it. Rome is at peace. These are the waning years of the Roman Republic shortly before the establishment of the Roman Empire. Gaius Julius Caesar, a former Consul of Rome, is currently the Proconsul or Governor of Transalpine Gaul, roughly the area of Provence, France. Over the next several years, Rome will establish its dominance and influence over nearly all of Western Europe.

During this glorious period, life is good for Roman citizens. They shop for the best goods and consume the best foods from the Mediterranean rim. They enjoy great culture and can choose great entertainment – anything from Greek and Roman plays to gladiator fights. The citizens are quite religious, ruled by gods they personally select for their family. Career choices are vast, but influenced by family tradition. They own slaves from around the empire, many of whom are well educated and very sophisticated. Medicine is based on a number of competing theories, but physicians are abundant. Roman surgeons most often learn at the side of another practicing surgeon, but the best learn their craft in the military.

By contrast, the Helvetians in present day Switzerland are considered barbarians. The few known facts about them are recorded by their Roman conquerers. Their religion, guided by Druids, is based on Nature. They live off of the land. Their career choices are limited to being either farmers or fighters. They frequently war against their neighbors, usually to acquire more land for their growing tribes. Chieftains who control their lives are discontent and ambitious.

Roman conquest of Europe begins when Caesar learns of the Helvetian Confederation's plan to migrate across Gaul to the Atlantic. He uses this excuse to raise two new legions to complement three seasoned legions from L'Aquila, east of Rome in what they call Italy. These five legions will meet Caesar's elite Tenth legion in the Province to chase the Helvetians and crush the migration. Afterwards, he will defeat and expel the Germans from Gaul. By the end of the campaign of 58 BCE, Rome will control roughly one-third of Gaul.

Chapter 1: Conscription

It was a day of firsts. Lucius, the oldest surviving son of the Calidius family, had every reason to be excited. That day, he turned twenty. It was the first day no one would call him a teenager. He had just finished four years learning the art of Medicine at the side of Theodosius, the physician to the Patrician families of Canino and his family's slave. That day, the venerable medic deemed Lucius ready to be an independent healer. On rounds, he was no longer addressed as young Calidius, but as Physician, the first in his family. Those events made him proud and exhilarated, but what energized him most was the task that lay ahead of him. That day, he would make his first cut into the human chest.

Lucius had grown into a handsome Roman. From his father, he inherited his muscular build, his thin straight nose, and his sharp mind. From his mother, he inherited his black hair, his penetrating dark brown eyes, and his incredible dexterity. He was average height for an Etruscan, but had a long stride. Theodosius, hobbled by old age and afflictions of the bones, held Lucius' arm trying to slow the pace of their rounds.

That day, house calls went lightning fast. Lucius was the first to examine the patients and make the therapeutic decisions. He performed so well that Theodosius had little to add to Lucius' assessments and treatments. When they exited the last villa, it was still morning and they had seen all of their patients, except for one. They headed home to cure the family chef.

The pair entered the Villa Romanus, the family estate, and went directly to the slave quarters. In one of the small front bedrooms was their patient, Basilius, the family's chief cook of many years. He and Theodosius were enslaved when the Romans defeated the Greeks at Cabira. Lucius' father, then a young legion officer, collected them and brought them home. Basilius kept the family well fed with exotic dishes that were the envy of all the citizens of their little town. Although he was a great chef, he had never gained weight the way many cooks did. He was proud that he had maintained his trim, muscular physic. However, at that point in his illness, he was emaciated, disabled, and confined to his quarters.

Lucius sat down next to the patient and stared at the bulging chest mass. His heart pounded. One moment, he wished his father, Senator Titus Calidius Romanus, was there to admire his surgical prowess, the next, he hoped Papa was nowhere near the slave quarters. He took a deep breath and pointed at the bulging mass.

"Right here," he declared.

"Are you sure?"

"Absolutely!"

"Well, you are not quite right, Lucius," said Theodosius. "Try it again. Remember, this is an empyema, not just any old boil on the back."

"Yes, I know," replied Lucius. "It is a collection of pus trapped between the lung and ribs. The patient can't cough out the pus, so it must drain out of the side."

"Correct. We can help it drain by cutting the chest, but we must choose precisely when the abscess is ripe and we must cut the ideal spot."

"Yes, I understand."

"Remember, if we cut the chest for any other condition, we could cause lung collapse and the patient might die. Then, in the eyes of Society, we would be murderers."

Lucius began to feel less sure of himself. He thought for certain he had it right. He had watched Theodosius do the same operation before and he believed he had mimicked the maneuvers perfectly. He did not want to screw up his first operation, so he examined the man again.

Basilius was in obvious pain, bent over toward the side of the empyema. His racking cough produced nothing, yet he was clearly deathly ill. He had contracted the disease in late winter, along with a great number of Etrucia's citizens and slaves. The epidemic spread rapidly to both young and old in less than a fortnight. Symptoms began with a high fever, nasal congestion, painful sore throat, and cough. Within days, the disease dropped into the chest and was associated with pleuritic chest pain and severe shortness of breath. Many died within days, including Lucius' recently betrothed, Acca Camilia Restita.

Those who survived, languished for weeks with a viscous pneumonia. They coughed up massive amounts of thick yellow and green phlegm. Some developed empyema like Basilius. Theodosius had cut the empyemas with surprising success, only losing two of twenty. Basilius was the last survivor with an undrained empyema. For Lucius, Basilius represented the only chance he would have that season to make a righteous cut into the chest.

When the outbreak began, Lucius pleaded with his father to be allowed to accompany Theodosius as he visited the citizens' homes that winter. His father, who had reluctantly allowed him to study Medicine, granted permission, but prohibited him from having contact with the infirm of the epidemic lest the disease jump to him and spread to the Calidius household. He could only observe the old physician examining and treating the sick.

Theodosius was always kind and spoke in hushed dulcet tones with the patient and the family. He began each session with a request for the family to pray and make offerings to the family's personal gods and to Aesculapius, the god of healing. He also prayed, asking Aesculapius to give him the necessary strength and knowledge to make the right diagnosis and to allow healing powers to flow through his touch. After these preliminaries, he interviewed the infirm, listening to every symptom and complaint. He paid particular attention to the sequence of events. He would ponder the facts, explaining to Lucius that he compared them to the vast knowledge he obtained from his schooling in the ways of Hippocrates and to his own experience gained through many years of healing.

After a ceremonial inspection of the body, Theodosius would place his hands on the patient beginning in a part far from the affected area. This, he told Lucius, caused the least pain and suffering to the patient. He gently and reverently touched every part. When he examined the torso, he would place his ear against the skin to allow the body's organs to talk to him. When he finally examined the affected area, he inspected it first, then gently touched it feeling for any deviations from normal. Examinations always concluded with a careful inspection of the patient's excretions to assess the four humors. Only after this would he speak to Lucius summarizing the patient's story, enumerating the abnormalities he discovered during his observation of the body, and describing the balance of humors. He would conclude by announcing to all his diagnosis and his opinion of the prognosis, then he would prescribe a treatment. Sadly that winter, the conclusions were always the same. The disease was pneumonia. He would quote the Hippocratic aphorism, "Pneumonia coming on pleurisy is bad." As always, the prescriptive was oxymel.

"Young Calidius, a flask of oxymel, please."

Theodosius firmly believed that the best way to learn about medications was to make them. Lucius made countless batches of oxymel that winter. He mixed one part vinegar, one part water, and two parts honey in a pot, then he simmered the mixture, slowly reducing it to a third of its original volume. While boiling down, the developing oxymel produced a frothy scum. Lucius had to stand over the pot and remove the froth as it rose to the surface. The vapors made him sick for hours afterwards. Once the liquid was reduced to goo, he had to bottle it in small flasks to be handed to each patient. Because of the gravity of the epidemic, Theodosius had instructed him to make massive quantities. Toward the end of the epidemic, he had used every available vessel he could find and still needed more vessels for the disgusting glop. Although he knew it might bring bad luck, he swiped all the flasks left at the altar of Salus, the family's primary goddess, whose festival they had just celebrated. Still needing more, he decided to plead with his prissy little sister Calidia to relinquish her perfume flasks.

"You want me to do what?"

"Donate your perfume flasks to fight this epidemic."

"You are insane! Why would I ever do such a thing?"

"Well, Cali, you know this is for a just cause."

"Cause? Whose cause? We are not ill."

"No, but some of the best families in the region are afflicted, even your friend Flora."

"I don't care. Besides, how do you know about Flora? You never liked her before. We haven't even visited her family in months."

"I found out when Theodosius and I attended to Flora's Pater, Vibius Flavius."

Calidia was twelve years old, but looked younger. Her baby fat made her look ridiculous in her bright green chiton. She was very self conscious about her appearance and tried to act sophisticated like her older sisters. She held her chin up high and looked down her nose to a point near Lucius. She would not look directly at him, as though she was talking to a slave. She swung her skirt as she turned and walked slowly away from him.

"Why do you want to follow that gnarled up old Greek? He's so creepy and spooky with a potion for everything. He pries into people's deepest private matters. He even smells and tastes urine and merda. Eeeww! I get sick just thinking about it." Calidia shuttered and gagged.

"Well, I want to be a physician to help our citizens stay healthy and live long lives."

Calidia spun back around and slowly paced back toward Lucius.

"I can't believe you won't follow in Papa's footsteps. After our poor dear brother Faustus was yanked from his horse and killed by those cursed Armenians, we all thought you would take his place in the legion. Maybe someday, you might even go to Roma as a decorated hero and assume a place of honor in the Forum. Instead, you choose to be a low class physician and I have to withstand the ridicule of my friends."

"You know Papa has given me permission to pursue my true passion."

"Yeah, right! After you told him what you wanted to do, Papa was angry for months. I thought he was going to turn you into a eunuch. He only relented when he realized you were a worthless dog who could never be a real legionnaire."

"Okay, okay. I admit I'm a dog, but I still need your flasks."

"What are you going to do for me? I will have to waste my precious perfumed oils. Uncle Nanius bought those in Iberia especially for me." Calidia regally paraded around as she spoke.

"How about you donate them out of concern for your fellow citizens?"

"Forget it. How about you buy me some more?"

"We need every flask we can get right now."

"Okay, then pay me for them."

"How much do you want?"

"They are precious to me. Uncle Nanius goes to Iberia only twice a year. It will be harvest time before I can get replacements, so it will cost you dearly. I want a Quadrans for each."

"A Quadrans? You have ten flasks! That's a fortune!"

"How do you know how many I have? Were you snooping in the women's chambers? I swear, I'll tell Papa!"

"No, I wasn't in the women's chambers.   I asked Calista, your handmaiden."

"Well, you're right, I do have ten flasks. So, that would be ten Quadrans."

"But, all I have are two Asses," he said showing her two gnarled and heavily etched bronze coins.

"I'm looking at one big asinine fool right now!" Calidia put her hand to her mouth and tittered, then she turned around to face Lucius and struck a regal pose.

"You always lost to Valeria and Serenilla, now you are going to lose to me."

"Valeria and Serenilla are a lot older than you. Besides, they're married. They're not here to help you."

"I don't need their help. I can make an ass out of you all by myself. I'll take your two Asses as downpayment." She grabbed them from his hand and mocked him in a singsong voice.

"Now you owe me twice as much! I expect payment by the harvest festival of Ops."

"Where am I going to get twenty Quadrans this summer?"

"That's your problem, you miserable dog!" Calidia spun around and folded her arms holding her head up high.

"Now take them and just go away, you beast!"

"Thank you," Lucius said with a smirk, then added, "I didn't lose to Valeria and Serenilla, I just let them win."

He entered Calidia's chamber, grabbed the flasks, and slunk out. He felt momentary guilt as he poured the foreign essences on the ground, but as he filled the flasks with the acrid paste, he vowed he would find a way to make his sister understand how important his work really was.

Lucius reached in his sack, fumbled for a flask, and handed it to Theodosius. The old physician immediately dispensed some to the patient with the instructions to chase it with diluted sweet wine.

"You should take this between meals since it induces coughing spasms," he would command.

Before leaving, if the patient needed to have his humors adjusted, Theodosius would also prescribe emetics and purgatives, which Lucius would dispense.

"I promise to return in a few weeks to check on your recovery and to see if you need any additional medications," he would say, reassuring the patient and family with solemnity, but he told Lucius it was to evaluate for signs of dropsy or the development of empyema.

For those who developed the dreaded empyema, Theodosius directed Lucius to produce a second, more potent medication. For this, he boiled squill bulbs in water until they were soft to the touch. Then, he discarded the soggy bulb and into the liquid mixed pounded almonds and roasted cumin and white sesame seeds. The electuary had an exotic odor, but was acrid to taste. He blended the mash with honey making a very gooey paste, which could be mixed with either oxymel or hot white poppy tea.

Like the other infirm that year, Basilius' illness began with raging fever, lethargy and miserable body aches, particularly in the articulations. Unlike the majority, his fever continued unabated until the evening of the third day when he became delirious. His Latin, which had never been good, eluded him. He babbled in a strange dialect of Greek calling on his long dead mother and father. He went on and on about a bad olive harvest. During the evening examination by Theodosius, he launched into a one sided conversation with an imaginary woman. Whatever he said brought first a smile, then a frown to Theodosius' face. Though he refused to translate, Lucius had the distinct impression that the woman was the physician's sister and the actions Basilius described were not honorable. Theodosius wiped away his momentary revulsion and quickly finished his exam. He instructed the servants to bathe Basilius. The cold water bath immediately brought down his fever and stopped the hallucinations. In the meantime, Lucius was dispatched to make more oxymel.

The illness dragged on for weeks with spiking fevers followed by frightening shortness of breath. It seemed as though each breath would be his last. He lost weight, not from the cupping to remove bad humors and not from the purgatives Theodosius administered, but simply from his inability to take in sufficient nourishment due to incessant coughing. Theodosius did not have to induce vomiting to clear the humors because the wracking cough often caused Basilius to vomit.

With time, the pains in his side gradually worsened. His fevers came only at night. The sole liquid he drank was tea made from white poppies dispensed by Theodosius. The concoction would relieve his pain for at least a little while. He no longer had the stamina to cook and was relegated to intermittent supervision of the family's staff, who had little experience in the culinary arts. The vile meals they produced made the entire household surly.

While Lucius examined Basilius again, Senator Romanus stormed into the cook's bedroom.

"Why in the name of Jupiter are you letting my son practice on Basilius? I swear, Theo, if this turns out badly, I will have you crucified!"

"Hush Senator, you know you wouldn't do that. Be patient with Lucius. Just over four years ago, you allowed—"

"Reluctantly allowed," corrected the senator. He grumbled looking for something to throw or kick. Several years ago, his eldest son, Faustus, had been killed in the battle of Tigranocerta. He had hoped Lucius would take his place in the Roman cavalry, but it was clear Lucius had his heart set on Medicine. Now, he was beginning to regret his decision.

"—reluctantly allowed Lucius to choose this profession," continued

Theodosius in his smooth lugubrious monotone physician voice. "Since then, he has been at my side. He is a fast learner."

"If Lucius has been with you that long and learns so fast, why has he not done this procedure on someone else already?"

"Because he simply was not ready," replied Theodosius. "Becoming a good physician takes time. After considerable deliberation, I deem him ready now. Let Lucius perform the examination again without disturbance, otherwise he might get it wrong. I will be at his side directing him through the drainage. If it goes badly, don't blame him, blame me."

Titus swung around and pounded the door lintel, then turned back to Lucius.

"You better be perfect, because if you cause disaster, Charon will never carry you across the Styx." He stormed out muttering insults mixed with exaltations to the gods.

An uncomfortable silence followed. Lucius bowed his head. His ears still burned from the admonition. He desperately wanted to be a surgeon. He hoped he would prove to his father that he was worthy if he performed the operation correctly. Failure meant he could cause the death of a man who had become a beloved member of the family. Eventually, Theodosius broke the silence. He spoke in a subdued, but reassuring voice.

"All right Lucius, show me again. Remember Hippocrates' aphorism that we always should do good, or at least do no harm."

Lucius slowly lifted the left arm of Basilius so he would not cause any discomfort and instructed him to clasp his hands on his head. The entire left side of the chest was swollen. The color gradually went from yellow on the upper chest by the shoulder, to red, to deep purple. The purplish area was as big as Lucius' head and covered the lower edge of the chest cavity. The yellowish areas had the look and consistency of dough. Lucius could make indentations in the skin that stayed for a considerable time before filling in again. The bright red semicircle was painful and did not indent. The purplish region felt like a thin wine skin with a great deal of fluid underneath. He could make fluid waves when he poked it with his finger.

As he examined the purple bulge, he realized his mistake. The first time, the spot he had chosen was on the bottom of the bulge. He understood that the pus was coming through the chest wall and collecting underneath the altered skin in a puddle, just like the wine in a wineskin. If the patient was upright, the bulge sagged to the bottom. If he was lying down, the bulge would sag to the back. The pus probably was coming through a hole in the chest cage far above the biggest part of the bulge. If he cut the skin where it bulged, the hole through the ribs would be covered up by skin and the pus would stop draining before it was all removed. The empyema would reoccur within days. He decided to choose a spot closer to the middle of the purple area.

"Right here?" He looked quizzically at Theodosius.

"You tell me."

He was no longer self-assured, but he had to be decisive, if he was to be a surgeon. He affirmed to the old wizened physician his newly chosen spot.

"So?"

"So, the pus is not coming out of the mouth when he coughs. I believe the next step is to release the empyema to the outside."

"You believe?"

"Okay, I opine that we must release the pus."

"And how are we going to do that?"

"I will make an incision..." Lucius began timidly. He knew he sounded weak. He cleared his throat and started again.

"I will make an incision with the scalpel across the spot the width of my palm."

"Okay, but before we cut, what should we do?"

"Well, we should try to minimize his pain. We gave him three cups of triple strength white poppy tea. His pain is the least it has been in days."

"So we have relaxed and comforted the patient as best as we can?"

"I believe so. No, I know so."

"Well, I gave him another important drug," said Theodosius. "I made a decoction of three henbane roots which I instructed him to chew and swill with wine. Did you not notice his dilated pupils and lack of saliva and sweat?"

Lucius bowed his head in embarrassment.

"Oh, yes, of course. You are right. I should have paid more attention to the exam of the whole body. Now he is ready."

"Here is the scalpel."

He took the knife and looked at the big purple area. It seemed to have grown since he last looked at it. He was mesmerized by the bulge. He remained motionless. Basilius looked under his arm and stared directly at the son of his master.

"Just cut. If you don't, I'll grab the knife and do it myself."

"We're all waiting, Lucius," the physician said. "Be sure to cut deep and smoothly in one motion like you would a leg of lamb."

He clenched his teeth and put the blade against the skin.

Immediately, the chest exploded. Lucius sat transfixed as a geyser of creamy greenish-yellow liquid gushed onto his neck above the top of his tunic and ran down his chest and abdomen into his pubic hair. He felt the warm viscous liquid slide down his inner thighs and drip into his sandals. It caused Lucius to gag and shudder involuntarily. He felt nauseous. As the flow of pus tapered off, Basilius developed a massive coughing spasm. A second geyser of goo spewed onto his tunic.

Theodosius placed his hand over the ruptured skin. The hole was now as large as his fist.

"Step away, boy!" he shouted. "How many times have we talked about not to letting pus drain too rapidly or the patient will collapse and die!" After checking that Basilius was still alive, Theodosius regained his composure and spoke in his usual reassuring voice.

"At least we are lucky the pus is not mixed with blood and it is not too putrid. I will handle the rest. Go clean up."

Lucius stared at his front. The greenish-yellow cream was nearly everywhere. Theodosius said it was not too putrid, but to him it reeked. He looked down at the puddle of pus in which he stood. His feet and sandals were engulfed in the puddle. He tried to pick up his feet but his sandals were stuck to the floor. He slipped out of the sandals and left the slaves' quarters. He ran through the atrium and the peristylum heading for the pool. As he ran through the tepidarium, he threw off the sticky tunic and took a leap into the pool. Even in the fresh water from the stream that fed the pool, it was hard to separate himself from the glop.

As he concentrated on pulling the disgusting muck from his groin, his little brother, Marcus, ran out from the main house.

"Come on, hurry up!"

"Hurry up for what?"

"You need to get out of that pool, put on your tunic, and join me in the city center."

"What are you babbling about?"

"Proconsul Caesar has sent a decree. The Helvetians are planning to cross the Transalpine province. He is raising two new legions so that Roma can crush the enemy."

"So what does that have to do with me?"

"Papa didn't tell you?"

"Tell me what?"

"You and I are going together."

"You must be sick. Go see Theodosius."

"No, I'm serious."

"I can't. My tunic and my sandals are covered in pus."

"I'll get you a clean tunic and dry sandals. Then, let's talk to Papa."

Marcus returned just as Lucius was climbing out of the water. He was free of the pus but he still felt unclean. The acrid odor of the purulence would not leave his nose. He pulled on the dry tunic, slipped into the sandals, and followed his younger brother to the peristylum where their father was contemplating the statuary.

"Marcus tells me I am going to war with him. What in Tartarus is he talking about?" demanded Lucius. Senator Romanus turned to face his incredulous second son.

"We have been at peace for some years," his father said. He turned to face the statue of Mars.

"It is not in our nature to be at peace. We find excuses to go to war. Now, Caesar is headed to protect our borders. He is an ambitious man and it has been rumored in certain circles that his real goal is to annex all of Gaul."   The Paterfamilias began to walk slowly toward the vestibule. He continued to speak to Lucius as the boys followed.

"Caesar needs the support of the old Etruscan families to win approval for his ambitious venture. Our family has a long tradition of supporting Roma. We were one of the first in the region to do so at a time when many families were against Roman expansionism. That support has been of great benefit to us over the years and has allowed us to develop great influence in the old provinces. Last week when Caesar passed through Orvieto on his way to Roma, he met with a number of Etruscan senators, myself included. We entered into negotiations with the governor for favors in exchange for our backing. One item on my list concerned the military career of Marcus." He put his hand on Marcus' shoulder, but continued to address Lucius.

"Now would be an auspicious time to start a military career. You know how much your brother wants to be a soldier, but I still consider him to be too young. Under the right circumstances however, serving in the legion during a defensive action would be an ideal way to gain experience without too much risk. Caesar's plans are strategically sound with a high likelihood of success, but funding is critical and he is desperate to win unanimous approval from the government. So, in exchange for my support on the senate floor, he agreed to all of my terms, including accepting Marcus into the new Eleventh legion so long as you go as well."

"Papa, you know I hate fighting!" Lucius was furious.

"That's the other part of the deal.   You will be among the immunes assigned to the medics of the Eleventh. Caesar assures me that you will be able to continue your training with his surgeons and battle physicians. Even though I am still opposed to wasting your life in such a way, at least I know that you will get well trained by the best Roma has to offer, and you will have an opportunity to serve the Republic as well."

Lucius could feel his heart pounding out of his chest. In a twisted way, it was a blessing from Abundantia. He never felt the goddess had bestowed luck on him before. Maybe now, she was smiling down on him.

While they were talking, the servants quietly brought two packs filled as they had been instructed by Senator Romanus.   They deposited them in the vestibule. When Marcus spied them, he grabbed his bag and threw the other to Lucius, then ran through the portico.

"Hurry, we're going to miss muster!"

Lucius picked up his bag, but paused before leaving.

"Say good bye to everyone, Papa," he called, but his Paterfamilias had already retired to the gardens contemplating what Rome would be like that summer.

Chapter 2: Confederation

Aia's world unravelled at the Imbolc ceremony long before she ever met a Roman. That day should have been the happiest day of her young life. She was finally allowed her turn as the Maiden in the ceremony, although getting the honor was not without a fight.

Aia, the middle daughter of the Druid High Priest and Priestess of the Tigurini tribe, was a beautiful tall willowy young woman with soft hazel eyes, a long thin nose, full lips, and dark chestnut brown hair that flowed down her back to her waist. The older folk often commented how she bore an uncanny resemblance to her mother, Adiega at that age. Aia's older sister, Ouenitouta had mousy brown hair and was quite zaftig. Sina, her younger sister, had not developed into a woman yet and still looked like a chubby little doll.

For the past two years, Aia had pleaded with her mother to allow her to be the Maiden. Each year, Adiega would reluctantly consent, but some incident would cause her to renege. First, it was Aia's refusal to help with preparations, then it was her poor performance in her sacred studies. Instead, Ouenitouta continued to portray the Maiden, even though she was married. Aia was convinced that her mother would pass over her for Sina.

That year, the sticking point was Aia's not so secret love, Lugurix. He was the biggest and strongest of the young warriors. Following completion of his training, he was in line to be a lieutenant in the Chieftain's elite guards.

Aia dreamed of Lugurix portraying the Dark Lord opposite her at the ceremony. Adiega did not approve of Lugurix, even though he was of noble blood. He was a warrior by birth and they were Druids. Adiega firmly believed that the two should never mix. The mother-daughter relationship, icy for months, came to a head while they made preparations for the ceremony.

"Tarbeisú should be your Dark Lord in the ceremony," Adiega announced. "He would make a good husband."

"Why, Màthair? Why should I ever consider that creep?" Aia moaned. "We have nothing in common!"

"You have more in common with Tarbeisú than you do with that warrior," her mother replied. "Besides, warriors have a habit of getting themselves killed. I don't want you to feel the pain and disgrace of being a young widow."

Ouenitouta sighed.

"I married a Druid at Màthair's wish."

"Oueni!" Aia exclaimed. "You told me you were in love with Frontú ever since you could walk." She turned to her mother.

"I don't love Tarbeisú. I don't even like him. I love Lugurix."

Sina wrinkled her nose.

"She has a point. Tarbeisú is a very sallow and melancholy fellow, and nothing like Aia."

Aia felt her face flushing.

"Besides, you gave permission to Toutios to marry outside of the Druids. Why can't I have the same privileges as my twin brother?"

"Yes," said Sina turning to her mother. "I'm really interested in your answer, Màthair. My turn will not be so far off."

"Oh, Sina, you have not even begun the journey into womanhood," Aia hissed.

"Shush you two!" admonished Ouenitouta.

Sina and Aia stared at one another for a while, then Sina folded her arms and spun around. Aia blew a lock of hair out of her eye and slowly turned back to the basket she was weaving, trying to act nonplused.

"With your father's blessing, Toutios was allowed to become a warrior at a time when our tribe needed every able-bodied man. He had to break his Druidic training. That cannot be reversed now. It seemed only right that his wife, when he chooses one, should be from outside of the Druids."

"You know, Màthair," said Ouenitouta. "I have a unique perspective on this since Frontú and Lugurix are best friends. Frontú tells me that Lugurix loves Aia. Doesn't that count for something?"

The three girls faced their mother, all hoping she would answer from the heart rather than upholding some ridiculous tradition. Besides, the Tigurini tribe had been at peace for over ten years and there were no prospects for war. During that time, many traditions had changed and even some rigid rules had been relaxed.

Aia fingered the charm that hung from her leather necklace. The charm, a Druid serpent egg was older than anyone in her tribe knew. It was a dark green stone harvested from the sacred mountains. A Druid master artisan had carved the stone into an egg shape and engraved the entire surface with interconnecting spirals. Adiega had a similar serpent egg. The two charms were always worn by the current and the next High Priestess. Aia received hers from her grandmother after she completed her first twelve years of Druidic training. She was instructed never to remove it. It was more than just a symbol of her exalted position. It had mystical powers that channeled energy from the Mother Goddess to the High Priestess. Aia hoped she could send some of the energy to her mother to influence her decision.

Adiega looked at Aia, so beautiful, yet so willful. She thought about herself. She had been rather willful at that age, but much more respectful of tradition. She never would have crossed her mother. Aia shared all the passion of her twin brother, yet in many ways, she still had the innocence of a child. She needed the protection and structure of the Druidic life. It would be easier if she married within the clan where Adiega could keep a watchful eye on her, but without love, she knew Aia would live in misery. Finally, after what seemed like an eternity, she replied.

"You know, I must discuss this with your father. He has the final say."

The girls grabbed each other and squealed in unison. Aia's eyes grew wide and wet.

Adiega shook a bony finger at Aia.

"Mind you, child, this is just for Imbolc. Let's see if you and that boy can act civilly for a day." Immediately, she got an enthusiastic nod of agreement from her second daughter. At that point, Adiega thought it best to take her leave and prepare supper.

The girls waited until their mother was well out of earshot, then hugged each other. Aia was overwhelmed. The sisters supported her until she could compose herself, then they all ran out into the snow to find Lugurix.

Aia's family home was situated in the center of the only Tigurini tribal village. It was located on the western edge of a long valley at the base of the Alps. Since her parents were the Druid High Priest and Priestess, their home was next to the Great Hall used for meetings and ceremonies.

Their home was just like all the other village houses. It was constructed of large rough cut timber beams and built over a short stone storage basement plastered inside with mud. The house was a two-story structure with a simple thatched roof over log rafters. Each floor was a single multipurpose room measuring about eight by ten meters with one window on each wall of the house. The main entrance led into the kitchen on the first floor. That floor also contained the eating area and the parlor. Upstairs was the sleeping quarters for everyone. Only a flimsy partition separated her parents from the space she shared with Sina and Ouenitouta. When Ouenitouta got married and moved to the countryside, Aia successfully negotiated a partition between Sina and herself. Although Aia got the larger space, Sina got the window.

The Great Hall was of similar construction. It stood two stories high, but had only one floor measuring twenty by forty meters. With the high roof, it seemed cavernous inside. The Great Hall, the home of the High Priest, and the homes of the chieftain and other dignitaries faced a small town square used primarily for outdoor ceremonies. Several hundred homes of the other villagers spread out behind the homes of the dignitaries. Tribe members, who were mainly farmers, lived on little plots of land scattered throughout the countryside. The village center was located to the east of a small river that ran freely throughout the year, even in the coldest winter.

The three girls crossed the open meeting area and headed north locating Lugurix with the other young warriors chopping wood for the evening fire. He was unmistakable. He towered over the other young men. He was all muscle and clearly the strongest among his peers. He was outgoing and always had a smile for everyone. He had light brown eyes, dark brown hair, and sported a full beard, which looked a little out of place on his youthful face.

Lugurix caught a glimpse of the girls as they approached and decided to give them a little show. He took off his coat and wiped his chiseled face on his sleeve. He stood tall and flexed his muscles. He pretended he did not know they were approaching. The girls stopped and watched him for a moment, then Sina kicked her sister.

"Ask him, Aia!" she whispered loudly.

Ouenitouta gave her a little shove. Aia took a hesitant step forward. Her two sisters pushed her again almost knocking her over. Lugurix was amused at the commotion.

"Oh, hello," he said as he pretended to notice them for the first time. "How are you beauties today?"

"Fine, thank you for asking," replied Sina. She looked at Ouenitouta.

"Aia has something she wants to ask you," said Oueni. There was an embarrassing pause. Then she poked her sister.

"Get it out, Aia," she coaxed.

Aia clasped her hands in front down low and swayed back and forth. She stared at Lugurix's feet.

"My mother, the High Priestess has allowed me to ask if you would be willing to portray the Dark Lord for Imbolc this year. I will be your Maiden." She continued swaying while slowly looking up toward his face. She gazed into his eyes. She felt breathless and lightheaded.

Lugurix looked at Aia's face, which was just visible under her hooded coat. Her eyes were dreamy and pleading, like a little doe. He could not help smiling at the whole production.

"Girls are so dramatic," he thought.

"You better say yes, or I'll get your best friend to make you," said Ouenitouta. This pulled Lugurix back to reality.

"Well, if your mother is okay with this, I would be honored to be in the ritual." He bowed as he replied.

Aia jumped up and down squealing for joy. When she realized what she was doing she was suddenly embarrassed. She retreated back behind her sisters.

"Thank you," she said curtly, then she turned and ran back home, her sisters following the clouds of snow she kicked up.

*   *   *

The days between Yule and Imbolc were filled with excitement for Aia. Lugurix was released from wood chopping duty to practice his part. Aia made him practice a proper stance. She demonstrated his steps and made him recite his lines until he could do it in his sleep.

After practice, they would go for long evening walks in the foothills near the fallow wheat and hay fields. Much of the time they just walked in silence. Aia would gather edelweiss and fashion a bouquet while Lugurix would dig out small rocks and launch them across the field.

One day as they approached the tree line, Aia took off running into the forest. Lugurix followed her as she darted from one tree to another. It reminded him of games they played as youngsters. He would be the wolf and the girls would be deer. Even though he was big for his age, the girls were quite strong and fast. His advantage was his stamina. Eventually, he would corner them and pretend to eat them. They would scream and giggle with pleasure.

Now, Lugurix was a man with warrior training. He easily outran and outsmarted Aia. He surprised her by jumping out into her path. She squeaked and backed up against one of the great chestnut trees. Lugurix stood over her with his arms against the tree. Aia's smile melted into that dreamy look she had given him on the day she asked him to participate in the Imbolc ritual.

They gazed at one another while they slowly caught their breath. Lugurix bent lower toward Aia's face while she stretched up to meet his. She closed her eyes. Lugurix kissed her tentatively on the lips. Aia threw her arms around him and passionately kissed him. When he held her around the waist, Aia pushed him back. He tried to embrace her again, but she slipped away and ran home leaving a very perplexed Lugurix alone at the tree.

The next day, the two practiced again as though nothing had happened. They talked and joked and shared family stories, but there were no more walks.

*   *   *

On the day of the Imbolc ritual, Lugurix spent the morning with the warriors before coming to the Great Hall. Ouenitouta and Sina spent the day preparing Aia. They stood in a small room at the back of the Great Hall where ceremonial paraphernalia was stored. Ouenitouta laced up the painted leather bodice over the white woolen gown. She combed out Aia's hair, which had grown even longer than at Yuletide and now hung down well below her waist. Sina attached to Aia's necklace a circle with a cross inside made of rushes. Ouenitouta gently placed a crown of mistletoe and edelweiss in Aia's hair making sure the mistletoe draped properly across her forehead. She adjusted the tails of the crown to lay directly in back as though they were part of her hair. She and Sina stood back to survey her.

Aia looked stunning outfitted as the Maiden. Her dark hair was a stark and beautiful contrast against the bright white gown and the pale white flowers and berries of the headdress. Although the wool dress clung to her, it was the leather bodice that added curves to her slender frame.

She stood just out of sight of the gathering while Sina peered around the door jamb. She could see everyone gathering into a circle with her parents, the High Priest and Priestess in the center. Lugurix stood in the shadows at the far corner of the hall. He was properly attired as the Dark Lord. As Aia had instructed, he wore the black robe with the hood over his head covering his face. All that could be seen was his beard, which he carefully groomed for the occasion.

The ritual began after sunset with her father, Drutos, intoning a greeting and setting the stage for the joining of the Dark Lord and the Maiden to begin the rebirth of the earth.

Come to us from the Earth's four corners
Soil and Air and Fire and Water
Bring your blessings upon our People

Then Adiega picked up the chant. That was Aia's cue to appear and move quietly into the circle. She walked through the door as the chant began.

Winter's spell is now passing
Buds will soon swell on the–

Adiega did not get to finish. Two warriors burst through the main entrance.

"Chief Bimmos has returned. He requests a council meeting immediately!" one of them announced. Then the two left as quickly as they had come.

The stunned crowd looked at one another.

Drutos shrugged and raised his hands in a gesture of frustration.

"We have been summoned. Sadly, our ritual must wait."

The circle disintegrated and the participants shuffled toward the door. Aia stood frozen to the spot with her mouth gaping. Adiega went to her devastated daughter and enveloped her in a motherly hug. Aia trembled and sobbed quietly into her mother's bosom. Her sisters joined in comforting her. The four women held one another until Drutos came over and placed his hand gently on Aia and Adiega.

"We must attend the council meeting," he said in as soothing a tone as he could. "Aia, I want you to join us. If this meeting does not justify disrupting such an important ritual, I want Bimmos to answer to you."

Aia looked up from her mother's caressing bosom, stared resolutely at him setting her jaw.

"Yes, Athair," was all she said.

As the celebrants dispersed, they were replaced in the Great Hall by members of the council. Aia had never been to a council meeting. They were rare events during her lifetime. Such meetings were held only in times of great distress or in times of war. The only meeting she could recall was held when she was only eight years old after a combination of war with a neighboring tribe and disease depleted their clan. The council decided to commit as many able-bodied boys as possible to the warrior class. Her parents had reluctantly sent her brother, Toutios for training. She and Toutios shared the tight bond of twins, but his strenuous combat training and her studies in the ways of the Druids left them little time together. Despite the distance, they often sensed each others' secret thoughts and feelings.

Aia stood beside her father clutching his arm as they watched Bimmos, the Chieftain, stride in with his staff. Along with the warriors was Ouillú. He was the Vergobretus, the most powerful man next to Bimmos himself. The Vergobretus acted as the Nation's judge and had power over the life and death of their people. He stood at the right of Bimmos. To Aia's surprise, Toutios stood to the left of Bimmos. He was the representative of the youth warriors and had accompanied the ambassadors at the most recent summit with the neighboring tribes. As they entered the room, she could sense a powerful anger deep within her brother. It would not be a good meeting.

"I bring you greetings from our brethren, the Helvetians, the Tulingi, the Rauraci and the Latobrigi," Bimmos began. "We had a very productive summit where we discussed with their leaders many important topics. Among them is the news that the tyrant Orgetorix is dead." He paused for effect. Murmurs arose from the council.

After the murmurs died down, he began to drone on for what seemed like an eternity describing the atrocities Orgetorix had committed during his attempts to seize control of all Helvetia to which their tribe belonged. Bimmos ended his little tutorial saying that the tyrant had committed suicide, although he suspected that he had been murdered.

During the dull speech, Drutos looked down at his daughter. She sat tall and straight. Her eyes were narrow and fixed on the Chieftain. Her teeth were clenched, and her grip tight on his arm. He was proud of her. Since she was a child, she had taken on the studies of the profession with zeal. She quickly learned all the ceremonies and songs, but when it came to the medicinal and ritualistic uses of herbs, she struggled. The tedium of learning the many facts bored her. He had to prompt her even that year. Despite her learning struggles, she was the bright flame among the young Druids of the next generation. His only regret was her relationship with Adiega. Mother and daughter rarely agreed. Since Aia flowered into womanhood, they seemed to fight constantly.

Aia elbowed him in the side and gave him a dirty look. He realized he was daydreaming and tried to refocus. He struggled to regain the thread of the discussion. He bent down next to his daughter.

"What did he say?" he asked.

"If you paid attention, you would know," Aia retorted and spun around to face their leader. She was becoming more curt with her father. She had seen him go from a spry and robust man to a pudgy and slow old man. He increasingly spent time daydreaming. He often lost track during chants and she cringed every time her mother had to prompt him. She wished she were older and could take over the duties as the High Priestess, but for now, she had to be an obedient daughter.

"We have been told," Bimmos continued, "that before he died, Orgetorix acquired horses and wagons for Helvetia to travel into new lands. The numbers are sufficient for the Rauraci and the Latobrigi tribes, as well as for our nation, if we wish. We all know our little valley barely supports our people. The new Helvetian leaders tell us of unoccupied lands in Gaul close to the sea where we can all have breathing room. They invite us to join into a new and magnificent confederation. They assure us that the Boii will join to make the Confederation of Helvetia stronger than any nation in Gaul. We will be able to seize the land for ourselves. Our plan is to travel past Geneva and through the northern edge of the Gaulish province of the despised the Roman Republic. This is the shortest and most direct route to our new land. We can complete this move before the end of summer if we leave immediately"

"I attended these discussions with Bimmos," said Ouillú the Vergobretus. "I have weighed the options and I concur with our leader. This is our best option to obtain lands that are better suited to us."

"I must agree"

Aia spun around in the direction of the voice. It was her mother. Her mouth dropped open.

"How can she want to abandon this beautiful land?" she thought.

Bimmos bowed to Adiega.

"I thank you for your support." He turned to Drutos. "Can we count on the support of all the Druids?"

Drutos thought for a moment, his face reddening. Then he stood up and faced the council.

"Our Chieftain brings us disturbing news and asks us to support a radical plan." His eyes welled up as he spoke.

"These lands have nurtured us through the ages. It is the land of our clan's birth. We neither know, nor care to know any other place. We were once a powerful nation when our great grandfathers defeated the dreaded Romans and made them our slaves. We have enjoyed tremendous freedom and gained the respect of our neighboring tribes. Over the years, foolish wars and disease shrunk our numbers and weakened our warriors. It has taken us more than a generation to rebuild our nation to a shadow of what we were." Before he continued, he surveyed the every member of the council.

"Our people want for nothing here. The rivers run fresh all year and nourish us and our crops. Forests of hemlock and laurel and cedar and willow provide us with magical medicines, and, when we need it, wood to build our homes and barns. We receive sufficient rain. Winter snows fall gently. They cover and protect our lands in darkness until the spring sun awakens them. The earth brings forth bounty every summer. Yet, you would have us forsake our earthly mother."

The speech took a lot out of the old man. Shaking, he called for Aia to support him. She jumped up with tears in her eyes and stood next to him. He put his arm around her shoulder and turned to face Bimmos. Before making his final statement he narrowed his eyes and stared at each of the leaders and warriors. All were silent.

"You seem to hold only contempt for our lands. You have stomped on our sacred rituals. Now, you ask us to make such a portentous decision in an instant, but I sense that you have already made the decision for us. Does our support really matter that much to you?"

As her father spoke, Aia was distracted by muffled noises beyond the doors of the Great Hall. She was uncertain of what was going on outside. She was curious, but she kept her attention focused on her father and their chieftain.

"You are as perceptive as ever, old sage," replied Bimmos. "Even as we conclude this council, our warriors are ensuring that we will all move to our new homes in Gaul." He gave an exaggerated bow and gestured toward the door.

"You are free to go."

When Bimmos gave the signal, the warriors threw open the doors of the Great Hall. Now, it was all too evident what was happening. In the square, there was mass confusion. Thick smoke blew into the hall. Villagers ran in every direction screaming for help. Mixed in with the crowd were warriors on horseback with torches.

Aia raced out into the melee. The little village she had called home all of her life was ablaze. Not a structure was left untouched. Warriors were chasing cows and sheep out of the barns and setting fire to the hay lofts. Several young warriors were stationed along the river bank with swords drawn preventing villagers from gathering water to extinguish the flames.

As she surveyed the destruction, a tall figure in the cloak of the Dark Lord approached her. He was carrying a torch. She could see the well groomed beard hanging out of the hood.

"Lugurix!" she screamed. "Why?"

"It is for the best, my darling. This is for the glory of all Tigurini! We will be a great and powerful nation again!"

She was ready to leap at him when her father grabbed her arm.

"Don't, my child," he said in a calm and resolute voice. Lugurix is only one of many warriors. It is Bimmos who has done this to us. We cannot fight such strength. Come, let us pray that everyone will be safe."

Aia yanked her arm away from her father, but stood her ground never taking her gaze off Lugurix. They stared at each other until Lugurix removed the cloak of the Dark Lord. He was in full armor. He threw the cloak to her.

"Take it," he said. "You will need it to keep warm tonight. In the morning, salvage what you can. I will see to it that your family has a decent wagon."

She let the cloak fall at her feet. She gave Lugurix the evil eye, then spit on his beard, spun around, and buried her head in her father's robe. Adiega picked up the cloak and joined her husband. She placed a comforting arm around her daughter, but felt a sharp pain in her side as Aia elbowed her with all her might.

"Get away from me, you witch!" she sobbed.

"Aia, please! I only want what is best for us. I had no idea our chieftain would do such a horrible thing."

"Whether you knew or not, how could you take me away from all that I know and love?" Aia pleaded. "This is my home. I love the valley and the mountains. The woodland creatures are my friends. How can I leave such a wonderful place?" She looked bleary eyed at her mother whose eyes matched hers.

"Please," Drutos said. "We have much to do. Now is not the time to be angry. We must come together and be strong for each other." He placed an arm around each gently caressing them. At the same time, he kept them apart while he guided them back home.

Chapter 3: Confusion

Lucius could barely keep up with his enthusiastic brother. His heavily packed sack cut into his shoulders with every step. Marcus, who was already as tall as Lucius, ran a hundred feet ahead splashing across the creek that coursed through the estate.

Of all the children of Titus Calidius Romanus, Marcus most lived up to the family name. Calidius meant fiery, lusty, eager, even rash. That was how his father described Marcus to his friends. That fire was reflected in his face. He easily flushed red whenever he became excited. He was mercurial, laughing one moment, crying the next, then picking a fight with anyone. His complexion was much fairer than Lucius and he had light brown eyes and hair. He was as muscular as Lucius and his demeanor was more suited to that of a soldier. Faustus never shared that intense passion. Romanus believed that may have played a role in his son's undoing at the hands of the inept Armenian forces.

On the other hand, Lucius was cut from a different cloth. He was quiet and thoughtful, even brooding. He favored his mother's family in temperament. Even though he was clearly the smartest of the Calidius children, he was athletic enough to hold his own against his brothers. He was most comfortable with the Greek slaves and learned a great deal from them and their collection of texts from the old empire. He particularly enjoyed studying the verses of Pythagoras and could recite them from memory as early as the age of four. He could calculate mathematical problems in his head with astounding accuracy. Although he was a quick study, he examined situations as though they were a puzzle and never made a decision without weighing all possibilities. His manual skills were well developed. His fine hand control allowed him to do intricate detail work. His sisters never could match his dexterity.

To his father, Lucius' worst trait was that he ran from conflict. He never picked a fight. If he was confronted, he tried reasoning with his opponent, usually to his detriment. For those reasons, the Paterfamilias had not forced him into the military. He allowed him to pursue a quieter profession.

The sun had reached its zenith and the open valley was unseasonably hot. Lucius was not prepared for the wall of heat. It was barely spring and already hotter than he could remember. He had been in the house dealing with the empyema from Tartarus. The villa was nestled between a line of trees and a creek in the shadow of a waterfall four times as high as the roof of the villa. That time of year, it was flowing fast and full from the melting snow of the far away mountains. It kept the entire dwelling cool, even on summer afternoons. The villa's pool was filled from the stream. The dip he took to separate himself from the disgusting pus had chilled him down and allowed him to recover from his shame and embarrassment. Already in the hot sun, he was sweating as he ran toward town. He wished he was still floating in the icy pool water.

The tiny town center was only a half mile from the creek just beyond the limits of the family estate. Most of the square was taken up by a two tiered fountain fed by the same mountain waters as the villa. Here, the town merchants and their animals could obtain water anytime they needed it. Already in the square were some twenty young men gathered around two soldiers. One was an infantry soldier standing at attention. Cradled in his right arm was a pilum with a sharp point that towered over the crowd. His belt held an impressive broad sword. The other soldier was an officer. Lucius had seen the uniform before when an honor guard came to escort the region's magistrates to Rome. He was probably a senior Tesserarius or guard commander. The Tesserarius was much older than the infantryman and quite stocky. He had a stern expression on his clean cut face. His arms, what could be seen of them outside of the armor, sported multiple scars.

It seemed odd, but Lucius and Marcus did not recognize any of those assembled. They were mostly farmers who worked the estates of the local families. As far as the boys could tell, they were the only sons of patricians. The reforms of General Gaius Marius thirty years before allowed non-citizens to become legionnaires with the possibility of achieving rights upon retirement. Lucius figured the farmers were looking for a better life for their families. The Tesserarius paced back and forth as he addressed the crowd.

"You will be joining the best fighting force in the history of the world. It will be your privilege to serve under Gaius Julius Caesar, the greatest commander I have seen in my career. Your mission will be to crush the barbarians who threaten our borders. When we are successful, Caesar has promised to be generous. For those of you who are faithful and perform well, you will be given great rewards. If you wish to join, you must travel down to the coastal town of Montalto di Castro. It's only ten miles from here. Tomorrow morning, the great legion supply train will arrive. You will see the Beneficiarius Classis, the quartermaster who will issue you some basic supplies. If you have a particular skill, be sure that you let him know. There is extra pay for certain professions."

"I wonder if we are in the right place," Marcus whispered to Lucius. "There must be another mustering area."

"When do we get uniforms?" someone yelled from the crowd.

"You don't get one! You are just Tirones until you prove yourselves. The usual time is six months. Under these special circumstances, you will need to be ready to face the barbarians in six weeks. You will get your remaining supplies in Placentia. So, if you want to serve Roma, you better get moving."

The crowd headed for the road leading southwest out of the town. As they cleared the square, Marcus approached the commander, Lucius silent at his side.

"Sir, is there another mustering area for the citizens? Where do the cavalry recruits go?"

The old commander let out a huge belly laugh.

"You are joking, right?"

"Well, I thought Papa had arranged—"

"Nobody arranged nothin, boy. You want to be in the legion? This is it. We're not recruiting cavalry here. We need infantry soldiers willing to run the barbarians through. Besides, we can't trust horses to Tirones like you."

"But—"

"But nothin, son. You want to make your mark as a soldier, you better get crackin'." Looks like the real legionnaires already left."

Marcus turned away, the commander's laughter ringing in his ears. Lucius tried to console his brother.

"Marcus, you know you don't have to do this."

"Of course I do! This is my fate. I know it. I just expected things to be a little different."

"Well, it won't get any easier."

Marcus brooded for a moment, then he brightened up.

"That's right, so let's get going!" He became enthusiastic again. He set his jaw and began to strut out of the square. Lucius, dumbfounded, fell in step behind his brother.

The road out of town was narrow and winding. Their little town was a good deal higher in altitude than the coast. They would have to descend more than six hundred feet over ten miles to get down to the little fishing village. Most of that drop occurred in the first third of the journey. They had made the trip many times before on vacations with the family.

Both Marcus and Lucius preferred to vacation on the lake, which was in the opposite direction. The distance to the lake was the same as to the sea, but the elevation was nearly the same as the town. The change in altitude along that journey was nearly imperceptible. The water of the lake was always cool and the shoreline interesting. It hid nests of turtles. As children, they hunted out the nests to harvest the eggs. Even Lucius' sisters, who hated leaving the luxurious surroundings of the villa, would delight in the egg hunts. They would proudly march back to the family's holiday dwelling with their quarry and present the eggs with great pomp to Basilius who did wonders with all foods. He would mix the eggs with salt and serve them with mushrooms freshly cooked in olive oil. The best eating came when they could corner a hare. Basilius would let Marcus break it's neck. Lucius would gut and skin the animal, then Basilius would braise the flesh until it was falling off of the bone mixing in chopped onions, olives and capers. Sometimes, if the children found fresh rosemary, he would stew the rabbit with onions and wine instead.

Those times seemed magical now. After the death of their older brother, Papa just rested and brooded while the children explored the craggy peninsula at Capodimonte. The view was spectacular from the summit of its little hills. They could see the mountains in the distance across the lake. If the water was calm, Papa would let them take a boat ride around the protected cove with one of the local fishermen. They were always kind to the children and gave them a portion of their catch for the family dinner. The children never knew that their Paterfamilias secretly paid the fishermen for their fish and their kindness.

On the other hand, the beaches of Montalto di Castro were hot year round. The land was flat with no good vantage points. The sea was endless with no mountains to view and daydream about. The sand was grayish black because it was mixed with volcanic pumice making it unbearably hot and impossible to walk on. Some of the pumice pieces were sharp enough to cut their feet. The estuary around the mouth of the little stream emptying into the sea was full of oozy mud at low tide. Although they could find many small creatures in the ooze, the smell was sometimes overpowering. Basilius would go to the docks and shop for the freshest seafood. He made wonderful tuna and sardine dishes, but there was little else to eat. Occasionally Basilius would vary the menu with mussels, but the children were not too fond of them. The creatures were black and smelly like the estuary.

With Marcus leading the way, Lucius negotiated the cut back trails. By the time the little trail straightened out, they were going directly into the sun as it moved lower in the afternoon sky. Neither of them were used to these conditions, because the family always traveled to the sea in the mornings with the sun at their back. They had to shield their faces and stop frequently for a drink from the stream that traveled next to the road.

Eventually, they arrived at the village, but it was long after the sun had set below the sea. They had a difficult time finding their way to the gathering of young men. There was only a sliver of moon. They followed the dull glow of a fire that had nearly burned out, but when they got there, no one was around it. They had to follow the sound of voices in the dark.   As they approached, the conversation seemed to get more animated. Some were shouting. By the time they reached the group, a few of the larger men had surrounded a youth. Marcus and Lucius could tell by his tunic that he was a citizen. In a flash, Marcus broke through the circle and stood next to the youth on the pumice sand.

"If you attack this citizen, you will have to go through me!" Marcus shouted.

"Stay out of this, dog. This is not your concern," said one of the tallest and obviously best built boys in the circle.

"Yeah, we don't want to rearrange two faces tonight," said another.

Marcus stood up as tall as he could and stared at the biggest man in the circle.

"Just try it!" he shouted.

In an instant, the circle collapsed on the two boys.   There were wild punches thrown in all directions.

After just a few moments of fighting, Lucius and a few of the onlookers started pulling bodies off and throwing them away from the melee.

"We're all here for the same purpose, and it's not this. Save your spunk for the Helvetians," said Lucius as he grabbed and launched boys away from the targeted combatants.

Finally, the only two left were the original youth and Marcus.

Lucius pulled them aside. Marcus obviously was worse off. His nose was bleeding and he already had facial bruising that surely would turn to black eyes by the morning. The other youth only had a few bruises on the head and abrasions from the substance that was a poor excuse for sand.

Lucius had Marcus pinch his nose and lean his head back to stem the hemorrhage. He reached in his pack hoping that Papa had instructed the staff to pack his sack with his medical supplies. Indeed, he found an unusually shaped jar and brought it out.   It contained a salve that his dearly departed mother had obtained when she was a child. The old woman, who sold it to her at the market, explained the unusual perfumed substance contained great healing properties. After his mother died, he had to fight Calidia for the salve. Luckily, his father sided with him. At the time, Calidia was too young for such a grown up prize. Romanus reasoned that she would just run through it in days, and ruled in favor of Lucius. He had used it only one other time before for a severe sunburn his little brother got from spending the whole day on the lake with the local fishermen.   The salve contained pine resin, mastic resin and moringa oil.   Theodosius made a similar ointment for open wounds, but his mother's salve seemed to have magical powers.

He opened it and the fragrance filled the air. Marcus protested.

"I don't want to smell like a girl."

"You want to heal and be ready for battle don't you?" asked Lucius.

Marcus finally relented and Lucius spread a thin layer over his abrasions. It was immediately calming.

Marcus slowly brought his head forward and removed his hand from his nose. He assessed his pugilistic partner. He looked quite young. He was skinny and very short, even for a Roman. He had dark eyes and straight black hair on his head, but practically nowhere else.

"So," Marcus said, "since I protected you from a serious beating, the least you can do is tell me a few things." He sounded oddly nasal.

"Like what?"

"Like your name, for starters."

"Quintus Pompillus."

"How old are you, anyway, Quintus?"

"I'm eighteen.   Yeah, I know I look like I'm only twelve, but I am old enough, trust me."

"Well, what did you do that got us in so much trouble?"

"I had a set of dice, so we started a little game of chance.   I was doing really well, nearly wiping everyone out of their coin, then some sore loser accused me of cheating with loaded dice.   That's about the time you showed up."

"Well, were they loaded?" asked Lucius

"Yeah"

"You mean to tell me I got myself nearly pulverized into merda defending a cheat?" Marcus was about to start up the fight again but his nose started bleeding. Lucius positioned himself between the two. He grabbed Marcus' hair on the back of his head and yanked it while shoving his hand back to his nose.

"All right!   You were the one who jumped in before you knew what the fight was about."

Marcus held his nose and sulked.

Lucius tried to restore calm again as he finished applying the salve.

"I'm sure you are not from here.   Your accent is different.   Where are you from?"

"I'm from Neapolis."

"Wow, that's a big seaport."

"Yeah, my family is in the shipping business."

"You're very far from home."   Lucius calculated in his head.   "You couldn't have traveled here just to join the legion. The word just came down.   You wouldn't have had the time."

"Yeah, well I was helping with a family job that didn't go so well and my Papa told me it might be best if I went away for a while.   I wandered up the coast and into here.   I saw the gathering on the beach and decided to check it out.   I got those dice from my uncle.   He's got a gambling business in Ostia.   The big spenders come down from Roma.   It's just a short distance and the place is always crowded. My uncle makes a good living, so I figured he wouldn't miss this pair."

"You stole them from your uncle?"

"Borrowed is more like it, but after the fight, I don't know where they went and it seems that I am light on coin as well."

"So, where are you going now?"

"Well, I hear Caesar needs an army, so I figure I would go along for the ride."

"You can't just drop in and out of the legion, you know.   It's a big commitment and if you desert, they kill you."

"Yeah, I know, but it could be a lot worse than that for me in Ostia or Neapolis right now."

Chapter 4: Homeless

Aia and her parents swiftly walked away from the Great Hall. Standing in front of what was left of the humble home of the Tigurini tribe's chief Druid were Ouenitouta and Sina. They clutched each other and sobbed quietly. Very little was left of the fire ravaged home. The roof had collapsed onto their belongings and the walls had caved in on top of the roof. The only recognizable area was the hearth. Pots and cooking utensils lay on the ground but seemed intact. The basement pantry where they had stored their ceremonial and medicinal flowers and herbs next to the dried meat and vegetables was incinerated. Everything was smoldering.

"We will stay next to our home tonight," Drutos told his family. "Oueni, stay with us for now. Your husband will be busy all night trying to corral livestock. He will know where to look for you when the time comes."

They cleared an area next to the hearth. The snow had melted and the ground was moist, but relatively warm. Drutos gathered his family into a circle and held hands with Adiega on his right and Aia on his left. They bowed their heads and he offered a prayer.

Oh Goddess, on this most auspicious day of Imbolc,
We were thwarted in our attempt to honor You.
Now we come to you in supplication.
Although we are devastated, bring us inner peace.
Allow us to forgive those who dishonored You.
Permit us time to show our devotion again.

Tomorrow, we are compelled to be travelers.
Give us the strength to survive this forced journey.
Guide the four winds to comfort us.
Bring forth an early spring to make serene our travels.
Inspire us with the fresh creativity you bring to all life.
Oh Goddess, guide us with love to our new beginnings.

Then, he hugged and kissed each on the forehead beginning with Adiega, then his daughters Ouenitouta, Sina, and finally, Aia. Aia trembled in his arms and he held her a bit longer until she was calm. Then, they all lay down to try to sleep.

Sometime in the dead of night, it began to snow heavily. The snows smothered the remaining fires and extinguished the embers throughout the village. It brought a calm to the livestock making it easier to corral them. Aia, who was snuggled between her sisters, woke to cold wet snow on her face. She grabbed the cloak Lugurix had thrown to her and covered the three of them. She was totally exhausted. She lay down again, falling into a fitful sleep.

Aia stood beside a large body of water. The winds whipping her face were moist and hot. Black clouds appeared on the West and grew to blot out the sun casting an eerie dark green light on the land. The clouds began to rain down spears and swords. The troubled waters stirred into giant white caps. As she watched, the white caps turned dark red splashing the shoreline with thick blood.

She saw her father struggling in the water. He was calling to her to save him. She waded into the bloody water, but he was far beyond her reach. She tried to call out, but had no voice. She felt the hands of her brother, Toutios, on her shoulders caressing and attempting to calm her. She turned to look in his face but saw only a bloody dark hole. She began screaming and screaming.

"Wake up, wake up, dear Aia!" she heard Ouenitouta saying. She grabbed her and held on tight until the images slowly faded from her eyes.

"You're all right," she heard Sina say.

She raised her head. The day was just dawning and the devastation from the evening before was painfully evident. Not a single structure was left standing, not even the Great Hall. It was all too real. Her father and mother came to her side.

"It's time," they said together.

All three girls rose and the family sifted through the rubble of their home. Only the pots and utensils could be salvaged. Sina wandered down to the river's edge and gathered a few reeds. She fashioned a cross inside of a circle like the one she had made for Imbolc and presented it to Aia. The two held each other and cried softly. Oueni said a brief goodbye and ran to join her husband in the fields with the livestock. As they were waving goodbye, Toutios rode up on horseback. Aia was thrilled to see her brother and hugged his leg. She could sense his anguish.

"Lugurix has prepared a wagon for you. Let me lead you there."

In silence, the family made their way to their designated wagon. They climbed on board. Toutios led them into position in the growing line of the tribe. They slowly moved away from the rising sun and headed out of the valley. Aia sat in the back of the wagon facing the village as it faded from view. She clutched Sina's circle and cross to her bosom, tears trickling down her cheek.

Arduous was the only way to describe the journey to Geneva. Some days, progress was measured in meters. Wagons were constantly getting mired in the mud and melting snow. Some wagons slid off the paths breaking axles. Blacksmiths had to set up and repair the damage with what few materials they had. Sometimes, the damage was too severe and they cannibalized the damaged wagons for parts. When they ran short of metal, families donated pots to be refashioned into wagon parts.

Ostara, the celebration of the vernal equinox, came and went without an acknowledgement from the Tigurini nation. Drutos and his family said a few short prayers that night when the moon rose. Otherwise, it was just another miserable day. Fights broke out between neighbors and within families over the advisability of the decisions of their chieftain. Unscheduled stops for tribal meetings were frequent. The nation nearly left the Confederation, but the elders recognized that they had nothing to return to and resolved to trudge on.

The last day of the trip to the border of the Helvetian lands was a beautiful cloudless day. The wagons traveled along the northern shore of a clear lake. The color of the water changed throughout the day with the angle sun. In the morning, it sparkled golden on dark blue. During the middle of the day, it shone like diamonds. Later, it became a deep blue again. All along the water's edge were homes built on pilings. The homes were wondrous in design. They were clustered in groups of three or four connected by piers. The buildings were never longer than twenty meters nor wider than ten meters. The floors hovered less than two meters above the water. The walls were made of boards roughly fashioned from the trunks of local trees. The roofs were thatched over wooden frames. At the edges of the peaked roofs, four boards extended beyond the tops like long skinny fingers. Some of the roofs sagged in the middle reminding Aia of a saddle.

Although the pile dwellings were intriguingly beautiful, they were empty. The tribe that occupied them must have joined the migration. Aia speculated as to why the structures were not burned to the waterline the way her village had been burned to the ground. The inhabitants must have gone willingly, sparing their homes. Most likely, the tribe was somewhere in the mass of humanity gathering at the Roman provincial border.

That evening, they arrived at the back end of the large camp near the Roman town of Geneva. They were so far away that they could see nothing of the town. Shortly, word passed down to them that their way was blocked by Governor Caesar and his troops.

Toutios came by the family wagon to give them details on the situation. Aia was especially glad to see her brother. However, she sensed in him not only anger, but also great despair.

"Ambassadors have just returned from the Roman's camp," he told them. "Caesar, their commander, agreed to consider our request to cross their territory. He said he will make a decision in two weeks."

"Is there a chance that he would be kind enough to let us pass?" Drutos asked.

"I doubt it," Toutios replied. "He reminded the delegation that it was our tribe that defeated the Romans and made them slaves. It turns out that the second in command of the disgraced legion was a relative of Caesar. The outlook seems grim."

Drutos's expression clouded over.

"That was the last time our clan was powerful. It is a distant memory, even for the oldest of us. Because of the plague that took so many lives years ago, none of the Romans and only half our population survived. Those soldiers who returned home from war with our neighbors were hit very hard. I thought we had answered for our sins then. Maybe I was wrong."

"The younger warriors are becoming very disappointed with Bimmos's command. Lugurix–"

"How is Lugurix?" Aia blurted out. She immediately regretted her emotional outburst. She loved Lugurix deeply, but still could not reconcile his behavior on Imbolc.

Toutios looked at his sister. He felt her anguish.

"He is healthy, but none of the young guard will be very happy if we are not allowed to cross Roman lands."

"I guess we are in for more hardship," Drutos sighed.

"Well, please pray for us all," Toutios said as he turned to resume his post.

Aia grabbed him. He turned back to face her.

"Please take care of yourself, dear brother. Every night I dream of Athair and you. I believe you are in terrible danger."

"I will always be there for you dear Aia."

She watched as he disappeared into the gathering dusk.

Each night, Aia's terrible dream revisited her. Each night, her father would cry for help. Try as she might, she failed to utter a word or reach her father's outstretched hand. Each night, her white Imbolc gown became more bloody. At first, it was only the tip of the skirt. By the time they camped outside of Geneva, there was enough blood to cover nearly half of her outfit. The dream always ended with the vision of Toutios's empty skull above his blood soaked clothing. Every time Aia saw her brother's mangled head, she screamed out in her sleep and had to be comforted by her family. Everyone was becoming bone tired and depressed.

The next day, they arose to hear that Caesar's troops were building high fortifications on the far bank of the Rhône. Soon, their path to Geneva would be blocked entirely.

"Toutios was right. Caesar will never let us cross the river and travel through Roman territory," Aia thought.

She went to her father and sat in his lap. She kissed his cheek and played with the front of his robe the way she did when she was a child.

"If we cannot cross the river here, do you think we can return home?" she asked.

"No, my child. There is nothing for us to return to."

Aia clutched her father's robe and became more insistent.

"But, we could rebuild our lives there."

Drutos smiled a fatherly smile.

"It would not be easy. Who would cut the trees and rebuild our homes? Who would protect us from our warring neighbors? Who would till the land and raise the livestock?"

"Sina and me and Oueni and Frontú. We could be your arms and legs. Please?" She grabbed his robe tighter.

He turned away so she would not see his tears.

"No, it is not possible. We must accept our fate, whatever it may be. If it is to die on the way, I will see you in the Otherworld, my dear sweet Aia."

During the encampment, Lugurix would come by daily to see Aia, but she hid and asked Sina to tell him she was ill. After several days of the elusion game, Sina refused to participate.

"No, I won't tell that man another lie!" She whispered angrily. "You need to tell him your feelings yourself, and the sooner the better!"

Aia knew Sina was right. She sighed and opened the back door of the wagon. Her heart jumped. Lugurix was in full armor, helmet included. He had trimmed his beard to a proper fighting length. He sat on a black stallion, who snorted and pawed the ground. He looked splendid. She wanted to hate him, but all she could do was cry.

"This is all your fault!" She tried to sound authoritative, but she sounded more like a pouting child.

"You are being too dramatic as usual," he replied. "My part was minor."

"You ruined our beautiful moment at Imbolc!" She stomped her foot, her voice wavering.

"I swear, I did not know the delegation would return at that very moment to break up the ceremony. I had every intention of enjoying the celebration with you. I was astounded that Bimmos stopped the ritual so abruptly. It would not have taken long to conclude the ceremony. Maybe our tribe would feel differently about this move had he done so."

She narrowed her eyes and gave him a look of incredulity.

"Believe me, I wish it were different." He paused then said, "Look, the young warriors are almost certain we will not be able to cross the river here."

"Then take over from this madman and return us to our home," she interrupted.

"Aia, it is impossible for us to go back now.   Our alliances and commitments to the Confederacy prevent it."   He sat upright on his mount.   "I promise you that things will change.   When they do, the Druids will again hold the exalted position they should always have, and you, my lovely Aia, will be the fairest High Priestess ever!"

She spun around and folded her arms, but said nothing.

Lugurix waited for a few moments to see if she would respond.   When she did not, he said,

"Be well, my love, I must be get back to duty!"   He kicked his steed and was off.

Aia's heart pounded to a bizarre rhythm of sadness and joy, but she kept her emotions to herself.

The next day word came down that Caesar refused the Confederation passage.

Chapter 5: On the Move

Marcus removed his hand from his nose and touched his nostrils. The bleeding had stopped. He stood up and walked toward the water's edge. He felt a constant breeze at his back. The sea seemed languid, barely lapping the shoreline. Occasionally, the waves deposited part of a broken clam shell on the beach giving the only contrast between the blackness of the sand and the dark waters.

His head ached and his vision was partly obscured by his rapidly swelling shiners. Despite the blurriness, the stars seemed brighter than usual. The lack of a moon and the clear air enhanced the sky. Back at the villa, the view to the North was blocked by the bluff. Here, like nights at the lake, he had an unobstructed view of the northern sky. He could make out Ursa Major a little above the horizon. To the West, Aquila hung low, ready to plunge its arrow into the sea. The Via Lactea stretched out broadly overhead. He could read nothing in the heavens that might help him foresee his fate.

He felt rather ashamed at that moment. After Faustus was killed, he pleaded to join the legion, even though he knew his Pater felt he was still too young. Lucius, who would inherit the villa someday, was intent on lowering himself to be a physician. Marcus felt that the business of the military naturally fell to him, but to pursue his dream, Lucius was forced to tag along as his protector, at least for a while.

He had assumed that he would be moving into a position of authority in the cavalry. To his surprise, he was neither in a position of privilege nor in the cavalry. He would be a line soldier, forced to live with non-citizens, slaves, and small time thugs like Quintus. Before he was officially part of the Roman legions, he jumped into a fight without thinking and got himself beaten to a pulp. As he stared out at the horizon, he resolved to prove to his family that he was a great warrior. He knew he could bring honor to the Calidius name.

As he turned around, he nearly plowed into Lucius.

"One of the Greek slaves who is here to join the legion gave me some hemlock leaves," said Lucius. "He swore they will take the swelling down. I crushed them to release their resin. I can't guarantee that this will work, Marcus, but take some of the crushed leaves in each hand, close your eyes and place this over them."

"How am I supposed to see with my eyes closed?"

"You can't. So, I'll bring you back to the campsite and you can sit with this stuff on your eyes until daybreak. Maybe by the time the quartermaster arrives, your swelling will be relieved."

It seemed like only moments had passed since they made their way back to the campsite when he could sense the first light of dawn. The sky went from a jewel speckled black canvas to gray, then to a deep blue. Almost in an instant, Sol popped up over the distant hills casting a golden light on the Mediterranean. On cue, seagulls began to circle the shallow waters surrounding the local fishermen just hauling their boats into the water.

Marcus realized he was hungry. Although the packs he and Lucius received from home were laden with delicious crusty bread and treats of dried meats and fruit enough for three days, Marcus had inhaled all of his provisions on the journey to the coast the previous afternoon. Excitement and anticipation of his new life made him voracious. That morning, he was famished. He craved everything from bread to eggs to roasted meat. It was only then that he realized the air was thick with the smell of freshly baked bread. He stood up, removed the hemlock eye patches, and looked in the direction of the village. Through his puffy eyelids and the low light of dawn, he thought he could make out a long table stacked with provisions.

He shook Lucius awake and dashed toward the table. As he got closer, he realized that the table was not as large as he thought. Stretching back from the table was a long line of youths, the region's recruits, waiting for the gift of breakfast prepared by the townspeople. There had to be several hundred already in line. Some already had the tunic of a Tirones and a few had weapons. Scanning the area to the North not more than a hundred feet away, he could make out a tent and a pile of gear. He and Lucius saw none of that the night before because they arrived in near total darkness. The quartermaster must have been there already and they were late.

By the time they made it through the food line, the sun was high in the sky. The day was heating up as usual and there was little relief from sea breezes, which refused to blow. A second line had formed for registration and distribution of military gear. They fell in at the rear. It moved slower than a snail. By the time they got to the quartermaster, it was midday.

The quartermaster sat behind a small writing table flanked by two soldiers of low rank. The quartermaster was a rotund fellow with thick black beard stubble. He was sweating profusely and his tunic under his armor was soaked. He chewed on what looked like a piece of tree bark and talked incessantly to no one in particular taking time out to order about his two soldiers.

"Blockheads and mushrooms! That's all Caesar is getting, blockheads and mushrooms! Roma would be better off with a legion of cattle. The fighting stock is polluted by mindless fornicating bastards – Scum! You can put a uniform on them, but they're still just mushrooms! Name and city." The quartermaster said without looking up.

"Marcus Calidius of Canino, sir." Marcus said in a rather high pitched, nasal voice.

The quartermaster looked up to see what creature uttered such a queer sound.

"Oh, Jupiter and all the gods! We are at the bottom of the barrel! He's a ruptured melon and he hasn't even seen a battle! Give him a tunic, a helmet and a gladius. Don't hand out any more pila until we see how these mushrooms function. All right pipsqueak, you're assigned to the Hastatus Posterior of the ninth cohort of the Eleventh legion. If there were a weaker cohort in the legion, I'd put you there. Your Centurion is Martial. Woe is you! What a criminal he is! You just better hope he doesn't run you through before he greets you! Grab your travel rations from the wagon over there, but hurry, you're moving out this afternoon."

Marcus trudged off.

"Next monkey," the quartermaster barked. "Name and city."

"Lucius Calidius of Canino, sir."

The quartermaster looked up sizing up the older Calidius.

"Well, you must be big brother! I suppose you're the scum bucket whose supposed to protect melon head over there. It don't work that way in Caesar's Army, got it hangdog? You will be in a different cohort."

"Well, sir, I was told I was to be assigned as an immune."

"Oh, mister fancy pants, you have a skill? Spill it."

"I'm a physician, well actually, a physician in training–"

"Stop blathering.   The medical train will be here later this afternoon. Report to Manius Fabricius Taurinus. You can't miss him. He is the old butterball with a white beard. We had to dig deep to get physicians to leave Roma right now. They're all making too much money and they won't part with their fortunes. I pray to the gods that none of us needs his services. Now, just go away and don't bother me!"

Lucius watched as the two soldiers struck the tent, then accompanied the hulking quartermaster who hobbled off.   On the road he saw rows of men awkwardly milling around while officers, obviously centurions, shouted orders with little effect. It took at least an hour for the recruits to line up sufficiently well to please the commanders.   They were joining a larger group of slightly better disciplined recruits who marched up during the day from mustering points further south.   Then, with more orders barked, the recruits began jogging, some losing their helmets. They were berated by the centurions while they picked up their gear and sprinted back into line. Although the numbers seemed countless, they were out of sight in minutes, leaving Lucius alone at the dusty campsite. He looked around as the townspeople returned to their everyday lives. Several men moved the tables back to a villa on a low hill. He began to wonder just what he was in for.

Lucius did not have to wonder long. He noticed a small cloud of dust slowly rising from the road to the South. As the dust cloud grew closer, he could hear shouting and clanking, then he could see on the crest of a low hill a line of ten wagons heading in his direction. The breeze was picking up off of the sea and blowing the dust up and away to the West. It allowed him good visibility as the wagon train moved past his position. He could see a rotund, nearly bald man with a short white beard driving the first wagon. He looked and acted remarkably like the quartermaster. He was chewing on a piece of bark and talking to himself. As the wagon approached, Lucius shouted over the clanking of the yokes and gear.

"Greetings, I am Lucius Calidius. Are you Manius Fabricius Taurinus?"

"The one and only!"

"I am to join you. I am a physician. Actually–"

"Well, climb on board you little monkey, cause we're not stoppin'!"

Lucius grabbed on and hoisted himself into the rumbling wagon.

"So, you're a physician!"

"Well, actu–"

"Great, because we're really shorthanded! Who trained you?"

"Theodosius, but–"

"Never heard of him, but it won't matter.   Forget everything you were taught. War is different. Your real education starts now."

"Thanks."

"Thank me when we are at peace, monkey."

Shortly after leaving town Lucius tried to get more information on their travel plans.

"When are we stopping for the night?"

"We're not exactly stopping.   This wagon train moves so slowly, we only stop to prepare and eat our meals and to give the mules a brief rest. We are up and on our way at first light and travel until well after Sol sets below the earth. Today will be a little shorter, since there is no moonlight. Luna soon will be waxing strong again and we will lengthen our travel time. Even at that rate, we will be a day or two behind those troops on a forced march. Next meal will be after dark, wherever that that takes us."

"Where are we headed?"

"I understand we are headed to the colony of Placentia. These two new legions need seasoning quick. They will learn marching on the way. When we reach Placentia, they will work on fighting skills, but they will simply be too green to win the campaign. I understand that Caesar is headed to the Eastern shore. It is peaceful there, ever since we beat the merda out of the Italians, so he is collecting three seasoned legions who wintered in L'Aquila. We will all meet at Placentia for the march to Gaul. We can only hope by then, the green troops will be ready."

"How long do you think it will take us to reach Placentia?"

"These newly recruited legions won't be able to march anywhere near as fast as the seasoned legions. I suspect it's about a three week journey."

Chapter 6: Learning the Ropes

"Halt!" shouted Centurion Martial in sequence with the other centurions. Marcus was exhausted and hungry. His feet were on fire and his neck ached from the extra weight of the ill fitting helmet he wore all day. It was the first break after what seemed like an eternity of marching in formation. They had jogged all afternoon along side of the Via Aurelia, the shoreline road constructed years earlier to connect Rome to the Republic's west coast towns. It was well maintained and many merchants traveled the road daily. The new legionnaires jogged on the ground next to the thoroughfare. They were told they could not obstruct commerce, but the real reason was so they could more quickly become accustomed to uneven terrain. Off the roadway, the ground was rough. Nearly every recruit turned at least one ankle that afternoon.

The sun was now low in the sky. That meant they had marched at double time for half a day. Marcus collapsed in a heap. As he did, he could hear the centurion's heavy armor clank as the infantry commander stomped up to his position and stopped.

Centurion Tiberius Didius Martial was a veteran of many campaigns. He came from a long line of legionnaires. His great-grandfather was the first to join the Roman Army, fighting in the successful third campaign against Macedonia. His grandfather participated in the destruction of Carthage at the end of the third Punic War. His father fought under Gaius Marius, first in Africa, then in actions to protect Cisalpine Gaul from invading tribes. For his service and valor, he was awarded lands in the new colony of Pompeii. Although all of Martial's forebears could have been officers, they chose to fight in the ranks of the legionnaires.

Martial joined the military under General Sulla at a young age. His first action was against Mithridates VI in Pontus. When his centurion was killed by an arrow through the eye into the skull early in the battle, Martial took the lead. Even though the legion was surrounded, he kept his century intact. He received a battlefield promotion to Centurion. He and his century remained together and fought valiantly for many campaigns. Later, during a few years of peace, he married his childhood sweetheart, Fannia Artoria. However, he was soon called back into service against Mithridates VI in Pontus and decided to remain in the military. He became renown for his ability to quickly train recruits.

When Martial's father died unexpectedly, he retired to Pompeii. He served as a government inspector of public buildings. However, he and Fannia had a stormy relationship. During Martial's many years away, she was seduced by the free and hedonistic Pompeian lifestyle. He was very conservative and did not approve of her unrestrained behavior. They clashed constantly. When the call came to form two new legions, Martial jumped at the opportunity. Fannia was so thrilled at the prospect of being alone and free again, she held a lavish reenlistment party in Martial's honor, which continued for weeks after he left.

Martial had been a handsome young legionnaire. He was tall and well proportioned. His military life kept him in top physical condition. He had chiseled features and was always clean shaven. Although he maintained himself, multiple battle scars had disfigured his face. One particular scar under his left eye had healed poorly leaving him with a thick, heaped-up jagged pink line across his cheek that gave him a fierce appearance. He often used his menacing face and his deep baritone voice to his advantage when training young legionnaires.

Martial glared down at Marcus, who had become the campaign's object lesson for the other recruits.

"I didn't give you permission to break ranks, scum bucket! You must be in need of a whippin'!"

"Pardon me sir, but I'm tired and my neck and feet hurt," Marcus whined.

"If it's pity you want, go back to your mother! You are in the Roman Army now. There's no complain'n and no disobey'n orders here. Maybe a whippin' is too easy for you. So, let's make that latrine duty!"

Several recruits around Marcus giggled.

"What's so amusing?   I didn't give you permission to laugh!   You just bought yourselves a pass to join this miserable ass! Fall out and march one hundred paces toward the shoreline and wait for orders."

Marcus pulled himself up and marched toward the water along with the other disciplined recruits. There were eight of them. Behind him he could hear the booming voice of his centurion.

"All right, the rest of you monkeys, Right turn! March!"

"Halt, damn you! When I say march, you start with your right foot! Didn't your mothers teach you anything? You never start on your sinister foot! Do you want to bring dishonor and misfortune on General Caesar? Idiots! Now, march!"

Marcus and his group arrived at their designated spot and turned to watch as the remainder of the column moved off of the road. He looked up the line ahead of their position and saw the same thing happening as far as he could see. Each century dispatched a small group toward the water, while the main force marched off the road to pitch tents. The old Centurion strutted up to Marcus and the others.

"OK, you filthy scum buckets, spread out ten paces from each other. Now, dig a hole two feet wide, three feet long and three feet deep. Pile the mud toward the water side. You must be done before the tents are pitched. So, get moving!"

"Sir, what do we use to dig the hole?" Marcus asked.

"Anything you can find, you ass! A sword, a knife, a clamshell, or maybe even your hands!"

Martial snarled down at his new charges. "One more thing. Don't talk to me unless I ask you a direct question! Got that, morons?"

"Yes, sir!" they all shouted in unison.

"All right, move!" He pointed at Marcus and shouted, "And you! I have my eyes on you!" He turned and marched back to yell more insults at his charges. They began digging.   Some used their hands, others used their stubby Spanish swords.

"Well, brother, you really pissed him off."

Marcus spun around to his left. He knew that voice.

"What? Looks like you saw a ghost."

"Quintus! Where did you come from?"

"I was in the rank right behind you and you never noticed?"

"No, you jail bird! I was concentrating on being sure I didn't fall down and get trampled. The last couple of miles, I thought I was dead already."

"That self absorbed, huh? I could have been next to you and you probably wouldn't have noticed."

"You're right. I don't even know who was next to me. The only one I could pay attention to was our centurion. He seemed to be yelling directly at me the entire march."

"Well, if you would keep your mouth shut, maybe he wouldn't know who you were."

"Yeah, well I've never been that way."

"Maybe you should start."

"Both of you better shut up and dig or you may be in for that whipping he promised," the recruit on their right said.

Marcus looked round and saw that the others were nearly done with their field latrines. He put his head down and dug like a madman to catch up. It was a good thing he did because the centurion was returning.

Martial slowly walked up one side of the latrine row and down the other, then stopped.

"All right, ladies," he mocked. "Looks passable. Now get out of those piss holes and find your tent. Everyone else is eating."

"What's for dinner?" Marcus realized as he asked that he had done it again.

"You! You must have mushrooms for brains! What did I tell you?"

"You said don't talk unless you ask us a direct question." Marcus hung his head.

"Right. So, why did you speak?"

"Sorry."

"You are one sorry ass, you moron! That just bought tomorrow's latrine duty for you and your mates!"

They all clambered out of the dark gray sand and trudged over to the camp. The centurion never stopped yelling insults at Marcus. They could see all the tents were erected already. Each tent was big enough for eight soldiers. There was a space where no tent stood, only a pile of material and poles. The latrine detail would be sharing that one for the night. As they arrived, Marcus realized there would be no meal like the one they shared at breakfast. Everyone was eating rations from their pack.

The group struggled to erect their tent rapidly. Their packs had been thrown in with the tent parts. They sorted out whose pack belonged to whom, although it did not matter, since they all had the same contents that first day. Marcus pulled out his rations: hardtack biscuits, a chunk of bacon, and a full wineskin. He was ravenous. He took a huge bite out of the bacon. It was like eating a block of salt. He opened his mouth and let the piece fall on the ground, then took a long drink from his wineskin. He did not even taste the flavor until the third gulp when he realized the water was heavily laced with vinegar. He spit out a large mouthful and groaned.

"Hey, brother, watch how you eat that stuff," said Quintus. "I hear that's three day's rations."

Marcus put his head in his hands.

"By Jupiter and all the gods! What have I gotten myself into?"

"You chose this, brother. I only joined because of temporary cash flow problems and the threat of serious bodily harm back home. You, on the other hand want to make this your life."

"You're right," Marcus said as he picked up the dust covered piece of bacon. He brushed it off and nibbled at the edge. Now, it was salty and gritty. He sighed.

"This is not an auspicious way to begin a military career," he thought to himself.

He put away the rations and lay down. He used his pack as a pillow and was asleep in seconds.

Someone was trying to tell Marcus something. He strained to hear it. The words were unclear and soft, but the cadence of the repeated phrases was the same. It got louder and louder until he was able to make out the words.

"Get up, you scum buckets!"

He slowly opened his eyes. The sky was dark blue with only a hint of light. Sol had not yet broken over the distant hills. Everyone else in his group was up and ready to strike the tent. He quickly rose as the tent collapsed. He ducked out of the side and ran directly into Martial.

"I see a night's sleep made you no smarter, melon head!"

"Sorry, sir"

"You and your tent mates are late! Get down to the latrines and fill them in, then line up for the day's march."

Marcus swore he had descended into Tartarus, the prison of the underworld. He felt like Sisyphus, the mythologic monarch who was doomed to haul a huge boulder up a hill only to find the next morning that the boulder was at the bottom waiting to be pushed up again. Every day became the same miserable routine.

They jogged half a day taking the briefest of breaks to take a swig of vinegar water and to relieve their bladders, then they jogged for the rest of the day. The eight tent mates became a tent group, a contubernium. They were rearranged in the century as the ninth cohort, the weakest of the weak.

The bulk of the new legions were recruited from Italy. The coastal recruits were to join the main force at Parma. Although the recruiters tried to choose the best men, some recruits washed out, either because they were not up to the task, or because they became sick or injured. Like the rest of the troops, the ninth cohort also lost a few men. Even though replacement recruits joined along the way, Martial kept the ninth cohort a man short.

Every day, Martial would find something to complain about. It gave him an excuse to place the ninth cohort on permanent latrine duty. Every evening, the cohort would pass out from exhaustion until shouts from their hard boiled centurion woke them for morning muster. The cycle seemed endless. The only highlight was the occasional food gift from citizens. When the recruits went through a village, the townspeople would come out and offer them food and wine. Quintus would take the treats offered to them and stuff them into Marcus' pack to be shared later.

On the evening of the ninth day of the forced march, they reached the mouth of the Flume Magra. Up to that point, they had marched parallel to the Via Aurelia and the Via Amelia Scaura hugging the coastline, but their goal was Placentia at the North central border of the peninsula. The quickest route from their coastal camp was through Parma where they would rendezvous with the other recruits. The Via Amelia Scaura continued along the coast and away from their goal, so they had to change course. The next morning, the legionnaires veered off the main roads and marched in a northerly direction along the left bank of the Flume Magra.

By the noonday break, the recruits noticed that they were in a shallow valley. They were surrounded by rolling hills to their right and left. They were still at sea level. Behind them lay flat terrain. Ahead were rolling hills of greater and greater height. They continued along the riverbank climbing steadily every day. By the evening of the fourth day, the trail became so narrow that they could only shelter in place.   Since they did not have to unpack and repack the tents, they gained two hours of travel time.   The next day, they faced north-northeast and ascended over the mountains, climbing two thousand feet and then back down again to arrive in the town of Parma.   There, they joined the recruits from Italy to form two full legions of over nine thousand men.   From there, they paralleled the Via Amelia.   The terrain was flat and led straight to Placentia.

Chapter 7: Mind Numbing Lectures

Lucius found his journey as tough as the line soldiers found the forced marches. Every day since climbing into the medical wagon, he had to endure the stories of Manius Fabricius Taurinus. Taurinus told the story of his youth, his education in the legion as a surgeon, and his unusual practice ministering to the senate in Rome. According to him, there had never been, nor would there be a better surgeon than he.

"They don't make surgeons like they used to, my boy! When I started, I was younger than you. My father sent me to be sort of an assistant to my uncle, who was a senator at the time. It was as boring as watching a tree stump. Then one day, this candidate for head of the Senate, Gaius Memmius, got murdered. This other senator, Saturninus, and his followers got blamed, and they got cornered in the forum. They negotiated a surrender, but as Saturninus and his associates came out of chambers, a couple of other senators stone them to death with terra cotta roof tiles. Blood was everywhere! Some of the soldiers guarding the culprits got injured. The private surgeon of Counsel Gaius Marius had to treat the guards. He needed help, so I was grabbed."

Taurinus always paused at that point and shook his head.

"What a fascinating thing – to watch a master surgeon operate! The injured guards were cleaned, bandaged, and removed to the barracks in no time. I never found out what happened to them, but I knew from then on that I wanted to be a military surgeon. I joined up the very next day, but I was too young to be a surgeon. I had to work my way up the ranks. I started as a medic in the Castra of the elite Roman guard. The troops spent their time drilling. They practiced battle movements and hand-to-hand combat. Sometimes, real fights broke out. My first job was carrying injured soldiers back to the medical barracks. I was supposed to drop them off and report back immediately, but I would stay there as long as I could. Believe me, I saw all sorts of injuries and operations. I would get berated by the chief medic for not doing my job, but the surgeons liked me because I would be there to help them whenever they needed anything. I soon got myself reassigned to the surgical team. I assisted all day and all night. I would skip sleep and meals just to be in the operating theater. Soon, I knew every operation the surgeons did. Eventually, they let me do simple procedures. I learned about everything from fractures to hemorrhoids. By Jupiter, those days were great!"

Each day, Taurinus varied his story with different embellishments, but the basics of the plot were always the same. A young man gets conscripted to help a master surgeon. He sees near miracles performed as the surgeon patches up soldiers. He decides to become a surgeon and ignores everything to be at the operating table. Nothing else mattered to him. Taurinus talked about treating patients with medicines as though he was shoveling merda.

"The only part my job that I really I hated was morning sick call. Every day in the barracks, we had to see any soldier who had a compliant. When we were out of camp at war, the soldiers had no time to complain about minor stuff, but in camp, our job was to return the troops to fighting strength. Whatever the condition, we were obligated to cure it. That meant treating coughs and rashes and conditions of the bowels. I hated it, I tell you! I would find any excuse to skip sick call duty, then I would help the surgeons with procedures."

Taurinus described in great detail his wartime experiences. For Lucius, he was forced to endure an unwanted history lesson told by a nostalgic old man who remembered only the successes and the good times.

"My first real taste of battle came when I was in my early 20's. There were uprisings of Italians southeast of the capital city near L'Aquila. That's the city from where our seasoned legions are coming. The Consul of the senate, Lucius Porcius Cato, took a force to Fucine Lake. Our legion was sent to the city of Asculum to join the siege of that town. Our siege was so tight that the Italians either had to fight or starve. They chose to fight. Our forces were stronger and healthier due to our great care, of course. We defeated them easily. What few Italians survived were cut down in a revenge killing. We spent days putting our forces back together, but we were proud and victorious. The return to Roma was a delight!"

Taurinus described in excruciating detail the parade and reception they received in Rome, including some incredibly hedonistic orgies. Initially, Lucius was shocked, but by the third time through the story, he was bored.

"We stayed garrisoned in Roma for several years. It was during that time that I met a young cook named Aulus Gratius Publicus. Coincidently, he is with the quartermaster corps in our legion. He and I became great friends. That's why I'm so fat now." Taurinus laughed and patted his rotund abdomen. "He makes a scrumptious Pullus Fusilis and a mean Isicia Omentata, but his desserts are to die for. His pancakes and his pear soufflé – unmatched! Maybe he'll make some for you when we get to Placentia." He poked Lucius and flicked his eyebrows, then settled back to continue his life story.

"Most of the time when we were in camp, I had little to do. By now, I was one of the chief surgeons. I had battle experience, so I was doing the teaching. After duty, Publicus would whip up something delicious. We would sit up all night and eat and talk, but most of all, we drank. I never saw another man drink the way he did. We would drain a barrel of wine every night. I really miss those times, but I am looking forward to much reminiscing with him during this campaign." He closed his eyes, took in a deep breath through his nose, and exhaled.

"I was getting bored and thought about leaving the legion, but a very important campaign began. It started in Greece under the command of a young general named Lucius Cornelius Sulla. Although I hoped our legion would move out and fight again, there was significant unrest in Roma. Sulla determined that we should remain there to protect the city and keep the peace. I thought I was going to die of boredom, but our next action came only a few weeks later in the battle at Mount Tifata south of Roma. The battle was swift and decisive because of Sulla. What a brilliant commander! After that, we joined the chase around Greece of the Samnites. It took three years, but eventually we crushed them at Nola. I loved it because our losses were light and the workload manageable. We were pumped up. We all wanted to remain in the field under the command of this great general." Taurinus sucked in his gut and saluted his favorite leader.

"That next year was a chase around the middle of the old Republic fighting skirmishes. Finally, we came back to Roma. We had to defeat armies of our own citizens who had risen against Sulla. The final battle was at the Porta Collina on the northwestern border of Roma itself. The battle was fierce and raged day and night before we were victorious. Of course, there were many casualties and we spent days operating on the injured. Fortunately, we had the resources of our great city to help us. Unfortunately for me, it meant we missed the triumphant march into Roma proper and the unanimous appointment of Sulla as Dictator."

That incident must have been one of the great the highlights of Taurinus' life, because he told the story the same way every time.

"That was a wonderful time to be in Roma.   Change occurred at a phrenetic pace. We were treated like royalty and life was good. Then, in less than a year, our idol retired. Sulla retired! Can you believe it? No one else could either. So, I retired. I didn't think I would see another genius like that, and I wanted no part of an inexperienced pompous commander. I established a little office near the forum. I would minister to the Senate while its members were in Roma. Mostly, I spent my days treating them for their sins. Nearly all of them developed bladder problems with dripping pus and blood. Often, I would have to cannulate them just to relieve their pain.

The senators were grateful and I was well paid, but to my disgust, some of them sent their mistresses for treatment.   Those women were all lunatics with ridiculous complaints. They were constantly getting pregnant. The senators were fearful of the publicity back home if some concubine delivered their love child. They demanded I perform abortions. It would have been easier to kill them, but that would have looked worse for those high and mighty politicians. I hated it. When I wasn't aborting them, I was compounding medicines to treat melancholy or phlegmasia.   I had to listen to their petty stories and drivel while pretending to be concerned. I had to make the senators feel that they were getting a good deal. That practice lasted nine years. I hated it. Hated, I tell you!" He cleared his throat and spit a large wad of phlegm over the mules.

"Then I got a chance to get out from under my miserable existence. There was a slave uprising. It became a real threat to Roma. This outrageous filthy chief of crimes, Spartacus, led the uprising. He recruited as many as 120,000 slaves. They defeated two of the Republic's legions. That was enough for the Senate. Ten legions were collected to defeat this scum bag. I knew they would need surgeons, so I volunteered again. I was immediately assigned to the High Command. What a rush! We raced north nearly to the Alps where the legions finally snuffed out the jailbirds. Our hospital saw innumerable wounded. We had to work for days to patch up those soldiers. We became very tough and efficient at our jobs. By the end of the campaign, our slogan was – Edite Ferrum, caca clavi! – Eat iron, shit nails!" Lucius smiled at the clever remark. The old man still had a few good lines. Taurinus took a drink of water before he began again.

"The most amazing thing, though, was what came next. The six thousand sorry criminals remaining in the slave army were brought down the Appian way and crucified one by one along the roadside. That was an awesome sight! Many citizens traveled that way just to see the power of Roma. It was a mighty statement to the slaves! I don't think they will try to rebel again."

Every day at that point, Taurinus took a ritual break. He stood up and urinated over the side of the wagon, then sat down with a plop.

"After that, there was little military medicine to do and I found myself back in my office treating lunatics and venereal disease. I have been doing that for the last thirteen years, then this opportunity came up. You can bet that I jumped at the chance to enlist again. Some said I was too old to serve, but we are in need of all the experienced surgeons we can find. So, here we are my boy! The next great adventure of our great Republic! I wouldn't miss this for all the denarii in Roma!"

The long winded tales went on, and on, and on. It was the same routine all day, every day. Taurinus suspended his recitation only when they camped for the night's brief rest. Immediately after the train stopped at the end of the day's travel, Taurinus would clamber down from the wagon and head straight for the quartermaster's wagon where he would meet with his old friend Publicus. Publicus would prepare a private meal and the two of them would eat and drink the night away.

Bacchus could not have gotten more intoxicated than those two. Before the meal was served, they were talking and laughing loudly enough to wake the dead. By the time the meal was done, both were mad drunk and pissing on the wagon wheels. Before long, they were slurring words, spilling their wine, and giggling like girls. Eventually, they would pass out by the campfire as if they were dead. As the sun rose the next morning, they would rise from the dead, dust off, and act as if nothing had happened. Taurinus would return to his wagon. Within moments of starting the day's journey, he would begin his life story again as though he had never revealed it to anyone before.

Lucius was fed up with the tales. To him, it was ancient history. He was interested in learning surgery, not reliving history. Some of the stories were so fantastic, he wasn't even sure if they were true. The old man's words bored into his head like trephine. After the third day, he did not even listen. He had most of the stories memorized. Unfortunately, he was captive. He had hoped that his experience with a veteran surgeon would allow him to learn surgical skills. Instead, he was the prisoner of a burned out, demented boozer who just blathered about the good old days. He felt like taking hemlock tea and just being done with it.

Every now and then, Lucius would try to change the subject or derail the recitation by asking questions. All that did was result in more digressions. On one occasion, however, his questioning did lead to a pleasurable experience.

"What is that piece of bark you are chewing?" He asked.

"This? Glad you asked, my boy." Taurinus was eager to have another story to tell. He took the piece out of his mouth and held up the wet chunk. "This is cinnamon. It is the latest craze to hit Roma. We first learned of the spice after an Eastern campaign when a legion commander brought some back. He only had a little bit, but it made a splash immediately. Still, very little cinnamon comes into the Eastern seaports. The bark is worth a small fortune. Only the richest citizens can get it. It is all the rage among the noble families of Roma. It's a status symbol. They say it has magical powers. Some burn it as a sacrifice to the gods. It gives off an incredible smell when burned. It does not dissolve in water, but when you boil it in sweet wine with honey, it imparts a delicious exotic flavor to the wine." He smelled the chunk and stuck it back in his mouth.

"Most of all, I like it for its mouth properties. When you suck on it, it sort of stings the tongue and cools the breath. Better yet, it changes the smell of your breath. Publicus makes great meat dishes, but they can leave your breath rancid. With cinnamon, I can have all the meat I want and my breath doesn't smell of it. Even the smell of wine goes away. Some say parsley works, but fresh parsley is hard to get when you are at war." He reached into his pack and pulled out two fresh pieces offering one to Lucius.

"Here, try it."

Lucius could see into the sack. It was loaded with cinnamon.

"How did you get so much?" He inquired.

"Remember, I had a very lucrative medical practice in Roma. A grisly practice, but a very lucrative one. I could easily afford to buy it from the merchants who came to the forum."

Lucius looked at the curious bark.   It was dry and curled forming a rudimentary tube.   It had a slightly rough surface and a sweet spicy odor.   It reminded him of terra cotta roof tile and was about as brittle.

"If I chew this won't it break?" he asked.

"Oh, yeah.   Don't chew it.   It crumbles and the particles don't dissolve. You get way too much of a dose.   Just suck on it.   You'll get the hang of it."

Lucius put it in his mouth.   Immediately, he felt the tingle on his tongue. As he tried to analyze the taste, he noticed that the bark sapped his mouth of moisture while simultaneously making him salivate.   The saliva rapidly filled the tube and dribbled out of his mouth.   He tried to stop it by closing his lips around the bark and breathing in.   When he did, some of his spittle flew rapidly out of the tube spreading the heavily spiced juice around his mouth and down his windpipe. It burned his throat and he coughed involuntarily.

"Watch out, boy, this is a very potent batch," warned Taurinus.   "Go easy with it."

Lucius placed it in the corner of his mouth and wet it with his saliva to slightly soften the bark.   When the little tube filled with saliva, he would elevate the end and allow the liquid to roll around his tongue and the floor of his mouth.   It was so potent that he had to remove the bark and spit out the liquid.   The tingly sensation lasted a long while, even though the bark was out of his mouth.   When it finally subsided, he tried sucking on the bark again with the same result.   His mouth had never felt that way before.   It took the rest of the day to understand how to use the substance.   Strangely enough, it was mildly addictive.

Lucius was glad to know of the bark.   He planned to acquire some to bring back home to the family and, especially, to Theodosius.   He felt the old physician might be able to add it to some of the prescriptives they made.   Maybe it could be used in the oxymel to spice up the goo.

He daydreamed about the medical practice he hoped to establish back in Canino.   He wanted to emulate his old teacher in all aspects of the art.   Theodosius was always available for the sick, no matter what time of day or night.   Even in the middle of meals or conversations with friends, the patient came first.

Theodosius never made the patient come to him.   He always traveled to the patient.   He did not want them to experience additional harm or expose their illness to other families.   He was always kind and gentle to his patients.   He made them feel at ease.   He always had time for the family.   He considered them part of his own family.   He always listened to the patient's entire story.   He allowed the patient to begin his story anywhere, even if it seemed to have little to do with the current condition.   After the patient concluded the story in their own words, he would ask a few probing questions and allow the patient to ramble again.

"Be a good listener, Lucius," Theodosius would say, "because the patient will tell you the diagnosis. They may not know anything about their illness or about the workings of the body, but in their story is the truth. You must allow them to tell it in their own way while listening intently for the clues they provide. The facts will never be in order, or explained with the right medical words. It is the truly great physician who can tease out the facts, assemble them in a logical fashion, place the right terms on the symptoms, and match the story with the diagnosis. Before you lay hands on the patient, you should already know the diagnosis."

His kind manner and deep expression of concern attracted many patients to Theodosius, particularly women.   The village women brought all of their complaints to him.   Lucius got to see some very unusual diseases limited solely to women.   While he knew they were important for his education, he felt very uncomfortable in these situations. The conditions the women related, particularly about issues of the vagina, were foreign to him.   He could not relate to their complaints and he had difficulty teasing out the important clues from the complex stories they told.   The women would unabashedly strip, bearing their entire form before Theodosius.   Their bodies fascinated Lucius, but frightened him at the same time.   He would have asked his mother for guidance, but she had perished many years before.   He knew he couldn't ask his sisters.   They would have used his ignorance of women to embarrass him at the most inopportune time.   He was just becoming intimate with his girlfriend and betrothed, Acca Camilia.   Unfortunately, she died only two months before in the winter's epidemic.   Theodosius would explain each illness, but Lucius was too distracted by the naked women and their intricate stories to retain any understanding.   He could only pray that his discomfort would gradually subside as he became more familiar with the maladies of women.

Lucius made many attempts to match abilities with Theodosius to obtain a diagnosis.   He always volunteered to interview the patient and collect the data for the physician.   Occasionally, Theodosius would allow him to do so and Lucius would emulate the old physician in every way.

Although he tried to listen carefully to the patients' stories and assemble the facts, he was never as good as his teacher.   Theodosius would wait patiently by his side, observing the conversation, then he would allow Lucius to present the information.   After the exchange, Theodosius would ask the patient additional questions.   To the satisfaction of Lucius, the number of questions had been diminishing during in the last few months.   Theodosius would force Lucius to make a diagnosis and give his reasons for his conclusion, then he would confirm or refute the efforts of his pupil.

After the encounter, there was always further discussion as they traveled to the next patient.   These discussions were give-and-take sessions, but Theodosius always reminded Lucius to study the old texts and manuscripts.   He freely quoted Hippocrates, because the great physician's guidance on obtaining a diagnosis and making a prognosis had stood the test of time and remained successful for him.

Once the diagnosis was established, the prognosis depended upon the type and severity of the disease.   Theodosius spent little time explaining the various possible outcomes to the patient and family, because he said it would only serve to confuse and frighten them.   He constantly explained to Lucius the importance of understanding the possible scenarios, but admonished him never to divulge to the patient what his fate might be.   He gave only optimistic prognoses.   Lucius did not agree with that philosophy and planned to give all the information to the family.   He firmly believed that they should know what to watch for and notify him immediately.   That way, he might anticipate any complications and possibly thwart them before they came to fruition.   He had expressed his thoughts to Theodosius, but had been rebuked, so he kept his plans to himself.

One aspect of Medicine that they both agreed upon was the importance of the physician touching the patient.   Unknown and unimaginable powers seemed to emanate from the physician's touch.   The power went both to and from the physician.   A firm handshake for the Paterfamilias reassured all in the household that the patient would be well cared for.   The addition of a hand on the shoulder conveyed a bond akin to being part of each others' family.   Laying a hand on the patient while the patient relayed his story made any others present for the interview virtually disappear.   The only important person was the patient and he had the singular attention of his healer.

Theodosius examined the patient first with a gentle touch. That allowed data to flow from the patient through the fingertips, the most sensitive part of the hand. One could sense the body heat as well as the heat of the affected part. To Hippocrates, heat was the life force. It emanated from the earth and seemed to be generated in the body in the same manner. Other important factors were the subtlety of variations in skin thickness, contour, and turgidity. These attributes seemed to convey messages from deep below the surface.

Flowing to the patient was the sense of kindness and gentleness of the physician who was demonstrating his deep respect for the patient. The soft touch of the physician's hand often brought a numbness to the area. After the gentle touch, patients could accept better a firmer hand examining markedly tender parts. Patients seemed to feel the knowledge and skill of the physician flowing into their afflicted areas, thus beginning the healing process before any medications had been prescribed.

Lucius observed that maintaining contact between the physician and patient was equally important during the pronouncement of the diagnosis and the prognosis. It was a shared bond between the two. Patient and physician were facing the disease or injury together. Together, they were stronger than the malady. The bonding during the discussion of the probable outcome of the disease could be as important as speeches given before a battle to the troops by a great general. Patients were always much stronger after such a bonding session. Although the healing hand was immensely powerful, the prescriptive was the real cure.

Theodosius knew all of Hippocrates' prescriptions by heart. He had picked up a few additional ones from the traders who came from lands east of Greece, but he was not very familiar with those to the west of Rome in Iberia and, of course, none from the northern frontier. What medicines he and Lucius compounded were quite effective for the narrow disease spectrum they saw in their little village.

They would gather ingredients throughout the year. Sometimes, they picked garlic, scallions, mint, and other herbs from the kitchen garden. Whenever Basilius discovered it, he would curse Theodosius in Greek threatening to give him tasteless food, but the histrionics were feigned. Basilius always planted more herbs than he needed. The pilfering never really affected the food preparation.

Medicines were handed out with great ceremony and pomp. The ritual enhanced the mystical powers of the drugs, Theodosius explained. Patients had to believe that the medicine would work, but only if their heart was pure and they took it with religious regularity. In that way, when the medication did not work, Theodosius could blame the patient. Fortunately, except for grave diseases like the pneumonias of the past winter, most people recovered.

Surgery on the other hand, was not a strength of Theodosius. He was excellent at preparing his patients for the knife. He would calm them by his touch and by holding a soothing conversation. He chose a topic of great interest to the patient, even getting the patient to relate a story or an amusing incident. The discussion led the patient's mind away from the dreaded moment of incision or cautery. The result was that few patients complained, even when experiencing the most excruciating pain and discomfort.

However, Theodosius was always clumsy with instruments. Sometimes, he cut in the wrong place and had to cut the patient again. Often, he dropped the cautery in the middle of a treatment. That resulted in the need to talk the patient down from the clouds while reheating the cautery over the fire. Sometimes patients would refuse completion of the treatment, or simply run away.

That winter, Theodosius had begun to prepare Lucius for surgeries. Before each planned operation, Theodosius would make Lucius recite the steps of the procedure the way Hippocrates had written them. The old Greek physician would interject some detail to the steps that he had learned over the years. He explained these pearls were nearly as important as the steps in the manuscripts. In addition, Lucius would need to state his plan if bleeding or some other complication occurred. Theodosius knew that would allow Lucius to be much more calm when operating.

Lucius believed deep in his heart that on the fateful day of the pus explosion, Theodosius knew beforehand what would happen when he drained the empyema. Allowing him to experience the spewing of pus in such a violent way was probably amusing at some level for the elderly physician, but Lucius did learn an important lesson. Now that he knew what was possible, he would be prepared the next time.

"Hey, are you listening to me boy?" Taurinus asked. "You seem miles away while I am giving you such important pearls of wisdom. You'll never be a surgeon if you can't listen." Taurinus spit.

"They sure don't make surgeons like they used to. By Jupiter! All we can attract to the surgical profession these days are tree stumps. How can I teach tree stumps?"

Lucius sighed and apologized. He sucked on his cinnamon and feigned attention. It would be another long day.

Chapter 8: Redirection

"What happens now, Athair?" asked Aia. She desperately hoped she would hear,"*We go home.*"

"We wait for our leaders to return from the Confederation summit and we have another council meeting," her father said.

Everyone was tired of council meetings by that point. Since that fateful day, the first day of Anagantios when Bimmos disrupted the Imbolc ceremony, the Tigurini had conducted over twenty different meetings to decide whether to forge ahead, leave the livestock, double up in wagons, or kill their few remaining slaves. Everyone was fed up with the discussions. They always turned into affirmations of Chieftain Bimmos's plans, anyway.

They were still on Helvetian lands. If the Confederation broke up, they could resettle at or near their old homeland. If the decision was to continue the migration, the path would be even tougher than their travels so far. Paths to the new territory were very limited. They could either go far to the North through the lands of the fierce Germanic tribes, or they could go through the Jura Mountains. It was rumored that the mountain trails were rugged and narrow with high rocky cliffs. The travel thus far had been tough because of the winter's heavy snows and the early spring thaw, but spring had not yet visited the paths around Mount Jura. That meant more hardship and the possibility that they might lose more wagons.

Such a journey required strong alliances with the Sequani tribe who lived on the other side of the mountains. Fortunately before his death, Orgetorix had begun the process of making peace with the Sequani. He offered hostage exchanges and arranged marriages of the hierarchy of the two tribes in hopes of assuring safe passage.

The Tigurini tribe was among the smallest of the Helvetian nations. They knew that the other tribes were determined to find a way to their perceived promised land. The Tigurinis felt that they would be lucky if they were allowed to continue to the new territory and not get left somewhere along the way like so much excess baggage. All was in the hands of Bimmos, their leader. According to some members of the delegation, he was a gifted negotiator, but to others, he was an arrogant blowhard. Regardless of his rhetoric, they had little real power to influence the decisions of the other nations. They could only await their fate.

Ever since their arrival in the outskirts of Geneva, Adiega had been coughing. She would feel an intermittent tickle deep in her chest that caused a coughing spasm. When it occurred, she could not stop coughing until the tickle subsided. Initially, it began as a dry cough, but by that point in the migration, she was coughing up large amounts of rusty brownish phlegm. She had no fevers or other symptoms, just the cough. Drutos instructed Aia to collect some sap of beech trees. It was late in the month of Cutios and the sap was just beginning to flow. Aia collected a pot-full of resin from several trees along the banks of the lake. She boiled the sap down to a thick, sticky consistency and mixed it with mulberry wine. She and her father administered it to her mother. The concoction was bitter and sent shudders through Adiega. The syrup made the cough disappear, but only for a short time. She required frequent doses.

That morning, Adiega felt a strange new sensation. At first, it seemed as though something was dripping into her chest. She felt a very slow, but constant drip in her right lung behind her breast. The liquid felt cold, like water dripping off an icicle. She tried to will it to stop, but it persisted. While she was reciting morning prayers, she developed a wheeze. As she did her morning chores, the wheeze became more like a bubbling. By taking very shallow breaths, Adiega was able to hide the wheezing from everyone. She decided to tell no one. By mid morning, she could feel rattling in her chest. She took an extra swallow of the foul tasting elixir to suppress her urge to cough.

Around midday as Adiega went to the lake to gather water, the urge to cough returned. She coughed and up a large amount of material into her mouth. She spit out a reddish brown lump of goo. She turned toward the water, took a deep breath, and coughed hard to clear the rattling material still left in her chest. Instead of phlegm, she expectorated bright red blood. There was so much blood coming up in her mouth that she could not catch her breath. She fell to her knees and allowed the blood to flow out.

Gradually as the flow slowed, she was able to catch her breath. After a brief rest, she noticed that the dripping in her chest had stopped and her urge to cough was better. She took slow shallow breaths until she could breathe normally. She looked down at the ground where she had expectorated. She was frightened to see that the blood and phlegm was enough to fill her two cupped hands. She looked around. No one had seen what had happened. She kicked dirt over the blood and decided not to mention it to anyone.

When Adiega returned with her water and her secret, she found Drutos and Aia preparing to go to the Council meeting. She made excuses for not attending saying it was going to take extra time to prepare dinner. Aia was old enough to represent her at the council, anyway. She turned away to tend to the fire. She felt dizzy and propped herself on the wagon so no one would suspect she was ill.

As Drutos walked toward the gathering place in the center of the campground, he spoke with his second daughter.

"You should have a talk with your mother. She thinks you are avoiding her."

"I am, Athair," she said. "I have nothing to say to her. She has been a witch to me." Aia looked away from her father and toward the large glassy lake.

"It is not healthy for our family to be angry with each other. We are the leaders of the Druids and we need to be strong for our people."

"Athair, you have always said that we should be true to our feelings because people will be able to tell if we are not being honest."

"Yes, but right now our clan is very vulnerable and needs to look up to us as an example of a family with strong bonds and faith in the future." He turned to her and looked in her eyes.

"You know, you two are very much alike. Your Màthair was a headstrong young woman like you."

Aia looked at her father.

Why is Athair trying so hard to get me to make peace with Màthair?

"I remember before we were married," he continued. "She fought with your grandmother over every detail of the wedding. She did not want to wait the prescribed year before marrying, but once we were married and she had children, she changed. She became focused on family matters. She lived for you children. Her thoughts and plans have been only for you." He fell silent and stared into the distance.

"Athair, are you all right?" asked Aia as she poked him gently in the side.

"Yes," he said refocusing on Aia. "Well, anyway, promise me that you will have a chat with her. She only wants the best for you."

She looked at the ground. She knew in her heart that her mother had sacrificed a great deal to give her and her brother and sisters the best, but sometimes, she was just plain infuriating. Every time they had a conversation, they fought. Their fractured relationship had turned from smoldering embers to a raging fire. She hoped for better, but she was unsure of how to change it. She loved her father and would do anything for him. Taking the initiative to mend fences would be hard for her. She breathed in deeply and gave a giant sigh.

"Okay, Athair, I will do it for you."

"Thank you, my child."

They finished their conversation just as they arrived for the council meeting. Nearly everyone was already there. Bimmos stood on a barrel surrounded by the young warriors including Lugurix and Toutios. Aia did not sense anger in Toutios's heart as she had on Imbolc. He seemed to be calm, although he was hiding something, even from her. Bimmos began to speak.

"Today, my kinsmen, I bring you good news from the Confederation. We remain united with our brethren. Our combined nations are stronger than ever! We believe as one great people, that our future lies in the lands where we will be able to see the afternoon sun touch the great sea. Yes, we will settle in new lands in Gaul!"

There was cheering, mainly from the warriors who circulated among the people. They goaded those surrounding them to cheer as well.

"As one nation, we have decided to go through the mountains to the northwest of Geneva. We estimate that it will take only a few extra weeks to work our way through this obstacle. We recognize that it will be hard, but our brethren who had an easier time getting here will support us with new wagons and supplies!"

Everyone's spirits were raised and a cheer arose spontaneously.

"Now, I, as your Chieftain, worked hard in our cause to secure the best position for this migration. The Helvetians, the nation which began this initiative, is the largest. They are a quarter of a million strong. They will lead us into Gaul. Of the other nations, we are in the best position. Although we are only 36,000 strong, we outnumber each of the Boii, the Rauraci and the Latobrigi tribes. Besides, our tribe is the only one to have faced and defeated the Roman Army. It was our great grandfathers who made the cursed Romans go under the yoke, and today, we have the finest and fiercest fighters of the Confederation. As such, we earned the privilege of being the rear guard of this fine new nation!"

There was more cheering, but Aia sensed dark emotions rising in her twin brother. She hoped she would have an opportunity to be with him soon and understand his concerns. Bimmos droned on.

"Because we have willingly taken on this important role, we have been assured that we will be allowed first pick of the new lands. We will be able to maintain our own governance and our own language and traditions. We will be masters in our new world!"

There was real cheering among nearly all Tigurini, but Drutos and Aia remained silent observing the crowd.

"Prepare to move out tomorrow!"

The council ended without anyone having an opportunity to make a comment.

"Typical of our Chieftain," Drutos told Aia. "At least he gives good speeches. The people seem genuinely happy and more upbeat than they have been in months."

As they began to walk back to their wagon, Drutos looked at Aia.

"Now don't forget to talk with your mother," he added.

"Okay, okay, I will. Just don't push me," she whined.

That night, Ouenitouta and her husband Frontú as well as Toutios joined the family for dinner. Toutios was taciturn. On the other hand, Ouenitouta was beaming.

"We have exciting news," Ouenitouta bubbled. "I'm pregnant! I have suspected for a few weeks, but today, the baby stirred. It must have happened between Yule and Imbolc before our troubles began. With luck, we will be settled in our new home before the baby comes!"

Sina ran over to hug her eldest sister. Drutos and Toutios congratulated Frontú. Aia smiled, but wondered if she would ever get married, let alone become pregnant.

"Oh, what joyous news!" Adiega said with deepest love. "I will be here for you, anytime." Then, she turned to Drutos.

"Well, old man, we are about to become grandparents," she said. "What do you say to that?"

Drutos was beaming. The marriage to Frontú had been a good one for Ouenitouta. Now they were blessed with the gift of life, and just at the appropriate time in the Druidic calendar.

"When we have sufficient time, we will arrange for a proper blessing," he said.

Aia hugged Ouenitouta and Frontú wishing them well, then she looked at her brother. Something was wrong. She just could not put her finger on it. She held out her hand to him.

"Come, Toutios, take a walk with me. It has been so long since we have been together."

He looked at her with sad eyes, but got up to join her. They walked down toward the lake. Toutios remained silent and pensive. She caressed his arm to reassure him that she was there for him. He stared up at the clear evening sky. The stars were beginning to come out. The moon was just rising, and its reflection sparkled on the calm lake waters.

"Athair tells me that Màthair is quite ill," he said.

Aia looked back at him.

"Is that what is bothering you?"

"Yes, among other things. I just found out tonight when I arrived for supper. Athair does not think she will complete the journey."

"But, she just has a cough," Aia protested.

"He thinks otherwise. He seems genuinely concerned." Toutios looked into her eyes. She could sense a deep sadness.

"Are you still having those dreams?" he asked.

At first she was startled, then realized that their twin bond must be as strong as ever.

"Yes," she answered.

"I have had disturbing dreams ever since the day we were refused safe passage through Gaul. I dream that we are swimming together in the river back home, the way we used to when we were very young. All of a sudden, the current becomes swift and the waters become bloody. We are washed down stream in a torrent of blood. We find a rock to cling to and find Athair clinging there. He is very weak and he is crying for help. He slips and we both grab for him. You try to hold him up, but he slips from your hand. I lift him up to you, but as I do, I lose my grip on the rock and get carried away by the current. I look back and see you alone on the rock, then I get pulled under the water and I wake up out of breath."

Aia became frightened.

"My dream is very much like yours, only I am on land and I can't reach Athair. You come to help, but..." she trailed off and threw herself into Toutios's arms and sobbed. After a few moments, she regained composure and pulled back to look into his eyes.

"What is to become of us? Are we doomed?"

"I do not know, but I will do everything within my power to keep our family safe," he said through clenched teeth. "Promise me you will pray everyday that we receive blessings."

"I promise."

As Toutios took his leave from the family, Aia vowed that she would attempt to make peace with her mother. She would try to cherish every moment she had with her parents.

Later that evening, Lugurix stopped by to see Aia. He was well groomed and wore the armor of an officer. He had a cuirass of bronze. His sword hilt was encrusted with stones. Although Aia felt like brooding, she received him with courtesy.

"My, my, Lugurix. You wear the armor of a leader. Must I bow to you?"

"No, please don't. I am still Lugurix." He stood tall and spread his arms. "I have been promoted to lieutenant directly under Bimmos. I have great responsibility now. I will not be able to come to see you once we are underway, but tonight, I wanted to spend a little time with the one I love." He extended his hand toward her.

Aia folded her arms and turned away, coyly glancing back.

"I still have not forgiven you for your part in displacing our tribe."

"I know, and for that I am truly sorry. It pained me to have Bimmos ruin our moment, but my duty is to the tribe as your duty is to keep us at peace with the spirits. Sometimes, our duties work at cross purposes."

Aia turned to face the man she loved.

"Lugurix, I need to know. If you had to choose between me and your duties, how would you choose?"

"You know I love you," he replied.

Aia tapped her foot. Lugurix looked at the ground and played with his sword trying to craft a careful answer.

"My duties...," he began haltingly. "My duties are to the Tigurini tribe... You are the princess of the Druids of the Tigurini tribe... So, my duty is to you." He finished with a feeling of smugness, but he tried to hide behind a look of deep caring as he reengaged her face.

"I wonder. That was too neat," Aia thought to herself. She turned away from him again.

"Hmm, I am not at all certain about your answer."

"Well, one thing is for certain," he said. "I love you deeply and I want you to be my wife when we settle in the new lands."

"Oh, Lugurix," Aia said as she spun back around, then caught herself and tried to act cool. She looked at her hands and inspected her cuticles.

"I must ask my parents. You know they are divided about you." She became pensive. "I must think about it too." She paused a moment, then looked back at his face with a glint in her eye.

"Show me at Beltane. Convince Bimmos that we must have ceremony in our lives. Our spiritual side is as important as his quest for new lands."

Lugurix smiled broadly. "I promise you, we will have a wonderful Beltane ceremony. You will be surprised at how things will change in the very near future."

"I'll wait for your surprise," she said, "but it better be good."

She tried to turn away, but he grabbed her by the arm and spun her around pulling her against his armor plating. They shared a long passionate kiss, then Lugurix released his embrace and dashed away without looking back. As she watched him disappear into the night, she tried to imagine what the future would bring.

Chapter 9: Nicknames

Lucius sat next to Taurinus on the wagon and chewed on his cinnamon bark. He was ready to start daydreaming the moment Taurinus began his stories of indestructible surgeons and the woes of a practice full of women with morbus indecens, but the speech was different.

"It's time we work on your training as a surgeon," Taurinus began.

Lucius turned to look at the fat old blabbermouth.

"What?"

"You heard me. All of your training so far has been about learning the art of being a physician. Sounds like your training was very classical, so you practice medicine in the ways of Hippocrates, am I right?"

"Yes, that's true. My mentor, Theodosius is Greek. He brought a manuscript copied from the texts of Hippocrates and made me memorize it," replied Lucius.

"Well, a lot has changed in Roma since the great one wrote down his thoughts. What were his words about those humors?"

Lucius felt like he was being tested the way Theodosius tested him.

"The body requires the balance of the four main humors: blood, black bile, yellow bile and phlegm. Blood brings warmth to the body parts. Lack of blood leads to coldness and lack of speech..."

"Okay, okay. That's enough. You certainly know the old Greek theories. In Roma, those theories have become passé. Don't get me wrong, I'm not saying it's for the better, but Roman physicians are pulled in different directions every day by competing theories. Hippocrates based his treatment on reasoning. Reasoning has fallen out of favor and has been replaced by a host of new theories. At least we can thank the gods that we have finally buried the idiotic theories of that quack, Cato."

Taurinus began to enumerate a variety of contemporaneous medical theories.

"Roman physicians of today want to have their own brand of Medicine, so they have created a huge variety of practices. One of the recent groups espouses diet as the only treatment. They say you can cure the body and keep it pure by altering your diet. Of course, even they admit it works best on the healthy." Taurinus laughed.

"Then there are the Empiricists who experiment by giving something or doing something to the patient. They wait to see what eventually happens, and choose the treatments that work the best. If I recall correctly, a physician from Alexandria named Serapion started it a couple of hundred years ago, and it is kept alive today by Heraclides of Tarentum." Taurinus spit out a mangled piece of cinnamon.

"The most recent craze comes from this guy, Asclepiades, who is only a few years older than me. He has a great deal of favor with Roman families, because he is dear friends with Cicero, and his major prescriptive is to take wine in excess. He abhors Hippocrates calling the great physician's writings on prognosis a meditation on death. His philosophy is based on this atomic theory of Democritus and Epicurus. It has something to do with pores that allow atoms to flow in and out of the body. He says, when these pores are altered, the body becomes diseased. To correct the disease, he either constricts the pores such as prescribing exercise in dropsy, or opens the pores such as performing a tracheotomy for breathing." Taurinus became more animated as he continued.

"Asclepiades has an insane disciple named Themison of Laodicea. This character goes even further by creating a new class of physicians called Methodists. He bases his theory on tight sinews, loose sinews, or some combination of both. They loosen or tighten the body with rest, massage, and stretching exercises. Those two lunatics have trained innumerable young physicians, so Medicine in Roma right now has diverging, bizarre theories and countless quacks."

Taurinus took a pause and relieved himself over the side of the rolling wagon. When he sat down, he continued the lecture.

"Anyway, I tend to favor the dogmatism and reasoning of Hippocrates, so you and I are similar there. I admire you for that. However, you know that physicians rarely cure disease. Rather, they keep the patient alive and comfortable until the disease either goes away or the patient dies."

Taurinus began poking Lucius in the chest.

"But, you. You, my boy. You want to be a surgeon! What is a surgeon, you might ask? Well, I define a surgeon this way: Medico qui curat! – A physician who cures!"

Lucius could feel a little excitement growing inside. He knew that he and Theodosius often had little effect the course of a patient's disease. Symptom recognition and knowledge of specific outcomes allowed them to advise and comfort the patient and his family. It helped them to better navigate the long and often unaltered course of the disease. Maybe now, he would learn how to cure some diseases and see some real results.

"I hear that surgeons do some incredible operations in Roma," Lucius said with a little too much excitement. "There are stories of complete cures never before dreamed of. For instance, we sent a citizen, who was blinded by cataracts, to be treated by the famed ophthalmologist, Livius Claudius Laurentus. He cured his eyes with no incisions!"

"Watch out, boy. Don't fall for all that false advertising. I know that guy. How do you think he got that cognomen? He crowned himself with a laurel wreath and went around bragging. He does only one kind of operation and makes it sound like he is a god. What he really wants is for citizens to buy his line of eye creams and ointments. Every woman in Roma pleads with her husband to bring home his latest anti-wrinkle cream or some drops to cure red eyes. He is a filthy rich scam artist!"

"But he cured our magistrate!" Lucius interrupted. "The poor man was going blind. We examined him and found opacities the color of sea water occluding vision in both eyes. When his term as the Curule Magistrate ended, we sent him to Roma with his family. He came back with only the smallest opacities and markedly improved vision. He talked about it for months. We were all amazed."

"I'm sure it's true my boy, but it's not magic, and it certainly was not done without an incision. He calls it no incision, but others who use the technique refer to it as a 'minimally invasive' procedure." Taurinus spit again.

"I must admit, Laurentus has quite the setup. He works out of his immense villa in Roma. He only accepts wealthy patricians as patients. He has a staff of beautiful young female receptionists waiting in his vestibule. They greet the family with praises to the gods and compliments for each member of the family, then they escort the entire family through the peristylum packed with statues of

Laurentus next to Aesculapius and Hippocrates and Jupiter knows who else! They allow the family to admire the artwork for a while, then usher them into the atrium where another beautiful voluptuous woman takes the family's expensive, nonrefundable examination fee and tells them about the services. She performs a cursory eye exam to confirm the cataracts, then calls in another voluptuous assistant to negotiate the fees."

Lucius could tell that Taurinus was passionate about the topic. His face flushed red, and after every few sentences, he spit cinnamon.

"After the fees and expenses are agreed upon, the patient is led to a sitting room while the family is ushered through a stunning vine arbor to the terraced garden where they are served a lavish banquet. Meanwhile, an apprentice reexamines the patient. Once the diagnosis is confirmed, the patient is pumped full of poppy tea and belladonna wine until he is snoring and having drug dreams. Assistants hold the patient down. Only then does Laurentus appear. He slides a specially designed straight needle sideways into the clear part of the eye. He works the cataract loose and shoves it into the depths of the eyeball. That's the whole operation! Assistants put dressings soaked in egg whites over the eyes and present the patient to the family. The patient and his family spend the night together in the converted summer house on the Laurentus villa."

Lucius was amazed.

"Sounds like a delicate procedure, but I am surprised that people say they see so well afterwards."

"Well, here's the answer to that, son," Taurinus said. "The day after the operation, the patient and his family are brought to the gardens by more of Laurentus' buxom assistants. Usually, the poor patient is still drunk from the high doses of drugs he received. There, in the presence of his staff of beauties and with a great deal of fanfare, Laurentus removes the bandages. The first thing the patient sees is an up close view of breasts. Cute, huh? As his eyes adjust, the girls step aside and he can see the beautiful gardens and the manicured grounds of the Laurentus villa. The gardens are on the northern side of the villa, so the patient does not have to look into the sun. For the first time in years, the cloudy yellow lens is gone and the patient sees unfiltered bright colors. It's like he died and went directly to the bosom of Juno! Nearly every patient is overjoyed with the view. Before there is time to critically analyze the results, Laurentus loads up the patient's wife and daughters with creams, ointments, and drops for which the patient is all too eager to pay. What a racket!"

"Amazing," was all Lucius could say. He had no interest in emulating that type of physician. His family was wealthy. As the oldest surviving son, he would inherit all the family's holdings when his Pater passed on. His only dream was to be his region's best physician and provide the finest medicine and surgery to his friends and their families and slaves.

After a pause to find a fresh piece of cinnamon bark, Taurinus went on.

"Yeah, there are too many crooked quacks running around the Republic. We need a good purge."

"Are there any honest surgeons in Roma?"

"To be sure, there are honest surgeons, but they are hard to find among the countless dishonest ones like Asclepiades and Themison and pseudo-surgeons like Laurentus." Taurinus spit out another chunk of cinnamon bark and continued.

"The good ones work hard. They drain abscesses all over the body. They remove teeth and tonsils, cysts and condylomata. They fix hernias and hemorrhoids and eradicate varicose veins. They can dilate the urethra and get old men urinating again. They remove stones in both men and women. Some can even fix a woman's vagina after being ruptured during delivery. Unfortunately, wealth has poured into Roma from around the world. Citizens demand the latest treatments. The temptation is overwhelming to specialize in doing only simple surgical procedures that have great results. It plays to the vanity of rich men and their families and their mistresses. Many talented surgeons fall into the money trap."

Lucius couldn't help himself. Taurinus had left himself open to the question.

"Isn't that what you have been doing for the last thirteen years?"

Taurinus spun around turning instantly red. Lucius thought he saw steam rising from the old man's bald head.

"You should be whipped, then crucified, you stinking gas bag!" Then he waited a moment, belched, and laughed.

"In a way, you are right, but I only charged minimum fees. The senators have been generous to me for my skill." He looked back to the road and drove on.

"And, I never advertised!" he added.

They sat in silence while Taurinus composed his thoughts, then he began in an instructive tone.

"Military surgeons have the best of all worlds. We have equipment provided and repaired by the greatest war machine known to man. We get unlimited dressings and supplies. We have young healthy men for patients. Once trained, they don't bitch and complain about every little cut or bruise or pimple. When they come to us, they need our help." He stopped to take a swig of water before going on.

"You see, we don't have to guess at the diagnosis. It is obvious. We can feel a broken bone or see where an arm has been hacked off. We can see an arrow, sword, or spear sticking out of a body part. We can see hemorrhage or merda issuing from a wound. It's easy to make a diagnosis. Not only that, we know the cause. It's battle trauma. We don't waste time on symptoms and signs. Our examinations are simple and direct. Treatments, however brutal, are applied quickly. We don't have a long list of potential procedures and argue about which one will get the best result. We have learned which treatments are effective and we don't hesitate to apply them. We don't have to waste time on the simple injuries, because they heal over time without our help. We don't have waste time on the dying, because we can't alter their course and they use up our resources. What's more, the soldiers and officers are grateful, because we patch them up so they can fight another day! So, as I always say: Vide, Cura, Exige! – See it, Treat it, Street it!"

"Won't we see and treat non-surgical diseases?" questioned Lucius. "Certainly an epidemic could strike us."

"Oh, we will see a little illness. Anytime you put this many men in a small space, there can be epidemics like the ones described by Hippocrates. Those usually occur when we are in castra, not during a campaign like this. We are under the open air and we move camp sites nearly every night. This way, we stay ahead of the diseases of overpopulation and stagnation. Besides, when we do build a new castra to house these legions, Caesar's engineers will use elaborate plans. The buildings will be well ventilated to keep away bad air. The hospital will be well divided to keep the diseased away from the injured. We will have running water for our baths and our latrines. This brings fresh pure water to us and carries away the stink and pollution." Taurinus was silent for a moment as he readjusted himself, then began again.

"Don't worry, son. Campaigns end after harvest time. You will have all winter to deal with medical illnesses and other types of surgical conditions. If you want, you can even do specialty work like gynecology in the village near the castra. The village folk provide you with an excellent opportunity to hone your skills. They will be very grateful. They will bring you gifts of food and wine. Why, they may even build you an office and provide furniture. For me, though, the best part of wintertime practice is that next year, we'll be gone. We will leave in the spring and we won't have to deal with any of the postoperative complications!" Taurinus grinned and patted Lucius on the back.

Lucius shuddered at the last statement. He wanted his practice to be family oriented. He always enjoyed seeing patients back, even if treatments had not worked out. He hoped the campaign did not last until winter. He was itching to be a physician back in Canino again with or without surgical skills.

That night after Taurinus went to find Publicus, Lucius left his wagon for the first time. He walked back to see the other medical wagons and survey the supplies. To his surprise, he discovered that he was not the only young medical immune. Five others were sitting at a small field table sharing stories with their supper rations. Lucius raised his arm.

"All hail!"

They looked up at the thin young Etruscan. Lucius felt a little uneasy. He continued.

"If you are well, so am I. I am Lucius Calidius of Canino. I am a legion surgeon. Well, actually, I—"

"Hey, don't be so formal. We know who you are. You're the poor sap stuck with Taurinus. Come join us. I am Priscus. This is Magnus, Petrus, Atticus and Modestus. We wondered how long it would take you to break away from the old fart."

Lucius greeted each in turn and sat down.

"All of you go by your cognomens."

"Yeah," said Modestus. "That's Manius Fabricius Taurinus. He likes to nickname nearly everything. Priscus never gives details, so I'll try to explain." He pointed to Magnus. Lucius looked at the big burly youth.

"This is Aulus Murrius. He is from Milano. He arrived in Roma to apprentice with Taurinus just as the call came to form two new legions. Taurinus conscripted him. Because he is such a big man towering over most Romans, he calls him Magnus. There will be many women in Roma who will be glad he is not in the clinic with Taurinus. Look at his hands!"

Magnus extended his hand. It was the biggest hand Lucius had ever seen.

"They tell me I would make women useless for a Roman." The others laughed.

"Except for you and Magnus, the rest of us have apprenticed with Taurinus. He conscripted each of us. The salary is right, and the experience should help us all when we return to practice."

Modestus introduced each young surgeon in turn. Horatius Novius was next. He went to Roma to work with Taurinus, but washed out early. He never could remember anything, thus he never developed adequate surgical techniques. Taurinus called him Petrus, because he was so thick headed.

Livius Aemilius also washed out with Taurinus. At first, he seemed like an excellent student. He was always attentive and asked questions, but the discussions wandered to topics well off the subject of medicine. He tripped from food, to plants, to buildings, and other random subjects. It was clear to Taurinus that Livius gained knowledge very slowly, so he became Atticus in mockery of his attention.

Marcus Amatius was the son of a physician, who had grown up assisting his father. He held many preconceived notions of Medicine and brought many bad surgical habits learned from his father. When he worked with Taurinus, he steadfastly held to his antiquated notions and habits. Taurinus nicknamed him Priscus for being Old School.

Silanus Valentis was the son of a senator, who had dreamed of becoming a senator himself, maybe even Consul someday. However, his father wound up on the wrong side of Sulla in the civil strife and was murdered. Silanus was forced to change his plans, at least temporarily, just to survive. Family and friends in the Senate got him an apprenticeship with Taurinus. When asked about his political views, he would always side with the majority sentiments in the senate. Since Taurinus closed his practice to go to war, Silanus was forced into becoming a surgeon. He was a reasonable assistant, but it was clear that his heart was not in it. Taurinus called him Modestus for his political correctness.

Lucius listened carefully to the very candid stories.

"You seem rather open about yourselves," he commented.

"In the business of surgery, your faults become common knowledge," said Priscus. "In the medical fields, you may hide yourself and your mistakes. Some, you just bury. Surgery is different. You become known for your skill, your results, and your personality. You must accept who you are and own up to your missteps. It's the only way to become the best you can be."

"Do I have a nickname?" Lucius asked with some embarrassment. Everyone laughed.

"Well, not officially," said Petrus. They all laughed again. Lucius was puzzled.

"You see," said Modestus. "Taurinus always says, 'Fortune favors the observant' and the one he favors now, we have dubbed Fortunatus. You have the misfortune of riding with the old gas bag every day. We have become fortunate, because he is busy with you. So, we nicknamed you Fortunatus. Even the old fart seems to like our choice."

"Thank you, I think," chuckled Lucius. They all laughed. After supper they shared a few hair raising stories about the old man and some of his less than compassionate encounters with senators' mistresses.

As Lucius went back to his wagon, he thought about his strange evening.

"Has fortune favored me, or will this experience be a giant gap in my education?" he wondered.

Every evening before turning in, Lucius prayed to Salus, the family goddesses. He prayed that he would gain knowledge, skill, and strength during his journey. To those prayers, he decided to add a short request of Abundantia. He beseeched her to keep luck on his side.

Chapter 10: Formal Training

Placentia was an easy three days' march from Parma. The town was established about a hundred years earlier. As an early Roman outpost, it had been a source of trouble. Consul Marcus Aemilius Lepidus built the Via Emilia to the West after it became a well established colony with fortresses both there and at its sister city, Cremora. A few years later, Consul Marcus Aemilius Scaura built the Via Amellia Scaura toward the Southeast. The roads connected Placentia to both coasts. At the time of the arrival of Caesar's new legions, it was a peaceful, solid center of commerce.

The River Po on the northern side of Placentia made lazy "S's" as it coursed through the valley on its long journey toward the Adriatic Sea. Just to the west of the town, the diminutive Flume Trebbia joined the Po at its most languid. As the river passed the banks of the town, it became wider and deeper, making crossing difficult. That spring, swollen from a massive snow melt, it was near its highest point in years, nearly overflowing its banks. Despite the extra water, it was less than one thousand feet across and only a few feet deep at the fording site.

When the legions were about two miles away, Marcus could make out the rampart towers of the city. The column of troops looked to be headed for the main gate. However, just before reaching the gates, they made a sweeping left turn and marched around the city to the banks of the Po. As they approached the West side of the walled city, they could see the buildings of a large military camp. They would be in real buildings for the first time in weeks. The legion halted just south of the buildings. Martial brought his troops around to stand facing west into the hot afternoon sun. He scowled and paced in front of them.

"All right you scum buckets, we have arrived at our rendezvous point. While we wait, we will billet in the castra. Don't get too used to these luxuries, because we are only here until the seasoned legions arrive, then we are off again. We only have a few days to whip you into the fighting machines that Caesar expects, so we will drill all day, every day. Tonight, you will get all of your remaining gear from the Placentia quartermaster. He is set up at the headquarters building. Then, there will be a meal prepared for you. Pick it up when you draw your rations from the granary. Don't linger. You little mushrooms need to get a good night's sleep. Be ready to jump to it tomorrow. After rising, meet out here with all of your gear, and I mean all of it. We will practice formation drills before breakfast. After breakfast, there will be combat training for the rest of the day, then it will be time for supper in your barracks. We will repeat the process every day until the legions arrive. Any questions?"

"Yes, sir," shouted Marcus.

"How did I know it would be gas bag here!" Martial spat on the ground.

"Will we get an opportunity to go into town?"

"Not if I can help it! And, if I find out you went there without permission, be prepared to be crucified! Any more questions? None? Okay, do not be late tomorrow. Dismissed!"

"Totally outrageous!" moaned Marcus. "We go through great Roman cities to get here, yet we don't see a single one. Surely there is enough time for one night inside the city walls."

Quintus came up and put his arm on Marcus' shoulder.

"You are whining like a girl! I thought you wanted to be the greatest legionnaire!"

"I do, but I need a break now and then."

"I have relatives living here. They moved up when the senate sent colonists almost a hundred years ago. The families kept up, so I know where to find them. Maybe they can help us sneak out for one night."

"Are you a lunatic? We could be killed for leaving the castra!"

"We will be fine, just let me handle the details. You'll see!"

Marcus didn't like the sound of that, but waited to see what Quintus was cooking up.

"All you need to do is give me some money."

"What?"

"You know I lost all of my money in that fight on the beach. Getting out for a night will cost, so fork it over."

Marcus reluctantly agreed and gave Quintus most of his remaining coins. He figured it was another ruse and he would be separated forever from his money with no rewards.

The two youths entered the castra through the West gate onto a broad street lined with one story buildings of varying sizes. Soldiers were running about in every direction. Marcus had never seen more than two centurions together at one time. Here, they gathered in groups and walked with one another in animated conversation. On their right was a row of larger, almost square dwellings for the senior cavalry officers. On their left was a row of long buildings extending back from the street with a small separate house in front. Watching the movement of the soldiers, he figured that these were the century's barracks and the small separate houses in front were for the centurions.

Just beyond the barracks was the headquarters building. It was set back from the street and had a fenced courtyard. A line of recruits was going in the left gate and through the headquarters building, then exiting to the right loaded with gear. They joined the line and received their armor and military tunic. They walked to the East castra gate, put on the new garments, and left their old clothing there to be burned that night. Next, they reentered the East gate and were told to turn to the right. They had to pass behind the houses of the Tribunes to reach their granary. They drew their rations and received some sort of stew in a pot to distribute to their other mates at their barracks.

They turned away from the granary toward their barracks. Unlike the ones on the main street for the first cohort, the other cohorts' barracks were lined up next to one another with the centurions' quarters facing the East wall. They surmised that they would form up next to the barracks and march east to the wall, then turn south following the wall to the gate. That would put them in the appropriate rank order formation.

When they entered the barracks, they were stunned to see that each of them had a cot. Marcus plopped down removing the new uncomfortable armor. He knew they he would have to get used to the extra weight and still travel as far and as fast as ever. Quintus distributed the thick substance called supper. The gruel contained almost no meat, a few carrots, and mostly barley. They ate quickly and everyone jumped on their cots. The cots were just material stretched out over a few strips of wood, but to these recruits who spent nearly three weeks on forced marches with little comfort, the bedding was as luxurious as any villa. Almost before Marcus' head hit the cot he was asleep. He neither saw Quintus slip out after dark nor heard him return a few hours later. The next thing that Marcus sensed was the centurion screaming orders.

"Get up, mushrooms! We don't have time for a beauty rest! Put your asses in a building and you become worthless mushrooms! I want all of you in uniform and outside ready to march this instant!"

Marcus and the others threw their clothing and armor on. They grabbed their pila, swords, and shields, and stumbled out into the first rays of dawn. They formed up with the rest of the century and marched out of the camp. The column turned south to join the other recruits. They were in traveling formation with each cohort behind the other as always. In front was the vanguard, now complete with cavalry and light infantry. These units would also serve as flankers and rear guard. The only elements not present were the medical wagons and baggage train, which were still a day or so away from joining the force.

The legatus for each legion had the centurions form the troops into their first real battle formation. The first lines were the Velites, the spear throwers. Next were the ten maniples of the Hastatii followed by the identical Principes and the Triarii. The last fighters were the heavy infantry who would engage the enemy directly in hand-to-hand combat. Internal orientation placed the strongest fighters on the right flank and the weakest on the left flank. Marcus found himself in the line of the ninth cohort of the Triarii Posterior, all the way on the edge of the left flank. Standing in formation, he realized that he would be among the last infantry to face an enemy as their lines clashed. Despite his lowly position, he could feel a surge of energy pulse through his body. When he did get his chance, he would finally taste battle and have his opportunity for the glory of Rome.

Centurions prowled up and down the formations moving individuals slightly to the right or the left , forward or back to achieve perfect alignment. At first, there was a cacophony of shouted orders as each centurion whipped his century into shape. With time, the orders diminished to infrequent barks. Soon, only sporadic shouts could be heard, then finally silence. They stood in silence for what seemed like an eternity.

Marcus heard hoof beats, but did not follow them for fear of garnering Martial's anger again. He just looked straight ahead at the horizon. Out of the corner of his eye, he saw the legatus with his second in command, the Tribunus Laticlavius, riding next to him. They went by slowly weaving through the lines inspecting the formation, then galloped back to the front. Moments later, the troops received the order to march in formation. They had never marched in battle formation before and it was disorienting for a while until they got used to the new cues for staying the appropriate distance from the four soldiers around them. They marched in that formation for a half mile, then new orders were shouted.

"Ad dextram – Depone! Right wheel! Turn!" came the command.

That meant the far right flank became the anchoring point of a great spoke in an imaginary wheel. Their movement was minimal. The first cohort essentially marked time as they slowly faced to the right. Each successive cohort to the left had to travel further and faster to keep the line straight. Marcus and his cohort at the far left of the formation literally had to sprint to keep their position.

It was a disaster. The line warbled and sagged, first in a comma shape, then an S-shape. Finally, it disintegrated into dots of confused motion. The commanders and centurions had a field day barking insults and orders at the men. They reformed the legions facing east and did it again with nearly the same disastrous result.   More yelling and barking helped the legions form up quicker. They did it repeatedly, first to the West, then to the North, then to the East, and so on until they could make the right turn without disintegrating into a jumble. Finally, they were allowed to take a break and eat breakfast. The sun was halfway to its zenith by then.

"Don't get too comfortable, melon heads." Martial said as he looked down at his subordinates. "That drill was so pathetic, the legatus has decided to continue formation training until we get it right. Hand-to-hand combat training will have to wait. If you weren't such a pack of mules, we could move ahead with the real fun. But, no! We're stuck on basics! So we drill again. Are you going to get it right this time?"

"Yes, sir," they mumbled in unison.

"I can't hear you!"

"Yes, sir," raising their voices.

"I still can't hear you!"

"Yes, sir!"

"Louder!"

"Yes, sir!"

"Louder!"

"Yes, sir!" They were all screaming at the top of their lungs by then.

"All right, form up again!"

The group hurried into line and marched back to the assembling legion. They mustered in battle formation and marched south for another half mile, then the next order came down.

"Ad sinistram – Depone! Left wheel! Turn!"

Marcus was glad that they did not have to sprint.   He and his group performed the maneuver well, but they watched the line to the right waver and break apart. Once the lines were reformed, the worst offenders were pulled to the front of the troops and whipped. That got everyone's attention. Turns improved immediately.

They marched through midday making first a right wheel, then a left wheel, then forming a travel column, then battle formation, and then more right and left turning.

It was late afternoon as they made a left turn.   Sol was low in the sky. They could barely make out the castra about three miles away. Now, they practiced something new.   They formed a battle line facing north and marched a short distance. Then, on command, they charged ahead and stopped after one hundred paces. After holding position for a short time, the front lines were ordered to fall back to the rear just in front of the reserves. They repeated that maneuver until the unit was back in the original formation. Then, they marched ahead and repeated the exercise until they were just outside the castra. They halted in formation while their Legatus rode to the front and inspected the line, then he addressed the troops.

"Today was the first day of real training. We have precious little time to prepare for the coming campaign. When Caesar arrives, we must be as good as the three legions from L'Aquila. This training may seem impossible now, but when you face the barbarians, you will be glad we worked so hard. Each of you must be able to do your job and trust that your fellow soldier will do his job. That is how we will always be victorious. Today, you were barely passable. In the next few days, you must become a fighting machine. Once you are, I will be proud to lead you into battle.   You will fight to keep Roma safe from foreign invasion.   Your families depend on you. Do not let them down! Dismissed!"

Quintus immediately grabbed Marcus by the arm.

"We are set for tonight, brother."

"What do you mean, Quintus?" All Marcus could think about was how tired and hot he felt, and how much his feet hurt.

"Yeah, we go to town tonight!"

"Get yourself out of here! What are you talking about?"

"I paid off the guards with the money you gave me and slipped into town. It didn't take long to find my relatives and get a new set of dice, then I came back and played dice with the chief of the guards. He lost big, but instead of taking all of his money, I only took a little and made him promise to let the two of us slip out for the night."

"So, you got another set of loaded dice?"

"I'm not saying," Quintus protested holding his hands in the air. "Let's go back and eat. Tonight, we stay awake until after bed check, then head right into town. There's a place there called 'Boys' Town' that you are going to love. My Cousin showed me how to get there."

"You better have this all worked out. I don't want to be killed before I get a chance to fight barbarians."

"It's going to be spectacular, trust me."

"That's what I'm afraid of."

They walked back to the domicile with the rest of their tent group trying to act nonchalant, but the more Marcus thought about it, the more he could barely contain his excitement. He would get real food for a night. Maybe, he would get a night of pleasure with a woman. Although his coming of age ceremony was held on the feast of Liberalia, just two months ago, he was still a virgin. After the ceremony, his father refused to introduce him to the opposite sex as many of his friends' fathers had done. He remembered Lucius had suffered the same deprivation. He was irritated at his father for not completing his education. He hoped to change that soon. He was so distracted that he barely touched his rations.

After everyone retired, he lay on his cot imaging his evening, marveling at the visions he saw dancing before his eyes.

"Hey, brother!" Quintus whispered at his portal. "It's time!"

Marcus, dressed only in his army issue tunic, hoisted himself out of the window. The two crouched low, darting from building to building until they approached the North gate of the castra. Quintus whispered something to the guard and they were allowed to pass. They moved through the gate and stood against the wall. The half moon was large in the eastern sky casting a suffused light on the plains and illuminating the brush that would be their cover as they traversed the half mile to the walls of the city. They worked their way along the wall to the city's north gate, which was the main entrance.

When they arrived at the gate, they found a great deal of activity. The portal was open and guarded only by an unarmed civilian sentry. Quintus greeted him with an embrace later explaining that he was one of his cousins who was in the family business. His job was to assure that all the "special" troops could access the wonders of Placentia. So far, they were doing well.

It was only a short walk from the gate to the house where Quintus had been directed. From the outside, it looked like all the other buildings, except for a banner depicting a smiling soldier sporting a giant naked and very rigid cock. Marcus could not perceive any light coming from the portals. The building looked abandoned. They entered the main door, which opened into a long dark tunnel of a hallway. He could hear music and smell garlic and spices as they moved through the arched passageway. At the far end was a burly guard with a Spanish sword standing at a curtain. Although he had a sword that looked like the military issued one Marcus carried, he wore no uniform. After a brief word from Quintus, the guard pulled back the curtain and the two boys entered a spacious courtyard.

There was a large crowd. Many men wore military tunics and some wore armor of high rank. Tables seating four were everywhere. He could make out several tables of centurions, but thankfully, Martial was not among them. He could hear the soft music from a lute playing in the distance.

They found a table with two empty seats and sat down. A young woman came over to them. She was clad only in a tiny two piece leather garment that did not cover her midriff. The top barely covered her nipples and the bottom covered only her groin. The bottom was tied with strings over her hips. She brought the boys each a goblet of beer and a round flat bread cut into four pieces and covered with garlic infused olive oil and aromatic meat. Marcus looked around and saw that everyone had the same fare. They would pick up a slice of the bread, fold it, and eat from the pointed edge. Marcus followed suit. With the first bite, he was transported to Mount Olympus. The beer, although bitter, gave him an instant buzz. He closed his eyes, leaned back, and enjoyed the feeling.

When he opened them again, he noticed that the courtyard was the center of a two story building with many rooms opening onto the space. At each door was a woman. They were mostly clothed in peplos like the ones his sisters wore, but they were dyed the most unusual colors. From that distance, he thought it looked like a beautiful mural, but the women did not stand still. Some leaned over the balcony beckoning to the men. Some would undo the shoulder button and show a breast. Some were pulling up their skirt to show more than their legs. As he watched, some of the soldiers would get up and talk with one of the women. He watched one centurion give a woman a few coins and the two disappeared into her doorway. Marcus took a bite of his bread and a long swig of beer. When he looked back in the direction of the darkened door, he saw the centurion coming out. The woman was slinking out behind him buttoning her peplos back into place. It seemed only moments before that they had gone in together.

He continued to watch in amazement as one by one, soldiers would choose a woman and disappear, only to return moments later. Quintus excused himself and did the same. On his return, he had a sheepish, but satisfied grin on his face.

"The second floor has some incredible young beauties, Marcus. They are irresistible. I heard one of them calling your name."

"Me?" Marcus looked over Quintus' head and saw a beautiful girl in a blue peplos pointing at him and gesturing for him to come up and see her.

"The stairs are back to your right." Quintus said. "Go on, it's paid for. I'm told she's the finest one here. Don't keep her waiting or she may get bored and choose someone else."

Marcus felt a powerful force moving through him. His heart raced and the buzz from the beer made his head swim. He felt exhilarated as he stood. He straightened up and walked like a champion gladiator to the stairs. As he exited the stairs on the second floor, he turned right. He had to pass several rooms with women calling to him.

"Hey, handsome!"

"Come take me, you hunk!"

"Hey, big boy. Bring your cock over here."

He could clearly see the girl in the blue peplos. She was giving him the hurry-up sign.

"Quickly, Marcus," she called. "I'm wet for you! Please hurry and give me your ecstasy!"

He puffed his chest out and strutted quickly by the remaining doors ignoring the pleadings of the other women. He was focused on only one, now. As he reached her, she sidled up to him caressing his arm and led him into her room.

The inner chamber had no window. It was softly lit by three beeswax candles. There was a small dish with incense burning that mixed with the smell of the candles. The girl was about his age with curly black hair flowing over her shoulders. She wore a small crown of eucalyptus leaves tied with ribbons that streamed down each side of her face. She smelled strongly of exotic oils and flowers. Her skin was alabaster white. Her hands were as delicate as his little sister's hands.

The girl stopped and turned to face Marcus. Her eyes were clear, her irises dark brown. When Marcus looked into them, he could not turn away. He felt an involuntary shudder as she slowly moved her hands down his sides to his hips. She grabbed a handful of his tunic on each side and slid her hands up brushing gently against his chest.

"Take off your tunic," she whispered.

Marcus obliged. He was covered in goosebumps. She pressed her firm breasts against his chest and stood on tiptoes and purred in his ear.

"Unbutton my peplos, Marcus."

He slowly raised his arms to do her bidding never deviating from her gaze. First he unbuttoned the right button. Her outfit fell to expose the top of her breast draping just above her nipple. He unbuttoned the left button. As he let go, the entire garment slipped to the floor. He could see her nubile form silhouetted in the candlelight. He could feel his penis swiftly swelling.

She placed her arms around Marcus' neck and stretched up to kiss him on the mouth. Marcus remained transfixed to the spot. He was aware that his ears were throbbing and he was suddenly warm. Her perfume filled his nostrils and made him lightheaded. She pressed against his body and opened her mouth to kiss his lips, first gently then with more passion. He began to reciprocate feeling the warmth of her body. Now his head swam and he began to float.

As they kissed, he sensed her hoisting herself. She climbed him like a pole. She was surprisingly light. Her skin against his chest felt so smooth. Her nipples rubbed his chest like two fingers, exciting him beyond anything he had ever imagined. He put his arms around her. He felt his rigid cock slip underneath her pubis as she picked up her legs and wrapped them around his waist. She moved her hips out slightly and he felt himself slip into her warm moist vagina. Her pubic hair against his groin brought a rush that was indescribable.

All he had to do was hold her. She did all the work. Her skill was flawless. She slowly moved her hips up and down. The motion brought her away from him slightly, her breasts massaged his chest. With the sensitive tip of his penis he explored the walls of her vagina as she moved. Once, twice, three times – he felt an explosion in his groin followed by aftershocks as his throbbing cock spurted his essence deep into her.

He held on tight until the rhythmic pulsations subsided. As he breathed deeply in the aftermath trying to comprehend what had just happened, she lifted up her hips, disengaged, and jumped down. She grabbed his tunic off the ground and shoved it into his chest.

"Put it on," she commanded.

Stunned, he followed orders while she pulled up her peplos and quickly buttoned it.

"We're done, Marcus. You can join your friend now."

She grabbed his shoulders, turned him around, and pointed him to the door.

Spent, out of breath, and a little embarrassed, he walked toward the door with her pushing him all the way.

"Good bye, soldier."

Urged along by the little lupa's prodding, he put one foot in front of the other. As he stepped out, the courtyard seemed bright and the sounds coalesced into a throbbing din. He tried to calm down. He turned and walked past the women who had beckoned to him just a short time before. Now, they ignored him calling out to other soldiers and imploring them to visit. He plodded down the stairs wondering how things had gone so quickly. At the bottom of the stairs he looked up. Quintus was motioning to him. He came back to the reality of the moment, straightened up and strutted to the table.

"Well, was she good?"

Marcus gave a sheepish grin.

"Yeah, I really got cranked. She is one smooth operator."

"I thought you'd like her."

"It all went so fast," he mused. "I felt there should have been more."

"Marcus! I only had one night to make these arrangements. This place costs buckets of money. I had to gamble all night to make this happen. Be satisfied with what you got."

"You're right. At least I had a few moments of ecstasy." He looked around beginning to feel self conscious.

"Let's go, Quintus."

"That's good for me, since I am just about out of funds."

They quickly made their exit. When they left the walled city, Marcus realized how little time they had spent in Boys' Town. The moon was directly overhead. Only about a quarter of the night had past. The moon lit the path well and they quickly traversed the half mile back to camp. As they approached, the sentry stepped aside. The boys darted back to their barracks and climbed in through the window. They shook hands and went to their cots. Marcus lay on his back smelling the exotic residue the girl left on his body. He tried to bottle his feelings. Before he knew it, Morpheus overtook him and he fell into a deep sleep.

"Get up melon heads!"

Marcus woke immediately with the first command. He sat up quickly. His head began to spin and he knew he was going to pay for his night of pleasure. He put on his armor and grabbed his sword and shield. It would be a bad day.

When they formed up, he saw Quintus looking bright and standing tall as though last night had not occurred. He had no idea how Quintus could do it, but he knew he needed to do the same. So, he straightened up from his slouch and tried to forget about his aching head.

The morning drills were the same as the day before, except everyone seemed to perform better. No one wanted to get whipped. Both legion Legatii were pleased enough that they gave orders to begin combat training. Marcus' century and the tenth century formed up and marched together toward a stand of trees on the Western perimeter of the field. As they approached, he could see a pile of short stout poles no longer than his Spanish sword. These had been laid out by the quartermaster's assistants while they were marching that morning.

"All right, scum buckets," Martial bellowed while his troops ate their breakfast. "It is time we begin some real training. First, me and Protus, the centurion of the tenth century, will show you the Roman technique of combat. Then, you will fight a member of the tenth century. To make this exercise more exciting, the winners and those of you Protus and I feel deserve it will move up to the tenth century. You will use these wooden swords today, so you don't kill each other before we go into real combat. Fight well, you little monkeys, because those of you who are victorious today could be part of the front line and the first to kill barbarians."

"Finally, an opportunity to show our fighting abilities," Marcus said to Quintus.

"You can fight as hard as you want, but I am not going to be the first to get whacked by any barbarians. Let some other whip dog have that privilege."

Martial and Protus demonstrated some basic moves. Marcus realized that he knew these from his play with his father. He had used those moves and more sophisticated ones to beat his friends when they played Legion back in Canino. He felt ready to be one of the victorious as they lined up in a row facing the tenth century. At the command, Marcus charged his opponent pinning him to the ground with his wooden sword in only three moves. Quintus, on the other hand, lost in as many strokes.

"Winners, line up on the East," commanded Protus. "You will fight the next line with the advantage of the sun at your back. Losers, move out with Martial for remedial training."

For once, Marcus was not under the thumb of Martial. He relished the moment, forgetting about his hangover. The matches went on all afternoon. He fought like a wild boar winning all of his fights to join only a handful of undefeated recruits. By that point, the losers were returning to the area with Martial. The centuries formed up while the victors stood at the front awaiting orders. Protus approached each asking name and town, then he positioned them in his century. All except Marcus.

"You are to stay with the ninth century, son," Protus told Marcus.

Marcus was dumbfounded. "Why, sir? I fought better than everyone else," he pleaded.

"Sorry, those orders came from a lot higher up than me. You fought well, but orders are orders." Now report back to Martial."

He turned around and plodded back to the ninth century. He was boiling inside. He knew it was the work of his father. He figured his father was just trying to protect him, but so far, all he did was obstruct Marcus' ability to demonstrate his worth.

"Back in line, scum!" shouted Martial.

As he took his place in front of Quintus, he realized that his entire tent group was still intact.

"Not quite what you expected, huh brother?" asked Quintus.

"Go to Tartarus!"

"Whoa, brother. That's no way to treat a friend."

"Just shut up and don't bother me," Marcus barked. His military career was not starting out the way he had envisioned it. He sulked the entire march back. He did not even notice the wagon train pulling up to the castra.

Chapter 11: Death and Renewal

Travel across the Jura Mountains was miserable. The first day was spent organizing the Confederation into a traveling column. Because the Tigurini tribe was the rear guard, they were forced to stay in camp near Geneva an extra day while the Confederation column formed up. Although the trip to Geneva was difficult, they were only one nation. Now, they were the tail of an ungainly monster many times their size. The train of nations stretched from Geneva to the tiny village of Gex, the last outpost of the Helvetian lands and the gateway to the Jura pass.

On the second day of the great migration, the Tigurini learned the perils of bringing up the rear. It was fair to say that no one among the proud nation had ever experienced such humiliation. The trail was heavily rutted from the innumerable wagons that had traveled before them. The roadside was littered with garbage and human waste. The farms along the way were deserted and ransacked. Storage bins and silos were empty. On the second night of the migration, they arrived in the remains of the town of Gex. The village was destroyed. There were smoldering fires in the rubble. A terrible stench rose from the rotting, partially eaten carcasses and piles of human filth.

Grumbling among the Tigurini, which had plagued the tribe since leaving their homeland, now reached a climax. They gathered around the Druid wagons hoping that the religious leaders might be able to influence the warrior leaders. Drutos and Adiega tried to calm the complainers. They offered prayers and blessings that everyone had made it safely to that point. Eventually, the crowd dispersed for their evening meal.

Aia and Sina tried to prepare supper. Their mother hovered over the proceedings. It was obvious by then, that Adiega was very weak. Her persistent cough had sapped her energy. She grew more pale and skinny every day. Her efforts that evening trying to calm the crowd drained her remaining strength. The sisters tried to get their mother to rest in the wagon. Even though she was too weak to provide much help, she insisted on dictating the girls' every move. She stood beside them commenting on each aspect of cooking. Sometimes, she pushed in to demonstrate. Sometimes, she attempted to take over when she felt they were not listening to her. Sina just let it roll off her back, but Aia stewed. After the fourth interruption, she boiled over.

"Màthair, shut up! We know what to do!" Aia shouted. "We can prepare supper without your help. You hover over me like a hawk criticizing everything I do, then you redo it as if it was all wrong. You never think I am good enough! I wish you were dead!"

The three stood in icy silence. Aia and Adiega were shooting daggers at one another while Sina looked alternately from one to the other. Adiega felt a twinge in her chest. She gave a few stifled coughs, then began a violent coughing spasm. Blood began to spurt from her mouth. She could not breathe in, because the blood was coming out so fast. Her eyes became big and she clutched at Aia with her bony fingers. She stared wildly into her daughter's eyes, then collapsed. Sina grabbed at her mother. Aia stood transfixed to the spot. Blood continued to trickle out of Adiega's mouth, but she was not breathing. Her color was ashen.

"Help me, you witch!" Sina shouted to her sister.

Aia jerked back to life and knelt in front of her mother. She cleared the blood from her mother's mouth butshe just lay there.

"I didn't mean it, Màthair! I love you! Please live! Please live! I will be a good daughter!" Adiega lay lifeless on the ground staring blankly at the heavens. Aia began to panic.

"I call upon Epona, daughter of our Earth Mother," she shrieked. "Màthair is not ready to go to the otherworld. Please allow her to stay with us! We need her here!"

Aia threw herself on her mother's torso. That forced a large blood clot out of Adiega's larynx. It rolled out of her mouth and onto the ground.

Adiega, still unconscious, noisily drew in a long breath. She lay motionless for what seemed like an eternity, then drew in another breath. Aia sat back on her knees and prayed silently.

The gasping between long pauses continued for some time. Sina moistened a cloth in the water they had gathered for supper and began to wipe Adiega's face to clean off the drying blood. Gradually, the gasping subsided and breathing became more regular. When she inhaled, her chest shuddered, but she did not move. Aia caressed her mother's cold hands against her cheeks and sobbed.

Drutos came running to find out what the commotion was all about. Adiega still lay motionless. The girls were kneeling – Sina at her head and Aia on her right side. He knelt down at her left side and placed his cloak beneath her head, then bent down to kiss her cheek. He lingered there. Adiega's eyelids fluttered open. He could see her eyes rolled up with the white part showing. Aia took off her cloak and offered it to her father who used it to cover his wife.

By that point, the sun had set. There would be no supper that night. Drutos picked up Adiega and brought her to the wagon where the girls made room for her to lay down comfortably. They would take turns sitting with her through the night. Slowly, normal breathing returned and she regained control of her eyes and limbs. Aia borrowed some hot water from the wagon behind them and made willow bark tea. It was not as strong as it should have been. It usually required half a day to steep. Still, it made Adiega feel better. By the morning when it was time to travel, she could sit up with assistance.

That day and the following day would be the toughest traveling yet. They had to ascend twelve hundred meters in a day, then down five hundred meters the next. Although it was late April, almost no snow had melted on the mountain passes. Since no new snow had fallen, what snow was on the ground had become hard packed. In many places, it was just slick ice.

By the time the Tigurini started up the trail, the ruts worn in the ground the day before had frozen over. Horses lost footing and frequently pulled the wagons out of one set of ruts into another. The jolts threw the contents of the wagons from one side to the other. Any organization was quickly undone.

The tossing forced Adiega up to the front bench. She remained quite dizzy and passed out several times. Aia sat next to her mother to support her and to cushion her from the bouncing. She knew she had to make peace with her mother soon. Her outburst before the nearly fatal hemoptysis only made it harder for her to find a way to begin. She looked ahead at the endless line of struggling wagons and bit her lip, her mind a total blank. Then she felt someone stroking her hair gently and rhythmically. It was her mother. She turned to face her. Adiega's eyes were bright and focused on Aia's face.

"Thank you for saving my life, child. Athair told me it was you who brought me back to life. I have no memory of it." Adiega looked away in the distance, sighed, and looked back at her headstrong daughter.

"I saw the otherworld, Aia. It is beautiful. It looks like our valley, only all the spring and summer flowers are in bloom together. There is a warm gentle breeze. The river is full and bubbling over the rocks in a pleasant quiet song. The birds are chirping and there are children everywhere running and laughing. All of my long dead relatives were together. I saw your grandparents and their parents. They were beckoning to me. There was the most beautiful princess in the middle of the village square. She was radiant wearing your Imbolc dress, sporting a crown of spring flowers, and holding the circle and cross Sina made. Everything was wonderful. I truly felt at peace. Then it all faded away and I woke in Athair's arms here in the wagon. I know now that we will all be fine. We will be together in peace." She stroked Aia's hair again.

Aia's eyes filled with tears at the beautiful story. She wondered why for all these years she could not get along better with her mother. Now, she could not think of a more beautiful place to be than beside her dying mother. That thought made her heart skip a beat and she hugged her mother and let her tears flow.

"Okay, dear. You're choking me. I can't breathe."

Aia realized that she was holding on for dear life and relaxed her grip. She pulled back to look into her mother's eyes.

"I'm so sorry, Màthair. I'm sorry for every worry I ever gave you. I'm sorry for every angry word. I'm sorry for ever doubting your wisdom and spurning your guidance."

Adiega stroked Aia's hair again.

"It's okay, dear. Everything's okay." They embraced.

"Now, tell me about you and Lugurix. Do you love him? Have you forgiven him for burning the village?"

Aia told her mother about their last rendezvous outside of Geneva. She spoke of her undying love for the man and his passion for her. She spoke of her concern that he was more interested in warring than being a good husband. Then, she told Adiega that she had given him a test. It was almost Beltane. He would have to show his love for her and for the Druids by celebrating with her.

"Well, I am sure he loves you and he will find a way to pass your little test," Adiega said. "Just remember, he is a warrior and warriors have a tendency to die young."

"Yes, Màthair." Aia looked down. "I remember you told me that," she said quietly.

"It's okay, dear, I give you my blessing. If you are truly in love, then I am happy for you."

Aia was overwhelmed again and hugged her mother. She cried tears of joy. Mother and daughter talked all day. By late afternoon, Adiega was worn out. The heat of the sun on the trail had melted the top layer of hard pack and the ruts were not as firm, but the path remained slippery. Sliding was better than the jostling of the morning. Aia offered her lap to her mother. She placed her head down on Aia's leg and was fast asleep in no time.

They arrived at the summit late in the day. The area for camping was surprisingly small. It was hard to imagine how all the nations had camped there before them. Luckily, only their tribe was left at the summit.

Aia eased her mother's head off her lap and placed it on her rolled up cloak. She climbed down, stretched, and walked to the edge of the mountainside.

In the darkening shadows, the edge seemed like a shear drop into an abyss. She could see the fires of the nations in the valley ahead of them. She backed away and looked for a place to relieve herself. She surveyed the campsite. The homes of the little summit village had been stripped bare.   There were piles of garbage everywhere. The only area with some cover was the forest at the edge of the village.

She headed into the tree line to the east of camp. The shadows were long there and she found an untouched spot.   As she finished, she heard hurried footsteps of warriors. She dove forward and clasped her hands over her head. Her dress was still around her waist. The footsteps grew louder, then stopped several feet away. Slowly, she peered out from between her arms. She could see Lugurix and Toutios along with four other young warriors. They were nearly close enough to touch. She quietly edged her way behind a boulder and peered out. She heard one of them whispering.

"When are we going to end this tyranny?" one asked.

"Not here. Not today," Lugurix replied. "There is too little room around this town."

"The longer he is in control, the more disgruntled our people become," said Toutios.

"That's the point. Give him enough time and the people will thank us."

"But we can't wait much longer. He will find out about our plan and we will be the ones to die."

"Tomorrow, we will be off the mountain and in the valley. We can accomplish the task easily during the night."

"Let's go over the plan one more time. We may not get another chance," said Toutios.

"Okay," said Lugurix. "Shortly after sunset, Bimmos will eat and drink like a pig, as usual. His bodyguards never leave his side until they go to the edge of the camp where Bimmos will relieve himself. The lighting will be poor because they can't bring the torches into the forest. We will already be in the woods on both sides of their group." He pointed at the young warriors. "Before they can get back to the open field, you four jump the bodyguards. Toutios, you and I will take Bimmos ourselves."

"We will gather on the edge of Bimmos's camp tomorrow and wait for your word," they said.

"Stay apart from one another from now on. Otherwise, he will suspect something is up."

"Right. Until tomorrow evening." With that, they were off.

While the others moved away, Toutios remained a moment. He turned and stared in Aia's direction. She jumped behind the boulder and leaned on it facing the other direction. She knew her brother sensed her presence, but she was unsure if he had seen her.

Toutios squinted into the darkness. He sensed his sister was there and he was sure she had overheard the plan. He decided to rely on their twin bond to make her understand that she had to keep the plan secret. He closed his eyes and sent his message to her, then quickly left to join the rest of the warriors.

Aia stayed hidden for a long time after the footsteps disappeared. She was now certain her brother knew she was there. She silently prayed until she was sure no warriors were around. Then, she stood up, straightened her dress, and walked nonchalantly back to the wagon.

When she arrived, her mother was hovering over Sina, who was stirring a pot of stew. She was supporting herself on Sina's shoulders and speaking into her ear. In order not to surprise them, Aia circled around to approach from the front.

"Ah, you have returned," Adiega said when she caught sight of Aia.

"You should be resting," Aia said in a mock scolding manner.

"I know, I know, but I can't help myself." She stood up holding on tightly to Sina.

"Come, Màthair. Let us take care of you." She took her by the hand and led her back to the wagon. It took Aia a while to hoist her mother into the back of the wagon and get her settled. When her mother was comfortably situated in the wagon, Aia went to back to help Sina. She peered into the pot and took a deep sniff drinking in the aroma.

"It could use some thyme," she said off handedly.

"You know we don't have any herbs," Sina hissed.

"Oh, yes," she said in a distracted manner. "How silly of me not to remember."

Sina spun around to look at her. Aia started giggling. Soon both were giggling uncontrollably. They hugged and shared the comfort of sisterly love. Sina returned to tending the supper. Aia watched for a while in silence. She so wanted to share her new secret but she did not want to jinx Toutios and Lugurix. She would just die if anything happened to her brother and her true love because of something she said.

Supper that night was wonderful. Everyone ate quietly. Aia tried to seem carefree. She engaged her father in a discussion of the coming holiday of Beltane.

"We should be in the valley when the day comes. Can we ask our Chieftain if we can celebrate?" she pleaded brushing against his side. Drutos just brooded.

"We have not been given the opportunity to celebrate any sacred days this winter or spring. I can ask, but don't get your hopes up."

"Thank you, Athair." She kissed him gently on the cheek.

That night, Aia could not sleep. She lay next to her mother staring into the darkness inside the wagon. She kept playing in her mind the events of the last two days. She wondered if these things were predicted by the dream she and Toutios shared. She finally concluded that it did not fit. Her mother was not part of any of the events.

What else is coming?" She buried her head in her cloak and sighed.

The next day's travel was hazardous and frightening. The cliff, which seemed to be a sharp drop off in the dark, was not much better in the daylight. Aia could see the trail down the mountain zigzagging back and forth all the way into the valley. Although the vertical distance was short, it would take them the entire day to descend.

The north side of the mountain was away from the sun and the entire road remained frozen. At every cutback turn, the horses lost footing. Wagons slid ahead of the horses injuring the animals and breaking wagon wheels. Three wagons detached from their horses and careened out of control. Two slid off the side of the trail into scrub pines. The little pines offered no resistance to the wagons as they tumbled unimpeded down the mountain. Both came to rest at the edge of the next cutback trail.

As their wagon rolled past the wrecks, Aia could see the broken lifeless bodies of the occupants. She touched her charm and said a silent prayer for them. Drutos requested time to retrieve and bury the dead, but Bimmos refused to stop the march saying that it would be better to get down the mountainside in the daylight to avoid further disaster.   Mercifully, the day ended without further incident. Eventually, the road broadened and flattened out. Once all the wagons were off of the mountain, Bimmos ordered them to make camp.   He was disappointed that they had fallen behind the main body of the migration and hoped to make up speed in the open valley the next day.

Aia helped Sina and her mother make supper, although her heart was not in it. The darker the evening became, the more agitated she looked. She shook as she ladled out the soup.

"What's wrong, child?" Adiega asked.

"Nothing, Màthair. I must be shaking from hunger," she lied. She hoped her mother did not see through her charade.

"Then let me serve it," Sina snapped. "You seem to be a worthless witch today."

"Sina! Watch your language!" her mother admonished.

"Sorry. I don't know why, but I have been very cranky and depressed for several days."

Aia tried for some sarcastic humor.

"I don't know why, either. Everything has been so wonderful since we left Geneva."

"No, I mean it! Everything is irritating me."

Adiega understood. Sina had been moody for a few days and complained of constipation, cramps, and bloating. She was almost twelve and had not seen womanhood yet. It was time. She stroked Sina's hair.

"Let's you and I have a little chat after supper, just the two of us."

Aia was about to say something, but held her tongue. At least her mother's attention was off of her.   Evening slipped into night.   No news came from the headquarters tents. Aia crawled into the wagon and lay down, but again she could not sleep. In a way, she was glad. Whenever she closed her eyes, whether it was day or night, her terrible dream revisited her.

At first light, a horn sounded calling everyone to the center of camp. Aia rushed ahead of Sina and her father, her heart pounding. She pushed her way to the front and was thrilled to see Lugurix in his bronze armor with Toutios standing at his right. She quietly thanked every god and goddess she could think of. Lugurix raised his arms for silence, then spoke.

"Bimmos and his guard met their end last night.   We felt our nation's anguish under his tight fist, and we have freed you from his tyranny!"

A murmur swept through the crowd.

"Today, we are reestablishing our old order.   Even though we cannot return to our homeland, we can live free. No more tyranny!"

Everyone cheered. Lugurix again held up his hands up for silence.

"We recognize the importance of prayer in our lives and ask that the Druids help us get back to what is most important to us. It is almost time for the festival of Beltane. We will travel to the end of the valley and hold our ceremony there. It will put us two days behind our Confederation, but we will make up the distance over several days."

Again, more cheering. Lugurix held his hands up again.

"We must return to communing with our spirit world. As for Bimmos and his guards, we have buried them already. There will be no special ceremony of the dead for them. Instead, after we break camp this morning, I ask that our High Priest conduct a ceremony for all of our departed brethren, especially for those whom we left on the mountain."

The tribe moved quickly to break camp and return for the ceremony. Drutos had just enough time to prepare himself.   Aia and Sina got their mother ready. They moved to the center of the camp where Lugurix had just addressed the assembled. Drutos stood in his cloak with hood pulled back. Adiega in her cloak with her hood pulled over her head stood near Drutos supported on the left by Aia and the right by Sina.   Aia and Sina wore their cloaks with their hoods up as well. Drutos addressed everyone.

"We are gathered here under unusual circumstances. As such, this will be a brief ceremony, especially since we cannot retrieve our dead from their mountain grave. Please remember Chieftain Bimmos and his guards as well." He pulled his hood over his head and began.

We all come from the Goddess
And to Her we shall return like rain falling into the ocean.

Now Adiega raised her head and began in a raspy voice.

Journey on now, brothers and sisters.
We will follow when we can.

At that point, Adiega began a rattling cough. When she stopped, her voice was too weak to be heard. Drutos elbowed Aia. She looked at her father.

"Go ahead, child. You must carry on for your mother."

Aia felt her heart pounding heavily in her chest. She could not remember the words.

"May you return to the same time..." her father whispered.

The words came back and she raised her head.

May you return to the same time and place

She sounded like she was whispering.

"Louder, child, they can't hear you."

She stood up straight and tall, took a deep breath, and began again.

Journey on now, brother and sister.
We will follow when we can.
May you return to the same time and place
To those you knew and loved.
May you know them and love them again.

"This concludes our shortened ceremony," Drutos announced. "Keep our dead in your hearts." Then, he turned to Adiega.

"Let's get you back." He picked her up and carried her back to the wagon. From that moment on, she did not leave her traveling bed.

The next day was a whirlwind for Aia. They traveled only a short distance to reach the end of the valley. Lugurix asked her to choose a sturdy tree to be used as the Mât enrubanné for Beltane. Warriors cut it down and brought it to the center of camp where they removed the limbs, dug a hole, and erected it. Usually, they would attach long ribbons to the top and use them during the dance, but there was no cloth to spare. They would have to dance without the ribbons. Using the tree's branches and several additional trees, the warriors built a pyre to be lit by the High Priest and Priestess at dawn the next morning.

"You will have to stand in for Màthair as High Priestess tomorrow," Aia's father told her.

"Yes, Athair, I know," she sighed.

"That also means you will not be able to dance with Lugurix at the celebration."

"Yes, I know that too," she whispered. She bowed her head. It seemed to her that she would never get to be with Lugurix.

"However, I have arranged with Lugurix that you may join him privately after supper tomorrow."

She turned to look at her father.

"It's okay, my child. Màthair and I discussed it. You have our blessing, but your formal marriage ceremony will have to wait until we reach our new homes."

She leaned over and hugged her father's neck. Her eyes welled up as she kissed him gently on the cheek.

"Thank you. I love you Athair."

Drutos patted her then pushed her away.

"We have work to do. You must know your part for tomorrow morning."

Drutos asked Aia and Sina to spend the night with Ouenitouta and Frontú so that he and Adiega could be alone. Aia could not sleep. Too many thoughts raced around in her head. She could not concentrate on any one thought without another popping in. Maybe her luck was changing and the Mother Goddess was smiling again.

In the predawn, Sina slipped out while Aia stayed in the wagon for a few extra moments to gather her thoughts as she prepared for her role as High Priestess in the ritual.

When she exited the wagon, Drutos was waiting for her. Sina was with him. She had made a charm for the ceremony.

Aia was cold in the morning chill. She wrapped her cloak tightly around her. It was going to be a strange Beltane.

"Before we go, Sina wants to talk with you," her father said.

Sina gave her the charm. It was a garland made with spring flowers from the valley. It was braided into a circle like a wreath. Aia estimated that if she unwound the wreath, it would have been twice as long as she was tall. She knew she could depend on her little sister to make the most beautiful charms.

While she was admiring the garland, Sina grabbed Aia's arm and pulled her out of earshot of their father.

"I am ready for the coming of age ceremony," she whispered. Her eyes were bright.

Aia gave her a quizzical look at first, then it dawned on her.

"You mean—"

"Yes," said Sina. "Last night, I was visited by the spirit of Brigantia. At first, I did not understand what was happening, even though Màthair explained it to me yesterday after supper. I felt moist and squishy. It was only this morning that I realized what was going on."

"Well, I guess we will be having another ceremony soon," she whispered back. Aia knew she would have to conduct that ceremony and probably all future ceremonies. She began to realize the burden of responsibility she was shouldering as High Priestess.

"I should have studied harder," she thought.   *"At least I can depend on Athair to help me when I need it."*

She hugged Sina and promised to conduct her ceremony soon, then returned to her father. The two moved quickly to the center of camp. A crowd was already gathering to witness the lighting of the new flame.   Some brought their livestock to experience the power of the spring fire.

Drutos and Aia worked together.   Drutos used his bow drill on a small plank of wood.   Aia took bits of dried moss and placed them where the heat was generated on the wooden block.   In short order, the moss was smoldering.   She gently blew on the moss until a flame jumped up, then she added straw to enhance the flame. When it was large enough, Drutos took a dry branch and lit the end. The two got up and walked slowly protecting the flame, then lit the kindling at the base of the immense pyre that the warriors had built the day before. It took two tries, because the wood was so green and unseasoned.   One of the herders, who had brought some extra hay, gave it to Aia. She used it effectively to feed the flame until it was a roaring fire.

Aia turned around to the sea of people who had gathered while she and her father had been occupied.   She raised her hands to present the fire. A great cheer arose as the fire lit up the dawn. Everyone enjoyed the fire as it roared. Many tribe members lit new torches and took them back to their wagons to make breakfast. Some brought back food and treats to celebrate the day. When all had made their offerings, Drutos and Aia moved on to the site of the Mât enrubanné where the Beltane ceremony would be held.

When everyone had gathered around in a circle, Drutos gave Aia the cue. She turned to the pole and intoned,

Mother Goddess,
Queen of the Earth

Then Drutos said,

Father God,
King of the sky

Together, they recited,

We celebrate Your union as nature rekindles life.

Aia took the charm that Sina made and placed it at the base of the pole. She looked up and said,

Accept my gift in honor of Your union

She walked back and joined her father. Together they said,

May Your mating bring new life;
May it cover all lands,
Oh, Ancient Ones,
We celebrate with You!

One of the bards played a spritely tune on his pipe while another sang inviting all to sing along. After the song was done, Drutos announced that the Maypole dance would begin. The dancing went on until the dull filtered sun was high in the sky. As the day wore on, young couples would drift away to emulate the God and Goddess. Drutos and Aia remained at their post and greeted all who came by. Many of the older men and women inquired after Adiega's health as they left their gifts and food. Drutos would say, "The journey has been hard on her. We hope, with rest, she will recover. Thank you for your kindness."

The greetings went on well into the afternoon. When they were finally done, Drutos had the gifts brought back to their wagon where he spent the rest of the day trying to get Adiega to eat. Aia was too excited to eat. When she arrived at their wagon, she threw off her ceremonial cloak and sprinted to the stream that ran through the valley near the road. She bathed quickly, then walked back slowly collecting wildflowers along the way.

It was the perfect time of year for wildflowers. The variety was immense and Aia lingered trying to find just the right ones. She gathered up the front of her dress like a basket to cradle the flowers. She collected pink Snowbells that grew low to the ground around the stream to represent the passing of winter. In the open meadow, she picked white Pasque flowers with yellow throats that looked like eggs to symbolize fertility. She found intensely yellow Alpine Primrose to bring her confidence. On the side of a rocky hill, she located pink Alpenrose for friendship and love, and the blue Snow Gentian to represent healing. Finally, she picked the deepest purple Columbine to symbolize the divine Mother Goddess.

When she could carry no more, she returned to the wagon and quickly fashioned a flower crown. She rummaged through the few pieces of clothing she had left and pulled out the white Imbolc gown. She held it to her bosom and closed her eyes thinking about how she felt when she was decked out for Imbolc before the troubles began. She changed into the gown and carefully placed the crown on her hair. She decided she would wear her cloak with the hood up so she would not be so conspicuous when she went to Lugurix. Then, she sat down to wait and promptly fell asleep.

Aia was standing alone, deep in the forest. She was wearing her gown and her flower crown, but the cloak was gone. She turned around slowly. At first, she could see nothing in the dark. Then, she saw a flickering light of a fire in a small clearing just a short distance away. She thought she could hear voices. She cautiously approached the clearing. As she did, the forest opened up to reveal a stunningly beautiful maiden in a flowing white linen dress. She had long straight silky white hair and pale features. Although the forest was still, there was a breeze blowing the maiden's hair and dress backwards to expose the contours of her frame beneath the gown. Her eyes were closed and she was straining upward as if to kiss someone, but no one was there. As she parted her lips, a man appeared out of nowhere to kiss her. He was taller than anyone Aia had ever seen before. He was dressed in the armor of a Tigurini warrior. His cuirass was silver and studded with gems. His scabbard held a sword with a jewel encrusted handle. His muscles rippled as he reached out to hold the maiden. As he did so, the maiden turned to look directly into Aia's eyes. Before she knew what was happening, the maiden was gone and Aia stood where the maiden had been. She was wearing the maiden's gown. She looked up into the warrior's face. He was clean shaven. His hair was long, straight, and black. His eyes were darkest brown. He gently held

her by the waist. She could not take her eyes off the warrior. Then he grasped her
arms firmly and shook her violently.

"Wake up, Aia!" It was her sister Sina. "There is a soldier here to escort
you to Lugurix!"

Aia blinked as she came back to reality. She had difficulty focusing after
having no sleep for days, and now, getting only a short uninvited nap. She looked
around. The sun had set and it was dark. She pulled herself up with Sina's help,
rubbed away some drool at the corner of her mouth, and took a deep cleansing
breath. The chill wind was still blowing. She gave her sister a brief hug and went
with the warrior.

He deposited her in front of Lugurix' tent where a guard let her in.
Lugurix was not there. She looked around. She had never been in a warrior's tent
before. It was large, supported by four corner posts and a longer center post. The
door flap had two posts of its own. The contents of the tent were spare. It
contained a chair, a small table with a single large candle, and a cot with a woolen
blanket. She walked over to the cot and passed her hand gently over the blanket.
It was thick, thicker than any blanket she had ever seen. She wondered how long it
had been since the animal wore it.

"You are still in your cloak. Come, let me take that."

She turned around and looked up. It was Lugurix. He was not wearing
his armor or his sword. He had on his long sleeve shirt and leather pants. He still
wore his boots, which were unlaced. Her eyes focused on his face. He had combed
his beard.

While they stared at one another, Aia reached up and pulled back her hood
to reveal the flower crown. Then, she undid the one tie of the cloak and let it fall
on the ground next to the cot.

Lugurix's eyes drifted down from her face to the woolen gown.

"That brings back memories," he said.

"I didn't have anything else to wear," she replied.

They just stared at one another until it felt awkward. Finally, Lugurix
broke the silence.

"I'll put your cloak on the chair." He stepped forward and reached down
to pick up the cloak. Aia stood still and closed her eyes. As Lugurix came close, she
could smell his sweet sweat. She took in a slow deep breath as a tingle ran up and
down her spine. He stood up with the cloak in his hands and stared into her eyes.
He reached back toward the chair and, without looking, dropped the cloak. It hit
the edge of the chair and fell to the ground in a heap.

As they stared at each other, Lugurix grasped Aia's hands and bent in to
kiss her. She removed her hands from his and placed them lightly on his chest, then
parted her lips and closed her eyes. She felt him delicately press his mouth against
hers. She pressed her lips against his and reciprocated. Beneath her hands, she
could feel his heart thumping in time with hers. After a long embrace, they broke,
breathless.

She rested her forehead against his chest for a moment and closed her
eyes, then slid her hands and arms around his neck. She raised her chin and he met
her lips in another long passionate kiss. She sensed his hands slide down her body
to her hips and felt him raise her dress. She let him bring it to her chest, then
pushed back slightly so he could take the dress over her head. He threw it in the
general direction of the chair. She stood back arms' length from him, completely
naked.

As he admired her, she took his shirt and slowly pulled it over his shoulders. He let her try to get the shirt off his head, but she wasn't tall enough. He finished removing the shirt and tossed it toward the growing pile of clothing. She put her arms around his neck and pulled him toward her. She first kissed his chest, then his cheek, and finally his mouth. As they embraced, she allowed him to bend her backwards, lift her, and place her gently on the woolen blanket. He stood to remove his shoes and pants. She watched intently as he did so. He stood to her left, silhouetted by the candle. The only other male parts she had ever seen belonged to her twin brother. That had been many years ago when they were both still very young. She was amazed at the size and hairiness of Lugurix. She coyly raised her right leg to let him see her crotch.

Lugurix put his left knee between her legs and his arms on either side of her, then lowered himself to hover just above her breasts. They looked in each other's eyes for a moment. He gently kissed her starting with her forehead, then her cheeks, then her mouth. He moved down kissing her neck, her upper chest, and her breasts. She closed her eyes and again realized she was breathless. She panted to catch her breath while her entire body flushed red hot. Lugurix rested his elbows on the cot while caressing and kissing her breasts. Her breasts became soft and supple to his mouth. She was a lump of clay in his hands. She trusted his touch and allowed herself to melt into the blanket.

Lugurix placed both legs between hers. She accommodated by raising her knees and spreading her feet. She could feel her bottom becoming moist. He was warm and hard against her belly. She enjoyed the new sensations as he moved his penis down her front to rest between her legs. Instinctively she arched her back and welcomed him into her. At first, there was some resistance, then a tingle as he slid in. She felt a rush of warmth to the spot. She gave an involuntary moan as Lugurix rhythmically moved his pelvis. She pushed back when he pushed and relaxed when he pulled back. The tingling became greater and greater until he pushed deep within her. Then, she felt rhythmic pulsations inside and a strange spreading warmth. She yelped with surprise and pleasure and threw her arms around him pulling him down.

The two lay embraced until they were breathing slowly in unison. Aia slowly released her hold on Lugurix. He looked down at her and kissed her mouth. He rolled to her right and she followed placing her leg over his hip. They kissed again and drifted off to sleep.

Sometime later, Aia awakened shivering. She realized she was totally naked laying above the blanket. She pulled her leg back. Her movement woke Lugurix and they crawled under the blanket together. They kissed. She felt the warmth return to her bottom and she pulled Lugurix to her rolling onto her back. Lugurix obliged and they coupled again. Aia floated through the experience. They held onto one another until they fell asleep.

After what seemed only a moment, a guard knocked on the tent pole and announced to Lugurix that it was time to rise. He woke Aia who slipped out of the cot and dressed. They embraced one last time and she went outside into the crisp predawn air. A warrior escorted her back to her wagon. As they approached, she saw her father and Frontú sitting on the front of the wagon.

"Athair, Frontú, what are you doing up so early?" she asked.

"Màthair passed on to the otherworld last night."

Chapter 12: Sick Call

Taurinus finished the daily recital of his life's story just as they pulled into the castra at Placentia.

"Just two days behind the troops," he declared. "Not bad for an old stinky fart like me, but we've got much work before we can rest today."

"What do we need to do, sir?" Lucius was curious.

"We need to unload all of our medical equipment and set up the hospital. Won't be any patients in it to speak of while we are in camp, but these troops have had no medical care since enlisting. Tomorrow morning, we will hold our first sick call, then we begin some training for the battles to come."

They pulled up to the North gate and climbed down from the wagon. The hospital building was just past the granaries and the barracks of the third and fourth cohorts near the headquarters building and the house of the Legatus. They watched as a detachment of recruits quickly unloaded the instruments Taurinus had transported from Rome. These would be the basic surgical tools for the campaign. Lucius would finally get to see real surgical weapons. So far, the only instruments he knew were a simple scalpel and a cautery. Theodosius used instruments only if medicines failed and shunned the fancy armamentarium of the surgeon.

He had read the great manuscript concerning surgery written by Hippocrates. He had memorized the basics and felt prepared, at least theoretically. Hippocrates described the essential components of an operation as the operator, the patient, the light, and the instruments. Lucius knew that the surgeon should have good light. Hippocrates preferred artificial rather to natural light. The surgeon should be able to position the light on the opposite side of the patient's body part. The light should not be too oblique and the surgeon or assistant must not stand in the light, because that would cast a shadow on the operating field.

Although he did not know the instruments and their uses, he knew they needed to be prepared and laid out beforehand. After use, they needed to be cleaned and made ready for the next patient. There might be a number of instruments prescribed for each operation and Hippocrates directed that the assistant must always be ready to hand the surgeon the appropriate tool. Since Lucius did not know the conduct of any operation except for minor ones, he would need to observe and learn the steps from actual procedures.

Surgeons require incredible dexterity and Hippocrates instructed his students to practice well. Lucius had always trimmed his fingernails short as Hippocrates prescribed. He practiced the basic hand position with his index finger opposed to the thumb like an O. He positioned his hands opposite one another and worked hard to make his left hand work as well as his right. However, practicing with his left hand was not easy. From birth, all Romans were taught that the right hand was dominate and had to do everything. When no one was watching, Lucius would eat, write, and perform tasks with his left hand. Sometimes, he got caught by his father, who would lecture him in the social and military importance of the right hand. Over time, Lucius made his sinister hand function nearly as well as his dexter hand.

Hippocrates spent a great deal of time describing the types of bandaging. It had confused Lucius, so he only learned the simple bandaging that Theodosius used. Now, he wished he knew more about that aspect of surgery. It surely would be an important factor in wartime. Lucius knew he was as ready as anyone could be for someone who had only picked up a scalpel a few times before.   He was determined to learn the trade, even if he had to listen to the life story of Taurinus a thousand times more.

Taurinus was standing over the treasured instruments of his trade. He considered surgery the noblest profession, even if society looked down upon him and his colleagues. He knew from many years of work in the field and the clinic that disease and trauma could take down even the greatest of men in the prime of life. Pain and suffering associated with surgical conditions could reduce men to crying babies begging for relief. Even if they considered physicians and surgeons quacks, deep in their hearts they realized prayers to the gods alone would not cure them. So, they submitted to the ministrations of the practitioners they decried. It brought a smile to his face. Particularly now, the only persons able to salvage the wounded were the surgeons. With fire in his eyes, he grabbed Lucius. He stood as tall as he could and beamed.

"Legion surgeons are the victorious gladiators of medicine. They are not just another immune, they are untouchable.   Their power in the hospital is unquestioned. Even the Legatus would do our bidding if we commanded. They depend on the us to keep the fighting force healthy and whole."   Feeling empowered and rejuvenated, he swept his hand in a grand gesture across the table.

"Here, my boy are our weapons."

Lucius surveyed the armamentarium. The array was immense.

"Let's start with the sharps. Every operation needs them. Here are the scalpels – magnus and minimus. This long straight set is for deep use. This set is for superficial use. Note how the superficial scalpels are more rounded and sharp all the way around like a myrtle leaf to allow one continuous cut. You can start at the neck and, in one stroke, incise clear down to the anus without lifting your scalpel off of the patient."

He picked up a knife as long as his forearm turning it over to catch the glint of the light. He admired it as he slowly traced the edge with his finger.

"Now here is my favorite – the amputation knife. I could perform an amputation in the blink of an eye when this baby is sharp. We'll make it sharp again." He called out to one of the medics to sharpen the blade with a special stone kept with the instruments.

"Next are the forfex or scissors. These are crude and used mostly to cut hair and bandages. Next, the osteotomes for cutting, whittling, and shaping the bones. Note they come in right handed and left handed styles, and they are double ended. We even have rasps for grinding down sharp bony edges. We also have sharp and smooth tissue hooks. We use those mostly for elevating bones, but I have used them for obstetrical purposes. Don't think that will happen during this campaign." He laughed.

"Thank Jupiter women don't fight!" He stopped for a moment thinking about the possibility, then shook his head and moved on.

"We have other bone instruments as well. We have bone elevators of various sizes to help us align fractures. We have bone forceps to keep the bones aligned while we secure them." He gathered these instruments and placed them in a separate box.

"Next we have tissue forceps. They are about the length of your hand and are used to hold the skin and superficial sinews. This set is our abdominal forceps.

They are long and the tips come in smooth and rough.   Next are the epilation forceps. These are small and delicate, mostly for hair removal from facial abscesses. Finally, we have the staphylagras for removing the uvula." Taurinus turned it over admiring the long double curved device.

"I love this instrument, but we won't have much use for it here. It's mostly for curing snoring. Had my uvula removed a few years back, see?"

He opened his mouth wide, but Lucius only took the briefest of looks.

"I see," he said quickly.

"You couldn't have seen anything, boy! Damnation, you are just like the rest of today's trainees! You glance and pander to me thinking you would loose face if you said no, or if you did not make your observation instantly. I'm not doing this because my mouth is cleaner than anyone else's! I do it so you can see with the eye of a surgeon. How do you expect to see what my eyes see if you don't look? Now take a look again and describe what you see. Use that torch for light." Taurinus opened his mouth again.

Chagrinned at muffing his first real surgical lesson, Lucius obeyed. He held the torch in his left hand and peered in.

"I can't see because your tongue is in the way."

"Good, my boy!" Taurinus sounded encouraging. "I did that on purpose." He grabbed a broad flat piece of metal. It looked like a long straight scalpel but had no sharp edge. He placed it on his tongue and held it down. Now Lucius could see the entire oral cavity. In the back of the mouth where he expected to see the hanging fleshy curtain of the palatine arch with the uvula dangling off of it, he saw only a shriveled curtain and no evidence of a uvula.

"There is no uvula and the palatine arch is atrophied."

"Precisely!" Taurinus beamed. "That's what I expect out of you next time, and every time. If you don't see something, you need to direct the team to expose the area for you. That's the way we work. Each member has responsibilities and we need to preform flawlessly to fix the body." Taurinus returned to the instrument table for the next lesson. Lucius took a deep breath. He made a mental note to be more observant and to be less timid when acting as the surgeon.

"Most importantly in our armamentarium, we have cautery instruments. These help us stop or prevent hemorrhage. Notice the variety." Lucius admired the unusual shapes of the points and lengths of the handles.

"Blood letting is good for Medicine men, but surgeons abhor bleeding. Soldiers lose too much blood on the battlefield, so we conserve all the blood we can. That's why we have so many cauteries. Some are long so we can stay away from the source." Taurinus got an amused look on his face.

"The anus is a good example of an organ to stay away from. I have seen a cautery ignite an actual fire when a man farts." He chuckled. "Don't want to singe the hair on your hands if you are too close." He pointed to other designs. "Some are short for better control. Some are pointed and some are flattened like a spatula, depending on how much tissue we plan to cauterize." He moved to the next group.

"Now for some assorted instruments. Those double curved tubes shaped like an S are male cannulas for relieving the bladder. Again, we won't use that much in the field except on the senior soldiers. Hope we don't have much of that. It's hurts and it's not a pretty sight."

They moved to a collection of oddly shaped devices.

"Here we have instruments we will use on the infirm, but not the wounded. You should know these already. We have cucurbitulae or cups for drawing. We heat them and apply them to the back to draw out poisonous humors. Here we have clysters for giving enemas. Here are a variety of spatulas and probes for compounding and administering medicines."

"Yes, I am familiar with these," Lucius said. "We used these back in Canino, but what about those over there? You haven't mentioned them."

"Oh those. Most of those are gynecologic instruments. We won't have much call for them during the campaign, but I brought them just in case we need to treat a barbarian woman or a prostitute. Those are specula of various sizes. I left the rectal specula over there. Those, we will use during the campaign. We'll see hemorrhoids galore among the recruits. The young soldiers are not used to the legion's rations. Almost all will get constipated during the first six weeks. As you know, too much straining will produce hemorrhoids and bowel prolapse."

Taurinus stood up and looked at his newest apprentice.

"Well, there's the lot of 'em. Memorize them before we break camp in a day or two. We may need to use them sooner than anticipated." After his monologue, he did what he had done every evening of the trip. He left to find his old buddy Publicus to get a fine meal and to drink the night away.

Lucius ate with the other surgical trainees. As they ate, he realized that he was the youngest of the physicians. Most of the others had been apprenticed to other physicians or had their own practice for a few years before apprenticing with Taurinus. Except for Magnus, they had assisted in procedures and knew the instrumentation already. Lucius knew he would have to work hard to catch up.

Following supper, he went back to the table of impressive instruments. He picked each up in turn, marveling at the unique designs. He felt the weight and balance of each. They fit so well into his hand. They could have been made just for him. He wondered how there could be so many highly specific designs. Surgeons like Taurinus and many who preceded him must have designed them, but they seemed to have had divine inspiration. Roman surgical tools evolved gradually from crude instruments used eras before Hippocrates into the designs Lucius held in his hand. They had been tweaked by innumerable practitioners of the art and now, he would get to use the finest, most modern surgical tools in the world.

From the stories Taurinus told, those very instruments had been used to fix fractures, amputate limbs, and probe and cauterize wounds of thousands of legionnaires and senators and their concubines over the forty years of the old surgeon's career. Maybe Taurinus would turn out to be the surgical teacher Lucius needed. He went to sleep hoping he would learn volumes from the old curmudgeon.

Next morning, Lucius got up with the dawn. He had a wonderful night's sleep on a hospital cot. It was far better than the floor of the wagon. He felt refreshed and ready for the sick call Taurinus talked about. He found the old surgeon already standing in the atrium of the hospital. That part of the hospital was a sizable space with few support beams to impede traffic. The front doors of the hospital led directly into the atrium. Spaced out evenly in the middle of the room were six tables with one chair and a torch mounted on a pedestal. The other young surgeons were assembled, each manning a station. Lucius took his position at the open table next to the doors. Taurinus hoisted an apron over his head.

"Today will be a very busy day," Taurinus told them. "Remember, you must do as I tell you. It will make our lives easier for the coming war. We have six stations, which means we can handle six patients at a time. I will help each of you with the first two or three patients, then you will be on your own. I will be available for questions if they come up, but if you follow my instructions to the letter, there won't be many." He turned to the medics.

"Now, open the clinic."

Two medics standing by to assist the surgeons opened the double doors. Immediately, everyone's hearts sank into their sandals. They saw a line four deep stretching down the length of the castra and around behind the barracks. That morning at muster, the Centurions had announced that the hospital would be open for the care of maladies accumulated during the trip to Placentia and the wounds received the day before in combat training. It seemed that nearly every legionnaire in Legion XI took advantage of the first sick call.

"All right, surgeons, be prepared!" Called Taurinus.

A medic ushered in six soldiers. Each went to one of the stations. The recruit in front of Lucius complained of foot pain. It had started on the second day of the march and persisted. The pain was in the center of his right foot. It was always present but was exacerbated by walking and running. It felt like he was being stabbed repeatedly in the foot. Nothing he did seemed to ameliorate the pain.

"What's the complaint, Lucius?" Taurinus said as he came to the station.

"Right plantar pain, sir" Lucius replied expecting the lad to get an ointment or a bandage and time off to allow the pain to subside.

"Prepare him for a rectal exam."

"A what?"

"You heard me. Prepare him for a rectal exam."

Lucius was perplexed, but they had been instructed to follow orders explicitly. He directed the soldier to lift his tunic, bend over the table, and hold onto the edge. In the meantime, Taurinus dipped his index finger in oil and jammed it into the surprised youth who sucked in a quick breath. Taurinus ceremoniously waved his finger around a few times while humming softly to himself. When he pushed down compressing the prostate gland, the soldier exhaled, moaning and crying for the old surgeon to stop. At that point, Taurinus removed his finger and gave the prescriptive.

"Give this recruit castor oil, salt, and vinegar."

Lucius was stunned.

"Sir! That's an emetic and a purgative!"

"Don't question the prescriptive boy!   Just administer the dose as directed!"

While Taurinus was performing the rectal exam, Lucius noticed the medics delivering barrels labeled "Sick Call Medication" to each station. He withdrew an aliquot from the barrel as Taurinus moved to the next table and plunged his finger up the rear of recruit number two. Lucius dispensed the combination medicament and watched as the dazed soldier downed the dose. Then, the legionnaire hustled out of the hospital while the next patient was ushered over to the exam table. By that point, Taurinus was waving his finger around in the rectum of recruit number four.

The next soldier complained to Lucius of a large bruise he had received in combat training the previous day. During the fighting, he took a blow to the base of his neck sending lighting down his arm. The sparks shot into his hand and he quickly yielded to his opponent. Even after the fight, the pains persisted. The bruise on the neck was the size of his fist, and he still had residual numbness in the thumb and forefinger of his left hand.

"What's the matter with this soldier?" Taurinus called as he strode over from the sixth table where the patient was getting up from his rectal exam and receiving his combination dose of emetic and purgative.

"Numbness in the left thumb and index finger, sir"

"Prepare him for a rectal."

Lucius did not question the crazy old man as he had with the first patient. He just prepared the young legionnaire. Taurinus performed the same thorough exam declaring the prescriptive to be "castor oil, salt, and vinegar." Lucius dutifully gave the dose to the recruit, who was now pale and wide eyed.

All morning the legionnaires' scenarios changed, but the surgical routine did not. Taurinus went down the line performing rectal exams on all recruits, regardless of their complaints. When the next recruit came to his station, Lucius barely listened to the complaints of back pain. Taurinus gave the same orders and performed a lengthy rectal exam prescribing the same medication.

"Got the routine, Lucius?"

Lucius raised his eyebrows but there was no mistaking the plan. He was to perform a rectal on any soldier who came in that day.

"Yes, sir, understood."   Each of the other young surgeons in turn acknowledged the orders.

"Right! Then, get to it! The line is long and if you don't get going, you may be here all night. I'll be in the next room taking a nap. Disturb me only if you have a legitimate question."

Still a little perplexed, Lucius did exactly as he had witnessed three times at his table and three times at each of the other tables. Eighteen men had come in with varying complaints. Each was the recipient of a very thorough rectal exam and a large dose of the specially formulated emetic and purgative.

For what seemed like an eternity, Lucius emulated the old man. He no longer listened to the complaints. When the soldier came up, he instructed him to bend over. He performed a rectal exam, then gave the medicine. All six surgeons in training performed the same routine. It took them until late in the evening to finish. They all had sore index fingers. Each trudged off while the medics cleaned up. They ate together in silence contemplating the strange day. Lucius had lost exact count, but figured he had done over five hundred rectal exams. If they each treated the same number of legionnaires, that would have been more than three thousand. Legion XI only had a total of four thousand five hundred soldiers.

Lucius chuckled to himself.

"There aren't many virgin rectums left," he thought.

Lucius fell back on his cot and was out in an instant.

The next morning, the Centurions again announced that the hospital would be open for sick call. Any soldier who still was in need of medical or surgical care was excused, but word of the exam and medication had spread like a virus through the castra. The recruits would not make the same mistake twice. From now on, they would only go on sick call if they were dying. When the medics opened the doors, only seven soldiers were standing in line. Two of them were Marcus and Quintus.

Chapter 13: Forces are Joined

As the young surgeons gathered at the hospital atrium for sick call, the medics broke the news – almost no one was on sick call.

"The old man isn't crazy after all!" thought Lucius to himself.

Taurinus had sent a message to the soldiers. Their duty was to fight, regardless of minor problems. No one was going to get a free pass to the rear from the Legion XI surgical team. Rome's legions were serious business and there was no room for slackers. The message to the surgical teams also was clear. Their job was to take care of real wounds and treat debilitating diseases, not malingering slackers.

Lucius looked at the line. Only seven scraggly recruits shuffled toward the front of the hospital. He squinted into the light outside the portal. One of the recruits looked like Marcus, but he was much thinner and he was deeply suntanned. As the line came closer, he realized it was his brother.

"Marcus, it's great to see you, but you look wretched."

"I don't feel too slick either. We need help."

"We?"

"Yeah. Quintus and me."

"Well, there are six of us and seven patients. I'll take both of you." Lucius ushered them over to his station. "What's the news, little brother?"

"We'll fill you in on the details some other time. If you are ever on a forced march for weeks and have to eat dirt, you'll understand. This morning, I woke up with pain in Cupid's rudder. I went to urinate and pus dribbled out. Quintus told me he had the same thing."

"Anything else?"

"Yeah, pain like fire when I piss," whined Marcus.

"It's like pissing through crushed oyster shells," moaned Quintus.

"Let me see. Lift your tunics and milk your staff." Lucius already knew the two really needed rectal exams.

Both boys lifted their tunics and did as they were instructed. Both had a thick greenish dribbling discharge from their penises. Lucius examined their genitals and performed a rectal on each in turn. In his time with Theodosius, he had not encountered that set of symptoms and physical findings. He knew it was a sign of an infection but he could not imagine why. It was time to ask the old man.

Taurinus was just lumbering over to the clinic area to enjoy what he knew would be a short workday. He saw the worried look on Lucius' face.

"What's up, Lucius?"

"It's my younger brother and his friend. They both have nasty pus issuing from their mentulae. It started this morning."

"Let me see." Taurinus examined them. "Did you perform a rectal?"

"Yes, sir. They have minimal tenderness, but their prostates are boggy. When I mashed on the prostate, more pus issued."

"Well, I don't know much about medical diseases, but this one I do know. You boys took some liberties, am I right?"

They looked at one another.

"We don't know what you mean, sir," said Marcus.

"You spent a night in Corinth," said Taurinus. The boys shrugged.

"You explored the ditch," Taurinus continued, "sheathed your sword, got ridden, got laid, ground down–"

"Okay, okay," admitted Quintus. "We snuck out to the city and got some action."

"Is that true, Marcus?" asked an astonished Lucius.

"Yeah, we got some," Marcus admitted. He could feel himself flush. He had wanted to become a man. He felt some pride at accomplishing something his older brother had not yet experienced.

"We fucked, but it was a righteous fuck, and we fucked well!" he added striking a manly pose.

Taurinus was condescending.

"You may have fucked well, gentleman, but she stuck you back. She did more than just polish your jewels. She gave you morbus indecens. Almost every physician refuses to treat it, but that was my specialty in my little clinic near the Forum. Those politicians paid me well to treat their social secrets. I also saw their women. I am not sure why some of the senators thought of those women as Laelias." He looked in the distance for a moment thinking of the concubines, then shuddered. "Some of those exams were foul, but I treated them and did what I could to make them acceptable again. Their male partners would come seeking cures as well."

"Can you cure us?" Marcus asked.

"Well, cure is a strong word, son. If you do as I say, the pus will stop in a few weeks."

Taurinus left to compound a medicament. While he was gone, Lucius pried the details out of the two rather contrite youths. As they described the scene, the beautiful women, and the moments of ecstasy they both had experienced, Lucius was visited by Priapus. He had all he could do to conceal his erection. He stood behind the chair. He did not want to give any sign that he was enjoying any part of the story, and tried to maintain his clinical composure about the whole affair. Taurinus returned with two flasks filled with a murky oily substance and gathered the young surgeons around him.

"These flasks contain Bubonium. For the trainees here, it is compounded from fresh Aster Atticus that grows in abundance along the banks of the rivers in this region. The only other area where I believe it grows is on the estates of Cicero just across the straits of Messina in a small northern Sicilian village. It cost me dearly to obtain that flower for my practice in Roma, especially since Cicero was such a prude. He would have called for my crucifixion if he knew I was treating morbus indecens in the shadow of the Forum. Anyway, the petals of the flower are mixed with swine's grease that I got fresh from the castra's kitchens where they were preparing a fresh batch of bacon for the campaign. Both ingredients are fresher than I have ever had before, so this batch should be unusually potent."

"What can we use this substance for?" Magnus asked.

"Well, Crateus wrote a text on a large variety of herbs. He was the rhizotomist and physician to Mithridates VI who was defeated by Sulla in our war in Pontus. The text was lost, but we heard stories about the use of this oil for treatment of anyone bitten by a mad dog, or as a shrinking agent for a swollen throat. It is said he believed that if one inhaled it, it drove away snakes. However, we found it is particularly useful for this malady." Then, he turned to the two young chagrined soldiers.

"Hold out your hands and cup them," he commanded. The boys did as they were told.   Taurinus dispensed a generous aliquot of the grease into their palms.

"Rub that into your groins and onto your serpent every morning and night. You should be well in a fortnight."

"This feels a little strange," said Quintus as he applied the grease.

"It might be, my boy, but other than smelling like bacon and attracting all the dogs within miles, it won't hurt you," chuckled Taurinus.

"Is there anything else we can do extinguish the pain?" asked Marcus.

"Not much," Taurinus said patting Marcus' shoulder.   "The army-issue vinegar water seems to have some affect on keeping the urine flowing, so drink as much as you can get your hands on.   Other than that, you can pray.   The women used to pray and make offerings to Juno Fluonia for return of regular menstrual flow and for fertility, but I doubt that would do either of you any good.   Some men prayed to Liber.   You can try that.   For sure, I would pray to Bacchus for a better party next time."   Taurinus couldn't help letting out a belly laugh.   He was especially proud of himself.

As his laughter subsided, shouts and commands could be heard all over the camp.   Everyone was being mobilized in a hurry.   Marcus and Quintus took their medicine flasks and left swiftly to join their cohort.   Lucius hailed a centurion who was running by.

"What's the commotion? Why is everyone in such a panic?"

"Caesar and the legions from L'Aquila have arrived!" he shouted.   "No one was prepared for them to arrive this soon.   We did not expect them for another two or three days.   A member of Caesar's vanguard rode ahead to warn us.   We have less than a quarter of a day to prepare the troops for a parade in his honor."

As a child, Lucius used to kick ant piles to watch the crazed and confused ant hordes scurry to rebuild their damaged nest.   The entire camp looked just like a disturbed ant hill.   Everyone was running.   Equipment and supplies were being stacked neatly.   The ground was being raked.   Every soldier was in full dress and headed out of camp to form up.

"Well, we won't have much to do until we break camp in a day or two," Taurinus said to the assembled medical team.   "Let's put everything away and watch the festivities."

They gathered the few supplies they had taken out for the day's sick call and replaced them.   Medics placed the surgical instruments back in their crates ready to be loaded when the order came.   Taurinus led the team to the South gate where they all climbed in one of the empty watch towers to observe.

They did not have to wait long.   The two new legions formed up stretching out from the camp.   They faced left and began to march quickly south to the area where they had practiced their turning maneuvers, then turned to face east.   In the distance, the surgical team could make out motion to the South.   First thing they could discern was the cavalry of the vanguard.   It was most impressive, because it was the combined vanguards of all three legions.   The columns of troops stretched behind them to make a formidable army.   Because they were seasoned troops, they made about a third more distance every day than the greenhorns.   When marching with the new legions, they would force the recruits to come up to their speed.   As they approached the field, the commanders stopped and shouted orders.   In a flash, the three legions transformed into battle formation.   They seemed to stretch on for miles.

To the right, they heard the orders of the legatii of the new legions.

Legions XI and XII marched further south to the line of the three legions from L'Aquila. On shouted orders, the new legions reformed into their battle line facing the seasoned troops. They were a little slower and definitely more sloppy than the older legions, but they were able to make a well formed line.

At that point, a single general rode to the center between the two troop lines. It had to be Caesar himself. After riding up and down the entire length of his troops, the five legatii joined him in the center for a brief conference. The legatii returned to their legions and shouted orders.   Then they, along with Caesar's personal guards, rode around the formation and headed for the castra.   Behind them, the troops broke rank and began to pitch their tents.

"That's it, gentleman," Taurinus said. "This means the legions have gone back to the field.   We won't see another barracks until this year's campaign is finished. It will take a day to fully supply these five legions, then I wager we will be going through the Alps. Let's get down from the guard tower. Caesar won't like his immunes occupying strategic positions."

The following morning, the medical team loaded all their supplies into the wagons. Taurinus now had a new routine. He came in to the hospital area and asked for specifics on morning sick call, then he left to go to some sort of meeting leaving the young surgeons to finish up the packing.

*   *   *

In the field, supply stations had been set up. The troops were lined up to get any broken armor replaced, then they were to report to the camp's granaries to be resupplied with field rations.

Neither Marcus nor Quintus had any broken equipment, so they headed directly to the granaries hoping to get a little better rations. When they arrived, they got in the line that was just forming. When they got to the front and opened up their sacks for supplies, the quartermaster's assistant dropped in three days of field rations. Standard rations included one mina – about two pounds of bacon and one congius – about a gallon of sour vinegar water, but no hardtack. Instead, they received the ingredients for making hardtack: one half peck of coarse flour and one acetabulum of salt.   Another quartermaster's assistant was reciting the recipe for making hardtack.

"Pay careful attention. You are being given these instructions in the event the supply train gets separated from the legion and you have to make your own food. The ingredients you received will make one dozen biscuits. Use your helmet to combine the ingredients. Put in the salt. Take the empty acetabulum and fill it twenty times with water and mix it in thoroughly. Next, add all the flour to make the dough. If needed, add more water. The dough should be mixed just enough to stick together.   Bring your dough to your legion's ovens. Spread out the dough on a paddle to make a sheet one cubit by two cubits.   The thickness of the biscuit is important. If it is too thick, it will be too moist and it will spoil. If it is too thin, it will be too dry and it will crumble. Make cuts in the dough – three on the short side and four on the long side. Do not leave it to dry. Thoroughly bake the dough in the oven.   Our ovens will be available this afternoon only. We will be making hardtack all night and packing the biscuits away for distribution during our march. Save your own biscuits for our battle days and for times when the supply wagons fall behind the march."

The assistant continuously repeated the announcement as the recruits picked up their rations.

"Jupiter be damned!" Marcus cried in disgust. "Isn't there anything better you can give us? We know the officers get better rations."

"When you're an officer, I'll give you better," replied the quartermaster's assistant who was distributing the rations. He was covered in grain dust from shoveling barley and wheat flour.

Quintus joined in.

"Come on, brother. We know you slipped others a little something extra. We saw someone just ahead of us get a treat."

"That soldier was getting supplies for his centurion."

"I know you're lying," Quintus said. Then, he whispered into the assistant's ear.

"What's it worth for you to slip us some of that honey?"

The young cook thought for a moment, then he brightened up.

"Get me the medical standard," he said.

"You want us to do what?" Marcus blurted out.

"Hey, if that's what it takes, we'll do it," said Quintus pushing in between the floured assistant and Marcus.

"It'll be okay, Marcus. Let's move on." He pushed him out of line. "We can do this. I have a plan"

"Your last plan got us into deep merda."

"This will be an easy matter. We get your brother to let us borrow it for the afternoon."

"If we get in trouble again, I'll personally kill you."

"Deal."

The two youths slipped over to the hospital where Lucius and the others were almost finished packing. Standing in front of the hospital was the medical standard. The pole stood about eight feet tall with a conical cap on top. Just below the cap, three rings were carved into the pole. Below the third ring were cascading diagonal spirals carved out of the wood going down about three feet. Below that were another three rings.

"Hey, Lucius!" Marcus said in an unusually cheery voice. "Can we borrow your medical standard for a while?"

"Borrow the standard? You know how much trouble we would be in if it is lost?" Lucius was quite upset.

"We only need it for a little while," pleaded Quintus. "We guarantee that we will have it back before the afternoon is gone."

Lucius was suspicious but did not want to know the details.

"Don't tell me any more. This conversation did not occur. I am going inside for a lesson from the chief surgeon. That standard better be there when I return."

"Thanks, Lucius! I'll repay you later," said Quintus.

He and Marcus waited for Lucius to disappear into the hospital, then hoisted the pole and ran around the corner to the backside of the granary. They propped up the pole at the back of the building, then approached the young quartermaster's assistant from the rear.

"We got your pole," Quintus said. "Now make good on our deal."

The assistant looked over their heads and saw the top of the standard propped against the rear of the granary.

"Get out of here! You really did it!"

"Yeah," Marcus said. "Now give us some of that honey."

The young quartermaster reached down and handed each of them an acetabulum sealed with wax. Marcus and Quintus grabbed the jars and sprinted away, Quintus in the lead. As they approached the gate, Quintus abruptly stopped.

"Do nothing, Marcus," instructed Quintus. "I'll do the talking. Just walk with me and follow my lead."

They tried to act naturally as they walked slowly through the gate.

As they approached the guard, Quintus said loudly to Marcus.

"Can you believe that guy? How brazen can a soldier be?" The guard cocked his head to pick up the conversation.

"Yeah, brazen," replied Marcus.

"He just lifted the Medical standard and took it to the granary like it was his!" exclaimed Quintus.

"Who did what?" The sentry demanded. Quintus knew his plan was going to turn out well.

"Right. This quartermaster's assistant by the East granary stole the medical standard! We couldn't believe he did it in broad daylight! Isn't that right, Marcus?"

Marcus nodded enthusiastically.

"Yeah, broad daylight."

The sentry called over the guard commander and Quintus repeated his story.

"Thanks, fellas. Now get back to your cohort. Don't loiter around. I wouldn't want you getting into any trouble." The Tesserarius called two sentries out of the guard house and they left in the direction of the granary. Quintus and Marcus walked out of the gate. When they were well away from the camp, they broke into a dead run back to their tent.

*   *   *

Taurinus was regaling Lucius with his life story again when he was cut short by the bellowing voice of the Tesserarius. Lucius went out to see what the commotion was about, hoping not to see Marcus and Quintus in chains. When he peered out of the doorway, the two sentries were replacing the medical standard.

"You lost something very important here," the commander said. "Luckily for you, two soldiers alerted us to the theft. You are probably too new to know how important standards are in the legion, so I will just warn you. Do not let your standard out of your sight. Next time, it could cost you your life."

Lucius thanked him profusely. He watched the contingent round the corner of the building. As he went back inside, he wondered what his brother and his buddy had done. He was glad he didn't know and vowed never to ask.

*   *   *

During that day, the ninth cohort acquired their final recruit. Decimus, a lad from Placentia, arrived while Marcus and Quintus were on sick call. Appius, who previously served as an auxiliary and had joined as a legionnaire, introduced them. He volunteered to be responsible for bringing their newest member up to speed.

During the evening meal, Marcus and Quintus gave their tent group a detailed account of their escapade. The diversion was a good way of starting their campaign to hunt down the Helvetians. The boys shared a little of their booty with their mates and devoured the rest. They knew it would be the last treat for a very long time. Next day, they would be marching into the Alps. Marcus and Quintus vowed to watch each other's back forever.

Chapter 14: Comfort

Aia stood next to her father staring into the shallow grave where they had just interred her mother. It was supposed to be a big travel day, but plans were changed because of the untimely death of the Tigurini High Priestess. Lugurix sent his condolences and relieved Toutios of duties to be with his family. Sina stood beside Aia while Toutios stood opposite Aia on the other side of the grave with Ouenitouta and Frontú.

Adiega had spent her last night in the arms of her husband. They would face the inevitable by themselves. Sina again spent the night with Oueni and Frontú while Aia was with Lugurix. Adiega drifted in and out of consciousness. When she was lucid, she and Drutos informally said prayers together for her safe travel to the otherworld. It would be her last act as High Priestess. After prayers, she lay there recounting the wonderful moments of their lives and eventually drifted off to sleep. Drutos leaned his head back and soon was asleep himself.

Early in the morning he was awakened to Adiega's final coughing spasm. She was unconscious throughout the episode. As she coughed, she began to spit up blood. It was a trickle at first, but soon became a torrent. Drutos watched in horror and sadness as she exsanguinated on him. Her coughing spewed blood all over the inside of the wagon. Almost everything was soiled.

The morning skies were overcast and a light snow fell on the gravesite gathering. Aia was frozen. Her teeth chattered and she shivered in her cloak. She had no time to change or clean up from her night with Lugurix. She wrapped the cloak around her both to keep warm and to cover her gown. The dress had gotten soiled on the ground. She felt as dirty as her clothes. She glanced at her family hoping no one noticed.

Drutos turned to her.

"Aia, please begin the burial ritual."

"Oh, my dear Mother Goddess!" she thought putting her hand to her mouth. *"I am the High Priestess now, and my first official act is to bury my mother!"*

She closed her eyes and took in a deep draft of morning air. It was sweet with the smell of the wildflowers and the newly turned earth. Tears welled up in her eyes. She gulped hard, then began,

This is a place which is not a place
In a time which is not a time
Halfway between the worlds of
Gods and of mortals.

One by one, they each picked up a hand of dirt and spread it on the grave. Drutos was last. He stood for a long time just staring. Tears came to his eyes as he sprinkled his handful of dirt, then he looked skyward and intoned,

We all come from the Goddess
And to Her we shall return like rain falling into the ocean.

Then, Sina gave everyone tiny wreaths she had fashioned from wildflowers she had quickly gathered that morning. Toutios and Frontú covered the grave. Drutos asked that everyone recite the last prayer in unison.

Journey on now.
We will follow when we can
May you return to the same time and place
To those you knew and loved.
May you know them and love them again.

They each kissed their flowers and dropped them onto the mound of dirt. Toutios and Frontú fashioned a circle with a cross inside from stones laid flat at the head of the grave. All stood and said a silent prayer in the increasing snow shower. Aia raised her charm and kissed it, then kissed her fingers and extended her hands sending her love to her mother one last time. Then, they all headed back to the wagon train, the three sisters supporting their father and each other.

When they arrived at their wagon, Drutos became agitated.

"The wagon and everything in it cannot be used."

Frontú, who had removed the body and knew the horrific scene, jumped in front of the wagon door and spread his arms.

"It's best we just leave it here. Please join Oueni and me in our wagon. It may be tight, but at least we will be together."

"That is kind of you," Drutos said. "Please lead the way."

Toutios took his leave and returned to the front of the column.

Everyone traveled in silence that day. The trail took them past a roaring waterfall and strangely beautiful rock cliffs. The rocks looked like layers of blankets that had been pushed together forming folds and ripples. Occasionally, the rock blankets broke into peaks. All day, they struggled through the snow crossing over rolling hills and through tight valleys. They passed a small village along a stream. No one was in the village to tell them its name. The villagers had cleared out when the migrating Helvetian hordes overwhelmed the little town. The Tigurini made camp there that night and crossed the bridge built by the villagers the next day.

The snow stopped overnight and the sun shone brightly. Although they had to navigate many more hills and tight valleys, traveling was much easier. They began to make up time and caught up with the main migration column. As they set up camp, word came down that a council had been called. Drutos and Aia dutifully went to the center of camp. Lugurix was greeting everyone as they arrived. The tone was already different from the previous councils of that year. When Lugurix saw them approach, he sprinted to greet them. He embraced Aia and led them to the front row of the council. He raised his hands for silence and began.

"My countrymen, I bring only good news. Through negotiations, the old Helvetian chieftain Divico has secured the promise of passage through the Sequani territories where we have just arrived. Their ruler, Dumnorix has stated that we may cross their lands as long as we do not make war against them. I need your approval that we will obey the treaty. Are there any questions?"

"We are running out of supplies," shouted someone from the back. "What assurances do we have that the Sequani will provision us?

"What if they don't?" yelled someone else. "Can we take it by force?"

A few grumbles could be heard in the assembled council. Lugurix put up his hands.

"I have been assured that the Sequani will provide us food for a fair trade. We have arranged to trade provisions for gems from the armor of our leadership."

There were murmurs among the council, then Drutos stood and spoke.

"Lugurix has treated our neighbors, the Sequani, with respect the way he now treats you with respect. We should approve this plan unanimously and immediately. All in favor..."

A great roar arose from the crowd.

"Any opposed to this fair and just plan..."

There was silence. Drutos turned to Lugurix.

"You have passed your first test, my son. Enjoy your victory, but remember how you acted today. Respect will bring you respect." They shook hands heartily. Lugurix raised his hands again to silence the assembly.

"Thank you for your confidence. I will try to earn it every day. Our council is done. Go in peace and hope."

Aia was filled with pride. Lugurix had turned out to be a wonderful leader. She hoped that they would enjoy a long life and have many children. She took solace in the fact that her mother had blessed the union before her death.

Aia thought about her torrid night with Lugurix. Her cheeks flushed as she recounted to herself the details of their shared passions.

"This is the way we will make babies together." She thought smiling, then noticed her groin was aching.

The days that followed were much happier. The small villages they went through were populated and the townsfolk were friendly. Unfortunately, by the time their tribe came through, they had little to sell or trade. That was the price they paid for Bimmos's prideful negotiations that put them at the rear of the migration.

Lugurix provided supplies from headquarters where they traded their jewels for much needed food. Drutos took a set of clothing from Frontú. Aia borrowed clothing from Oueni. As her pregnancy progressed much of her clothes did not fit anyway. Sina rapidly made friends with some of the village children and traded clothing for a lesson in making charms.

During the days they were traveling cooped up in the wagon, the sisters shared stories. At one point, Sina asked Oueni what it was like to be pregnant.

"At first, you just feel different," she said. "One day, Frontú told me that I was more moody than usual. I dismissed him and blamed it on our depressing winter and spring, but then I noticed other things. I woke up queasy and sometimes the smell of my favorite foods made me ill. Later in the day, I would get ravenous and eat like a warrior. I felt like I had gained weight, but figured that was because of all the food I was eating. Every time our wagon stopped, I had to relieve myself, but I remained constantly bloated and constipated. My breasts were swollen and hurt when I rolled over on them at night. Frontú would get amorous, but I had to stop him because his caresses hurt. Then, I felt my lower belly growing and getting hard. By that point, it was very obvious."

"I felt some of that when I had my first period," Sina said. She started to describe her crabbiness and her cramps the days before she flowed.

Aia had been listening intently to Oueni discuss pregnancy, but lost interest when Sina described the feelings she knew all too well. It had been over two weeks since her last cycle and she knew she would be feeling soon what Sina was describing. She did not need to hear the details again. She moved to the front of the wagon. Her father was dozing, so she poked him awake.

"Hello, Aia," he said sleepily. "I thought you were getting caught up with Oueni."

"I was, but I wanted to talk with you," she said holding his arm and resting her head there.

"You have to help me with my duties."

"How is that, child?"

"I am the High Priestess now. I am supposed to know everything."

"Indeed you should. You have had years of excellent training," he replied.

"Well, I am very unsure of myself. When I was studying in school, I could make mistakes and the teachers would correct me. At Beltane, I lost my focus and you had to prompt me. I just feel overwhelmed."

"It is an awesome responsibility to take on all at once, but I trust you will rise to the occasion." He patted her on the knee.

"Would you please review everything with me? Please?" she pleaded.

"You know it would be my pleasure to help you, Aia, but remember, even I won't be here forever. You will have to be a quick learner."

"Oh, thank you," she said and hugged him. "Can we start today with the medicinals?"

"Let's wait for tomorrow," he said. "today, I need rest."

The next morning as they pulled out of camp, Aia was already up in the front of the wagon insisting that her review begin.

"All right, child." Drutos pushed her away at arm's length. "Let's start with the basics. As you know, we can use the same herb or plant in many ways. What are the forms that we use?"

"Oh, Athair, that is so easy!" She turned away pretending to be insulted.

"Well, you wanted to review. So, let's be sure that you know everything."

"Okay," she folded her arms and turned back around. She recited her lesson in a singsong voice the way she learned long ago.

"Teas are made by extracting the essence of a leaf or flower and delivering it in a pleasant manner. Tinctures are made to give a concentrated amount of essence in a small dose. Syrups are made to help us swallow icky tasting stuff and to coat the throat and stomach. Fomentations make a warm soothing skin application, and salves are made so herbs can stay put and act for a long time."

"See my dear, that wasn't hard was it?"

Aia feigned a pout.

"You make me repeat things like I was eight years old. I'm ten plus eight now."

"Well, this stuff is confusing sometimes, and requires memorization like you did when you were a little girl. Besides, you did a fine job."

She briefly looked at him and playfully pushed her shoulder into his side.

"Thank you, but let's get to the more complex things."

"Okay, you want to do the complex? How about the figwort?"

Her eyes got wide.

"I didn't mean the hardest stuff!" Then, she shrugged and relented.

"Okay, let's just do it your way."

"All right, let's begin with the medicinals in alphabetic order."

Aia sat up and pretended to be in Druid classes again. She recited the answers as her father named the item.

"Anise—"

"Anise is best for coughs. Pound and make a syrup with honey."

"Good. Blackthorn–"

"Blackthorn is a diuretic. It is best given as a tea."

Drutos assisted Aia in successfully reciting the straightforward flowers and herbs used for the more common problems. As Aia went through the list, she seemed to gain a little confidence only to lose it each time she faltered. When she hesitated, Drutos had to hold her hands to keep her calm and focused. Despite her lack of confidence, he only had to prompt her a few times.

The list included basil fomentation for rheumatism, tincture of caraway and tea of ginger for dyspepsia, chamomile tea for stress, dandelion and dill syrup for colds, tea or tincture of elderberry for fever, and eyebright salve for inflammations. Foxglove tincture was a heart tonic, garlic salve was to aid in healing wounds, hawthorn fomentation was for inflammation, and horseradish tea was for dropsy. Tincture of juniper was both a laxative and a diuretic, lavender tea was for sleep, and mint tea was for both intestinal spasms and female cramps. Finally, willow bark tea was for fevers and for inflammation throughout the body.

By that point, Aia was exhausted and lightheaded. They took a break and ate a small meal of sunflower seeds and honey. After the food, she felt better and they began on the sacred herbs.

They spent a great deal of time on mistletoe. Drutos made Aia discuss which colonies were the most sacred. She had to describe the proper way to harvest them. They were best harvested from the oldest oak trees five days after a new moon. They were to be caressed gently and never allowed to touch the ground. Aia knew the reasons were mystical. Her father instructed that it was believed that they sprouted spontaneously in the air and should be surrounded always by air, even when stored. Wherever they touched earth, power drained from them.

Drutos requested that she describe how to tell the difference between male and female colonies. She cheerfully described the pale yellow and green flowers which began to appear in early spring and bloomed until early summer. She pointed out colonies in bloom in some of the birch and oak trees they passed. She described how the female colonies developed sticky white berries in the late fall. Next, she recited how to preserve them for the Yule and Imbolc rituals. Drutos had her describe in detail the use of the plant as a stimulant and a heart tonic. He reminded her that teas and tinctures of mistletoe had to be made just right, because too large a dose was highly poisonous.

Aia described the use of rowan as a protectant, particularly against a woman's evil eye. Although she knew how to use it, she hoped that she would never need it. Drutos helped her understand the teas and tinctures of skullcap for anxiety and lunacy. That plant also required many precautions during preparation, because of its narrow therapeutic range.

Finally, Drutos felt that Aia's confidence was strong enough to discuss figwort and yarrow. He eased her into the topic by reminding her that these two plants had multiple uses. The easiest way to remember how to collect them and how to use them was by reciting the appropriate incantations during the gathering and preparation. Aia always was good at incantations and easily sung them for her father. Frontú listened in as he drove the wagon.

I will pluck the figwort,
With the fruitage of sea and land,
At the flow, not the ebb of the tide.

By your hand, gentle maiden.
The kindly Sucellos directing me,
The hellish Curoi protecting me.
Whilst bride of women beneficent
Shall put fruitage in the cattle.
As the King of Skies ordained.
To put milk in breast and gland,
As the Being of life ordained.
To put sap in udder and teat.
In udder of badger,
In udder of reindeer,
In udder of mare and of sow,
In udder of heifer,
In udder of ewe,
Of udder of doe, and of cow.
With milk, with cream, with substance.
With rutting, with begetting, with fruitfulness,
With female calves excelling.
With progeny, with joyance, with blessing.
Without man of evil wish.
Without woman of evil eye,
Without malice, without envy.
Without one evil.

Aia discussed the method of fomentation to optimize the yield of useful figwort. Although she was feeling very confident about her performance, her father gave her no time to savor the moment. He requested she recite the incantation for yarrow.

I will pluck the yarrow fair
That more benign shall be my face,
That more warm shall be my lips,
That more chaste shall be my speech,
Be my speech the beams of the sun.
Be my lips the sap of the strawberry.
May I be an isle in the sea.
May I be a hill on the shore.
May I be a star in the dark time.
May I be a staff to the weak.
Wound can I every man.
Wound can no man me.

Drutos pointed out that all of these sacred flowers and herbs should be gathered in birch or willow baskets made fresh specifically for the harvest. That enhanced the powers of the herbs.

Aia enjoyed reciting her lessons so much, she did not realize it had taken the better part of the day. Even so, it seemed that Frontú was pulling the wagon to a stop very early. She peered around to see the wagon train ahead had stopped. She shouted to a warrior riding down the line.

"Why are we stopping so soon?"

He pulled his horse up short.

"We have come to the end of the Sequani territory. There is a large river they call the Saône. We need to organize our nations to cross this river and head to our destination. We are going to make camp here."

Chapter 15: The Coldest Summer

Departure from Placentia was hectic. That morning, Taurinus woke up Lucius and the other assistant surgeons before dawn. He supervised them securing the remaining medical supplies and hitching the mules to the wagons. The old surgeon grabbed Lucius to join him in the first medical wagon. The next five medical wagons were each staffed by an assistant surgeon and two medics. All the remaining medics would walk next to the wagons. The first wagon contained all the surgical instruments and the torches they would use. The second and third wagons carried the bandages needed for the troops. The troops each carried simple dressings for quick bandaging in the field of battle, but many more were needed for the field hospital. The third and fourth wagons carried the tents that they would set up as their field hospital. The final wagon carried the cots for wounded soldiers and for those felled by illness. All the wagons carried chests of compounded medicines and ingredients to compound more.

They drove their wagons around to line up facing the troops. That maneuver put the Po at their backs and the rising sun to their left. Even though it took them a while to get organized, the legions would take considerably longer to make their formation and ford the Trebbia, the small Po tributary that was the western border of the castra. It was quite swollen from the rapid snow melt during the hottest spring anyone could remember. It gave Taurinus an opportunity to have didactic time with his trainees. He gathered his team around him for a morning session. Taurinus took his position in the back of the wagon where he sat on the steps. The six trainees stood in a semicircle around the wagon and the medics stood behind them. Everyone could see Taurinus and very few had the sun in their eyes.

"I understand from our commanders that we will parallel the Via Amellia Scaura for the next several days, then travel on flat lands until we reach Ocelum, the last outpost before the Alps. After that, we will have a much more arduous journey and Caesar is anticipating combat action. Most of the injuries will be handled by the surgeons of Legions Seven, Eight, and Nine. During the trip, spend your time thinking about your duties and reviewing the special compounds we use. When we get to the other side of the Alps, we need to practice as many procedures and bandaging techniques as possible so we are fully prepared to be efficient in the heat of battle."

Taurinus took out a fresh piece of cinnamon and stuck it in his mouth.

"Now, a little history lesson." The trainees shifted, but no one objected.

"On the other side of the Alps, the first territories belong to the Vocontii. They are well assimilated into our culture but are a cold and aloof people. They are not as much of an ally as the Allobroges whose territory lies between the Isere and the Rhodanus rivers, but they were key allies in defeating the Cataline conspiracy just five years ago. At the time, they were approached to be coconspirators to overthrow Cicero who was supreme Consul. Instead, they went to Cicero with the letters of intent from the conspirators. Cicero had the papers read aloud in the senate and the coup attempt was over before it started. The Allobroges are very friendly to us and will help us prepare. I have already arranged with Command to get the supplies we need. Now back to business."

Everyone was relieved that the old man did not digress into a long reminiscence of past wars.

"I have been a legion surgeon on and off for more years than I care to count. I have worked with a number of hard nosed commanders in my time. So, you need to heed the words I am about to say. I cannot make this point too strongly. Caesar, our supreme commander for this campaign, needs to subdue the barbarians. Our prime objective is to keep the soldiers in fighting trim. Our success will be measured by the number of wounded whom we make able-bodied again. Although we are assigned to Legion Eleven and report directly to our Legatus, we will receive wounded from all legions. No soldier from the Eleventh takes precedence over any other legionnaire who has equal injuries. To have the best outcome for our general, we must learn to triage our wounded." Taurinus pointed to the back of the group.

"This begins with the medics." He had the medics come to the front next to him so he did not have to shout.

"When it is time for battle, we will erect the tent hospital. Next, we wait for our signal. Under no circumstances are you to go onto the field of battle until we receive the signal. First, the Cornicen will blow his horn. This will be the signal for the medics to go out to retrieve the wounded. I want no more than one-third of you on the field at any time. As the first group returns to the hospital, the next group may leave. Collect those injured legionnaires whom we can potentially help. Do not bring the dead or dying. It is a waste of our resources. Likewise, do not bring those who can walk on their own or with the help of another comrade. They will come to us. Do not bring those with mortal wounds such as open chest injuries or open wounds of the hypochondrium where the entrails are ruptured. This leaves the soldiers with extremity wounds or those with actively hemorrhaging wounds. For soldiers with hemorrhaging wounds, use their field dressings to stem the flow of blood before you move them. Carry them back directly to me. I will be at the entrance to the hospital along with two medics." He chose the two he wanted at his side.

"I will look quickly at the injury and tell you where to take the soldier." At that point, he released all the medics and directed his comments toward the young surgeons.

"For the surgeons, I want three stations with two of you at each. Two stations will be for general injuries and one for bone fractures and dislocations of the articulations. Once hemorrhage is controlled and the fractures and dislocations have a proper bandage in place, the medics will move them to cots in the hospital. Of course, some operations will need to be done immediately. Try to keep this group to a minimum for efficiency. If the surgeons determine that the wounds are mortal, the medics will move them to the rear of the hospital. Once we have filled our cots, we will go around and reassess each soldier. Those that require a procedure will be moved to the surgical tent for the operation. Once the operations are completed, we will repeat the sequence until the battlefield is cleared of potential survivors. Remember how we were able to manage sick call? That came from following my orders to the letter. If you do the same in battle, we will accomplish our mission for General Caesar."

Taurinus offered small pieces of cinnamon to each of his trainees, then launched into a discussion of the wounds he considered salvageable. Next he demonstrated his method of ligating bleeding vessels and had the surgeons practice tying knots. Each surgeon took a two foot length of thin rope and looped it around a hook on the side of the wagon. Taurinus went around inspecting and critiquing the knots. Those who had worked for Taurinus before knew his usual critique was a curse leveled at the trainee and an admonition to perform the ligature just the way he demonstrated it.

"Magnus, those are the biggest, clumsiest fingers I have ever seen! If they were donkey dicks you couldn't do worse!"

"Atticus, why do I waste time on you? By Jupiter and all the gods! Can't you remember right over left?"

"Lucius, not bad for your first time. It's wrong, but not bad. Here, one last demonstration." Taurinus flew through the tie and finished with a flourish. "See?"

Lucius, remembering his previous rebuke.

"No," he replied.

Taurinus stopped, stunned.

"What?" He flushed red immediately. Lucius took in a breath.

"Sir, you said if I do not see something, I need to speak up."

Taurinus looked dumbfounded, then slowly he loosened his screwed up face.

"So I did, so I did, but you are supposed to get it the first time."

"I apologize, sir. I need another demonstration, but slow down and show me the steps."

Taurinus stared at Lucius. He blinked a few times, but obliged his newest immune. For that demonstration, the histrionics were gone and he carefully went through the knot explaining his hand movements as he went, then he talked Lucius through a perfect tie.

"Got it?" he asked.

"Yes, sir, got it."

"You damn well better, because I expect perfection from now on!" Taurinus demanded, then he moved on to his next victim.

"Petrus! I would call you a tree stump, but tree stumps disintegrate with time. You never change! Worthless!"

"Modestus, what is that? – The knot of Hercules? No one is getting married today, and if you don't get it right, no one will want to marry you!"

"Priscus, that is not right and you know it! There are only two ways to tie – my way and the wrong way!"

Time passed slowly as they took berating after berating. Thankfully, before the sun reached its zenith, they received the signal to head out. Lucius and Taurinus climbed aboard the first wagon. As they pulled out of camp, Taurinus addressed Lucius in a calm voice for the first time that day.

"Lucius, you are the one I have chosen to be my second surgeon."

Lucius looked at him stunned.

"Why so quizzical, Lucius? I see everyone's work. You clearly have the most talent and dexterity. Although you have the least experience in surgery, you will catch up and surpass the others in no time. Besides, you are clearly the best listener. I have been able to talk with you like no other trainee before. Most of them escape after a few days."

"That's because I had to ride in your wagon for three weeks," Lucius thought to himself. *"Even if I wanted to run away, there was no place to escape to."*

He squelched the urge to blurt it out.

"How about another piece of that cinnamon bark?" he asked instead.

*   *   *

The troops had been allowed to sleep until dawn, but once Sol peeked over the plains of the Po Valley, the officers began shouting orders.   Each Contubernium struck their tent immediately, packed it on their mules, and moved into formation.   The usual travel column would place each legion in numerical order from seven to twelve, but since they were anticipating fighting in the Alps, the legatii changed the standard rules. First order of business was to quickly cross the Trebbia. Legions XI and XII went first. They changed to battle formation making the crossing shorter.   The two legions marched double time into the river not knowing what to expect. Despite their training to that point, they stumbled and slid their way across the bottom.   Even though the river was only waist deep, most legionnaires were wet to their necks by the time they emerged on the far bank. Marcus knew that there would be more rivers to ford. He hoped in the future, they would be able to perform the task more efficiently.

After crossing the Trebbia, Legions XI and XII moved to the south of the fording site and waited. The legions from L'Aquila forded by number. The three legions crossed without incident in less time than it took the two green legions. At the same time, all the supply trains pulled around and used the small bridge of the Via Amellia Scaura to swiftly cross the river and join their respective legions. Then, the travel positions were assigned.   The Tenth legion, which was deployed at Geneva, would join them after the legions crossed the Alps. First in the column would be Legion VII, which would lead the expedition from that point forward. They would be the first to engage the enemy. Next was Legion XI, then VIII, then XII, then IX.   By using this formation, both green legions were bracketed by experienced legions, and both vanguard and posterior guard were battle tested. In addition, the new legions would be pulled and pushed to keep pace with the seasoned troops.

Now, the forced marches had a purpose.   Their goal was to reach the Helvetii without delay. The troop line marched off of the Via Amellia Scaura and followed the Po for the next four days.   At that point, they turned to face the afternoon sun and marched nearly due west for three days reaching the confluence of Flume Bormida and the Flume Tanaro.   The location was just south of a small Roman village situated on a hill. The confluence was completely flat and the rivers had nearly stagnant flows. They camped for the night. Although it was late May, the weather turned chilly overnight.   In the morning, a thick fog enshrouded the low land. With the pulling and pushing of the experienced legions, the greenhorns forded both rivers before the sun rose to its zenith. The wagon trains bogged down in the soft mud between the two rivers. During heavy fighting or in pursuit of an enemy, they would have been left, but the legions were allowed to wait for the supply trains. All forces camped on the left bank of the rivers that night.

Another two days' march brought the expedition to Ocelum, the last outpost before the Alps and Gaul. Caesar had just completed a permanent castra only a half day's march from there. His troops also constructed a bridge over the River Po to reach Geneva just six weeks earlier. Because only one legion without its baggage train had crossed the bridge, it required inspection before allowing the entire Army to cross.   The engineering contingent went ahead to inspect and prepare the bridge for the next day. Because the castra was designed for only one legion, all forces spent the night in the field. Only the supply trains were sent into the castra to restock. By morning, the Army crossed the Po and headed into Gaul.

As they marched, they could see the Alps stretched across the horizon growing taller and taller. They headed nearly due west into a wide valley with mountains taller than Marcus had ever seen. By the evening of the second day from Ocelum, they were camped on the valley floor surrounded by white capped mountains. The spot chosen was near the end of the wide valley in which they had been traveling. To the right of the column was the stream they had followed through the valley. The local tribe called it the Durien, but the Roman Army labeled it the Dora Riparia or the gods gift to the river banks, because of the lush vegetation that grew near it.

The valley easily accommodated the usual tent formation of each legion. The air was decidedly cold. They all noticed how much colder the temperatures were since they had crossed the Flume Tanaro. Marcus and his tent group decided to make a small fire, but when he and Cornelius, one of his tent mates, ventured toward the tree line, they were turned back by the guards.

"Let me take care of this," said Quintus. He went toward the tree line but was stopped by a guard.

"Bet he gets turned around like we were," said Cornelius. However, after a brief conversation with the guard, Quintus was allowed to pass into the forest. Soon, he was back with an armful of dry wood of various sizes.

"How did you manage that?" Cornelius asked.

"It was easy," Quintus replied. "I gave him an amethyst."

"You gave him a what?"

"I'll show you after we build this fire."

They worked together to build a crackling fire. Quintus got a second load of wood while they worked. The eight Tirones sat around the fire warming their hands.

"All right, show us what you gave the guard," demanded Cornelius.

Quintus reached into his sack and pulled out a tiny pouch made of sheepskin tied with a dried strip of sheep intestine. He opened the pouch and dumped the contents into his hand. He stretched out his hand to show them stones of all sizes and colors. They sparkled in the flames. The boys recognized these as stones used in women's jewelry. Several took stones to examine more closely.

"Where in Tartarus did you get stones like that?" demanded Marcus.

"From my uncle."

Marcus was angry.

"You lost your uncle's dice and your money weeks ago on the day I met you on the beach," Marcus said glowering at him. "How could you have such wealth while asking me for money?"

"I had them hidden very close to me," Quintus beamed

"You were severely beaten that night. Your tormenters should have lifted them from you."

"Not where I hid them."

"And where was that?"

"They were inside of my entrails."

"How–?"

"Simple. I swallowed them."

"So that means–"

"Yeah, I had to sift through my merda for a couple of days to recover them."

Every one of the Contubernium groaned in disgust. They could not return the stones to Quintus fast enough.

"Okay, party's over you mushrooms!" It was Martial, their Centurion. "Kill that fire. We are in enemy lands. Don't draw attention to yourself. Get some rest. The combat action picks up from here."

The boys did as they were told. They threw dirt on the fire and turned in. Appius and Decimus huddled together to keep warm.

With first light, all legions were up and packing. Breakfast for the ninth cohort was in silence. They all were still thinking about the disgusting history of the jewels. Shortly after breakfast, they were back in formation and moving out. Although the valley continued to the West, the Army turned south.

Since Marcus was on the left of the formation, he could see Legion VII make a half turn away from the river. They were headed up a small rise and into a pass. Much taller hills were on either side of the pass. While watching the legions climb the gentle slope, he could see the peak of both hills. At first they seemed to be undulating, then it looked as though both hills were alive with ants. He felt a thump in his chest and became immediately nauseated as he realized the hills were thick with Celtic Mountain men.

All of a sudden, the air was full of spears. Marcus was filled with dread for his comrades. Then, the legion did something he had never seen before. The outer legionnaires turned their shields outward and the inner legionnaires put their shields above them, and all pulled the shields in to touch each other making a shield box. The maneuver was done so rapidly that no spear reached any of the infantry. However, some of the lateral cavalry were not so lucky. No soldier was hurt, but several horses were killed. The cavalry soldiers who lost their mounts ran into the formation for protection.

The Mountain men who threw their spears ran part way down the hills on both sides hollering and brandishing their shields but approached no closer. A second wave of spear throwers appeared on the hill and the process was repeated. Those spears harmed no one. To Marcus' amazement, the enemy did not charge and did not venture any further down the hill on either side. The box formations opened up and the Velites launched their spears at the barbarians, which scattered the attackers back over the hill.

After waiting a quarter of a day, no further attacks came. The order came down to move out at double time. The legions traveled for the better part of the afternoon stopping earlier than normal. During the afternoon march, they climbed another thousand feet. Now, they were on an open valley floor. The bordering hills had become small mountains. The camp site was in the center of the valley. That position was more defensible and gave them full view of the enemy before they could get close enough to throw their spears. There were three open exits to the valley making it difficult to box the Army in. Martial addressed his century.

"Today you saw the Centrones tribe. They are typical of the tribes living in the Alps. We will see them or their brethren again before we leave these cursed mountains. Since Caesar arrived so quickly, we did not have time at Placentia to teach you the Testudo or tortoise formation. So, we will spend the rest of the afternoon practicing here. You can imagine what would happen if the spears hit you, so you know this lesson will be important to you. You can easily learn this maneuver, but you will need speed to protect each other."

Martial positioned each legionnaire and walked them through the maneuver. Once he was satisfied that they had the basics, he began the drill.

"Ad Testudinem! Form the Testudo!" he commanded.

The century practiced until they could make nearly impenetrable boxes. Then, they worked on speed. They were able to make it before Martial could say, "Caparum Romanus - Ad Victoria!" At that point, Martial was satisfied and dismissed his troops to make camp.

Marcus noticed for the first time that he was really cold. The sky was grey and the wind had picked up. It seemed to be coming from every direction. They were not allowed to pitch their tents, so they would be sleeping in their armor to be ready to assume battle positions, if necessary. To make matters worse, they were pulled for guard duty.

Because of the attack, all legions double posted guards around their perimeter. Marcus and Quintus were paired together. Although they could have each taken a portion of the watch while the other rested, they both agreed to do the guard duty together. They spent the night staring into the dark open valley. By now, the moon was nearly invisible and the landscape black. The boys passed the time complaining about military life and how cold they were. After what seemed like an eternity, they were given relief and stumbled back to their group. They passed out immediately, but were soon awakened to prepare for the day's march.

After the usual cold breakfast, the troops formed up and moved out. The valley remained wide and the ground smooth, so the march to the next stopping point went quickly. They did not notice that they had climbed continuously most of the day.

The next camp site was near the location of a tribal village at the confluence of three valleys. Marcus could see the small village on the top of a hill in the open valley. Just before dismissal, Martial told them that scouts had surveyed the village and found it deserted. That did not sit well with the commanders and they anticipated another attack. They were now at the border of the lands of the Caturiges. That tribe was known for fierce fighting and would be expected to launch a charge on the Army. Again, double guard postings would be necessary.

The Army stretched from the northwestern valley to the eastern valley past the village. The valley to the south of Legion VIII marked the middle of the army column. Legion XI was to the west of VIII and camped in the open confluence of the valleys below the village. That positioned the ninth cohort very close to the beginning of the Legion VIII. Again, Marcus and Quintus pulled guard duty for the third watch. Martial positioned them looking directly toward the village. Although they were to spell each other, they had difficulty deciding how to plan the night.

"Marcus, why don't you take a rest first, and I will stand watch," Quintus said.

"No, I'm not tired right now. Why don't you take a nap?"

They went back and forth arguing who would take the watch first without resolution. Finally, they decided to take the first shift together until one of them was ready for a nap. They sat on the valley floor and speculated about the empty Caturiges village and where the warriors had gone. After griping about the cold, the lousy rations, and the lack of shelter, conversation waned. They both just stared silently out into the void. Marcus thought of his comfortable bed back in Canino.

"I wish I could sleep in my own bed right now," he thought.

That was the last thing Marcus remembered until clanking and shouting penetrated his consciousness. He heard footsteps running past him, then a loud clank jerked him awake. Dawn was breaking. To his left, not more than one hundred feet away, he saw legionnaires and Caturiges locked in fierce combat. He realized that he had fallen asleep sometime during the night. He turned to see Quintus still asleep. He shook Quintus and the two groggy guards jumped to their feet. As they looked to the right, they could see that the other sentries of the Eleventh legion also had fallen asleep and were slowly coming to their feet.

During the dark of night, the Caturiges warriors had reoccupied the village and, with the first hint of dawn, stormed down the hill directly into the belly of the Legion VIII. The legion's sentries were alert and sounded the alarm in time for the cohorts to wake up, grab their weapons, and engage the enemy. Marcus realized that if the attack had been on their legion with all the guards asleep, the Caturiges would have overrun their position and slaughtered much of Legion XI. He vowed he would never allow that to happen.

He and Quintus turned back to the left to see the attack being repulsed. The first and tenth cohorts of the Legion VIII had moved out to form a U and were closing the circle on the enemy. When the Caturiges sensed the maneuver, they ordered a retreat. They ran back up the hill with the cavalry close on their heals.

The Romans waited for a second attack until the sun was above the mountain top, but none came. The soldiers were ordered to break camp. They formed a traveling column and moved in a westerly direction. Sporadic sorties continued, but were easily repulsed by the lateral guards. No significant damage was sustained.

As they traveled, they could see that many of the mountains were capped with snow. It was a marvel to most of the recruits who came either from sea towns or regions where their mountains were devoid of snow by that time of year. As the day progressed, the skies clouded over and the wind picked up. Everyone was glad that they were moving. At least they were able to keep warm.

That evening, they reached the highest point of the entire expedition. They were over a mile above sea level. The storm clouds that hung around all day began to sprinkle. However, as the sun disappeared behind the mountains, the temperature fell rapidly. The rain changed first to sleet, then to snow.

Quintus looked up and held out his hand to catch a few fakes.

"What is this falling from the sky?" He asked.

"That's snow. Haven't you ever seen snow before?" snorted Cornelius.

"No, and I have never been this cold before either," replied Quintus.

"He's from Neapolis," added Marcus. "He only knows rain."

"That's right, and I wish I was there now," whined Quintus.

"To stay warm and dry tonight, we will need our tent," declared Marcus. "There is only one way we will be able to do that."

He left his group and approached Martial.

"Sir, with the snow, we need shelter tonight. May we have permission to pitch our tent?"

Martial spun around to look Marcus in the eye.

"You little monkey! If we were still in Placentia, I would have you whipped and your tent group digging latrines again!" Then, he gave a big sigh and put his hand on Marcus' shoulder.

"Now son, let me give you some advice. You are a soldier. Your only job is killing barbarians. Others are responsible for your wellbeing. You do the fighting and they will keep you well. Just now, we have received permission to pitch tents as long as we can strike them and be on our way without delay in the morning. Had you waited, your request would have been unnecessary and I would not be mad at you again.   Next time I won't hold back my anger."

Marcus brought back the news, but left out the part about nearly getting everyone in trouble again.   They rapidly erected the tent and huddled under their blankets.   They soon realized that they would be warmer if they slept close to one another.   They arranged their gear to the outside and moved next to each other, except for Appius and Decimus who huddled together away from the rest.   Snow continued to fall most of the night.   The skies dropped nearly three inches of white powder on the Army.

With first light, they were up and striking their tent even before the orders came down.   They were beginning to function better as a team, and their speed matched the seasoned legions in front and behind them.

The morning march was downhill and the Army covered a considerable distance.   The further they moved from the previous night's camp site, the less snow they saw.   All were glad to be moving out of the snow covered valley.   By midday, the valley was green again and opened into a broad plain about a mile across and about eight miles long.   They moved quickly to exit the plain.   There were two different potential exits.   The one to the right went only a short distance before it narrowed down considerably.   The way to the left was wider.   It was the direction the Army took.

Before the vanguard could secure the exit, a new tribe of Gauls, the Graioceli, rushed out of the hills to block their path.   In response, Legion VII moved into battle formation and marched directly into the enemy.   The barbarians fell back without engaging the Romans.   They were not expecting such a huge army, and disappeared deep into the smaller valley.

The skirmish delayed the Romans' departure and they had to spend the night there.   Legion Seven drew up a defensive line across the exit to the valley. Legions Eight, Eleven, and Twelve stayed in the middle.   Legion Nine spread across the valley to the rear.   The supply wagons were placed dead center along the travel path for protection.   The night passed without incident and the Army formed up and moved out at daybreak.

The trail out of the valley was just wide enough to accommodate the standard travel column.   They marched next to a noisy little white water stream.   As they rapidly descended out of the Alps, they had to ford the stream multiple times as it twisted toward the valley floor.

Eventually, they left the mountains behind and followed the right bank of the stream for five miles to its mouth, which emptied into to the Isere River.   It was the gateway to the lands of the Vocontii.   The tribe's leaders met the Army at the river.   They had constructed a magnificent bridge and Caesar's legions easily crossed into the friendly frontier.   While Marcus and his colleagues made camp in the shadow of the Alps, they knew it would be only a brief break before they continued their race to catch the Helvetii.

Chapter 16: Practice, Practice, Practice

Taurinus incessantly lectured Lucius as they negotiated the Alps. Lucius was less annoyed by the lectures, because Taurinus talked less about himself and began to instruct him on becoming a surgeon.

"Remember, we are only treating healthy young men, so we only need a few basic tools and medicines for non-surgical diseases. Our medical tools are clysters for enemas and cucurbitulae for drawing out bad humors or pus. Our medicines include some of the ones with which you already should be familiar: oxymel, poppies, castor oil, salt, vinegar, wine, belladonna, water for bathing to bring down fevers and garlic as a diuretic. Some of these double for uses in treating trauma. We keep our supply of medical items low so we have more room for our surgical supplies and medicines."

Lucius asked a few simple questions to get an idea of how Taurinus wanted him to treat medical diseases. His approach was much more direct than Theodosius. He would elicit the main symptoms and prescribe for those. He hoped that diseases in the young healthy legionnaires were limited and that youthful bodies would heal with only a little help. Lucius understood the logic – get the fighting man back to work without delay.

When they stopped that night, Taurinus was still in a didactic mood.

"I guess this is about as good a time as any to review our surgical supplies. Leave the evening preparations to the medics and join me in the back of the wagon."

Lucius let the old surgeon clamber into the wagon first. He huffed and puffed his way in the darkness, then threw open the back doors. Lucius picked his way to the back to join him. In the rear was a chest. Taurinus opened the chest to reveal many large drawers.

"These drawers contain the most important items we will need when the injured start to come in," Taurinus said. "Along with water, which is multipurpose and important for cleaning any wound, and vinegar, which we use to wash our instruments and swab the skin before we cut it, we have cleansers." He pointed to the first row of drawers. "Here are pumice, balsam, pine resin, turpentine, copper and antimony sulphide. Next row of drawers contains the items we use to stop bleeding. Of course, severe hemorrhage from arteries and veins we control with a clamp and ligature like we practiced the other day. Are you still practicing your knots, son?"

"Yes, sir," Lucius lied.

"Well, back to the bleeding suppressants. Here are copper ore, copper flakes, antimony sulphide, potter's clay, and the most important item of all, alum."

"The copper and antimony are repeats from the cleansing agents," Lucius observed.

"Yes, you're right. Because they are used for more than one purpose, we need a bigger supply. So, we have extra drawers of them. It's not easy to get some of this stuff in foreign lands."

Taurinus snapped his fingers.

"Oh, I almost forgot. We also use dressings and lint to stop hemorrhage. Lint works very well for amputations or when a wound is oozing. We don't have time to apply these more precious substances.   Besides, they often wash away in brisk bleeding."

He went on to the next subject.

"Sometimes we need to bring out an abscess.   This row of drawers contains what we need.   Here are myrrh, balsam, frankincense, bitumen – called powdery clay by pagans – and sulphur. We also can use fat, oil, and goose grease, but those we get from the quartermaster."

"I am not really familiar with the use of any of these ingredients," he said surveying the drawers.

"Well, you will be in no time," replied Taurinus.   "When we get into a battle situation, there will be so many injuries, you will use these ad nauseam. After your hundredth trauma victim, you will know them like the back of your hand."

Taurinus went over more ingredients during the next several days of travel. There were agents to erode a wound or to draw out purulence from a wound. There were caustics. There were substances to produce scabs and agents to soften or remove scabs.   There were even agents to make flesh grow and fill in a deep wound.   Many of the agents had several uses.   Some agents were simple such as wax, figs, milk, and egg whites. Others were strange and even curious such as oak galls, pigeon dung, and ox bile.   Lucius surmised that the only way to become proficient at the use of these medicaments was to memorize their uses. About the time he felt comfortable sorting them out, Taurinus threw in a twist.

The day after the first attack, Taurinus knew he had to teach Lucius more quickly before they were in a battle situation. He knew that their legion probably would be the last to be committed to a battle, but raids like the first one might involve the new legions before they had witnessed a true Roman battle. The young soldiers might sustain considerable casualties, forcing Taurinus to work handicapped with unprepared medics.

"Today, you need to learn the way we combine these substances. Listen closely. I will try to be clear and concise. One thing that distinguishes a surgeon from a physician is the careful categorization of treatments.   It will require memorization at first, but I will give you a framework upon which to build. Ready?"

Lucius was game. At least it was better than the lousy stories of the career of Taurinus, "The Great Surgeon."   It was morning, they had passed the night without an attack, and they had eaten a solid breakfast.

"Ready," he said.

"Except for controlling excessive hemorrhage, we do not use these agents singly, but in combination.   There are three types of compositions: emollients, plasters and pastils. Emollients are made with combinations of flowers and their stems. They are applied to intact skin. Plasters and pastils are made with metals, earth, and other dry ingredients, but no fat.   They are intended to splint an extremity or cover a wound. For plasters, we mix the dry ingredients first, then add the appropriate liquid just before we need it. Sometimes it is necessary to melt the dry ingredients over a fire. Plasters are laid onto the affected area. Pastils, on the other hand, are premixed. If necessary, a little liquid is used to get the ingredients to mix properly. If so, we dry out the mixture before storage. When needed, we simply add the appropriate liquid to the premixed pastil and smear it on. Are you with me so far?"

Lucius felt the lesson was easy.

"Yes, sir.   Emollients are made of flowers and rubbed onto the skin. Plasters are mixed and applied to the affected part and allowed to dry there. Pastils are liquified when needed and smeared onto the affected area."

"Right," said Taurinus. "Now let's address emollients. There are thirty-six."

"Great," groaned Lucius.

"Don't despair," said Taurinus. "We only use a few. The first one on the list to eliminate is the only one that is designed to cool. It is for gout, which we will not see out here. Generally, the purposes of emollients are for one or more of the following –" Taurinus counted them on his fingers as he recited the list. "–relieve pain, alleviate a bruise, disburse diseased matter, extract pus, treat scrofula, relax a body part, soften induration, or open pores. We will not be treating scrofula, so that eliminates ten more. Also, we can eliminate those used to treat pains caused by diseases we cannot operate upon. That eliminates another four. We will eliminate redundant emollients that are used for similar purposes and compound only specific ones for specific purposes or make ones that can serve multiple functions. That leaves only ten to learn. Of these, one contains only four ingredients, one only five ingredients, and four only six ingredients. The others four contain ten, twelve, fifteen and twenty ingredients each."

Lucius felt a headache coming on.

"Let's begin with the most versatile and, of course, the most complicated – the emollient of Andreas. This is used when diseased matter has to be extracted. It also relaxes sinews, draws out humor, matures pus, and when it is matured, ruptures the skin and brings a scar over the wound. It is applied to abscesses, both small and large. Likewise, we apply it to painful joints. Further, it repairs any part of the body that is contused and draws outwards splinters of bone. In short, it is useful in all cases in which heat is of benefit. If you have to learn only one emollient, memorize this one. Learn to make it fast and smear it on everything. The twenty ingredients and the amounts are wax, mistletoe juice, tears of sycaminus, round and long peppers, ammoniacum for fumigation..."

Here, Taurinus began to drone on with a constant meter to his voice. It was the way he had memorized the formula. Lucius' mind began to drift.

"Hey, pay attention, son! This has to be in your head. We will not have time for you to ask me how to do this simple stuff when we start to treat the injured."

"I'm sorry," Lucius apologized. "The recitation is so boring."

"Stick with me, son. I am only doing this for your good. Besides, it will get easier as we go on."

Lucius promised to be more attentive and Taurinus began to drone again. He completed the ten emollients and began the plasters.

"Now, there are twenty-eight plasters, but only five indications, so we use only five formulas. The most important is for fresh wounds. It is a covering to agglutinate the wound, repress inflammation, and induce a scar. The best of these is the plaster called Barbarum. It contains twelve ounces of scraped verdigris or corroded copper, twenty ounces of litharge or corroded lead, one ounce each of alum, dried pitch, and dried pine-resin, to which is added one hemina or one cup each of oil and vinegar."

Taurinus described four more plasters. One was indicated for extracting fluids or for collections which form under the skin. One was for debridement or for dissolution of dead tissue in a wound. He described one suitable for bites and one for superficial wounds that only needed a mild dressing.

"Are you with me, son?" asked Taurinus

"I'm holding on," replied Lucius.

"Good.   Because we are almost done.   How many pastils do you think there are, my boy?"

"I don't know, sir. Twenty?"

"No, you're way off. There are only six — and all for the same purpose. So, you only have to learn one and one modification of the basic formula."

Lucius leaned forward, rested his chin on his fist, and knitted his brow. The lesson was getting ridiculously boring, and even though he looked attentive, he had gone back to Canino in his mind.

"Pastils are used for many purposes, but in battle, we use them for their agglutinating properties. The pastil of Polyides nicknamed 'the seal' is, by far, the most celebrated. It contains one ounce split alum, two ounces green copperas, five ounces of myrrh and aloe, and six ounces each of ox-bile and pomegranate heads. Rub them together and mix with enough dry white or red wine to form a paste. The modification is this. If the wound involves sinews or muscles, it is better to mix the pastil with a cerate composed of wax or resin — eight parts of the pastil to nine of the cerate."

Lucius could not believe he had made it to the end of these dry and boring lectures, but as he thought about it, there were only a few things he would have to do: stop bleeding, cover a wound, make a scab, dissolve a scab, draw out pus or fluid, and make a pain patch. He was grateful that the scope of his work would be so narrow.

"Okay, recite the formula for the pastil of Polyides." Taurinus commanded.

Lucius' heart jumped.   He did not think he needed to memorize the formulas already.

"Are you serious?" he blurted.

"By Jupiter and all the gods! I am dead serious!" exclaimed Taurinus.

Silence...

Lucius knew it was the last formula he had heard, but clearly, it had gone right through his head. Mmmmmm...

"Spit it out, son!"

"Alum... Pomegranate..."

"Well, at least you got the first and last item."   Taurinus frowned.   "I thought you might get this formula. Let's try to make it easy. Six ingredients: alum, green copperas, myrrh, aloe, pomegranate heads, and ox-bile. Three amounts: one, two, five, and six ounces. The first, second, and third ingredient are mineral, the fourth, fifth, and sixth are vegetable. Each group is in alphabetical order. First mineral, one ounce.   Second mineral, two ounces.   The third mineral and first vegetable, five ounces. The last two vegetables, six ounces."

"Mmmmm..." Lucius was lost.

"Okay," said Taurinus as he sat back.   "You need to develop your own method of memorization."

Then, the old surgeon gave Lucius a wry smile.

"I have one more surprise for you. Open the bottom drawer of the chest."

Lucius obliged.   There were four stone tablets with lettering chiseled into them.   Lucius stared at them and discovered that the first two contained the formulas for the emollients.   The third tablet had the plaster formulas and the fourth had the pastil formula.

"Why didn't you tell me this before?" Lucius was puzzled.

"Because you would have paid even less attention than you did today."

Taurinus grinned. "Now, you have until we cross the Alps to memorize these. Then, the tablets remain in the bottom drawer and the formulas must be chiseled into your skull."

Lucius spent the next two days learning to recognize the various agents without prompting either by the tablets or by Taurinus. Each night, he passed out from the mental exhaustion. The last night, he did not even notice that it had snowed. The next morning he looked out of the wagon surprised to see the three inches of snow.

Taurinus was just returning from his usual nighttime activity of dinner and drinks with Publicus. He kicked the snow around.

"Commanders tell me that it snows year round on the mountaintops here," he told Lucius. "Even so, it is not unusual to get snow in the high valley this time of year. The few friendly locals say it may snow here even up to the end of this month. Before I climb on and sit there for the day, I need to release." He pulled up his tunic, grabbed his penis, and urinated his name in the snow – Manius Fabricius Taurinus.

"Wine definitely is a great diuretic," he called over his shoulder.

"Right." Lucius was disgusted. He crawled back to the chest to study formulas. At least while he studied, he did not have to listen to the old curmudgeon's stories and ramblings. That day, Taurinus seemed to be breathless and often stood up to urinate over the side of the wagon, something Lucius really had not observed up to that point in the trek.

Taurinus remained quiet most of the day and that night when they camped, he did not leave to meet Publicus. He made excuses that he was not hungry. He just sat up in the front of the wagon and went to sleep there. Lucius found his actions curious and sat beside him for a moment. He noticed that the old surgeon's breathing was erratic and his color was slightly ashen. His lower legs and ankles were swollen. Lucius deduced that Taurinus probably was exhibiting early signs of dropsy. In carefully thinking back over the journey thus far, he remembered other times when Taurinus had difficulty breathing, but that episode was definitely the worst.

The next morning, Lucius tried to bring up the subject, but was met with a string of curses and insults. So, he just retreated back into the wagon to study the formulas again. By midday, Taurinus was back in his usual state of loquaciousness. That night, he again made his pilgrimage to Publicus for an evening of debauchery. Lucius decided it might have been just a passing illness.

He returned to the business of learning the formulas. They were all nonsensical. He tried rearranging the ingredients to make rhymes. He tried singing them. He tried word associations. Nothing worked. Finally, he resigned himself to straight memorization. He went over and over the list until he could say them in his sleep. By the time they crossed the Isere, he was able to recite them flawlessly to the great satisfaction of Taurinus.

"Now, we need to get your surgical skills up to speed." Taurinus declared the following morning.

"How are 'we' going to do that?" Lucius asked. "We don't have any one in our legion who is injured or in need of surgery. The few legionnaires who are injured are being taken care of by their own legion surgeons."

"Never underestimate me, son." Taurinus put his finger in the air, then to his temple. "I have methods. Publicus and I have worked out a plan. The Allobroges tribe is very friendly. Publicus has arranged for them to give him a flock of sheep. Some will be used for Haruspicina."

"Haruspicina?" questioned Lucius. He was unfamiliar with the term.

"You know, reading entrails for the High Command to assist them in strategic decisions. It has become big business." He cleared his throat in a disapproving manner, then went on. "Some of the flock will be used for milk. Some will be used for dinner. And, Publicus is in charge of all of them."

Lucius was puzzled.

"How does that help me learn surgery?"

"The sheep that will become supper need to be butchered. Those are the ones we will get first. Along with your fellow trainees, you will practice the various responsibilities of the surgical team. Each of you, in turn, will be the providers of light, holders of the animals' legs, surgeon, first assistant and instrument assistant. Each will have an opportunity to see and do simple procedures. We will make and sew wounds, make and set fractures, and perform amputations. Although sheep are not built like we are, they have the same kind of organs, and hot blood runs in their veins. The similarities are close enough for you to become familiar with the basic skills you will need to work independently from me. You will find this time invaluable when it comes to a real battle."

Now Lucius understood. They would have an opportunity to practice operations and to learn some of the subtleties of each job. By going through a simulated operation, they would be better equipped to anticipate each step in the procedure, and they would be better prepared to render assistance. Working together and rotating jobs would allow them to understand the needs and limitations that were unique to each position. It might dispel some myths about particular tasks. Each person had different capabilities and each job had different responsibilities. Working out the kinks under controlled conditions might prevent some misunderstandings.

"Not bad, old man," Lucius thought.

That evening, the six young surgeons gathered between the wagons. Medics had set up two tables. One held the instruments and equipment laid out and ready for use. The other was to be used as the operating table. Quartermaster's assistants carried in six sheep. They had been shorn by the Allobroges sheepherders before being turned over to the Romans. The quartermaster had slaughtered and dressed them before sending them to the medical area. The assistants dropped one on the operating table and the rest on the ground.

"We will be back at sunset to collect the meat," one of them said as they left the area.

Atticus and one of the medics were assigned to position the animal on its back and hold the legs out against the table. The positioning exposed the abdomen and chest. Modestus was assigned to stand by the head to observe. Taurinus said that job would change in a few days. Petrus was assigned to hold the torch. Priscus was the instrument assistant. Lucius was the first to act as surgeon and stood on the right side of the sheep. He was assisted from the other side of the table by Magnus. The abdomen had been opened down the center and the chest and abdominal cavity were empty. Taurinus stood at the head of the table and barked orders.

"Sew up the hypochondrium," came the command.

Priscus picked up a sturdy linen thread, which had a needle attached at each end. He handed one needle to Magnus and the other to Lucius.

"Begin on the inside at the top. Put a needle through each side. It must go through all tissues – muscle, fat, and skin. Now, take the needle on the right and put it through the left side from inside to outside. Pull the suture up tight and hand it to the assistant to hold. Now, do the same with the left needle through the right side. Magnus, keep tension on the suture and let go only when Lucius pulls it out of your hand. Re-grab the suture and pull through the skin until it is tight. Now you must hold both sutures for Lucius. Continue sewing until the entire abdomen is closed. Tie the two ends together. Good. Now, cut out the suture and rotate positions."

Lucius followed instructions carefully and was able to perform the procedure without getting yelled at. As he stepped away from the table, his animal was removed and a new animal was brought by the medics. Next, he became a holder, then he rotated to torch bearer. He stood between the hind legs in front of the leg holder. He positioned the light over the wound between the surgeon and the first assistant to provide light for both. Next, he became the instrument assistant standing at the right side of the surgeon with the instrument table oriented sideways on his right side.

In turn, each surgeon became the recipient of vitriol from Taurinus. Each yelling session seemed more shrill than the next. Finally, they reached the last practice run. Lucius rotated to the first assistant's side of the table. The surgeon was Petrus. Petrus got into difficulty immediately.

"No, you mule head!" shouted Taurinus. "Make sure the suture goes through all the layers, not just skin. Put the needle in deeper. No! Deeper! Deeper! Okay, next stitch. No!"

The yelling went on for each stitch. By the time all had finished their turn as surgeon, everyone, including Taurinus, was exhausted.

"That's all I can stand today," wheezed Taurinus. "Tomorrow we will work on fractures and amputations. Now, get out of my sight!"

Lucius could see that Taurinus was having difficulty breathing again. His normal ruddy complexion had turned ashen.

"Are you sure you are all right?" he asked.

"Just don't bother me. Get out of here!" Taurinus snorted.

"Sir, please sit down," Lucius pleaded.

"I'll be okay," Taurinus said breathlessly. "Just, get out of here."

Lucius backed away, but kept an eye on him. Taurinus leaned back against the makeshift operating table and supported himself with his hands. Slowly, his breathing came back to normal and he mumbled a few orders at the medics who quickly cleaned up the instruments and stowed the tables in the wagon. Taurinus hobbled toward the quartermaster wagons leaving Lucius and the others alone. Lucius turned to Priscus.

"Have you ever seen Taurinus this way?"

Priscus thought for a moment.

"He used to get a little short of breath after a long screaming match with a senator, but this seems worse than I remember."

"Well, let's all keep an eye out for any more episodes," Lucius whispered.

By the next morning, Taurinus recovered both his breath and his surly demeanor. That day passed without incident. In the evening, the medics again set up the tables and the quartermaster's assistants brought three more killed and dressed sheep from the Allobroges. That session, they practiced setting fractures. They worked in pairs, two per animal. One would act as the surgeon while the other assisted. Taurinus, with the help of Magnus, broke the humeri and the femurs of each sheep, then he discussed the general method of assessment.

"The upper arm and thigh are handled the same way. The forearms, lower legs, and digits are similar in management to the arm and thigh. That is the reason we will use these breaks as the lesson. Also, the bandaging is similar. Now, the least troublesome type of fracture is the simple transverse fracture. The multiple and the oblique ones are worse, but the worst are those where the fragments are pointed and stick through the sinews. You will see all three types of fractures in battle." Taurinus brought the young surgeons over to one of the sheep and grabbed the leg.

"First you must assess how the bones are aligned. Rarely do the fractured bones remain in place. More often, they slip and overlap each other. The distinction is easy. If the fragments are in contact, they make a sound and produce a stabbing pain when moved. You will not feel a lump under the skin. If the bone fractures obliquely, the limb will be shorter than the other, and the muscles swell up. When that is the case, we must stretch out the limb to proper length and set the bones. Usually, you will have to hold it in place until a proper bandage can be applied. If the bone is not set soon after fracture, inflammation sets in and we must wait until the swelling goes away. If not, there is a high chance for gangrene and the need for amputation." He looked up.

"Lucius and Atticus, come here and we will demonstrate setting the fracture."

Taurinus had Lucius hold the hoof and Atticus the pelvis.

"Now, pull... Harder." The boys strained to pull the leg out in a straight position.

"To get the bones back to position, they must be pulled beyond the normal position and guided back to the right spot." Taurinus guided the bones as the two gradually released pressure. The bone was now back in its normal position.

"Watch closely while I bandage this leg," Taurinus instructed. "You will need to do this for every kind of fracture to maintain the bones in place while they heal"

He folded a standard issue cloth bandage three times and dipped it in both wine and oil, then wrapped it around the leg.

"We will use six bandages including this dressing," Taurinus explained. "The first makes three turns in a spiral going upwards. The second makes three turns in the opposite direction. Next, place a thick pasty create on the layer. If bone projects through the skin and you can't reduce it, place a triple layer of wool soaked in wine and oil around the bone. Now, place two more spiral layers in opposite directions covering the fracture. These should be smoothed out over that create layer."

Taurinus worked swiftly. Without stopping, he asked Atticus, "As we smooth it out, what do we say?"

At first Atticus was puzzled, then he remembered.

"Frica Sicut Ama – Rub It Like You Love It!"

They all mumbled the phrase.

"Frica Sicut Ama."

Taurinus glowered at them.

"I don't hear you."

In unison, they recited the phrase three times. Taurinus beamed.

"That's better. Make the bandages snug but not too tight to allow for swelling. Otherwise, you risk gangrene. By the third day, the bandage will need adjusting, because it will become loose as the swelling goes down. After that, change the bandages every five days. Always wash the limb with warm water when the dressing is removed." He finished the bandage and turned to face the six surgeons.

"Healing times are slightly different depending on the site of fracture. The lower jaw, cheek bones, clavicle, sternum, shoulder blades, ribs, spine, hip, heel, and the bones of the hands and feet heal in two to three weeks. Bones of the leg and forearm take twenty to thirty days. The longest to heal are the upper arm and thigh, which take up to six weeks. These times are important because we must give a report on the sick and wounded to the Legatus. He needs to know how many men are disabled and when he can expect them to return to active duty. These reports are due every morning immediately after sunrise. Any questions?" He surveyed his charges.

"No? Then, start practicing. Each of you set one foreleg and one hind leg. Speed and accuracy are both important. Call me when you are done with each so I can inspect."

Lucius and Atticus had to remove the bandage that Taurinus applied before they could reset the fracture. Each group had a medic assigned to support the leg once they set it. Everyone worked rapidly, but the results were far from the same. Magnus and Petrus wrapped their limbs too tightly for Taurinus and they had to redo every one. Priscus and Modestus wrapped their layers with varying tension making the bandaging look sloppy. Taurinus ripped it off as he hollered at them. Lucius and Atticus made the best bandage. As they unwrapped the bandages applied by Taurinus, they observed and felt the tension he used to dress the wound. The delay also allowed them to hear the rampages by Taurinus as he observed the others. The pair were able to make corrections before they were inspected.

While they worked, they could hear Taurinus yelling.

"No, you ass! Frica Sicut Ama! Frica Sicut Ama!"

Lucius and Atticus first began to say it in jest, but soon it became a sort of battle cry. It was easy to wrap the limbs to the rhythm of the words.

"Fri-ca Si-cut Ahh-mahh, Fri-ca Si-cut Ahh-mahh, Fri-ca Si-cut Ahh-mahh."

First down, then up, then down, then up, and so on. It made their bandages go on smoothly with even tension.

The session became pleasant for Lucius and Atticus as they used the rhythm to make perfect dressings. The only awkwardness was Taurinus himself. Each time he came to inspect and approve their efforts, he was wheezing worse and worse. By the end of the exercise, he was more blue and short of breath than the day before.

"Should we say something?" whispered Atticus.

"No," said Lucius. "The last time I asked him about his breathing, I was nearly crucified."

As they talked, Taurinus stumbled and almost fell. Fearing a fit of apoplexy, they grabbed him under the arms and eased him to a seat on the wagon. Taurinus continued to wheeze for a moment, then he put his finger down his throat and induced vomiting. Shortly after that, he seemed to breathe a little easier and yelled at the six to clear out of the area and leave him alone.

They all went around to the quartermaster area to let the assistants know they were finished with the sheep. On the way back, Lucius addressed everyone.

"I have seen this condition many times before back home. I fear that Taurinus is hiding dropsy. If we leave it untreated, he will almost certainly be seized with apoplexy."

"He needs blood letting," said Priscus.

"He may need it, but the old gas bag will never submit to it," said Modestus. "If we ask him, he will surely have us flogged."

"Can we get him to take a diuretic?" asked Atticus.

"If he refuses, I will just hold him down and you can force it down his throat," declared Magnus.

"Right. Then we can all just climb on a cross because he'll crucify us when we release him," moaned Petrus.

"Then we just have to trick him," said Lucius. "Atticus, run over to our medications chest and grab Parnassus seeds. I'll go talk to Publicus and we will put it in his wine. That way he gets his medication and none of us are directly to blame."

"Great idea," said Modestus, "but let me talk to Publicus. I learned excellent powers of persuasion from my Pater before he was murdered. I will get the quartermaster to do our dirty work. We will all survive and Taurinus will miraculously get well again as though he was visited by the gods."

They all agreed to the plan. Atticus pilfered three times the usual dose and Modestus told Publicus that it was in Taurinus' best interest to take the medicine, even if he did not want to admit his sickness. He convinced the old quartermaster by suggesting that a daily dose would allow the two friends to have many more nights of reminiscing together. The boys all went back to their respective wagons to wait for the dawn of the next day and prayed the old curmudgeon did not discover their plot.

The following day, Taurinus was constantly going to the back of the wagon and urinating onto the ground in front of the mules pulling the wagon behind them. He was more quiet and introspective in between trips, but his breathing was significantly improved. Most of his conversation with Lucius was about being a leader.

"You see, Lucius," he said as he returned from his third relief trip that morning, "this job is tougher than just being a medicine man. Surgeons must be leaders. Surgeons never work alone like a physician does. Surgeons must perform their work quickly and efficiently. To accomplish that, he requires a team. The surgeon must be focused on the patient and the procedure. He must have appropriate light, proper exposure, and the right instruments to perform the task. Only he knows exactly what resources he needs and where they need to be, so that he can conduct a smooth operation. The staff and assistants are willing to do your bidding. If you communicate well with them, they will respond. If you don't communicate, or you yell and scream and berate them, their cooperation will diminish. They may do your bidding, but they will find ways to sabotage you at another time."

"The way you yell and scream," Lucius mused to himself, *"your assistants always want to run away."*

"I know what you are thinking, Lucius," Taurinus continued. "I have my reasons for yelling at all of you. You need to learn how to be effective surgeons in a few days. I don't have the luxury of guiding you with a gentle hand. I have precious little time to impart my knowledge. I don't know any other way to do it."

"I understand," Lucius said without really meaning it. He knew arguing would be pointless.

"Being a surgeon is similar to being a general. A general uses his troops like a surgeon uses his hands. Troops make maneuvers and kill the enemy at the direction of the general. The surgeon's hands perform the operation at the command of the surgeon. Both the general and the surgeon need resources to be effective. The general directs his resources to support his troops and supply what they need when they need it. The surgeon directs the lighting and exposure while requesting the right instrument at the right time to perform the task."

Lucius listened. The analogy was not bad, but he thought it had a fundamental flaw. His years of study under Theodosius using the Socratic method made him sharp at debate. He could not help himself.

"While I understand your basic point," Lucius argued, "you must admit that battles can be won without a general, while an operation cannot be performed without the surgeon." He felt a little smug at his logic.

Taurinus scowled.

"I'm in no mood to have a debate with the son of a senator."

Lucius spun around to look directly at him.

"Yes, I know your father. He may be one of the most respected and principled men in the senate, but that won't get you a pass to the head of the class. You must be better and work harder than the others to gain their respect. The long arm of your father cannot reach you here on the battlefield."

"I understand, and I apologize."

Taurinus sat back.

"No need. I may not be the best logician, but my point is clear. A general's intelligence and experience allow him to direct his troops so the army has the best advantage for victory. A surgeon must have the skill and experience to perform a successful operation. He is the team leader, but the team would be ineffective without a surgical leader. Despite your insolence, you have the right qualities and you certainly have the intelligence to be a great surgeon. In assessing the others, I think Magnus may have some of those qualities as well. I am not so sure about the others. You will have to help them develop into more effective surgeons."

"What about you? Aren't you going to do that?" Lucius asked.

"Considering the way my body is acting during this campaign, I am not sure how long I will be with you. I know you slipped me a diuretic. I know you think I have dropsy." He headed back to relieve himself again while continuing the conversation. "I may well have dropsy, but while I can, I plan to ride your ass and the asses of the other five to make us worthy in the eyes of Caesar. I swear by Jupiter that we will become the best and most efficient surgical division in this army."

"So he had noticed," Lucius thought to himself as he blushed. He would need to pay attention to the few remaining lessons if Taurinus only had a little time left. Lucius knew it was the only way he could become independent quickly. The training might be brutal, but it was the only way Taurinus could mold them into the best surgical team.

"One more thing," Taurinus was saying. "In the military, the lead surgeon must be the medical general. He must assure that his team is well supplied. He must train his medics to be ready for casualties. He must have a plan for all eventualities. He must position his resources so that they may be used optimally. He and his teams must be prepared not to be overwhelmed by casualties. Most importantly, he must assure the morale of his teams. Surgeons will need to make hard decisions about who can and who can't be saved. Some of the mortally wounded will cry out for hours before they die. Some of those you and your teams try to save will die despite everyone's best efforts. This will be hard on the uninitiated. Even I find it difficult at times to bear these burdens, but the lead surgeon must always be prepared to help his teams to do their best. It is the only way you will sleep at night."

Lucius silently pondered the heavy words.

"Of course, a keg of wine helps," Taurinus added with a chuckle.

Early that afternoon, they arrived at the Flume Rhodanus, the provincial border of Transalpine Gaul. Lucius watched as Caesar's engineers prepared the bridge they would use to cross the river the next morning. They would move into the territory of the Sequani, the territory immediately beyond the province. As the medics set up camp, the quartermaster's assistants led in three live sheep. The young surgeons looked at one another wondering what the old man had planned for them that evening. Lucius had a good idea. Taurinus gathered the young surgeons around him.

"Today is the last training exercise before we might engage the enemy and incur significant casualties. Although our legion will be in the reserves for the first battle, we never know when we will be needed by our own troops or when we might be directed to help other legions. So far, we have operated on dead animals. That definitely will not be the case from now on. We can't help the dead, only the quick. This evening, we will practice amputation techniques. These live sheep will scream like us. They will struggle like us. They will bleed like us. So, we must perform our operation quickly and efficiently."

He gathered his trainees around the first animal.

"Amputations will be necessary in cases of gangrene. Regardless of how well we treat the original injury, some limbs inevitably turn to gangrene. The only cure is amputation. Now, the soldier with a bad limb usually is in a weakened condition and some even die before the procedure. In some instances, the soldier may die from too much bleeding during the amputation. We are not going to let that happen in our legion. We are going to be vigilant and amputate limbs early. When planning the amputation, look for a spot well above the diseased tissue but below a joint, if possible. Use the amputation scalpel. Remember, it is the long blade that is sharp on one side. Cut the flesh all the way around in one motion, but just the skin. We are trying to cut each layer in turn so your assistant can pull back the layer once it is cut all around."

"How can we cut only one layer at a time?" Magnus asked.

"We do it by feel," replied Taurinus, then he added, "I know that may be hard for you with those big clumsy hands." He stopped for a moment and stood up to face his trainees.

"Think of it as cutting through a melon. The outside is thick and hard while the inside is soft and moist. You want to cut only the rind. After a few amputations, you will begin to develop a feel for the point where you cut through a layer. The knife just cuts with a different tension. The skin is hard, the fat is soft the muscles are firm, and the sinews are like lute strings."

Everyone remained silent, feeling unsure that they would be able to sense the same tissue changes Taurinus described.

"Why is this so important?" Petrus asked.

Taurinus spun around.

"Don't question technique, you marble head, just do as I say!" He took a breath and softened his tone.

"Look, if we cut each layer in turn and pull it back, then cut the next layer at the new location of the previous layer, what happens when we pull the layers back into position?"

There was silence. Eventually, Lucius ventured a guess.

"We get an inverted cone?"

"Precisely!" Taurinus was pleased it was Lucius who got the answer. "If the deepest part of the wound is the bone, the tissues will easily heal over it making a manageable scar. If you cut it straight through, then the bone sticks out and the wound suppurates. Then, we must revise the amputation. Revisions lead to more deaths. Understood?"

Light was beginning to dawn on the trainees' faces.

"Good! Now where was I? Oh, yeah. When bleeding occurs, compress it with lint. If there is a large artery or vein, seize it before you cut it. If possible, tie it with a ligature above and below where you intend to cut, then cut all the way through. If you cut it before you seize it, clamp it on the sound side of the patient and forget the diseased side that you are cutting off. The diseased side will stop bleeding when you remove the limb. Once we cut the sinews, we bare the bone by pulling back the flesh and cut the bone with the amputation saw. Smooth any rough edges with a rasp. Then, draw the flesh over the bone. The flesh must be sufficiently loose to easily cover over the entire bone. If not, pull the flesh back and recut the bone. Place a sponge soaked in vinegar over the wound and bandage it with a Barbarum plaster. This will help the wound heal."

"Questions? No? Okay, then. First, I will demonstrate, then we will practice in turn. Each surgeon will rotate jobs. Those of you who hold the animal are much more important now. With a live animal, there is one additional holder for the head. Lucius, you get that job first. Try to keep the animal still. Suppress the utterances and try not to get bitten. Priscus, since we have done a few amputations together in the past, you assist me. The rest of you, choose a job and be ready. By the way, don't throw the amputated leg away. It will be part of dinner."

Lucius found his new job quite difficult. First, the lanolin in the skin made the animal slippery. With the wool shaved off, the head was hard to grasp. Second, the ewe had no intention of submitting to her inevitable fate. Positioning the animal took extra time, because the holders had to subdue the bleating struggling sheep. Before the operation began, Lucius and the medics could barely manage to restrain the beast. Once the incision was made, their job was nearly impossible. The bleating became blood curdling screams. She struggled ten times harder and began to bite. Lucius did everything he could to keep the sheep's mouth closed, but still suffered multiple bites.

For his part, Taurinus performed a swift operation. The skin was cut, the main artery and vein clamped and ligated, and the bone exposed and sawed off before Lucius could recite the first half of the *Precatio Terrae*. He found it oddly appropriate for the amputation.

Goddess revered. Earth. Mother of all nature,
Engendering all things and re-engendering them from the same womb.
Because only you supply each species with living force,
You are the divine controller of sky and sea and of all things.
Through you is nature hushed and taken into sleep.
Likewise you renew the day and banish night.

You cover Pluto's shades and immeasurable chaos.
Winds, rains and tempests you hold back,
And at your will, let loose, and so convulse the sea,
Banishing sunshine, stirring gales to fury.
And likewise when you want, you rapidly bring the joyous day.
You bestow life's nourishment with never failing faithfulness.
And, when our breath has gone, in you we find our refuge.
So, whatever you bestow falls back to you.

As they packed the wound, rotated jobs, and prepared to hack off the next limb, he recited the second half of the prayer.

Deservedly you are called Mighty Mother of Gods,
Since in dutiful service you have surpassed the divinities of heaven,
And you are that true parent of living species and of gods,
Without which nothing is ripened or can be born.
You are the Mighty Being and you are Queen of divinities.
O Goddess. You, Divine one, I swear I adore you
Graciously grant me this which I ask of you
And with due fealty, Goddess, I will repay you thanks.
Give an ear to me, I pray, and favor my undertakings
This which I seek of you, Goddess, grant me willingly.
All herbs which your majesty brings forth,
For health's sake you bestow upon every race
Entrust to me now this healing virtue of yours
Let healing come with your powers:
Whatever I do in consonance from now on, let it have a favorable result
To whomever I give those powers or receives the same from me, please make whole.
Finally now, O Goddess, let your majesty grant to me what I ask of you in prayer.

The next amputations done by the trainees did not go as well as the one Taurinus preformed.   Only Magnus held the sheep's mouth closed. All the others' efforts were feeble and the screams were murderous. The noise was beginning to attract a crowd. The medics had to cordon off the area to keep out the curious. The screams from the animal were nothing compared to those of Taurinus as he berated each trainee in turn.

No one was able to see and control the artery before cutting it. Everyone, including Taurinus, was drenched from the blood bath. Each had to remediate by amputating a second limb.   During that round, Lucius, Modestus, and Priscus managed to see and clamp the artery and the vein before cutting them. Taurinus ordered two more sheep and Magnus and Atticus muddled through. They managed just to nick the artery before clamping it.   They received a begrudging pass from Taurinus. Petrus failed again on a third attempt and received kicks in the legs and buttocks from Taurinus, but to everyone's relief, he did not make Petrus try again.

While the medics did what they could to tidy up, Taurinus mercifully killed the animals before they were taken away. They all took a quick dip in the Flume Rhodanus. When they returned to the wagons, Taurinus told them their lessons were concluded. From that point on, they were on their own. He wanted no part of them.   Lucius knew that attitude would change when the next day dawned. Fortunately, the diuretics saved Taurinus from another breathless episode and he was able to enjoy the company of Publicus.

Chapter 17: The Hunt Begins

After crossing the Isere, travel was dull and unremarkable for Marcus and his fellow legionnaires. Now they were on the left bank of the Flume Rhodanus about to enter foreign territory. Martial told them they were not to disturb the local tribes. They were considered friendly. The local tribes included the Allobroges who had holdings along the lower part of the Arar River and the Ambarri and Aedui tribes who lived on either side of the of that river. The troops' job was to cut down the Helvetii when they caught up to them, no one else.

The march across the bridge was easy. Caesar's most trusted Tenth legion, which stood against the Helvetians and built the fortifications in Geneva, waited on the right bank of the Rhodanus. They defended the Army's flank as the other legions crossed into Gaul. Once all were over safely, the column picked up speed.

They marched through lands that were nearly flat with only an occasional rise. The late spring days were already hot and particularly sticky. One morning, clouds covered half the sky at daybreak. They were stately white billowy clouds, moving aimlessly about. They were playful, constantly changing shape. First, they combined to form monstrous pillows, then split into smaller ones that grew again. All morning they played hide and seek with Sol.

The last time the Army had seen precipitation was over a week before when it snowed. Here, the ground looked like it had not seen rain for a month. The earth was made of a grayish clay that powdered easily. The wind was hot and moist. Occasional gusts kicked dust off of the narrow paths. The fine dust covered everything and everyone. It got into Marcus' sandals making his feet ache as he marched.

The open fields were covered with young crops. It was impossible to tell exactly what crops were growing that early in the season. Many of the new plants looked the same. Marcus surmised that the local Gauls planted wheat for bread. In the distance away from the roads, they could make out herds of cattle and sheep grazing on patches of short grass. They did not see any Gauls. The only living beings they saw were the animals.

Everyone was restless, eager to find the enemy and annihilate them. They began to chatter among themselves about what they would do when facing the barbarians.

"I can't wait to get my hands on those barbarians. I'm going to cut them down to size," declared Marcus.

"So you think they are tall," said Appius.

"I heard they are monsters. They're a cubit taller than us with fangs like dogs," said Cornelius.

"Yeah," said Memmius. "They have yellow hair and blue eyes."

"You're describing the Teutones," said Appius. "I heard the Helvetians look just like us."

Marcus was surprised.

"How can they? They're barbarians, aren't they?"

"Not all barbarians are monsters," said Appius.

"That's right," said Decimus. Although he swore he was sixteen, no one believed he was even fourteen. It was rumored someone paid off the Prefect of the camp to allow him to join.   Ever since volunteering, he had been shadowed by Appius.   No one else knew much about him.   It was the first time he joined in conversation with the rest of the cohort.   He told his story with great emotion and augmented it with expansive hand gestures.

"My great uncle used to tell stories about the lost legion of Lucius Cassius who was consul nearly fifty years ago.   They fought the Tigurini, a Helvetian tribe and lost.   The Tigurinis made them slaves.   Only a few escaped.   A few years later, they were supposed to join the Cimbri tribe who are truly monsters and take over the alpine province.   My great uncle was in the legion of Gaius Marius.   In some incredible battles, they nearly annihilated the Cimbri.   The Tigurini decided not to come down from the Alps.   It was rumored that they went home when they heard that the Cimbri were defeated.   The Tigurini people are our height with dark hair and brown eyes.   They speak some strange language, but use our alphabet to write their words.   Uncle showed us a stone fragment with their writing.   It was curious because the letters so spiky."

"That's enough yammering!" yelled Martial.   "Save your breath for the fighting.   You don't need to know what your enemy looks like.   You will just kill them on my orders.   That means you will destroy anything and anyone I tell you to.   Is that clear?"

"Yes, sir!" they shouted in unison.

"Now march!"

After a few moments of trudging in silence, Quintus began a cadence for the century.   He would sing a line and they would repeat it.

Amabo, mea dulcis Ipsitilla,
meae deliciae, mei lepores...

I beg you my sweet Ipsitilla
My scrumptious charming Laelia
Summon me to your midday rising
And if you're willing, help me there;
Don't let anyone block the door
And don't go out wandering
But stay there and prepare yourself
For nine successive fuckings!
Honestly, if you want it, order it now
I've eaten!
I'm sated!
And now, I'm supinated!
I am poking right through
My tunic and the covers!

Everyone was giggling through the last lines.

"Where did you come up with that one?" Decimus sniggered.

"From this guy Catullus," replied Quintus.   "He likes to hang around my uncle's place in Roma.   He is always writing stuff.   Some of it is crazy good and some of it is just crazy.   He writes mostly for the lupas, but he occasionally writes about his friends and even his enemies.   One day, one of Catullus' favorite lupas stole all of his poems.   He was so pissed, he even wrote a poem about that.   He told anyone who would listen that she was a putida moecha, a vile harlot."

"Hey, I thought your uncle's business was in Ostia," said Marcus.

"I told you, he does all right for himself. Besides the place in Ostia, he built private thermal baths near Pompeii. They are for citizens who want to get away from Roma and not be seen. He also has a small villa near the Circus Maximus for those who prefer to stay in the big city for their leisure and gambling."

"I think I've heard of your uncle," said Terentius. "I wager his name Niraemius, right?"

"Yeah," answered Quintus. Terentius went on.

"My pater used to tell stories about the time when he helped build the Forum Baths of Pompeii. One of his favorites was a story about Niraemius. He was a big deal back then and might have been a Duovir Magistrate, but something happened. I can't quite remember what it was... Didn't he steal marble from the construction site to build his own villa?"

"Whatever you heard, it's not true," snapped Quintus. "He got that marble direct from the quarry. The trouble came when he was Aedile Magistrate in charge of Pompeii's public buildings. He tried running for Duovir, but the other candidate, Lucius Caesius accused him of stealing. Even though it was never proven, it cost him the election. But now, my uncle has the last laugh. All the previous magistrates from the early construction boom either died or mysteriously disappeared and Uncle Niraemius makes a fortune in the shadow of the public baths. You can still see his campaign slogan in the old town." Quintus stretched his hands out in the air to demonstrate the slogan. "Homo Honestus!"

"That is everybody's slogan," complained Marcus in disgust. "Even my pater used it. Now, he goes for endorsements, instead"

"Still, he is a fine man," countered Quintus.

"Can I meet your uncle someday?" asked Cornelius.

"Sure, I'll take all of you when we get back –"

"If you get back," yelled Martial. "Now march!"

"Got any more cadence songs?" asked Appius as they tried to regain some composure.

"Sure," said Quintus and he started up again with everyone repeating the refrain.

I just caught
A little boy
Thrusting away
Into a girl
So I banged 'em, and,
If it pleases Dione,
I drove my boner
Like a spear!

The last line was shouted and it put everyone in a better mood. Suddenly, a huge gust of wind drove dust into every orifice. They had not noticed that the clouds turned from playful white pillows to dark gray, nearly black menacing monsters. They were twice the height of their early morning brethren and all of them had flat tops. They even seemed lower to the ground. In the distance, the cohort saw a squall line with lightning. At first, the thunder came late after the lightning, but soon, the lightning and thunder were nearly on top of one another. Within moments, the heavens opened up and they found themselves in a downpour.

The dust they had been cursing all day transformed into slimy slippery mud. The dust on their arms and legs washed down in rivulets onto the ground, which was rapidly becoming a thick ooze. Almost instantly, the wagons became stuck and the drivers had to get down and push the wheels and whip the mules to make any progress. Soldiers began slipping and sliding on the muck. Those troops who could stand in the wind were becoming mired in the clay. Marcus and Quintus slipped and fell in the mud. Nearly everyone was covered head to toe in clay.

Orders came down to make camp on the spot and wait until the next day to move again. All were relieved because they were making no progress anyway. Marcus and his tent mates quickly moved off of the road and pitched their tent near a small shallow lake. The water's edge was congested with reeds that stuck up about an arm's length above the water line. The center of the lake was clear. Marcus watched the rain splashing into the lake and the wind blowing the reeds in every direction.

The rain lasted half the afternoon. As it gradually let up, the clouds broke revealing the hot afternoon sun. The warm wind quickly dried the clay on Marcus. He felt like he had a new coat of armor. He looked at the rest of the crew. Everyone had gray clay everywhere, but he and Quintus were the worst off. They were covered in so much clay, they could have been statues.

"Let's go wash off this merda in the lake," Marcus told Quintus.

Before Marcus could say another word, Quintus bolted toward the water.

"Last one in is a catamite!" he yelled over his shoulder.

Marcus jumped up and sprinted ahead of Quintus while the others were not far behind. He was the first to splash into the water pushing the reeds out of the way to get to the open lake. He was followed closely by Quintus.

"You're the catamite, Quintus," shouted Marcus.

"You're a bloody rotten mentula," retorted Quintus.

"And you lick it!"

They chased each other splashing geysers of water at each others' faces. Soon, the clay was just a memory. Others in the cohort joined them in the lake frolic. Exhausted but free of mud, they came back to the shore spreading the reeds again to climb out of the lake.

As they approached the tent, Decimus, who had not joined the escapade, noticed they had something on their legs.

"Hey, what are those black things on you?"

They looked down to see their legs nearly covered with black worms no longer than a finger. They had coronal reddish brown ridging over their whole body. The end that was attached to the skin was as thick as a thumb pad. The body gradually tapered to a small tail.

"What in Neptune's name are these?" exclaimed Quintus.

"That lake is cursed!" cried Marcus. "Look, they're getting fatter as we watch them!"

"They are holding on to my leg, but they don't hurt," said Quintus.

"Come on, let's go see my brother. Maybe he has an instrument or a medicine to help us."

The youths sprinted as fast as they could to the medical train at the rear of the legion. They found Lucius and Taurinus just climbing out of the wagon after guiding it out of the gloppy clay muck. Lucius looked up as he heard their screams. He recognized his naked brother and his buddies.

"Lucius, help us! We are attacked by monsters!"

"Marcus! How barbarian of you to drop by so unexpectedly," Lucius quipped. "Good to see you, Quintus, and to the rest of you, Salvete."

"Help us, we are being consumed by worms!" they pleaded as they arrived running headlong into the side of the wagon. Lucius and Taurinus now saw what they were screaming about. All of them had black creatures attached to their legs. The creatures were not moving. Each was growing in thickness as they watched. Some that were the fattest just fell off onto the ground leaving blood trickling down their victim's leg. Lucius had not seen such an animal before.

"Those, gentleman, are leeches," announced Taurinus. "They are harmless critters. They suck your blood until they are full, then they just fall off."

"They may be sucking my blood, but they don't hurt," said Cornelius. "I don't feel them biting. They are just slimy and heavy."

"That's right," said Taurinus. "They seem to be able to do their work without causing pain."

"Look," said Quintus. "I'm still bleeding where that one dropped off of me."

"You'll keep bleeding, probably overnight. Looks like your first war wounds are from a worm!" Taurinus chuckled.

"I have never seen these before," said Lucius. "We do not have them either in our lake to the East or in the estuary by the seashore."

"You won't see them at the seashore," Taurinus lectured. "They only live in fresh water. They like to hide in reeds by the shallow waters of a lake. I suspect your lake is high in the hills and has no shallow shore line for reeds to grow."

"That is true," Lucius said. "Have you seen them around Roma?"

"No," Taurinus replied. "The only reason I know about them at all is because of this quack Themison of Laodicea and his crazy Methodists. You remember we talked about them the other day?"

Lucius could not forget.

"He brought some from Greece and Armenia. Instead of making cuts for blood letting, he used them to suck blood. Come to think of it, these creatures give me an idea." He turned to a medic.

"Go get the rest of the team and bring some acetabula filled with water. We'll collect them as they fall off. Maybe they will be of use if we need to bleed anyone. Oh, and bring some alum. We'll mix it with this clay to suppress bleeding." He scooped up some semi dry dirt.

"Oh, no!" moaned Marcus. "We just washed that stuff off. Now you are going to smear it on us?"

"You want to stop bleeding, don't you?" Taurinus growled.

"Yes, sir," they all said reluctantly. They stood around while the necessary equipment was assembled. They sat and watched as one by one, the bloated creatures dropped off and the medics collected them in jars. As the last leeches fell off, the medics dried the soldiers' legs and applied a slurry of clay and alum. When it was dry, they were allowed to return to their tent. Marcus was the first to stand up. As he did so, things began to swirl before his eyes and he staggered into the wagon.

Taurinus poured some wine in a cup and diluted it with water.

"Here, sit and drink this," he instructed. "Wait until you feel stronger."

He did as instructed. Within a few moments, he felt stronger and warmer. The others had similar experiences requiring a dose of wine. Quintus had a second dizzy spell. Taurinus handed him another goblet admonishing him not to try a third spell. He got the message. Once everyone was feeling stronger, they all thanked Taurinus and walked back together. Their tent was already erected, so they went right for their rations. They ate greedily. Soon afterwards, they all passed out where they sat as the sun set.

What seemed just moments later, Martial was yelling at them like he had the first day.

"Let's go you cursed tree stumps! The war has begun!"

Marcus opened his eyes. At first, everything was spinning and he had a headache. Slowly, with a great deal of effort, he was able to focus. It was first light and the legion was breaking camp. He looked up at his commander.

"What's up, chief?"

"You moron," Martial bellowed. "General Caesar moved out last night during the third watch with Seventh, Eighth and Ninth Legions to engage the enemy. He is expecting us to back him up as rapidly as we can get there."

Chapter 18: Dreams Realized

As the Tigurinis moved toward their designated camping area, Aia got her first look at the entire Helvetian Confederation. The headquarters tents stood near a wooden bridge stretching across the lazy Saône River just north of the mouth of a small tributary. The little stream made a gentle curve and paralleled the Saône about two hundred meters away. The Confederation was encamped between the two bodies of water. Wagons stretched out beyond the headquarters as far as Aia could see. The Tigurinis had to travel the rest of the afternoon past the entire nation and beyond the beginning of the tributary to reach their campground.

Once they reached the origin of the stream, they turned toward the Saône. To their right was a second, much shorter tributary that curved lazily away from them to the North. The distance between the beginnings of the two tributaries was no more than five hundred meters making the entrance to the camp fairly well protected. The campsite for the Tigurini tribe would be in the curve of the northern tributary.

The area was horseshoe shaped. From the entrance to the apex of the horseshoe was about five hundred meters. The distance between the northern tributary and the Saône was the same as the southern stream – no more than two hundred meters. The wagon train entered two-by-two and traveled along the tributary. They parked by the banks of the stream and the river. That gave everyone easy access to fresh water. They were no further than one wagon width away from the stream or the river. They also preserved a great space in the center for council meetings and ceremonies.

Aia jumped down and assisted her father as he clambered out of the wagon. They walked from wagon to wagon as High Priest and Priestess greeting their tribesmen and welcoming them to the campground. They wished blessings on each family as they went. The walk did Aia a great deal of good. It not only allowed her to stretch and work out the kinks from the day's journey, but also kept her mind off of her troubles. After greeting everyone, she took leave of her father and walked across the central open space imagining the placement of a campfire and the location of potential ceremonies. There was a large tree stump that could serve both as an altar and a dais. The tribe would be in camp for several days, at least. She felt the campsite would make an ideal place to catch up on rituals they had missed.

Walking back to her sister's wagon, she noticed for the first time that the stream was lined with a variety of trees. There were birch and oaks and willows. She marveled at the birches and oaks because they were loaded with mistletoe colonies. She knew the best specimens grew on old oaks. The oldest growth began directly across the stream from their wagon and continued down to the river. Aia began planning a harvest. That evening, she pulled her father aside.

"Athair, we need to have a coming of age ceremony for Sina."

Drutos raised his eyebrows and nodded.

"So, she has become a woman." Then he looked at Aia. "I am sure there are other girls who have come of age this spring. I know they would like to have a ceremony as well. This should be a major celebration, not just for your sister, but for all the girls. Come to think of it, there should be a number of boys who have achieved manhood. That means a dual ceremony."

Aia was pleased that her father was agreeable. She was excited with the prospect of returning to some normalcy.

"We need a few days to arrange such a large ceremony. We can harvest the mistletoe we need, then we can hold the ceremony on one day for the boys and the next day for the girls. What do you think, Athair?"

Drutos looked into his daughter's eyes. For the first time in months, he could see that she was excited and focused.

"Okay, my dear. You may begin planning."

She kissed him on the cheek and immediately ran to tell Sina the good news.

The next day, Aia conducted an informal census to identify all the children who were ready and willing to make the ceremonial step to adulthood. She organized the young Druids in training to survey every family and get commitments from all the children who wanted to participate. She was overwhelmed to find out that there were eighty-five boys and ninety-nine girls who had blossomed in the last four months. Nearly all wanted to participate. Planning a dual ceremony of that magnitude was more than she had bargained for. Before she had time to become stressed over the project, word came to them that they should gather for a council meeting.

It was late afternoon when they assembled. Lugurix and his lieutenants strode in from the warrior tents which were set up at the mouth of the horseshoe. As they approached, Aia saw that Lugurix had a stern look on his face. She had not seen him since their night of bliss and she was disappointed with his demeanor. From Toutios who stood at Lugurix's right side, she sensed deep sadness. She prayed that everything was well, but knew there was some sort of trouble.

"My dear, dear family and friends," Lugurix began. "I must relate bad news. Today, the bridge created by the Sequani was opened with the hope that we would cross into new territories. The Rauraci were given the honor of crossing first. Divico, our Confederation leader, took a small party of warriors across as a symbol of unity. They crossed without difficulty. Unfortunately, when the Rauraci families began to cross with their wagons, the bridge gave way and four wagons were tossed into the river. All occupants drowned and Divico and his men had to wait for a Sequani boat to bring them back to this side of the river. The Confederation will hold a ceremony for our dead tonight. Drutos and Aia, I ask you as High Priest and Priestess to join Toutios as our representatives at the ceremony. There will be a Confederation council meeting tomorrow to determine how the replacement bridge will be built. We will meet again when the council has concluded. Thank you for your attention and please remember our brethren in your evening prayers."

As the council members left, Toutios approached Drutos and Aia.

"We must do our best to make a showing of solidarity with the Helvetian nation," he told them. "Bimmos nearly ruined our relationship with the other tribes. Lugurix has tried to repair the damage, but he needs our help."

Drutos patted Toutios on the back.

"We are here to do whatever you ask, son." Aia stood next to her brother. She sensed his sadness and tried without saying a word to lift his spirits as she had done when they were children. A young warrior brought three horses. They mounted and rode out of camp in silence.

Their journey was an eyeopener. Up to now, they had only followed the other tribes and viewed the devastation they left behind. Although they had ridden past the camp two days before, trees along the stream blocked their view. Even in the gathering darkness, the threesome saw first hand how the other Helvetian tribes lived. The camps were not well organized. Wagons were set up haphazardly from riverside to stream side. There were no organized central meeting places. The children were filthy and ran in packs. Trees had been stripped bare of their unripened fruit and nuts. Aia was disgusted, but held her tongue. She did not want to create any trouble with the tribes who would be their neighbors in the new land.

Fortunately, the funeral ceremony was short and they did not have to say anything. When it was concluded, the three expressed condolences and immediately left for the Tigurini camp. Aia had never been away from her tribe before and loathed every moment of the trip. When they arrived, she was exhausted, but happy to be in the company of her countrymen.

Although things were somber for the next few days while the Confederation held council, Aia tried to lift the mood with preparations for the coming-of-age ceremonies. The shear volume of participants and the lack of resources meant that the ceremonies and rituals would need to be pared back. Lugurix was at the council, so she prevailed on her father to arrange the ritual tests for the boys.

In conjunction with some of the senior warriors, they arranged two feats of skill. For the first feat, the boys would have to swim across the stream and back holding a scabbard without getting it wet. For the second feat, the boys would need to shoot an arrow thirty meters into targets constructed by some of the non-warrior fathers. Usually, there would be a feat requiring the boys to obtain a domestic or wild animal in whatever manner they could, but their living conditions made that impossible. Their livestock were depleted along the way and their camp was too near the disgusting Helvetian scavengers, who had already captured and eaten most of the local wild animals.

Aia had to be more creative in her planning. The girls were supposed to give up their childhood toys as symbols of the sacrifices they had to make during their journey to womanhood. Unfortunately, most girls lost their possessions when the village was burned. The stress of the arduous travel made the young women even more sentimentally attached to their few remaining possessions. Aia decided she would ask each girl to give to the Maiden, the woman representing the Mother Goddess, a replica of something they cherished that had been destroyed, lost, or left behind.

Also, each girl needed to give a token gift to the Maiden. Traditionally, it was something handmade. Aia suggested that the girls make amulets of wildflowers. Because the amulets would not last long, Aia planned to have the girls pick their flowers and make their amulets while the boys held their games. Once made, Aia would share with each girl a bit of the mistletoe she planned to collect, so that each amulet would have a little jewel. The girls' ceremony would be held the day after the boys' ceremony. Rather than having all the girls go through the detailed ritual, one girl would represent all. She felt fortunate that all the girls agreed to have Sina represent them.

That afternoon while Aia and her father were sharing their preparations, Lugurix returned and called for a quick council meeting. Once everyone was assembled, he shared the news from the Confederation.

"My dear family and friends, we finally have an agreement," he said with solemnity. "The first bridge was built to be a permanent structure. Poles were planted in the riverbed and planks laid on top like a proper bridge, but it was done quickly and the quality of the wood was not checked. Important sections were constructed with weak poles and planks that easily gave way resulting in this terrible tragedy. The new bridge will be a pontoon bridge joined by ropes with planking placed on top. This gives us two advantages. First, the bridge will be more stable, since it sits on top of this river that has so little current. Second, once all have crossed the bridge, we can easily destroy it so that any enemies following us will have to build their own bridge."

A cheer rose from the council. Shortly, small groups began to discuss the proposal among themselves.

"Where are we going to get these boats?" someone shouted.

"Ah, yes indeed," Lugurix said. "There was a great deal of rancor over this. However, out of adversity comes advantage. We gained a great deal of respect and new trust by proposing that each nation provide a share of the bridge based on their fighting force. The delegations from the other nations were impressed and agreed unanimously with our just proposal. That means that our tribe must provide one-sixth of the bridge. That comes to ten boats."

"We have no boats," someone angrily shouted.

"None of us have boats," Lugurix shouted back. Then, in a softer tone, he said, "We must build them fast and we must build them well. We realize the intense hard work necessary to construct them. We have specifications for the size and shape of the boats, which was agreed upon by the Confederation. They must be flat bottomed boats that are two meters wide, two meters deep and five meters long. We must provide the planks for the bridge path as well. The path must be four meters wide to accommodate the wagons and the animals. We estimate that it will take two days to collect the wood, three days to prepare the wood, two days to make the boats and two days to seal the boats with pitch. That is nine days if we are on time. So, the Council wants us to be ready to cross the river in twelve days."

He paused to allow everyone to absorb the magnitude of the job. After some discussion, Frontú stepped forward.

"Chief, we are at your service, but it will take every able bodied man and boy to do this in the allotted time." Murmurs from the council indicated that there was general agreement.

"Thank you, Frontú. We hoped everyone would be up to the task." Then to the entire assembly he shouted, "Thank you, my countrymen. I am proud to be a Tigurini. We begin in the morning."

Aia turned to her father, but Drutos held up his hand to hush her.

"I know what you are going to say. The ceremonies will be thrown aside, but the boys have a very important job to perform. They will not need a ritual task. The boat building will be their ceremony. You may hold the ceremony for the young women as planned. Now, let's collect the mistletoe."

They donned their white robes and gathered the needed supplies, then went out of camp walking around the origin of the small stream. Drutos told Aia that the men would most likely use birch as the primary wood, because it was softer and more pliable than oak and the bark was waterproof. They would first collect any colonies in the birch trees, but to have a sufficient supply, they would collect some of the most sacred mistletoe from the oak trees. They had to collect as many colonies as they could before a tree was felled and the colonies touched the ground. They worked well into the evening collecting twenty-one colonies. Aia was concerned that it might not be enough for the ninety-nine girls, but she had no choice.

Early the next day, the men and boys were hard at work chopping and hauling trees into camp. First, they cut all the trees on the camp side of the stream and river. The following day, they chopped down the trees on the far side of the stream and dragged them around the stream's origin and into camp. Not a single birch escaped the ax. Aia surveyed the scene from the center of the grounds as she prepared the meeting site for the ceremony. The trees decked in summer greenery had made a colorful backdrop behind the wagons. They enveloped the camp in the same comforting way that a cloak protects against the wind. Now, the edge of camp was clear cut, making the wagons naked against the plains and the sky. Only a few majestic oaks survived along the far bank of the stream. The few weeping willows that were spared seemed to mourn constantly in the wind. The whole scene was bleak and depressing. She felt suddenly cold, even though she stood in the bright sunlight. She hugged herself and went back to the wagon for her cloak.

That night, Aia's nightmare returned. It had not visited her since she and Lugurix shared Beltane together. The dream began the same way, but the scene was not ocean side. It was their stark ugly campground. The waters were no longer a sea but the Saône and its tributary. Her father was on the bank of the stream pinned to the ground by an unknown force. She was horrified again to see her brother's bloody skeleton face. Her entire dress as well as her arms and legs were soaked in blood. She woke in a sweat out of breath. She vowed not to sleep until they left that wretched camp.

To keep her mind off of her visions, she would meet with the girls twice a day to ensure that they would be ready. She employed the help of the mothers and her sister Ouenitouta to answer any questions the girls had about womanhood and the eventuality of marriage when they arrived in their new lands. The girls remained excited and cherished the few moments that they could relax.

Each day in camp was increasingly difficult because of the lack of firewood. Initially after the trees were cut down and split into planks for the boats, they had plenty of scraps. Now those were gone and there were no trees left that would produce decent wood for fires. The women cooked as much meat as they could with the remaining fuel. They hoped the food would be enough until the estimated day of departure. Each family retained a tiny stockpile of what precious wood remained in case their departure was delayed.

Aia watched as the boats took shape. They went from amorphous wood piles during the first days to ships' frames lined in a row. In the evenings, the frames silhouetted against the setting sun looked like skeletons of giant beasts come to life from the legends that the old crones told to the children. Gradually, the planks were fashioned, the skeletons covered, and the pitch applied. That meant the next day, the boats would be hauled away by the men and boys. They would stay by the river to build the bridge. She sent word to the girls that their ritual would be held the next morning.

That afternoon, she watched as the men rested and the girls left to gather the flowers to make their amulets. She remembered back to her own coming of age ritual. It was only a dreamy memory in a distant land of another time. She looked down at her soiled and tattered hand-me-down dress. It was nothing like the beautiful linen gown she wore for the ceremony. For her ritual, she gladly gave all of her childhood toys to be sacrificed. She made a willow basket to carry her flowers as her gift to the Maiden. After she had done her best, Sina put the finishing touches on it. Even then, Sina had a gift for crafting. It was the most beautiful basket she ever owned. She felt so grown up then. Now, she knew what it really meant to be grown up.

As the sun set, she dreaded the darkness and the possibility of her nightmare returning. She tried to resurrect other happy memories. She was lost in her thoughts when a young warrior taped her on the shoulder. She jumped at his touch. The warrior snapped to attention.

"Pardon me, Your Grace," he stammered.

She found it odd to be addressed formally. She was still uncomfortable as the High Priestess. The soldier wore a fine woolen cloak fastened with a bronze brooch signifying that he was a member of the Chieftain's personal guard. It only reinforced to her the gravity of her position and how revered her profession was to the Tigurini. She acknowledged him with similar formality.

"How may I be of service, my noble warrior?"

"I am very sorry to disturb you, Your Grace, but Chieftain Lugurix wishes to see you."

Her heart skipped a beat. She had not seen him since the council meeting. She had barely seen him since Beltane. She stared at the ground, put her right hand up to pull back a lock of hair, and placed her left hand over her breasts.

"I'm not prepared. The High Priestess must make herself presentable."

"Pardon me again, Your Grace," he replied, "but the Chieftain asked that I bring you directly."

Aia stared up at the boy. She and the young warrior were nearly the same age.

"We are too young to hold these positions," she thought. *"We have grown up too fast. The joy of life has been sucked away."*

He averted his eyes toward the horizon.

"Please come with me. You may gather your cloak first," he said stiffly.

"What choice do I have?" She sighed. "I am the servant of the people and my Chieftain calls."

She reached into the wagon and snatched her cloak. She quickly wrapped it around her and pulled the hood over her head. She followed the boy warrior who set a fast pace to the command tent.

When they arrived at the tent, the young guard knocked on the tent pole and announced that the High Priestess was there.

"Let her enter," was the command from within. He opened the tent flap and stepped back for Aia to enter, again averting his eyes to the horizon. She gave him a faint smile and walked through the opening, then stopped abruptly. The table was in the same place as in her last visit, but it was covered with a cloth upon which were two goblets, a flagon of wine, two candles, and plates of food. Beside the table were two chairs instead of one. Standing next to one of them was Lugurix. He was dressed the same as Beltane night.

"This is the last of the Sequani supplies," he said. "I saved a small amount for us to share." He extended his arm gesturing for her to sit. She looked from the table to his eyes. Suddenly she lost her appetite. Her heart was pounding out of her chest. She reached up and slowly pulled her hood back. They stared in each other's eyes briefly, then she leapt into his arms. She kissed his mouth passionately. At first, Lugurix was surprised, then he surrendered to her passion. In moments, they were ripping each other's clothes off. They made love on top of the lush blanket as they had on Beltane.

Climax came easily for Aia. She floated in pure pleasure. As her passion slowly subsided, her emotions overwhelmed her and she began to sob. Lugurix rolled off of her and held her close to him stroking her hair and caressing her until she was quiet. Soon, she drifted into a deep dreamless sleep. When she woke, Lugurix was asleep next to her. They were on top of the blanket as they had been after the first time they made love. Now she was hungry. She nuzzled at him until he opened his eyes.

"Is it time for some food?" she asked.

Lugurix stretched and looked at her.

"I guess so."

They got up. Aia wrapped the blanket around her and sat down. Her hunger had grown to a ravenous appetite and she devoured her plate of food. Lugurix watched her. Even chewing on a leg of lamb she was gorgeous. When she put the leg down and picked up the wine, he took a deep breath. He had to give her the bad news.

"From now on, I will have very heavy responsibilities that will keep me away from you. This crossing of the Saône must go well. Our position in the Confederation may be greatly improved if we pull this off."

She looked at him over the goblet.

"When will I be able to see you again?"

"If this crossing goes well, I will be asked to join Divico as his lieutenant. I will be at the front of the nations. I will assign your brother as commander-on-site until we arrive in Tolosa."

"That's a very long time," she said slowly tracing the lip of the goblet with her finger.

"I know," he said turning his head to the left toward the entrance of the tent, his thoughts running far away.

Aia put down the goblet and allowed the blanket fall off of her. She rose and sat in his lap. She put her arms around his neck. He kept looking away. She placed her hand on his left cheek and kissed his right cheek as lightly as the touch of a butterfly. With gentle pressure, she turned his face back to her. She planted delicate kisses on his cheeks and around his mouth. As she completed the circle around his mouth, he grabbed her and passionately kissed her lips. He carried her back to the cot and made love to her again. Aia was in ecstasy. As he finished, she wrapped her arms and legs around him and squeezed. She became part of him floating weightless across time and space. She closed her eyes and allowed herself to fall asleep again.

She woke up on her left side with Lugurix snuggly fitting against her back. They were under the covers. She had no idea how long they were that way. She slipped out from under his arm and slid off the cot. She went to the entrance to the tent and peered out of the flap. The entrance faced south. She looked to the West to see the waxing gibbous moon low in the sky. The first light of dawn was visible in the East. Suddenly she remembered that it was the day of the girls' ritual. There was no time to waste. She quickly dressed and gently shook Lugurix awake.

"I must go," she whispered. "I have duties today."

He opened his eyes and sat up. She kissed him gently on the cheek. He grabbed her shoulders and kissed her on the lips. Her knees were instantly weak and her pelvis ached. She wanted him again, but she pushed herself back.

"No, really I have to go," she pleaded. Lugurix threw his legs over the side of the cot.

"Then this is good bye for quite a while," he told her.   They both understood.

He watched longingly as she stood in front of him.

"Let me get your cloak," he said.

He stood in front of her and placed the cloak around her tying it under her chin. Then he put his arms around her and gave her one last passionate kiss. Aia pressed herself against him with her hands on his chest. She felt the fire rising again in her pelvis and pushed away.

"Send for me when you can," she whispered, then swiftly exited the tent.

By the time she arrived at the wagon, the first rays of sunlight were peeking over the horizon. She quickly ran to the stream and took an abbreviated bath. She ran back to the wagon and got her mother's High Priestess garments. She caressed them realizing they were the last of her mother's possessions. She slipped them on and collected the baskets of mistletoe. She opened the wagon doors to see the girls in their finest dresses with their amulets lining up to receive their mistletoe. She felt out of breath and exhausted, but she had made it.

While she handed out the mistletoe flowers to the girls, she could see the boys and men gathering at the boats. One by one, the boats and platforms rose and formed a line with humans acting as their wheels. The wooden parade crawled out of camp followed by the men who would help assemble the bridge.

When the last girl received her mistletoe, Aia had only wilted broken leaves in the baskets. She had depleted her entire supply, but at least every girl would have a magical jewel in her amulet. She put the baskets away and headed for the open meeting ground. The girls and their mothers had already gathered and were placing their reconstructed toy at the altar. She arranged the girls in a circle around the large tree stump that served as the altar and dais. Mothers stood behind their daughters. She brought four grandmothers to serve as the four winds and Ouenitouta to serve as the fertile Maiden. Aia persuaded her older sister to take the role because she was very pregnant. Also, she explained to Oueni that it would give her the best vantage point to see Aia in her official capacity and Sina representing all the young maidens transitioning to womanhood.

The ceremony went smoothly. Aia called for one girl to represent all the young maidens ready for the journey. Sina briskly stepped forward. Aia in turn presented her to the four winds beginning with the East. At each stop, she announced loudly so everyone could hear,

I present to you the maiden who wishes to join the ranks of womanhood.

At each crone, Sina would bow deeply. Each crone would place her right hand on Sina's head. Sina would raise her head and give her hand to the crone who would guide her to the next wind.

After the last presentation, all moved toward the altar where Ouenitouta stood. The group approached with two crones flanking each side of Sina. Aia stood behind her. When they were assembled in front of the Maiden, Aia intoned,

I present to you the maiden who wishes to join the ranks of womanhood.
She has journeyed the four corners of the earth to see you.

Sina knelt before Ouenitouta and bowed deeply, then looked up and extended her hands holding her amulet saying,

I present to you a gift made by my hand.

It is offered in innocence to your pure heart and fertile body.

Ouenitouta accepted the amulet, smelled the flowers and held it high above her head. She turned slowly around showing the amulet to all assembled saying,

I accept this lovely token representing the fully opened blossom you have become.
You are no longer to be called a child.
You are Woman.

Then she returned the amulet to Sina and said to her,

I return the gift to you as the Mother Goddess returns her bounty to us.
In turn, you will live as the embodiment of the Mother Goddess,
Bringing forth the gift of life to your family.
Keep this as a remembrance of your duties as a woman.

At that point, Sina rose. She and the four winds turned to face Aia who then stepped aside raising her left arm to Sina.

Behold, I present a new woman.

She gestured with her right hand to the girls in the circle.

May you be loving and caring, fertile and nurturing.
May you experience the joy of receiving love and returning the gift of life.

She gestured for all the girls to hold their amulet above their heads and said,

To all the new women today, I congratulate you.
Go now.
Be with your families.
Rejoice.
You are Women.

The circle broke up into small groups of girls joyfully hugging and kissing one another. Aia thanked the grandmothers who left to be with their daughters and granddaughters. She turned to Sina and Ouenitouta. They hugged. By the time they relaxed, each was crying. Sina was beaming.

"Thank you, Aia, for making this happen. I will always cherish this special moment with you and Oueni." Then she grabbed both and cried, "I hope Màthair is watching from the otherworld." They all sobbed for a while, then walked back to the wagon arm in arm.

That evening, the men returned and everyone returned to their normal routines. With her sacred chores accomplished, Aia began to feel depressed. She took a walk to the West end of the camp to relax and view the Saône. It was a languid river but it sparkled gold reflecting the setting sun's rays. Across the banks were a few fires lit by the vanguard of warriors. Down the river, she could barely make out the bridge in the twilight.

"The crossing will begin tonight for the Helvetians. Soon it will be our turn," she thought. *"That means this is one of our last nights in this wretched camp. Maybe after we cross, I can bury my dream here."*

She returned to the wagon in time for the evening meal. It was meager and the meat was going off. It was just as well for her, because she had no appetite. Despite the joy of the day, she had been nauseous since she left Lugurix. Maybe she had eaten too much of the Sequani's generous food gifts.

She left the family and sat in the back of the wagon with the doors open. There were few fires because of the wood shortage. The lack of light would normally make the night good for star gazing. She loved to watch the stars as a child. In her years of study to become a Druid priestess, she learned about the behavior of the stars. The knowledge had taken away some of her wonder. That night, however, the moon had risen already and dimmed her view. She stared out across the stream. Except for two massive oaks and three weeping willows, her view of the plains was unobstructed to the horizon. Everything was still. She tried to imagine her life in a new land, but all she saw was a blank.

The following morning, the skies were heavy with dark clouds and the air smelled of dampness. Life was the same dull routine. Aia had only dozed during the night. She was nauseous again and grumpy. She decided to wander about the camp and talk with the young women with whom she had spent the last week. Most were busy with daily chores and had little time other than to pass pleasantries. Her wanderings took her back to the West end of camp. She could see the bridge was packed with wagons. The camps on the right bank of the river were swelling to accommodate the new arrivals.

Suddenly, the dark skies opened up. Aia was caught in a deluge without shelter. The rain came down in buckets. At first, she tried to shelter next to a wagon near the end of the line, but it was no protection. She just gave up. She was drenched to the bone. She knew she could get no wetter, so she decided to walk across the open grounds. Although she had excellent balance, she slipped and fell twice on the suddenly slick clay. She was covered in mud and thoroughly miserable. She slowed her pace to a crawl and allowed the rain to wash the mud off of her. By the time she returned to the family wagon, she was soaked, but free of mud.

Looking out on the meeting place where she had slipped, she saw lakes of water. Several young children chased by their mothers were running and jumping in the large puddles. She wished she could be a child again without fear and responsibility, but she knew that could not happen. Her nausea overwhelmed her and she vomited until there was nothing left but bile. Eventually the rain stopped and the sun came out. It would take the rest of the day for the puddles to dry out. While she was daydreaming, several warriors rode down the wagon line informing the tribe that soon it would be their turn to cross the river. They would move out just before dawn.

In spite of the state of the campgrounds, there was activity everywhere. They had precious little time left to prepare. Everyone gathered up what they could and piled it into their wagons. Aia sat on the back steps of the wagon like a lazy frog allowing Ouenitouta and Sina to do all the work. She just stared at the stream.

Aia spied a duck with her ducklings in a line behind her. They paddled down the stream toward the river. Aia followed them moving into the Saône. As she did, she caught sight of a grand oak tree. She idly surveyed the tree and its branches noting several low hanging mistletoe colonies that she and her father had not harvested. Since she had depleted her entire supply for the ritual, she decided to harvest them by the light of the moon. She figured it would be her last chance until they reached their new homeland. With a task at hand, she felt a little more energized.

As she climbed down from the wagon, Aia saw Lugurix and his guard return to camp. He was pointing this way and that, giving orders. Warriors were running around to do his bidding. She sighed. She knew Lugurix would not call for her that night. He would be too busy governing the tribe and assuring a smooth crossing. She savored their last time together and their shared passion. She longed for the next time, hopefully in a happier place and time.

She skipped supper again keeping to herself. Sina wanted to scold her and shame her into joining them, but Drutos intervened. He wanted Aia to join them as well, but felt he had to give her space. Everyone crammed into the wagon with the few supplies they had left. They would be ready for the crossing.

Once everyone was asleep, Aia slipped into her white imbolc gown because the robes had been packed away and she did not want to disturb anyone. The gown would help her to make the harvest as close to the ritual rules as she could under the circumstances. She gathered two baskets and the sickle to cut down the colonies and eased out of the wagon. She stayed close to the bank of the stream and worked her way around its origin to the opposite bank. By the time she reached the great oak, the moon was past its vertex and beginning its descent. She looked up and saw that the colonies were higher than she thought. She had to climb part way up the trunk and reach out arm's length with the sickle. She fell several times before she worked out her balance and cut the first colony down. It rolled down the branch and bounced off the trunk into the stream where it floated into the Saône. She hoped for better luck with the next one.

Her luck did not improve. The second colony bounced on the branch below and launched itself onto another branch. As she stretched to reach it, she lost her balance. She grabbed for the branch to stop her fall and knocked the mistletoe out of the tree. She was unsuccessful at holding on and fell directly on top of the colony crushing it.

"That makes it nearly useless," she muttered to herself.

She struggled to her feet and brushed off the bits of moist grass and twigs that stuck to her hair and dress. Thoroughly disgusted with her efforts, she placed what little she could salvage of the mistletoe colony in her basket and started back.

She kept her eyes down as she walked kicking small stones into the water. She felt even more depressed than she had that afternoon. She did not notice the commotion in camp until she saw several fires reflecting in the stream. She looked up. Nearly the entire camp was ablaze. At first, she could not make out any people or activity because the wagons were all parked against the stream blocking sounds and shielding her view of the camp. The intense flames blinded her. She dropped her basket and sickle. Listening intently, she could hear metal clanking against metal. She heard men shouting in a foreign tongue. A few figures staggered to the stream and collapsed.

Aia jumped in the stream and waded back to the bank at the edge of the camp. As she approached, the shouts and screams were becoming fewer. She heard more commands in a foreign language, then near silence punctuated only by moans. She stood at the edge of the stream. The wagons were nothing but smoldering hulks. She peered around one to see the devastation. Families and warriors alike lay on the ground in grotesque positions. Warriors in strange metal armor and helmets carrying short broad swords roamed the camp hacking at anything that moved until there was no sound or movement anywhere.

Aia quietly went back to the bank of the stream and worked her way toward her sister's wagon. She stopped by one burned hulk and peered around it. Early morning light was beginning to illuminate the devastation. She waited until the warriors left the area, then she timidly looked at the people near the wagon. With horror, she realized it was her own family's wagon. Her heart nearly jumped out of her chest. Frontú lay face up in a pool of blood with his neck slashed. Ouenitouta lay next to him, her belly cut open and her gravid uterus chopped out. Not far away was the headless body of Sina still clutching her amulet. Further in the open, she recognized Toutios laying motionless, his mangled helmet lying next to his bloody head. She looked around, but did not see her father at first. Then, she noticed him standing in front of the wagon.

She crawled slowly on her belly through her brother-in-law's blood pool to view her father. He was impaled by a spear through his right chest and was propped against the wagon. While she watched, he stirred and dropped to the ground. He groaned as he thumped down. Aia sprung over to him covering his mouth to prevent him from making noise and attracting the attention of those brutal warriors. She whispered a lullaby into his ear until he relaxed and closed his eyes.

Aia looked across the camp. Only a few Tigurini warriors survived. They were in chains in the center of the meeting area. She recognized Lugurix among them. At first, she was overjoyed, then overcome at the sight of the inevitable. They were being led one by one to be beheaded on the tree stump, cum altar, cum dais. Standing in front was a commander with short curly hair outfitted in gold armor, hands on hips observing the proceedings. She had to look away. As she did, Drutos groaned. She soothed him again.

Aia needed a charm to place on her father. She slid back to Sina trying to remove the amulet from her hands. She could not pry her lifeless rigid fingers off the amulet and still keep it in one piece.

Aia removed her leather necklace with its serpent egg. She looked at the dark green stone. As High Priestess, she knew she should never remove it. It was a symbol of her office and her most prized possession, but none of that mattered now. She had to save her father and it was the only charm she had. She kissed it and placed it on her father's chest near the wound and whispered the incantation of lasting life.

I place this charm on your body,
The charm of the Goddess of life
For your protection.
The charm that the maiden of the flock
Put round Nuadu's fair neck.
Between sole and throat,
Between pap and knee.
Between back and breast,
Between chest and sole,
Between eye and hair.
The sword of Lugos on your side.
The shield of Lugos on your shoulder.

She heard a loud clang from the center of the camp and was startled into silence.   Slowly she turned around to see Lugurix run through with a pilum and thrust down on the stump.   She looked away and cringed as the large ax clunked into his neck.   After a brief silence, she heard the Roman contingent march out of camp.   She looked up to assure that there were no more foreign warriors in the area and returned to whispering the incantation.

There is none between heaven and earth
That can overcome you.
No spear shall rive you,
No sea shall drown you.
No woman defile you.
No man shall wound you.
From the crown of your head
To the soles of your feet.
The charm of the Goddess is on you now.
You shall never know disgrace.
You shall go forth in name of your forebears,
To the Goddess of life you belong wholly.
And to all the Powers together.

She stopped to catch her breath.   She laid her head down onto her father's chest to rest for a moment.   When Drutos stirred, Aia opened her eyes.   The sun was setting.   She did not know how much time had passed, although it was at least one day.   She quickly looked around.   Nothing had changed.   It was not a dream.   It was all to real.   She recollected where she stopped in the incantation and quickly finished.

I now place this charm,
In passage hard, brambly, thorny.
Go with the charm about your body.
And have not the least fear upon you.
You shall ascend the crest of the hill
Protected you shall be behind you,
You are the calm swan in battle,
Preserved you shall be amidst the slaughter,
Stand you can against five hundred.
And your oppressors shall be seized.

Tears poured from her eyes onto her fathers face as she finished the incantation of the charm.   She kissed his cheek.   It was cold and moist.   The kiss awakened him and he turned his defocused eyes in the direction of his daughter. He tried to say something but no sound came out.   He closed and opened his eyes in an attempt to focus.   The strain was evident on his face.   He finally managed a few whispered words.

"Sùghment...sùgh ruz..."

He uttered a few more inaudible syllables and passed out again.
Aia rolled the words around in her head.
"Great wave, red wave... He must have seen the slaughter before he was

skewered.   The sight of gushing blood from so many must have been overwhelming." She concentrated. *"I have heard those words before, but where?"*

Then she remembered her lessons. It was not a comment on the slaughter. He was trying to say another incantation – the incantation of red water. She took his hand in hers and said the prayer for him.

Great wave, red wave,
Strength of sea, strength of ocean,
The nine wells of Acionna
Help on you to pour,
Put stop to your blood.
Put flood to your urine.

Aia kissed his hand, closed her eyes and laid her cheek against his limp fingers. When she opened them again, she caught a shadow out of the corner of her eye. She froze as the shadow of a man came over her shoulder and stopped. She slowly turned around to see the shoes of a Tigurini warrior.   She gazed up recognizing Toutios and gasped. He stood with his sword in his right hand, his slashed and broken shield in his left. His front was covered in congealed blood. Hair hung down and stuck to his bloody chest. She saw his scalp hanging down over the left side of his face exposing his skull and a blood filled eye socket.

She covered her mouth and squelched a scream of joy and revulsion. She pulled herself up and hugged him mixing his blood with the blood of their family that soiled her dress. He just stood over her like a statue.

"You're alive!" cried Aia.

"I am dead," he replied flatly pointing to his side. She looked down and saw his cuirass had been cut and dark blood mixed with thick greenish bile oozed from the jagged gash.

She could not look.

"What savages did this?"

"Romans.   They came out of nowhere and everywhere all at once.   They overwhelmed us in moments." He fell silent.

She gave him another hug and pointed down.

" Athair is still alive."

Toutios looked at his father.

"He needs help," he said without emotion.

"Then help me. We must get away from here and try to reach the Sequani. They have been a blessing to us in the past. Maybe they will help save him."

"I have little strength," Toutios said, "but I will give you my all until I die." He sheathed his sword, reached under Drutos' armpits, and dragged him between the line of wagons and the bank of the stream.   He nearly collapsed under the effort. Drutos groaned and coughed.

Aia quickly assessed their surroundings.

"We can't go across the stream, we have no boat and we can't drag him through the water, it's too deep. We will need to go around the camp and out, but that will take us almost into the Romans."

Toutios looked blankly at his sister.

"Allons."

Chapter 19: Catching a Tiger by the Tail

Marcus and his mates quickly struck their tent and prepared for the march. The rest of the legion moved quickly. Some fidgeted in line and complained about the early call to assemble, but Marcus was excited. He knew that they were finally on their way to fight the enemy. Soon, he would have his opportunity to show his bravery and his loyalty to the Republic.

Rumors of the engagement spread rapidly through the green legions. Caesar had sent out scouts the evening of the debacle of the leeches. They discovered the Helvetians not more than half a day's march up the Arar River. Caesar could not pass up such an opportunity and mobilized three of his seasoned legions at the third watch. He marched them double time under the moonlit sky. They caught the Tigurini tribe completely by surprise with no exit. It was as easy as slaughtering a flock of cornered sheep. Marcus hoped that there would be a few barbarians left for him.

Time passed quickly as they raced at top speed to catch up to the battle line. They moved close to the Arar River where the land was flat and the obstructions few. Trees lined the banks. Beyond the trees and the path were fields of wheat. Because the crop was young, it recovered well from the storm of the previous day. The path was well traveled and Marcus could make out the footprints of the three legions that had just negotiated the road in the moonlight.

The line moved away from the river's edge as they approached a stream that paralleled the Arar. He could see a bridge constructed of boats and evidence of recent encampment on both sides of the river. The seasoned legions had moved into the camps and an engineering contingent was inspecting the bridge.

They made a left turn and entered the area. To his right in an open unplanted field, Marcus noticed small mounds on the ground. At first, he made nothing of the mounds surmising that these were just rocks. As he focused on the mounds, he began to make out shapes of humans. He saw the piles of dead bodies contained women and children, not just warriors. The fallen warriors were all dressed in tunics and wore leather boots. A few wore sleeveless coats made of animal hides with the fur side turned in. Their shields and spears were small in comparison to Roman standards and their helmets were made of leather with only a little metal.

Clearly, the battle was over. Nothing was alive. The bodies of the barbarians lay in piles. Some had their heads split open right through the helmet. Swollen brains and blood oozed out of the broken skulls. Amputated body parts were strewn everywhere. Blood collected in lakes. Swarms of flies danced above eviscerated bodies. In the distance beyond the grotesque mangled bodies, he saw smoldering hulks of wagons lined up against a horseshoe shaped stream.

As the legion moved around the edge of the battlefield, Marcus heard several of the young troops vomiting. Small groups of legionnaires were piling the bodies and setting them on fire. Orders were shouted and Legion XI halted directly opposite the killing field. Martial ordered them to make camp without tents. They needed to be ready to move out at a moment's notice.

Marcus and his cohort were chosen for guard duty on the Tigurini camp's outer perimeter. Martial deployed them next to the origin of a stream that was also the end of the wagon line. The guard line of Legion XIII covered the outer perimeter from one hundred feet on the outside of each stream extending in a long arch across the eastern frontier. The Eleventh faced the mangled dead barbarians. After detailing their assignment, Martial sent them to rest and get ready for the second watch.

Marcus was astonished at the terrible might of Caesar's seasoned troops. Not more than twelve feet in front of the spot where Decimus would be deployed was a young warrior about his age. He was run through with a pilum. He lay face up on the ground. Rigor had set in, freezing him in the moment of death. His face was swollen and blue. His mouth was open and his right hand held his sword. A soft breeze out of the Northeast blew the smell of death toward the young legionnaires. He had to swallow hard not to vomit.

   *   *   *

Lucius and the medical wagons were just behind the guard line. Taurinus persuaded Command to give them their first combat assignment. About one hundred legionnaires received wounds during the brief, but intense slaughter. Caesar wanted his four seasoned legions to pursue the Helvetians rapidly and the injured would only slow them down. So Lucius and his medics were assigned to patch up the wounded at the rear of the Army and send them back to fight as rapidly as they could.

Even before the wagons stopped rolling, the medics pulled the tables out and set them up. They piled supplies for dressing the wounds and brought out vinegar for cleaning, bandages, and ingredients for making plasters and pastils. Once the setup was complete, the wounded were brought to the medical area by their comrades and medics from the combatant legions. They dropped off their loads and sprinted back to their units ready to move out when the order was given. Lucius assigned Priscus to compounding the plasters and pastils. He took Magnus to assist him and to restrain the soldiers if necessary. Atticus, Modestus, and Petrus would nap and be ready to relieve them in several hours if they were not finished.

One by one, the soldiers presented their wounds. Most injuries were bruises and scrapes requiring little direct treatment. They would have been considered slackers by Taurinus and he would have given them the castor oil, salt, and vinegar punishment, but Lucius decided it would be better for the fighting force to send them back with no reprimand and let their Centurions deal with them. They were left with four serious, non-life threatening injuries. He felt fortunate that they would not have to amputate any body parts that day.

First to be examined was a young legionnaire who dislocated his right shoulder. Magnus took that one because he was so much bigger than the legionnaire. He grabbed the soldier's right wrist and had Lucius grab on to the soldier's chest. Then, he placed his left foot in the soldier's armpit and applied gradually increasing pressure. The shoulder slipped into place without a whimper from the soldier. What pain he had, disappeared immediately. They released him back to his unit.

Next was a legionnaire with a nasty gash on his left arm. His shield slipped out of his grip and slid forward exposing his upper arm. A Tigurini warrior took advantage of the opening and swung his axe. It sliced the legionnaire's exposed deltoid nearly in half. He fell to his knees, but was protected by his cohort who covered for him. When they closed ranks, he retreated to the rear where another soldier wrapped a tight dressing over the wound to staunch the hemorrhage.

Lucius took off the dressing and examined the wound. Bleeding had stopped. The wound was three inches long. The sides were separated by nearly an inch. He could see little in the depths of the wound, so he had Magnus hold the soldier's arm to the table while he washed it out with vinegar. The soldier screamed in pain but couldn't move under the grip of Magnus.

Now Lucius could see the cut belly of the muscle. The slice was clean and deep, but the bone was not exposed. He called to a medic who brought him suture and two needles. He rapidly laced the wound taking deep bites the way they had done on the abdomen of the sheep. He worked with both hands plunging both needles into the gash at the same time. He was surprised at how facile he had become in such a short time. He was grateful for Magnus' strength to hold the wound still for the procedure.

Priscus brought a pastil and he and Lucius applied the dressing smoothly. With the wound closed and the dressing in place, the legionnaire's pain was diminished. Lucius consulted with Magnus and Priscus. They decided a wound that deep would take three to four weeks to heal and carrying a standard shield would inhibit healing. They put his arm in a sling and told him to report to Legion XI's quartermaster for assignment and commanded that he return to the medical wagon for reevaluation in two days. He thanked all the staff profusely and dragged his equipment toward the quartermaster's wagon.

The third legionnaire was an old veteran. He had learned not to take chances and had survived over twenty-seven years in the ranks, moving from one legion to another. This time, however, his luck had finally run out. As his line came up for the third wave of the attack, several Tigurini warriors countered to his left. They felled the soldier to his outside shoulder. He turned to cover the opening and took a sword to the face. It knocked his helmet askew and the sword sliced him from his left temple across his eye and into the bridge of his nose. He was carried to the rear by his mates who used their field dressings to compress the bleeding. He had lost a great deal of blood and could not hold the dressing in place. A buddy held the compression dressing for him. When they arrived in the medical area, the buddy handed him to one of the medics and ran back to his cohort.

Lucius carefully pulled back the dressing. The slice on the temple had stopped bleeding and did not look too bad. He covered it up again and looked at the nose. The cartilage of the nose was cut to the bone and the nose dangled exposing the turbinates. The area still bled briskly. He placed fresh lint in the gap and added a cotton dressing over the area. With the temple and the nose bleeding controlled, he took away the remaining dressing to examine the eye. The eye socket was filled with a blood clot. Lucius could see no evidence of an eyeball. He pulled all the dressings off the socket. With gentle probing, he confirmed that the eye had deflated. The injury was beyond anything he had seen before. He knew he was not prepared to deal with that sort of damage. He sent for Taurinus.

"Well, old man," Taurinus told the veteran. "Looks like your career is over."

"Go to Tartarus, you scum bucket!" The old veteran spat blood at the feet of Taurinus.

"I may be a scum bucket, but you are useless to Caesar with only one eye."

"You're kidding, right?"

"No soldier, I'm not. You'll have to stay in the rear until the campaign is

over, then hope Caesar will grant you citizen's rights and a piece of land. You've
been loyal for many years. At least you have that in your favor."

Taurinus turned to Lucius.

"Fashion a leather mask that covers the nose and the eye and can be tied in
the back. The nose bleeding should stop in another day. Pack the eye socket and
nose, and pull the mask tightly over the area. No duty for him, but send him to the
rear. Have him sent back every day for a check. He should heal in one to two
weeks." Taurinus lumbered away waiting for darkness and his standard dinner
appointment.

Priscus cut out the mask and Lucius packed the wounds. The old veteran
cursed through the process but did not flinch, even when Lucius pushed the vinegar
soaked lint into the socket. He was led away by a medic to the supply train.

The final legionnaire took an arrow in the leg just as his line attacked. The
arrow was still in the outer aspect of his right thigh. Lucius noted the entrance
wound was near the knee and the arrow point was just under the skin of the middle
of the back of the thigh. From the trajectory, it seemed that the arrow was shot
directly from the ground, but the soldier said he felt it enter as he stepped over a
tree stump. So, the tract was a combination of leg position and angle of the arrow
in its flight. The legionnaire reckoned that it must have been shot from less than a
hundred feet away.

Lucius used the help of both Magnus and Priscus. Magnus held the
soldier's leg and Priscus pushed the arrow backward so that it tented the skin.
Lucius cut the skin and the arrow head popped out of the wound. Priscus cut the
arrow at the entrance site and Lucius grasped the arrowhead and pulled the arrow
through the leg. They immediately wrapped the leg to prevent bleeding. After
cleaning up the instruments, Lucius removed the dressing. They watched for a
while, but no bleeding occurred, so he redressed the leg and instructed the
legionnaire to rest in their camp overnight. If reevaluation in the morning showed
no further bleeding, he could join his legion.

The three young surgeons sat down to rest. Lucius pulled out three pieces
of cinnamon bark and passed them around. They chewed on them for a while.

"So, this is what it will be like," said Lucius.

"Only a hundred times worse when our legion goes to the front," said
Priscus. "In this battle, our best troops pulled off a surprise attack on a tribe where
the women and children were mixed with the warriors. The warriors were
unprepared for battle. Our legion is green and much less organized. I suspect a
well prepared enemy will inflict many casualties on our young legionnaires."

As they ate their supper, they could see the second watch being deployed
into position. The sun had set long ago, and the moon was only a small wedge.
The only lights were stars and the medical area torches. Marcus waved to his
brother as he took his position. Lucius waved back. Marcus was deployed one
hundred feet to the right of Decimus, who was directly between the enemy camp
and the medical tables. Quintus was a similar distance to the left of Decimus.
Martial placed Decimus between Marcus and Quintus in an attempt to prevent any
more nighttime guard incidents.

*   *   *

Just out of sight at the edge of the last burnt out wagon, Toutios dropped
his father and collapsed. Aia bent down over her brother. He was exhausted and

depleted from his mortal wounds. She knew they would not be able to travel the long distance to the nearest Sequani settlement. She looked into the Roman camp. In the flickering light of the torches, she could make out dressings and medications on a table. There were only three guards near the area and she could see no one near the pile of dressings. At a table in the distance were three Romans not dressed in armor talking and eating. She quickly made her decision.

"Toutios, we must change our plans."

Her brother looked up at her.

"I am nearly spent. I cannot go much further."

"I know, dear brother," she said with tears in her eyes as she stroked and kissed the intact side of his face. Then she wiped her tears away and sat up straight. "I believe this is a Roman bandaging area. If I can get in, I can steal some dressings and medications for you and Athair. Maybe, we can hide until they leave and the Sequani come to survey what remains in our camp. Can you get me past the guards?"

The warrior turned his good eye toward the camp. He could see a line of guards spaced out about thirty meters from one another. If he killed one of them, she might have a few moments to dart in and out before the other guards covered the distance and killed them all.

"You will have to be quick. You have only one chance."

"Do you have the strength for a fight?" she asked with concern.

"I will find the strength. I am going to die soon, but I would rather die fighting for us than dying here without honor."

Aia bent over her father. He was still breathing, but he was very weak. She found some unburned clothing and placed it under his head and kissed him on the forehead whispering a short prayer. She turned to her brother.

"Whenever you are ready."

Toutios surveyed the guards.

"The one directly in front of us looks young and very scared. He looks at our camp and the fires and he is not paying attention to his duties. I will attack him. I believe I can kill him. Stay right behind me until I engage him in battle, then run in and grab what you can. Do not pay attention to me. Get only what you need for Athair. The other warriors will run to the young soldier's aid and kill me. You must be in and out before his comrades turn on you."

"I understand. I will be swift."

At that moment, she realized it was the last conversation she would ever have with her twin brother. She gave him a firm hug and kissed him tenderly.

"I will see you in the otherworld."

He closed his good eye understanding the consequences of their actions and sighed.

"We must go now. Are you ready?" he asked.

"Allons"

Toutios slowly got into a crouch position and withdrew his knife. Aia crouched behind him and placed her hands on his back. He waited for the young legionnaire to fix his gaze on one of the makeshift funeral pyres where fresh bodies had been piled. Toutios stayed low, circling around to the backside of the soldier just out of his line of vision. Aia clung to her brother. When they were within two arms length, Toutios sprang up and swung the knife into the legionnaire's throat. The soldier let out an interrupted scream that degenerated into a gurgle. Aia darted past the struggle to the table.

*   *   *

Separated from Quintus, Marcus was a much more alert guard. He peered into the darkness and surveyed his area from right to left and back again. He hoped the night would be quiet, not like some of his previous guard assignments. The seasoned legions were such efficient killing machines, he expected nothing could live through their attack. He could only hope his watch would go by quickly. He thought about what he would do when he was off duty. Immediately after the third watch relieved him, he would eat his remaining rations and sleep.

As he panned back to the left, he saw two figures silhouetted against the fires where only Decimus should be. The second figure was on Decimus and he could see a struggle. Without thinking, he sprinted toward the fight with his Spanish sword drawn.

When he arrived, he could tell Decimus had lost the fight. He lunged at the Tigurini warrior running his sword to the hilt in the barbarian's chest. All three fell on one another in a heap. The torque of Marcus' attack caused them to roll on the ground. Marcus found himself at the bottom of the pile. He struggled to extricate himself from the pile but couldn't. At that point, Quintus heard the scuffle and headed for the fight. No one noticed the girl dart past the fight and head toward the dressing table.

*   *   *

Aia stood in front of the dressings. She began to grab at them realizing she had no sack or bag to place them in. She would only be able to take a little. She put them down and rummaged through the medicaments on the table. She recognized none of the substances. If the Romans used them, surely some of them would help her father. She opened one of the cloth bandages and began to load up as much as would fit.

Lucius, Magnus, and Priscus heard the commotion and jumped up. They could see a scuffle among the guards in the background and a woman soaked in blood from head to foot stealing their supplies. Lucius bounded over and grabbed her arm. She spun around to strike him, but he grabbed her other arm. She struggled to break free, but was rapidly subdued on top of the table by Magnus.

"Who are you? What are you doing?" Lucius demanded.

Aia twisted in his hands trying desperately to free her arms.

"Ma libera!"

"What?"

"Ma libera!" she panted, as she continued to struggle.

"That's some sort of Gaulish dialect," said Magnus. "I recognize the language. It is spoken in some parts of Milano. She is saying let me go."

"Then she is a barbarian," said Priscus.

"Of course, she's a barbarian!" Lucius exclaimed. "She certainly can't be a legionnaire!" He sized her up.

"She must be one of the only survivors. How desperate she must be to break into our camp for supplies." He looked at Magnus.

"Can you translate?"

"You're asking a lot, but I'll try." He stared down at her.

"Tge avair quaida? – What do you want?"

She looked at her captor. The man was huge, bigger even than Lugurix.
He seemed to know her language. Maybe he was Helvetian.

"Eluveitie?" she asked.

"She's asking me if I am Helvetian," said Magnus. He addressed her.

"Na, Milanese. Tge avair quaida?"

Aia was astonished.

*"How can he speak our language? They make us their slaves and force us
to learn their language,"* she thought looking at the beast of a man. The stories
were that the Romans never learned tribal languages.

"Co–?"

Magnus loomed over her.

"Jua dumand, ti respund! – I demand you answer!"

Aia squeezed her eyes shut and winced turning her head expecting to be
hit.

"Hey, a little help over here!" Quintus shouted. The three surgeons
looked up. Quintus was standing over a pile of bodies. The one on the bottom was
struggling to get out.

Lucius took charge.

"Magnus, stay here and see if you can make any sense out of her. Priscus,
let's go."

They ran over to the ball of humanity. On top was Decimus. He had a
knife blade sticking through his neck. Occasionally, he would make a motion like
he was trying to take a deep breath, but could not. The knife was shoved to the hilt
entering to the left side of his larynx and exiting the back of the right neck.   They
pulled him off first and lay him on his back. Blood mixed with bubbles oozed out.
His face was blue, his mouth open, his eyes cloudy and fixed on the stars.

"He's almost dead," said Priscus. "He can't be saved."

The next body was a barbarian warrior. He lay face down on Marcus.
Quintus helped Lucius lift the lifeless body of the barbarian off of Marcus who was
out of breath, but unharmed.

"I just reacted. I stabbed the barbarian in the chest."

"Thank Jupiter you are alive," said Quintus.

Lucius examined the Tigurini warrior.

"This one must have had super human strength. He looks like he was dead
before this fight started."

The group gathered around him for a minute looking at the scalp flap, the
empty eye socket, the bile oozing from the flank wound, and the sword sticking out
of his left chest. Blood was pulsing out around the sword.

"You finished him, but I am sure he was grateful you put him out of his
misery," Lucius said to his brother.

"I would have asked you to do the same for your comrade," said Priscus,
"but he just breathed his last." He looked at Marcus and Quintus.

"What's his name?"

"Decimus Gellius," they replied.

"Thanks. Now, You two should return to your positions. I will report this
to your Centurion."

They looked at one another.

"Right," said Marcus. He retrieved his sword, wiped it on the barbarian's
britches and sheathed it. They left to resume their posts.

Lucius and Priscus lugged the lifeless body of Decimus back to the medical area. Magnus and Aia were sitting on the table. He had released her and she sat with her head down, her tangled hair covering her face.

"She is no threat to us. She is a Druid. She tells me everyone in her tribe is dead except for her father. She came to get supplies for his wound. She wants us to try to save him."

"We can't help the enemy!" exclaimed Priscus. "We are here to destroy them, not help them."

Lucius understood now why Taurinus had given Priscus his nickname.

"We are here merely to prevent them from crossing our lands," he said.

"If that's what you think Caesar is doing, you are quite naive," Priscus retorted.

"What would you have us do, kill her and her father?"

"That is for the soldiers to do. We should turn her over to them when I speak with the Centurion."

Lucius winced. He did not have the will to be a legionnaire. It was all wrong to him. He looked Priscus in the eye.

"This is not the senate. Taurinus put me in charge, and we will do things my way. We will try to assist this woman to save her father. You may report the slain soldier to the Centurion, but not yet. Wait until we have left the area."

Priscus narrowed his eyes and clinched his teeth. He violently objected, but he respected authority.

"I will follow your orders, but if there is trouble, I will tell all."

"Agreed."

Aia watched the exchange. She could only guess at what was going on. The short surgeon who seemed to be in charge took her hand and spoke to the one who understood her language.

Magnus placed a blanket over her.

"Nus vegnin assister — We are going to help you," he told her.

Aia was astonished.

"Why would these thugs help me?" Still, she was grateful. *"Maybe they do have a soul."*

"Grazcha," she replied.

"Nua?" Magnus asked her, "Where?"

She pointed in the direction of the last burnt out wagon.

"La!"

Chapter 20: Deception

Lucius along with Magnus, who was shielding Aia, approached the Roman perimeter. He motioned for Marcus and Quintus to come over to him. He told them about his plan and asked them to watch out for them. Without hesitation, they agreed and returned to their posts. The threesome ran across the short open space to the wagon line. Behind the first wagon, Aia pointed down to her father. He was lying unconscious in the same position she had left him.

Lucius quickly examined the old man. In the dim moonlight, he could not fully assess the old man's skin color, but it was clearly darker and grayer than his own hand. Drutos was taking rapid shallow breaths. His pulse was weak and thready. His only wound was a through-and-through spear injury. The spear entered two ribs below the right nipple. The exit wound was just below the tip of the scapula.

Lucius could hear no breath sounds in the right chest. He felt for the thump of the heart. Usually, it was in the left chest just below and to the side of the nipple. What little he could discern, the thump was closer to the armpit.

He had Magnus help him roll Drutos on his left side. They broke the spear and slowly removed it from the back. As the end of the spear slipped through the front of the chest, a gush of wind along with bubbles of blood escaped. To keep the hole open, Lucius placed his rolled cinnamon bark into the wound. As if by magic, the old man took a deep breath. He looked up, his eyes still defocused.

Aia could not believe it. *Is this man a miracle worker? How could he revive an almost dead man? What wondrous powers flow through the fingers of this Roman dog?* She looked back at her father who was trying to get up. She fell on him sobbing.

Lucius looked at Magnus.

"You know that wounds of the chest are fatal. In the Republic, we are forbidden to cut the chest because it is murder. It has been written ever since the time of Hippocrates."

Aia looked up hopefully at the two surgeons.

"Tell her it is hopeless. I will get some medicine to ease his pain."

"Why do I have to break the news to her?" Magnus pleaded.

"Because you are the only one who can communicate with her. Besides, Taurinus says the surgeon should not be the bearer of bad news."

"Thanks a lot!" Magnus sulked for a moment then said, "Go ahead, I'll devastate her for you."

Lucius thanked him. With a grim expression on his face, he turned to Aia placing his hand gently on her shoulder. She looked into his eyes with a mixture of fear, wonder, and hope. He stared back with those sad, caring eyes he learned from Theodosius. He lightly rubbed her shoulder and gave it a squeeze, then rose and sprinted back to the camp.

In the medical area, Priscus had removed the dead legionnaire's soiled Tirones tunic, redressed him in the tunic of a full legionnaire, and placed a denarius coin under his tongue for the trip across the Styx to the underworld.

As Lucius approached, Priscus hailed him.

"This soldier's clothes are too soiled for a decent burial. Besides, the legion may need his armor in the future. We can give it to the quartermaster later."

"Nice job, Priscus," said Lucius. He pointed his right thumb over his shoulder toward the Tigurini camp. "We should be able to avoid any discussion of the woman. Her father has a fatal wound. I am going to bring him some poppies to sooth his journey to death."

"Tell me no more. I don't want to know."

"Okay, I understand. We should be back soon." He grabbed an acetabulum of poppies and a wine skin, then sprinted back to the Tigurini camp. When he arrived, Magnus was sitting back on his knees and Aia was sobbing and whispering in her father's ear.

"She took it better than I expected," said Magnus as Lucius knelt down by the old man. "She is saying prayers for his journey to the otherworld."

"The barbarian has religion?" he asked.

"Their religion is more involved than you think," Magnus growled. He wanted to lecture Lucius, but decided he would not understand.

Lucius crushed all the dried poppy flowers and mixed them with a little wine. The alcohol immediately drew out the pain killer from the petals.

"Wow, that is a powerful tincture!" exclaimed Magnus. "It could kill an elephant!"

"Right," replied Lucius. "We need to end this quickly and get back before we are all crucified."

Drutos was sliding in and out of consciousness. The brief improvement from releasing the tension pneumothorax was replaced by the effects of prolonged shock. Lucius carefully fed the tincture to his patient. He felt like he was a physician again, not a surgeon. Surgeons were supposed to cure. Here, he was assisting a fatally wounded man to die.

Aia held her father's hand as he drank the liquid in sips. The first sip he spit out. She had to coax him into taking the medicine. She watched as the Roman treated her father. In spite of her justifiable hatred, she had to admit to herself that he treated her and her father with kindness. She had never seen such compassion for one's enemies. The old crones, who told the history of their tribe, would swell with pride when they talked of Tigurini warriors torturing their enemies before sacrificing them to the gods of the otherworld.

Within a short while, Drutos lay motionless. His breathing became shallow, slow, and regular. As the moon rose to its vertex, he stopped breathing. Lucius sat up, looked at Aia, and shook his head. She knew what that meant. She folded her father's hands, closed his eyes, and said a silent prayer. Lucius and Magnus got up and prepared to leave. Aia jumped up as well.

Lucius became alarmed.

"No, you can't come with us! This was never part of the plan!"

Aia grabbed his tunic burying her head there. He turned to Magnus.

"Do something, man," he pleaded.

"Tia na vegns!" Magnus said bluntly. He turned to Lucius.

"I told her she can't come."

Aia stood up and stomped her foot.

"Pertge?" she screamed. Magnus turned to Lucius.

"She wants to know why."

"What do you mean she wants to know why? There is no way! She can't just tag along! Besides, no one would allow it."

"Somehow, I don't think this feisty little wench is going to understand

Roman logic, and I am not sure I could explain it."

"You've got to do better than that, chap," pleaded Lucius.

"Okay," Magnus sighed.   He gently put his hands on her shoulders and pulled her off to the side. They had a short, but heated discussion and returned.

"Seems we have a situation here, Lucius."

Lucius waited for the explanation.

"She believes she is the sole survivor of her tribe. She would rather take her chances with us than trying to survive alone in this land. She trusts you – I have no idea why. She thinks you can work miracles. She is willing to be your slave."

Lucius sighed and raised his eyebrows. He did not know how he was going to solve the dilemma. She was standing next to Magnus and directly in front of him. With the moon shining down, he could see her features. She was nearly as tall as he. She was thin and not very curvy. Her face was thinner and more prominent bones than his fiancée, Acca, who died during the spring epidemic.

Aia gazed deeply into Lucius' eyes. She could see Lucius was much shorter than Lugurix and nowhere near as muscular. He had angular features and a hairless chin. He looked wise beyond his years and she sensed a deep sadness in his soul. She was helpless and alone. He was a Roman. The Romans had just annihilated her clan. Yet, she knew that she could put her own life and her entire future in this stranger's hands.

While they stared at one another, Lucius hatched a plan.

"We will bring her with us." He turned and darted back to camp pulling Aia with him. The stunned Magnus followed on their heels.

When they arrived, the medical area was deserted. Priscus had gone to make his report to the Centurion and the medics were having their meal. Lucius removed the tunic from the dead legionnaire. He asked Magnus to tell Aia not to be afraid and to do as he said, then instructed him to take the body to the Tigurini camp and dump him by Aia's father. Once Magnus left, Lucius took surgical scissors and cut her hair.

Aia closed her eyes. Involuntary tears rolled down her face.

"What is to become of me? Is this the beginning of my torture? Is this what they did to all their conquests? What else does this man want from me? I thought I could trust him, now he is mutilating me."

She decided she had no choice but to submit. As he cut, she felt her locks falling off her shoulders and brushing past her hips. When he was done, she ran her fingers through her hair. It was incredibly short like a man's haircut.

She turned to look at him. He motioned for her to remove her dress. She turned away from him and removed her bloody dress. Lucius took the wet rag that Priscus had used to wash Decimus and wiped the blood and grime off of her. He cleaned her entire body, touching her where no man except Lugurix had touched her. As he did so, she closed her eyes and shuddered as much from the cool night air as from embarrassment and revulsion.

Aia took deep breaths to gain some semblance of composure. When she opened her eyes, Lucius was holding up the clean tunic that was recently on Decimus. He placed it on the table and gestured for her to put it on. She placed the tunic over her head and let it slip into place. It fit, but it was a little snug on her hips. She tried to get comfortable in the scratchy tunic. She adjusted it several times until she decided it was useless. When she looked up, Lucius was holding the dead legionnaire's armor. He gestured for her to turn around. She obliged and he placed the heavy body armor on her. He gave her the arm bands and helped her lace up the sandals.

Next, Lucius quickly compounded a plaster like the one he had seen Theodosius use for scrofula. It would burn the skin and cause reddening. He placed it on the front of her neck. Using some of the lint and dressing cloth she had tried to steal earlier that night, he fashioned a bulky dressing around her neck. As the materials of the plaster reacted with one another, the heat burned Aia's neck and made her wince. He put his finger to his mouth to remind her to be quiet. She settled down, even though it was terribly irritating.   She kept touching the dressing trying to lessen the pain. Magnus returned from dumping the body as Lucius tied the dressing into place.

"Ah, Magnus," Lucius called.   "I need your help again.   What is this woman's name?"

Magnus, surprised by the question, realized he never found out.   He turned to her.

"Tge es tia num?"

"Aia," she replied, fiddling with the bulky neck dressing.

Lucius placed his hand on his chest and said, "Lucius." Then he pointed at Magnus who put his hand on his chest and said, "Magnus."

She did the same and said, "Aia."

"Okay," Lucius said to Magnus.   "Tell her that from now on, her name is Decimus."

His eyes got wide as he realized what Lucius planned.

"Do you think you can get away with this?"

"As long as she follows our instructions we will."

Magnus looked at the faux legionnaire and shrugged.

"Why not?" He turned to Aia.

"Decimus tia num nova es."

Aia looked surprised.

"Dey-see-moose?" she pronounced slowly.

"Na, na. Dĕ-see-mŭs, Decimus."

"Decimus," she repeated.

"Decimus Gellius," Lucius prompted.

"Decimus Gellius," Aia said as she suppressed her disgust.   After gaining her composure, she stood up straight and pronounced the name with authority.

"Decimus Gellius."

"Gie, Gie," replied Magnus once he was satisfied she had her new name down.

She looked down at her costume and wondered what a cruel game these two were playing.

The puzzled look on Aia's face made it clear that she did not understand the deception. With the help of Magnus, Lucius explained Decimus Gellius was the soldier Toutios had killed to let her into camp.   She would replace the dead legionnaire, becoming a miracle of modern Roman surgical skill.   For purposes of the deception, Lucius would tell everyone that *his* larynx was damaged and *he* could never speak again. Slowly, she grasped the plan and agreed.

Lucius led her to his wagon. They explained that while she "recovered" as the wounded *Decimus*, he would make her his personal assistant. He ushered her into the wagon and allowed her to remove the armor for what was left of the night. He gave her his unfinished rations. Aia nibbled at the salty strange tasting meat and the dry tasteless hardtack.   She wished for her mother's delicious lamb stew. Unwanted tears came to her eyes. She fought them back. She knew her fate was not to die with her family, but her only chance for survival was to pretend to be the dead soldier. She knew warriors did not cry and she was determined to play the part. Somehow, she had to preserve her life to pass along her tribe's love of life and their knowledge to future generations. Right now, just surviving would be a chore.

Priscus returned just before dawn and peered into the wagon to see if Lucius had kept his promise to ditch the Tigurini. He was astonished to see the legionnaire.

"Lucius, who is he?"

Lucius looked at Priscus and swallowed hard.

"Here goes," he thought. Aia sat next to him wide eyed and petrified.

"It's *Decimus*. As we were cleaning up, *he* gasped for air and coughed out a giant blood clot. After that, *he* was better, but I am sorry to say, *his* voice is ruined. *He* can't talk. *He* will be useless to his unit. We cleaned up *his* wounds and placed a dressing. *He* can assist me while *he* recuperates. When we get to the end of the campaign, we can allow *him* to return home."

"By Jupiter and all the gods, I thought he was dead. I guess at least one of the gods must be his personal protector." Priscus started to walk away, stopped and came back. Lucius' heart skipped a beat.

"Has my ruse been discovered already?" he thought.   He tried to look calm, his palms sweating.

"Did you find the denarius I left under his tongue?"

Lucius exhaled.

"Why you cheapskate! You want your denarius back?"

"Don't be a stinky pile of merda! Of course I do! Where is it?"

Lucius realized the coin went with the real Decimus to the Tigurini camp. He reached in his pouch for a coin but the pouch was empty. His sister had cleaned him out before they left Canino.   He had no need of money in Caesar's Army. Everything was provided. His heart began to race.

"I must have misplaced it," he said at length. "I'll pay you tomorrow."

"You better, or I'll charge you interest! It will be a quadrans in no time."

"Yeah, you and my sister!"

"What's that, you gas bag?"

"Just shut up and disappear, mushroom!"

Priscus turned around and waved him off as he left.

Lucius began to hyperventilate.

"What a bizarre guy."

At least his deception held. All he had to do was borrow a denarius from Magnus to mollify Priscus. He lay his head back to rest, but Morpheus would not visit him.

"Hey, Lucius. Who is this?"

Lucius spun around to see Taurinus climbing into the front of the wagon after his nightly debauchery.

"Who, *him*?"

"Uh, yeah, him!"

Lucius knew the story that he and Magnus concocted was about to be seriously tested. If it did not work, he might lose his life.

"This is *Decimus* from the ninth cohort. *He* was stabbed in the neck by a deranged barbarian. Priscus thought *he* was dead and reported it to the soldier's

Centurion, but after he left, Magnus and I realized *the legionnaire* was still alive. We were able to save *him*. Although we did not have to perform a tracheotomy, *his* larynx is damaged and *he* cannot talk. Because of the seriousness of the injury and the precarious airway, I plan to keep *him* as my personal assistant. That way I can observe *him* closely until *he* is well."

Taurinus crawled into the wagon.

"That is quite a feat, son. To save someone with an airway injury is nearly unheard of. Let me see the wound." Before Lucius could react, he started to pull at the top of the dressing. Aia jumped back and put her hands on her throat dressing.

"Please don't disturb the bandage," Lucius stammered. "*His* bleeding was difficult to stop and I don't want it to start again."

Taurinus peered into Aia's frightened face. She could feel and taste his hot stale breath. It made her nauseated. She closed her eyes.

"Yeah, he is quite pale," he said. Then he turned to Lucius.

"Well done, lad!" He climbed back to the front seat of the wagon. "Oh, you said he was reported dead?"

"Yes, sir."

"On the morning report, you better correct that." Taurinus pulled out a piece of cinnamon bark and turned his attention to preparing to move out.

Lucius looked at Aia. He had duties, including the report. She would have to come with him. He motioned for her to put on the heavy armor and to follow him. They sat at the medical table as dawn broke. He wrote the report for the commander and gave it to a medic for immediate delivery.

They walked over to the unusually small sick call being conducted by Atticus, Modestus and Petrus. They had the privilege of sleeping through the night, so they had to work sick call. Lucius introduced his temporary assistant with the gargantuan neck bandage. He filled them in on the injuries of the legionnaires they treated and told them the imaginary story of the night's events. They seemed duly impressed.

Lucius went to visit Magnus who was snoring loudly in his wagon. Lucius woke him and whispered in his ear. Magnus stirred, dug into his belongings, and produced a twenty year old denarius. Magnus was from Milano. The city only began using Roman money recently. What money he had came from occasional merchants who traded with it when there was no other way to settle accounts. Lucius thanked him and promised to repay him. Magnus waved him off and went back to sleep.

Lucius and Aia circled around the medical area and located Priscus eating his breakfast rations. Lucius gave the old coin to Priscus who turned it over several times. He was pleased because the image on the coin was that of his uncle. It was more meaningful to him than the newer one he had placed in the soldier's mouth.

"I guess this worked out for the best," admitted Priscus. He extended his hand to Lucius. They grasped one another and Priscus apologized. Lucius gave an embarrassed acceptance.

Priscus took a look at the fake Decimus. He had only seen the recruit laying dead in the torchlight the night before. He eyed the figure from top to bottom. Aia felt as though he had undressed her. She was repulsed, but stood at attention at Lucius' side staring toward her old camp.

"My, my!" Priscus exclaimed. "He doesn't look a day over twelve! Someone must have paid off the recruiter to let such a young lad in Caesar's Army!"

"Yeah, well we don't pick them, we're just stuck taking care of them," replied Lucius.

"You are so right, brother! Hope he serves you well, Lucius!" He returned to his rations.

As they walked away, Aia realized she had been holding her breath. She exhaled hard and took in a huge gulp of air. Lucius squeezed her arm to quiet her and they walked stiffly away from the area. Before heading back, they circled past the quartermaster's wagon to obtain rations and a new back pack for the faux Decimus. Aia stood at attention while Lucius did a little fast talking. He hoisted the full pack onto her back. She started to topple backwards from the weight. Lucius told the quartermaster it was due to *his* weakened condition and loss of blood from the stabbing. He offered to carry it for *him* using grandiose gestures so Aia could understand.

"May I carry your sack until you are stronger, *Decimus*?" he asked her.

Aia bowed slightly and the pair walked away achieving another successful deception.

They returned to the wagon and climbed in. Lucius indicated to Aia that she could take off the armor. She was grateful because the heavy plate pressed on her breasts and made them ache. As they began to eat the morning's rations, Lucius heard commotion outside the wagon.

"I demand to see my legionnaire!" boomed Martial. "Where is he?"

Priscus knocked on the wagon door.

"Lucius, this Centurion wants to see your miracle patient."

"Will it ever end?" thought Lucius.

Aia looked at him wondering what the racket was about. He put his hand on her chest and forced her to the floor of the wagon with her feet toward the front of the vehicle and her head in the middle of the wagon. Then he covered her with his blanket leaving her head and neck with the gigantic dressing exposed and opened the doors.

"*He's* in here, sir," Lucius said, "but *he* is very weak and dizzy after assisting me this morning."

Martial peered into the interior of the cluttered medical wagon.

"I can barely see in that mushroom cave. Decimus, is that you?"

Lucius quickly reached under the blanket, grabbed Aia's foot and wiggled it up and down. Aia got the message and raised her arm.

"Remember, sir. The injury ruined *his* larynx. *He* will never be able to talk."

"What a crime!" Martial exclaimed shaking his head. "Are you in any pain?"

Lucius wagged Aia's foot side to side. She shook her head no.

"Your contubernium sends its best wishes and prays to the god Aesculapius for your recovery."

Aia raised her arm at the prompting of Lucius.

"You are a good man, Decimus. You were willing to die for Roma. With the approval of our commander, I am promoting you to the rank of Optio-in-Absentia. Although I know that you will never be able to fulfill your duties, I would have been honored for you to serve as my second in command."

He handed Lucius a Vitis staff made of grape vines as a symbol of the field promotion. Lucius placed it in Aia's right hand and gently pushed it upward. She raised it to the ceiling. Martial immediately stood at attention, snapped his closed right fist against his chest, and shouted, "Caparum Romanus - Ad Victoria!" Then, he turned and marched back to his troops.

When he was out of sight and the clank of his armor could no longer be heard, Lucius squeezed Aia'a foot. She slowly sat back up. Lucius gave her a weak apologetic smile. She returned it. They sat in silence and finished their rations as the legion pulled out.

Lucius put his head back, closed his eyes, and immediately fell asleep.

Aia remained jittery. She felt her nausea returning and shuddered. Before she drifted off to sleep, she wondered if surviving with the Romans was better than dying with her family in that unholy land.

Chapter 21: Discovery

A cheer spontaneously arose from the ninth cohort at Martial's report. Decimus was indeed alive, although he would not return to fight with them.

Appius, who sat next to Decimus' back pack sighed.

"I will miss him dearly," he said wistfully. He bowed his head.

"I loved the little guy," he whispered at the ground.

All of his tent mates patted him on the back as they gathered their belongs and prepared to move out.

"Come on, chap," said Quintus. "There are still seven of us. Cheer up."

Appius got up slowly. He removed a blue crystal attached to a leather strap from around his neck and slipped it into Decimus' pack, then walked to the rear and secured the pack on the mule carrying the unit's extra gear. He lingered for a moment with his hand on the pack before returning to gather his belongings.

"All right, you mushrooms, time for sentimentality is over! You are legionnaires. Act like it!"

Appius took his place in line leaving an empty space in front of him for Decimus.

"Close up ranks!" yelled Martial. "Leave no space for fallen comrades!"

Appius reluctantly stepped up. They all waited in silence for the next order.

Martial marched to the head of his century and stiffly turned to face them.

"Attention, listen closely!" They snapped to attention at the familiar command.

Martial looked up and down the ragged, depressed line. The veteran Centurion felt sorry for his trainees.

"I know how all of you feel. It is tough to lose a comrade, but we are legionnaires. It is our duty to fight for the Republic. We bring glory to the Republic by defeating her enemies, but even in victory, some of us will die. Those who die, do so with honor. Those of us who survive to fight another day must have no sorrow for the fallen, only respect for their sacrifice. So, let's send a message to our Optio-in-Absentia."

Martial came to attention.

"Caparum Romanus..." he boomed.

"Ad Victoria!" they shouted back.

"Caparum Romanus..."

"Ad Victoria!"

"Caparum Romanus..."

"Ad Victoria!"

Everyone's blood ran faster and spirits rose knowing they had officially saluted their fallen comrade.

Orders came down the line.

"Moveo! Accelera!" "March! Faster!"

Legion XI moved out smoothly leaving the killing fields behind. They marched past the area where the Helvetii had camped just days before and where Legions VII, VIII and IX spent the night after the slaughter. They turned and prepared to cross the pontoon bridge built by their enemy.

*   *   *

Ruts from thousands of Helvetian wagons made travel to the pontoon bridge a nightmare. The medical wagons swayed precariously right and left as they slowly negotiated the old campgrounds. The violent swinging woke both Lucius and Aia. Aia, completely disoriented, quickly surveyed the inside of the wagon. The horror of her situation crashed down on her and she tried to scream, but she only croaked out a raspy unfamiliar noise.

Her utterances were stopped abruptly by a hand slapped over her mouth. Her eyes dilated as she tried to break free. Lucius jerked her head around so he could look in her eyes. He shot a commanding look at her. She focused on his face and slowly reoriented to her plight. She relaxed trying to say with her eyes that she understood.

"That was quite a squeak from that boy," said Taurinus from the driver's seat of the wagon. "Guess his larynx was crushed."

"Yes, sir. I believe it was," answered Lucius as he cautiously removed his grip on Aia's mouth.

Taurinus expected the injured legionnaire to be exhausted from the blood loss and shock. He also assumed Lucius would be drained from his first real experience with violent trauma. He figured it would be best to drive the wagon by himself allowing Lucius and the boy soldier to get some sleep. He closed the front doors to the wagon to let them sleep it off.

Another lurch threw Aia on top of Lucius where she stayed. She placed her right arm around his chest and held tight. Lucius looked at the frightened barbarian. He decided he would try to offer her comfort. He made sure the doors were shut tight and Taurinus could not see, then he put his arm around her back. Aia buried her head in his chest. She began sobbing so hard she shook both of them. He stroked her head until she was calm.

"Why is this man so good to me?" Aia thought. *"He has no reason to keep me alive. He risks so much by hiding me in plain sight. He has been like Esus, god of protection. He demands nothing in return, but what do I have to repay him? Only myself."* She sighed.

Lucius squeezed her close to him. He had never held a woman that way before, even his dearest departed Acca. Acca's parents named her after the legendary foster mother of Romulus and Remus, who founded Rome. Lucius and Acca were betrothed only weeks before the horrible epidemic hit their village. They were just getting to know each other. They took long walks and talked about their future. Acca had slipped her hand into his as they walked. Her delicate hand in his sent a shuddering thrill that traveled quickly from his hand to every part of his body. Her adoring gaze made him weak in the knees. One evening, she kissed him gently on the lips. His heart had raced, his ears pounded, and his loins ached. Only days later, the cursed illness claimed her. She became desperately ill and would never recover. By the time he and Theodosius arrived, she was dead. That day, he held her hand for the last time. Even though it was cold and lifeless, he was captivated by the power of her spirit. He was at once filled with love and sadness, passion and grief. His chest constricted and he lost his breath.

Now, he was holding to his chest a woman even more beautiful than his own Acca. He rubbed and comforted her. They traveled in each others' embrace through the day. He had feelings of compassion for a fellow human being devastated by the loss of her family.   He wanted to help her, but he had only succeeded in weaving them into a web of deceit that threatened to unravel at any moment.

Aia felt warm and comforted by the Roman's caresses.   In his arms, no wrong could come to her.   She tightened her grip around his chest to feel his protection on her whole body.   She closed her eyes as he gently stroked her cropped hair and rubbed her aching back.   Without thinking, she lifted up and placed butterfly kisses on his cheek.

Surprised, Lucius pulled back, but Aia placed her hand on his cheek to steady him and planted more butterfly kisses near his mouth.   Then she kissed his lips, barely touching his skin.

Something strange stirred inside Lucius, as if it came from another life or another universe.   It rumbled up from the pit of his stomach shooting in all directions. His head and lips were instantly on fire. He felt his groin throbbing and Priapus made a swift appearance. He passionately pressed his lips against hers.

They broke panting hotly into each others' faces. Aia looked into Lucius' eyes.   He stared back at her with a fire she had not seen.   She placed her arm around his neck and pulled him toward her for another deeply passionate kiss. Lucius leaned forward to meet her lips. As they kissed, Lucius allowed the weight of Aia to pull them down to the floor of the wagon. He was swollen with passion. Aia slowly released her grip and Lucius gently kissed her cheek.

Aia felt the flames in her pelvis burning slowly at first, then increasing to a raging fire sending a burning warmth to her breasts.   She arched her back and pulled up her military tunic. Lucius felt her clothes moving under his belly.   Then he felt her grab at his hips and lift his tunic.   She guided him into her.   As she brought her hands up, she pulled her tunic up to expose her round full breasts. He began to hyperventilate.   She placed her arms around him and kissed his lips. Instinctively he began moving his hips.   The two danced to the rhythm of their hearts until his ultimate ecstasy.   He grabbed her and held tight as he throbbed deep within her. To Aia's surprise she too felt an explosion of ecstasy. She took in a swift breath then relaxed, floating.

A violent lurch of the wagon rapidly snapped the two out of their revery. They disengaged and sat up against the wall of the wagon. Aia placed her head on Lucius' chest and he draped his right arm around her.   Neither paid attention to their tunics.

Taurinus could barely control the wagon as he guided it out of the ruts to better stability. Once there, the ride was smoother, but slow. He figured Lucius and the legionnaire had rested enough and he opened the doors to give them a progress report. The afternoon sunlight shone directly into the depths of the wagon.

The flash of sunlight startled the pair and they quickly sat up and pulled at their tunics. Taurinus caught the movement. He squinted at the pair, but let his thoughts go for the moment. He would address the issue later.

*   *   *

It had been a strange day for the ninth cohort.   The deep ruts in the campground made double time marching a challenge.   No one was immune to stumbling. Even Martial stumbled while trying to buoy the spirits of his charges. Most of the march was in silence. The men pondered the loss of their comrade and the unusual behavior of Appius.   Quintus tried several times to start a bawdy cadence song, but no one was interested.   It would die out before he could complete one round.

Crossing the floating bridge proved problematic for the outside soldiers. Whenever cadence broke down, the uncoordinated marching augmented the swaying of the bridge, launching legionnaires into the river.   The column had to stop while the embarrassed soldiers were yanked from an unintentional bath.   To maintain order and reestablish a proper march on the bridge, Martial ordered Quintus to sing a new cadence.   He dug deep for something appropriate – something salacious, yet non-confrontational.   He remembered another poem of Catullus and belted out the lines.

My woman says there is none
With whom she'd rather stay.
Even if Jupiter asked her to wed.
So she says..., but women often lie.
What a woman says to her lover,
Quickly write in wind and water.

Everyone, goaded by Martial sang without passion, but it allowed the century to make it across without anyone getting dunked.   Once on the other side, Legion XI marched to the base of a small hill.

Sol was low in the sky by the time the entire supply train crossed the bridge.   Everyone was amazed that the entire army of six legions and their supply trains had crossed in one day.   It was a feat they would be able to share with their families for generations to come.   All legions set up camp on the right bank of the Arar.

*   *   *

Taurinus clambered down from the wagon and paced back and forth for a few moments.   Before heading to visit Publicus, he had to deal with Lucius.   After assembling his thoughts, he went to the rear of the wagon and pounded on the door.   Aia jumped at the sound, pulled away from Lucius, and ran her fingers through her hair.   Embarrassment returned as she realized she no longer had her beautiful long brown locks.   She instinctively used her arm to cover her tunic at the level of her breasts and raised her left knee.   Lucius opened the door to look directly into the red face of Taurinus.

"Step out, son. I need to talk to you!" he commanded.

Lucius' heart jumped into his throat.

"Have we been discovered already? Will we be crucified on the spot?" He jumped down as sprightly as he could while Taurinus squinted into the wagon at the scared figure.

"What's up chief?" Lucius tried to sound cheery.   "I see we made it safely to the right bank of this lazy river."

"Shut up, filth," Taurinus spat.

Lucius had never heard the old man say that before.   Now, he was petrified.

"Have you buggered that boy?"

Lucius was stunned.

"No, of course not!" he stammered.

Taurinus peered in again.   Faux Decimus sat with folded arms around raised knees, head down, and pushing *his* back against the wall.

"Are you sure? Because he is acting like he's been buggered."

"I swear by Jupiter, I would never do such a thing!"   Lucius' heart raced, his face reddened.

Taurinus pointed into the wagon in the general direction of the figure.

"That boy is your patient.   He is weak from his ordeal.   He is in a vulnerable position. He considers you a god for saving his life. As his surgeon, you have no right to take advantage of him. Remember, the entire legion depends on us to deliver swift, competent care. They trust us to do the noble thing. Treatment of a wound does not include a bugger job!"

He paced back and forth and spit.

"You disappoint me!   You are a patrician, the son of a decorated legionnaire and a noble senator! You are trained in classical Medicine by a disciple of Hippocrates! Yet, you act like an unprincipled Roman child of privilege waiting for his next trip to the circus or the baths! Maybe what they say is true! Maybe there are no more noble men in Roma! You disgust me!"

While Taurinus was expectorating his vitriol, Lucius turned to see poor wide eyed Aia plastered against the wagon wall. It dawned on him how it looked. He closed his eyes in embarrassment.   Taurinus grabbed him and jerked him around.

"Are you listening to me, son?"

"Yes, sir," Lucius said opening his eyes to face the tirade. Taurinus began to wag his finger like a dagger in Lucius' face.

"If word gets out that you bugger your patients, no one will seek your help.   Regardless of how competent you are, you will be useless to me and to Caesar!" Taurinus stopped for a moment panting hard and blowing foul breath and cinnamon at Lucius. Gradually, Taurinus caught his breath and his panting slowed. His fiery red face gradually returned to its usual ruddy complexion. He never took his eyes off of Lucius.

Aia watched her protector get roasted by the gruff ugly old man. She had no idea what the discussion was.   She feared she had been found out and she assumed it was her fault somehow.   She fully expected to be dragged out of the wagon and murdered on the spot.

"Please, sir." Lucius tried to be positive. "I swear it is not as it seems!" He thought to himself, *"If you only knew what was really going on!"*

Taurinus squinted at Lucius.

"Okay, son. You have never given me reason to doubt you before. If you give me your solemn oath right now that you have not violated that boy, I will believe you, but I must say it looks mighty suspicious."

Lucius raised his right arm high in the air.

"I swear by Jupiter and all the gods that I have not and will not bugger *Decimus* or any other legionnaire!" He secretly hoped Taurinus would never find out the truth.

Taurinus peered deep into Lucius' eyes. Finally he backed off.

"All right, I will believe you this time, but don't try anything so crude. It will bring disgrace on us all. Now, fix it so there is never any suspicion!" Then he stormed away to visit his friend, the chef. Lucius sucked in a deep breath.

Aia, still afraid she was about to be slaughtered, shivered uncontrollably. Lucius climbed back in the wagon. He had no idea how to explain the tirade to the poor wretch. He sat down beside her trying to figure out what to do next. They sat in silence as the evening sky turned dark. Thoughts swirled around in his head. They began to speak to him.

"She is not your patient. She is only pretending to be your patient. She is not a man, but merely playing the part. She started the passion, you merely followed her lead. Besides, how could you resist a woman of such haunting beauty and uncanny power?"

The voices gave him little consolation.

A loud clank broke the silence. Aia pulled away covering up again and Lucius peered into the moonless darkness. He saw Magnus behind them releasing the mules from the wagon for the evening and breathed a deep sigh. He pondered what he had done. His heart began to thump out of his chest.

"How did I allow myself to get into this?"

He turned to Aia. She looked at him with hope. It only made him feel more embarrassed. He felt her lure, but shook it off, took another deep breath, and tried to think of what to do next. As he did, he realized he had to relieve himself badly and that Aia might need to as well.

Lucius motioned for Aia to follow him out of the wagon. She felt self-conscious leaving the wagon covered only by the tunic. Lucius led her into the nearby tree line and motioned for her to take care of her business behind a bush. Then, he turned around, pulled up his tunic, and urinated on the ground. She crouched down and relieved herself. She was surprised how much she needed to go. She could not remember the last time she had done so. Once they were finished, he led her to where Magnus was feeding the mules.

"Magnus, I need your help!" Lucius whispered loudly.

Magnus looked up. "Lucius! Salve, and thank you!"

"Thank me for what?" Lucius was perplexed.

"You were the object of Taurinus' rant again tonight and the rest of us were spared. We were all able to spend a quiet evening while you took another sword for the team. Well done, chap! We are grateful!"

Lucius flushed.

"Did you hear what he said?"

"You know nobody listens to that old gas bag when he gets wound up."

Lucius was relieved. At least no one else knew what he was accused of, or what he had actually done.

"Please translate for me again," he pleaded. "I am afraid she is confused and I cannot explain it to her."

"You're making a habit of this, Lucius. Maybe I should start charging you for my interpretive services." Magnus chuckled, but Lucius seemed agitated. "Okay, my man, I will do it for you, but maybe someday, you can let me have her as an assistant for a night."

That was all Lucius could stand. He took a roundhouse swing at the jaw of Magnus but was easily blocked by the man's gigantic hand. Magnus grabbed Lucius by the forearm and squeezed.

"Calm down, chief. I said I would do it for you. I was just trying to lighten the moment."

Lucius regained his composure.

"Sorry. I guess the events of the last day have gotten to me. I didn't get much rest."

Magnus released his arm.

"It's okay, man. What do you need?"

Lucius rubbed his forearm where the much larger Magnus had nearly broken it.

"Thanks. Please tell her that she will need to be with me all the time. I will tell everyone that our faux Decimus remembers nothing of the stabbing. That way, we can say *he* has forgotten *his* Latin and only speaks and understands this Gaulish language. Everyone will need to communicate in simple sign language."

"Okay, that's simple. Is there anything else?"

Lucius swallowed hard.

"Yes, tell her that whenever someone is around, especially Taurinus, she cannot touch me. Also, when we are in public, I will treat her like scum. I will order her around and ignore her like I would a servant or a slave."

Magnus raised his eyebrows.

"You never treat anyone that way."

"I know, I know. Tell her it is part of this ruse. Tell her we cannot let anyone suspect us."

"What do you mean, Lucius?"

Lucius looked up and realized how that sounded.

"Oh, what I mean is she needs to look and act like a real legionnaire, otherwise her disguise will be uncovered. I must act as though I do not know her any better than any other member of Caesar's Army."

"Got it," replied Magnus. He put his arm around Aia and led her a few feet away. He leaned against the bar and began an animated discourse in broken Gaulish occasionally gesturing at Lucius.

Aia had watched the exchange between Lucius and Magnus. She sensed a new uneasiness in Lucius. As she listened intently to Magnus fumble for the right words in her dialect, the import of the instructions hit her. She folded her arms and squinted at Lucius who was wringing his hands.

"So, I embarrass him," she thought. *"He thinks I am a burden to him, but I know deep in my soul he has feelings for me. He shows me his passion in the wagon, but he is ashamed to show it in public. I know I need to play his game for my sake as well as his. Maybe someday, he can treat me outside with the same respect he has shown me in the dark."* She acknowledged the instructions and marched back to Lucius' side and made an about face looking back toward Magnus.

"I have done what I can, brother. Hope for your sake it works out."

Lucius thanked Magnus profusely and ushered Aia back into the wagon, but he left the front and back doors open. When they settled down, he pulled out the evening's rations. Aia nibbled at the crackers. She refused to drink the vinegary water or eat the bacon. She found them vile. After they were finished, Lucius put away the leftovers. Aia settled into his arms again. Lucius did not resist, but she sensed a new stiffness in his touch. Now it was her turn to soothe him. She sat up and massaged his back and neck until he let his tension go. Then she settled back into his arms and the two fell asleep.

*   *   *

Before the ninth cohort could set up their tent, they would need the tent parts carried by Decimus. Appius volunteered to get them. He ran to their pack mule, rummaged through their fallen comrade's pack and returned with only the pole and the tent fabric.

"Why didn't you bring the whole pack?" Marcus asked. "We could have split Decimus' rations."

"You're always famished!" exclaimed Quintus.

"Well, he's not here and the bacon should be eaten before it spoils. How about it, Appius?"

"There's no bacon left." Appius stammered.

"You're hiding something," accused Aulus. "We just got fresh rations."

"No, we ate it."

"You mean you and Decimus?" asked Marcus who was also getting suspicious. "Neither of you eat much. How could you go through that much bacon?"

"Let me see your pack," said Cornelius grabbing Appius' pack off the ground before he could get to it.

Appius stopped in his tracks. He would not confront any members of the cohort. He bowed his head.

Cornelius pulled out a pound of bacon.

"There is only one ration in here and it's yours. It's barely touched."

"I swear I am telling the truth!" Appius pleaded. Tears were in his eyes.

"Leave him alone," said Memmius. "Can't you see he's broken up over Decimus?" He turned to Appius and put his hand on his shoulder. "Tell us the story when you're ready."

Appius nodded but did not look up.

"I hate to break up the party, you mules!" thundered Martial. "Get your tent up and shut your stinking mouths! We are here to kill barbarians, so act like it!"

They quickly pitched their tent and sat together to eat their evening rations. Appius only nibbled at his rations and put the rest away. He stared into the distance and spoke to no one in particular.

"When Decimus joined us, he stuck close to me."

Everyone looked up. Marcus did not understand.

"What do you mean?" He asked.

"He was only fourteen and very vulnerable," he replied.

"So he was under age," Memmius said.

"I knew, but we kept it a secret" Appius said with his head down. "He told me he always dreamed of joining the legion when he grew up. His home in Placentia was near the castra. Every chance he got, he would sneak out to watch the legionnaires practice. He admired the brave men in the finest Roman armor practicing war games. Then one day, they just moved out. The castra was vacant for years. He thought they were never coming back. When our legions came to town, he figured it might be his only chance. He asked to join, but his family was against it."

Marcus thought about his own situation. He fully understood the passion of Decimus. Although he was sixteen already, his father did not want to let him join. He had to launch an intense campaign to convince him. Eventually, it still required co-opting his brother into the legion in order for him to get his way. It was a terrible price for his family to pay, but it was his only path. Appius was continuing his story.

"He got a friend to pay off the recruiter and he snuck out of town. By fate, he wound up in this cohort. By the first nightfall, he was so homesick he wanted to desert. That's when I began to help him. We would spend nights together. I held him and told stories about when I was in the fifth legion. He said he would feel stronger if I protected him. Every day, I whispered in his ear. You know how well he performed. He was never yelled at and none of you ever suspected." Appius began to cry softly. He eventually got hold of himself and continued.

"Once, when he became homesick again, I promised him we would be brothers forever if we exchanged mementos. I gave him my ring with the seal of the fifth legion. In exchange, he gave me a necklace. He said a magician from a far away seacoast town sold it to him. He promised that it would bring good fortune. We swore our love for one another. You never noticed, but after that, we spent every free moment together."

An uneasy silence fell on the cohort. Finally Quintus broke in.

"Well, that's it for play time, so I guess we go back to work."

The tent mates snorted at the comment, but the tension eased.

"Where's the necklace now?" Aulus asked.

"I feel ashamed to wear it, so I put it back in his pack."

"Is that why you would not bring his pack?" asked Marcus.

Appius nodded his head without looking up from the ground.

"It's all right, chap," said Fabius patting him on the back. "Go get the pack. We'll help you return it to Decimus."

"You're right," agreed Appius. "The pack and the necklace are his. He should have them. Maybe it will help him recover."

As Appius got up and trudged over to the mules, Quintus smirked and shook his head. Marcus gave him a quizzical look.

"What?" Quintus asked. "When you live in the big city, you see strange things. At my uncle's business, I saw men with women, men with men, men with boys, women with boys, women with women, women with girls—"

"No!" exclaimed Marcus. "You're a lying sack of merda!"

Quintus laughed. "You're such a country boy, Marcus!"

Marcus jumped up to challenge Quintus, but he was struck in the back of the head. He winced and turned around. Standing over him was Martial.

"That's enough, you criminals!" the Centurion boomed. "Word came down from command. Our scouts have the Helvetians in sight. We move out in the morning. Orders to attack could come at any time. We must be ready. That means you need to sleep when you can. Now, shut up and rest."

Quintus whispered to Marcus as he walked past.

"Men with donkeys."

Marcus gave Quintus a swift elbow in the gut.

The group stretched out, but no one slept.

Chapter 22: Cat and Mouse

As the Army tracked the Helvetians, Lucius reminisced about a lazy afternoon back home at the Villa Romanus. It was the day he first watched Dulceda, the family cat, catch a mouse. Dulceda was a spunky short-haired golden tabby who was descendent from a long line of cats that befriended his family during the building of the villa's gardens. From the early days of the villa, cats had an honored place in the family. They came and went as they pleased. Of the myriad of felines, Dulceda was the cat that Lucius most favored.

When she was born, Theodosius let him be the assistant midwife. He watched Dulceda's mother, Silvia, search for days around the villa to find the perfect place to birth her litter. She chose his room as her nursery. Once she settled in, he brought linen to make her bed. She accepted his gifts, but arranged them herself.

Lucius watched all day as one by one, seven little sightless progeny extruded from Silvia. She licked each one to life cleaning off the mucoid coating, then Lucius completed the cleaning for her. By the time the last delivery came, she was too worn out even to attempt a lick.

Theodosius quickly wiped the little kitten, but it remained lifeless. He cleared the mucus out of its mouth and gave it to Lucius who placed it up to Silvia's mouth. She ignored the kitten. Lucius picked up the kitten and rubbed it against Silvia's mouth and nose the way he had observed her do when she licked the other kittens to life.

Silvia opened one eye and looked directly at Lucius as if to say, "You really want this one don't you?" With obvious effort, she licked the kitten's nose and mouth. Shortly, the little ball of fir coughed and took a breath. After she completed the successful litter, Silvia rested for half a day while the newly minted kittens found their place by her belly to sleep with her.

Although the little kitten lived, she was the odd one out. She had to fight for a nipple at every feeding. Often she was the last to suckle after poor Silvia had gone dry. Lucius would collect an acetabulum of goat's milk and sweeten it with honey. He would dip his little finger in the warm milk and offer it to the starving little runt. She quickly got the hang of sucking the surrogate tit and soon preferred it to fighting for her mother's dry one.

Her markings were the prettiest of the bunch and she constantly purred in Lucius' hands. He named her Dulceda – Sweetness. Dulceda was anything but sweet to her siblings. She picked fights with all of them, including Scipius, the strongest male. She never defeated him and often lost hair in the scuffle, but he left her alone, allowing her to have her own space.

With time, her litter mates obeyed the feral call and wandered around the large grounds of the villa. Dulceda stayed in the house cuddling up at night with different members of the family, but only once with the Paterfamilias. One night, Dulceda climbed into bed with Titus Romanus and curled around his head. She enjoyed the elevated position it gave her and she purred contentedly. However, her body warmth on that summer night overheated Titus. He woke up feeling the weight of the young cat on his head. He slowly reached under her body while she purred away. Once his hands were in position, he launched her across the room. She hit the floor and rolled into the wall with a thud. She sprang up and darted out never to return to the Master's chambers.

At six years old, Dulceda became the matriarch of the Romanus felines. By then, she had graced the family with two litters of beautiful kittens. She mated first with her father, Corculus, then her brother, Scipius.

Lucius remembered her prowling around the gardens near the pool. He watched her move stealthily through the pampas grass. The leaves close to the ground had gone brown and her coloring allowed her to blend in almost unnoticed. Suddenly, she stopped in her tracks, her eyes focused some three or four feet ahead. She slowly, silently eased into a crouch position and sat motionless. Lucius looked at the spot on which she was focused. At first he could see nothing. Then, he noticed little abrupt movements of dried foliage. There, he made out a small brown mouse foraging for morsels.

Lucius alternated between watching the cat and the mouse. The mouse went about his business of finding a midday meal. Dulceda sat like a sphinx. After what seemed like an eternity, she began to inch toward her prey. Ever so slowly, she crept. Each move was just a short distance. Dulceda waited another eternity before creeping again. She never deviated her gaze from the prize. The mouse continued his quest without concern, never noticing his pursuer. When Dulceda was within two feet of her quarry, she pounced. The mouse had no time to react. She had him in her mouth without a fight. She stood up triumphantly and quick stepped her way to the corner of the garden near the house.

Lucius wanted to continue his observations, but she had hidden herself in the corner behind the low wall dividing the pool from the garden. He had to go into the house and peer out of the window to view her. She was sitting on all fours with the mouse less than a paw's distance in front of her owling as if the effort had worn her out. The mouse was stunned, but intact with obvious bite marks on the neck and upper torso. Periodically, he would make a move and Dulceda instantly slapped him with her right paw, claws extended. The prisoner would fall silent for a while, then try again, only to be slapped down immediately. Every time the mouse would try to run, Dulceda would claw him back to his assigned position. Occasionally, she would add a bite to the neck to emphasize the orders to stay put. The routine went on most of the afternoon until the mouse lay motionless. After an assessment that her quarry was dead, she gently picked it up in her mouth, as though it was one of her own kittens, and trotted off.

Later Lucius discovered that she had deposited the object of her day's entertainment on the door sill of the kitchen. Basilius told him that she often left gifts. Sometimes it was a grebe or a partridge. Sometimes it was a mouse or a rat. He explained it was her way of thanking the family for taking such good care of her and her offspring. He always accepted the gift by leaving her a saucer of fresh goat's milk. He never used the gifts to feed the family. He hid them in the garbage or the compost heap so she would not pick up the scent and think he was spurning her gift.

Lucius imagined Caesar was the cat and the Helvetians his mouse. His legions were ready and primed to pounce. He could strike anytime he wished. Yet, he toyed with his prey, staying just far enough away to prevent engagement, but close enough to harry them. He was biding his time until the advantage was all his. The legions traveled only forty miles and changed camp only three times in two weeks.

Unfortunately, while Caesar played with his quarry, their supplies dwindled. Each day they expected the Aedui to resupply them. The inhabitants of the territory harvested the early summer crops and promised to provide for the legions, but each day there was some new excuse. The quartermaster ran so low that there were few treats for Taurinus and Publicus to share. That made life in the Medical wagons of Legion XI increasingly intolerable. Evening dinners were shared with Taurinus who regaled them with vignettes of spectacular injuries and superhuman feats of surgery. No one believed these fantastic tales were real. During breaks when Taurinus was otherwise occupied, they would speculate about what really happened. After a few evenings, Modestus and Priscus refused to join the conversation. They joined the medics for the evening meal.

Nights for Lucius and Aia were miserable. Taurinus slept with them preventing any intimate time. Worst, by far, were the days. Taurinus filled them with surgical drills. There were no animals to practice on, so they preformed dry runs of operations. Taurinus was up at sunrise and rattled everyone out of the wagons.

Every day when Aia slipped away to relieve herself, she would take a little dirt and rub it under her eyes so she would look tired. She still had her neck dressing, but Lucius had decreased the size. The plaster had excoriated her throat and irritated her larynx. She hoped that soon, he would be able to remove the bandage entirely. The military tunic she wore was quite heavy, but it did not hide her breasts sufficiently, so she had to wear the chest armor all day. The heavy metal made her breasts quite sore. Every day, Aia took extra time to dress in the legionnaire's armor adjusting it until she felt she looked the part. That resulted most mornings in missing breakfast. Roman fare nauseated her, so that suited her just fine.

Immediately after breakfast, Taurinus would call for the medics to set up three operating tables. After his signal, he timed them by reciting out loud at a moderate pace, his homage to Priapus.

Jupiter controls the thunderbolts,
Neptune's weapon is the trident.
Mars is mighty by the sword,
Minerva, yours is the spear.
Bacchus fights with a flower,
Apollo shoots giant arrows we are told.
Hercules' invincible right arm holds a club;
Yet my engorged mentule makes me bold!

"You criminals! I had to recite the Priapeia three times before you completed the setup! Your goal is less than one time! Tomorrow all of you better improve!" After more tirades, Taurinus shouted orders.

"Lucius and Magnus, table one; Priscus and Modestus, table two; Petrus and Atticus, table three – Move!" He pointed to Aia.

"Decimus, help the medics!" He waved in the general direction of the wagons.

Aia stumbled in the direction of Taurinus' waving hand to the edge of the second wagon looking lost. One of the medics grabbed the faux Decimus, and together, they stood next to the surgical instruments.

Taurinus stood a few feet away from the tables and surveyed his charges. He scowled and spit, but secretly, he was pleased with their progress. He believed now, that he would have them ready when the first real patients came. He shouted his plan for the day.

"Table one, perform an amputation of the upper leg!   Table two, set a femur fracture! Table three, suture an abdominal gash!"

As Taurinus gave orders, each group called out to the medics to bring the instruments.

"Amputation set to table one! Fracture kit to table two! Basic pack to table three!"

Medics began to scramble. Aia followed the medic who had grabbed her. He turned and pulled at a box with lettering that Aia did not comprehend.   He motioned for her to grab one of the handles. She did as instructed. When they dragged the box off the wagon, the weight nearly pulled her to the ground. It took all of her strength to keep up with the medic who was quickly lugging the box to table one. They threw it onto the table. Aia did not let go fast enough and the inertia of the box transferred to her. She swung like a pendulum, twisted around, and landed in a heap at Lucius' feet. Her armor remained in place, but her helmet twisted around to cover half her face.

Lucius looked at her then toward Taurinus.

"Looks like *Decimus* is still too weak to help."

"You're right," replied Taurinus. "Thought he might be ready."

Taurinus looked down at the heap of armor.

"You're excused from the exercises. Just stay out of the way."

Aia just sat readjusting her helmet. Lucius gave Magnus a pleading look. Receiving the message, he helped her up and whispered in her ear. She nodded, stood up straight, and marched back to the first medical wagon where she stood at attention pulling in her chin and buttocks. Taurinus turned back to his trainees and soon forgot faux Decimus.

"Tables, count your instruments!"

"Do what?" asked Petrus.

"When you scratch your head, do you get granite flakes under your fingernails?" barked Taurinus.

"What?"

"Never mind," scowled Taurinus. "Before the operation, the assistant must assure that all the equipment is available.   To make that job easy, I have created instrument sets for our most common operations. The Medics made a tablet with the names and numbers of each instrument in your kit.   Today, all of your instruments should be in the kit. After a battle when we are going luny operating day and night, instruments may get misplaced. You do not want to discover in the middle of a procedure that you are missing a crucial tool.   So, count your instruments now. Match it with your list. One should read the list, the other finds them in the kit and affirms the list."

After a moment he started bellowing again.

"What are you waiting for? Get going!"

The three groups rummaged in the kits and found the tablet. Lucius asked Magnus to call out the names and numbers of instruments. Aia watched with interest, trying to understand what they were doing.

"Amputation knife – one..."

Lucius pulled out the long blade that looked like something his brother should carry.

"Here," he called out.

"Scalpels, magnus and minimus –"

Lucius rummaged, finding the objects.

"Here."

"Tissue forceps, two –"

"Check."

"Tissue hooks, pronged, two –"

"Check."

"Tissue clamps, two –"

"Check."

"Bone hook, one –"

"Check."

"Bone saw, one –"

"Check."

"Bone rasp –"

"Check."

"Cautery, short, medium blunt –"

Lucius picked up the foreboding instrument.

"Check."

"Cautery, short, spatula type –"

While still holding the blunt cautery, he picked up the spatula.

"Check."

"Needles, short and long, two each –"

At first, Lucius could not find them.

"Umm,"

"Look for the piece of lamb's wool," Taurinus prompted.

Lucius found a piece of cloth and turned it over. Weaved in and out were the needles.

"Right," said Lucius. "Check."

"Forfex, one –"

"Check."

"Uh, sir..." came a call from table two. "We have an extra cautery, long, spatula type."

"What?" roared Taurinus. "These kits should be perfect!" He stomped over to Priscus and Modestus.

"If it were anyone else, I would not believe them. Since it is you two, I'll check." He rummaged around for a long while. Finally, he had to agree. He spun around to the medics holding the extra tool in his right hand.

"Who put this together?" The one who helped Aia stepped forward. "I did, sir." Without a moment's hesitation, Taurinus swung a mean backhand striking the young medic in the cheek with the tool leaving a nasty gash.

"Don't let it happen again!"

"Yes, sir!" he replied. He returned to his post next to Aia, blood pouring down his tunic."

Aia who had allowed her attention to drift during the instrument counting was startled. She had never seen a teacher treat a student that way before. At the same time, she felt lightheaded and dizzy. Everything began to spin, then all went black. She woke up with Lucius kneeling by her and Magnus and Taurinus standing behind him.

"She's–" Lucius caught himself. "Uh, *He's* all right," he declared. "*He's* a lot weaker than I thought." He offered her some vinegar water.

Aia sat up, thoroughly embarrassed. She took the wineskin and drank only a tiny amount, but pretended to take a large swig. She felt nauseated again.

"Take him into the wagon out of the sun," instructed Taurinus. "If we had more food supplies, I would prescribe liver for the blood and nutritive properties, but we don't, so give him the wineskin. Hurry so we can continue our exercises."

Lucius helped Aia into the wagon, removed the helmet and chain armor, and laid her on the floor. He tried to give her more water, but she stroked his cheek and smiled.

"No, I must go back," he said as he gestured over his shoulder. She shook her head and lay back inviting him to stay. He patted her shoulder and left quickly. She sighed, closed her eyes and tried to ignore her nausea.

Lucius assumed his position at table one as he brushed himself off.

"Okay, now that the distraction is over, it's time for the next step," Taurinus growled.

"Table one, your amputation patient is delivered to you, what do you do first?"

"I examine him?" Lucius proffered.

"By Jupiter, I already examined him and told you he needs an amputation!" Taurinus grumbled.

"Yes, sir. I know you did the primary examination at triage, but you will examine so many injured during the battle. Maybe you might miss another important injury that might require our attention before the operation."

"You want to do a secondary examination? You think I could miss a serious injury?"

"Yes, sir, I think it is important to check the patient's head, chest and back."

Everyone held their breath waiting for the old curmudgeon's response.

"Not a bad idea," admitted Taurinus, "but it must be quick. Let's call it a survey, not an examination like your Greek physician would do."

"Yes, sir!" Lucius said, relieved he was not run in on the spot.

"Okay," said Taurinus. "The secondary survey is fine, what's next?"

"Position him on the table with assistants," replied Magnus.

"Good, good!" Taurinus nodded his head approvingly. "What's next?"

"Define the level of amputation," Lucius said.

"The wound is a deep cut from the outside into the knee. You can see the inside of the joint. Bleeding is controlled by a tourniquet in the mid thigh. He cannot feel the outside of his foot and it is cold and blue."

"We must perform an above knee amputation," declared Magnus.

"Right again! What's next?"

"Cut the skin," said Lucius.

"Ha! I caught you!" Taurinus yelled. "Clean with vinegar first! You want a clean surface to cut! Magnus, what's next?"

"Cut with the amputation knife," Magnus declared.

"Right. Vigoratus, how is that done?"

Silence. Everyone looked at each other. Taurinus pointed at Lucius.

"You, Vigoratus. How is it done?"

"Me?" Lucius inquired.

"Yes, you!" Taurinus was smiling. "Yeah, I know they call you Fortunatus, the lucky one, behind my back, but I choose Vigoratus for you."

Lucius looked at the others.

Taurinus continued.

"You're the only one who has healed someone so far. I'm going to call you Vigoratus, unless you prefer Fortunatus."

Lucius was stunned and embarrassed.

"Taurinus still has not uncovered my deception," he thought. *"How much longer can it stay hidden?"*

"Don't disappoint me, now!" Taurinus spit at him. "What is the most important principle during this operation?"

"Cut each layer in turn using one motion, pull back the layer and cut the next as close to the previous layer as possible."

"Right!" Taurinus turned to the others. "Remember this point above all else. If you do, you will have an inverted cone to pack at the end. Healing works better with that type of amputation than any other method!" He turned to Magnus.

"How do you assist?"

"I pull back the layers and cover them with lint."

"Right! Vigoratus, what about the sinews?"

"Recognize the blood vessels first, ligate, then cut."

"Good! What's next?"

"Expose the bone and saw it off," replied Magnus.

"Anything special about the bone?"

"Rasp the raw edges until smooth," he added.

"Vigoratus, what's next?"

"Sir, cauterize any significant bleeding and dress the wound."

"Well done!" Taurinus turned his attention to Priscus and Modestus. Lucius and Magnus relaxed. They felt relieved that they passed the challenge. Lucius watched as Taurinus grilled and gaffed the others. He wanted to be entertained, but he knew he needed to learn the operations. He listened intently to the sequence of steps.

Taurinus had at least one point to ram home with each operation. He would look for his opportunity, then he would pounce. He slammed Priscus for not distracting the extremity before attempting to align the bone fragments. He skewered Atticus for not examining a prolapsed loop of small intestine in the abdominal gash, reminding him if the bowel was damaged or dead, the soldier would die within two days.

When everyone finished, Taurinus instructed the trainees to place the instruments back in the kits and ordered the medics to put them away. Then after a short break where he told another tall tale of surgical daring-do, he started the exercises again, mixing up teams and tasks. They practiced deep into the afternoon.

Aia woke to the staccato insults of the old surgeon. It was well past noon. She peered out to see the scene had not changed since the morning. No one paid her any attention. She climbed down dressed only in the military tunic and slipped over to the tree line to relieve herself. She took a moment to look around. The trees were lush and the ground was covered with flowers and herbs. It gave her an idea. She was a captive of the medical team. Maybe she could use her Druidic medical skills in some way. She might be able to enhance the Romans' surgical prowess. First, she would need to examine their medicines, then she would gather what they did not carry. She returned to the wagon and waited for an opportunity to present her plan to Lucius.

Chapter 23: Waiting

At dawn before breakfast, each legion assembled in formation. Legions VII through X sent out cavalry and scouts, then marched out. Legions XI and XII remained at attention. At length, Legion XI's commander rode to the front of the formation. He gave a nod. The Cornicen sounded the trumpet, then the Signifier shouted the order to the Centurions who in turn shouted at his men.

"Ad aciem, Fungor! – Form Battle Lines, Execute!"

The troops quickly rearranged and came to attention. Moments later came the next order.

"Laxate!"

Marcus and his cohort moved smartly to parade rest. The next order told them they were in for another speech from their commander.

"Noto! Animus Attentus!"

Marcus felt that Legion XI deserved to be called "veteran" since they had marched together across the Alps and into enemy territory. They had taken their first casualty, even if it was from a half dead barbarian. He stood tall and looked straight ahead toward the northwestern horizon. He was ready for the order to march down the throats of the enemy and bring glory to Rome.

"Today," called the Legatus in his best command voice as he walked his horse toward the left side of the line. "Today, we have our enemy at hand. Yesterday, our finest cavalry rode forth to harry them, but our enemy would not bend to our forces. Throughout the day and night, they continued to test our troops, but it is child's play to us. Today our troops are hot on the trail of the Helvetian hoard. Soon, at the order of our supreme commander, General Gaius Julius Caesar, we will engage the barbarian scum and annihilate them. That day may be today. That day may be tomorrow, but when it comes down, we will annihilate them."

The Legatus turned his horse around and slowly rode just in front of the troops toward the right flank.

"We have been designated Caesar's first reserves. We must be ready to commit on his order. We are on highest alert and we will stay field-ready until every last barbarian is off our lands. That is all. Hail Caesar!"

In unison, Legion XI snapped to attention and yelled, "Hail Caesar!"

Martial spun around looking at his charges.

"Hear that, you mules? I want you at tactical alert. That means no tents and no whining. Be ready to assemble and march out on a moment's notice. Check your armor, adjust your bindings, sharpen your swords, secure your pilum." He scanned the young troops with a scowl on his face.

"Dimitto!" he bellowed.

Marcus dropped his shoulders.

"Looks like we sit on the side again."

"Stop blubbering," said Cornelius. "We can't change our orders. Let's just do as we're told. Maybe if we do our job without comments, Martial will leave us alone."

"Yeah," everyone said in unison while they poked Marcus.

Realizing he was stirring up trouble again, Marcus trudged back in silence to their base area and helped strike their tent.

Once the tent group cleaned up camp, they sat in the area and began to polish their armor. It wasn't long before the silence was more than anyone could stand. Quintus finally cut the tension.

"Wonder who's the top gladiator in Roma this season."

"I'm not that interested," answered Fabius. "My Pater says, since the consular legions crushed Spartacus and his slave army, the games have not been the same."

"Don't you think the anti-corruption laws passed five years ago during Cicero's consulship had more to do with that than the killing of a few slaves?" asked Memmius.

"Well, the games certainly have not been as lavish as they once were, but that hasn't changed the technical aspects of a fight," retorted Quintus. "Besides, the games are almost back to the way they were."

Marcus was keen to stir the pot.

"What do you consider a good fight?" he asked.

"Any fight that pits a Thracian against a Samnite. They have the best armor and weapons. The Secutor and the Retarius just run around the arena until the Retarius falls or makes a mistake, then a couple of jabs from the Secutor and it's all over. On the other hand, the big guys circle one another looking for the right opening, then pounce. The close hand-to-hand combat takes skill and stamina to prevent getting gaffed. If one of them strikes a true hit with those swords, the ground is covered with blood."

"You know, I heard the winners get a pot of gold," said Appius.

"Yeah, and the losers eat dirt forever!" retorted Memmius.

"Well, it doesn't matter who fights, I always win," declared Quintus.

"And just how does that work?" asked Marcus.

"I simply play the odds," smiled Quintus.

"I know better than to play with you," said Marcus shaking his head.

"I'm always lucky," said Cornelius. "I'll take you on."

Quintus gave a wry smile.

"Give me a denarius, Marcus."

"Why am I always the one handing you money?" he whined.

"Because you're my best friend. Besides, I always pay you back in one way or another, don't I?"

"Yeah," Marcus said with a hint of disgust. He flipped him the coin.

"Okay, just so you don't think I am cheating, let's have Fabius flip for us, agreed?"

"Agreed!"

"Here are the rules," said Quintus. "Before each flip you get to call heads or tails, and your bet. I call the odds, agreed?"

"Agreed!" Cornelius said eager to fleece Quintus.

Quintus turned to his buddy.

"Marcus, you keep score."

"Heads for a denarius," called Cornelius.

"The odds are even either way," said Quintus. By now, everyone had stopped polishing and watched the game of chance. Fabius flipped. The coin came up heads.

"Ha, ha! I won!" exclaimed Cornelius.

"Okay, want to try for two-to-one that it's heads again?" prompted

Quintus?

"Yeah! Flip, Fabius."

Fabius flipped the denarius. It was heads again.

"Ha! I won again! How much is that?" Cornelius turned to Marcus who scribbled on the ground.

"That's three denarii for you, none for Quintus" said Marcus. Cornelius smiled.

"How about three-to-one it's heads again?" prompted Quintus.

"What do you mean?" Cornelius narrowed his eyes.

"You get three denarii if it's heads, I get one if it's tails."

"I can't pass that up," Cornelius said as he rubbed his hands together. "Flip," he told Fabius.

The coin flipped and bounced on the dusty ground ending up tails.

"Okay, what's the total now, Marcus?" They all looked at the scribe.

"Three for Cornelius, one for Quintus," he declared.

"Want to go three-to-one on heads one more time?" asked Quintus.

"Right. Flip," he said a little less confident.

The coin rolled to a stop on tails.

"Three Cornelius, two Quintus," Marcus intoned.

"I want three-to-one on tails," Cornelius demanded of Quintus.

"Sure, sure! That's fine with me," agreed Quintus.

Fabius flipped the coin high in the air. It bounced twice, rolled toward Cornelius, and toppled over heads.

"That's three for Quintus and three for Cornelius," declared Marcus.

Quintus looked at Cornelius.

"Want to double your bet?" he asked slyly.

Cornelius narrowed his eyes.

"Yeah. I say all my winnings on tails."

Fabius flipped. The coin landed. Everyone looked. It was heads.

"Wow!" exclaimed Marcus. "That's six for Quintus, nothing for Cornelius."

Cornelius jumped up and put his hand on his Spanish sword.

"How did you do that?"

Quintus held up his hands showing his palms.

"I did nothing. Fabius is flipping and Marcus is keeping score."

"All right, I want a new flipper!" Cornelius demanded. He looked around. Terentius, who never said a word, had gone back to shining his armor.

"Terentius, flip this coin."

He looked up from his armor.

"Me?"

"Yeah, you," Cornelius demanded. "Flip me heads, double or nothing."

Terentius obliged. He got up, took the coin from Fabius and flipped it high in the air. It bounced once then spun landing on tails. There was silence.

Quintus allowed the last flip to sink in, then put his arm around the dejected and stunned legionnaire.

"Listen, Cornelius, I am a reasonable guy. How about I forget the debt. I don't even care what the total amount is. I'll give you an opportunity to make it all back and more. I'll let you bet on the great Flamma and I will bet on whoever he is fighting against this season. When we get back and find out who won, we will settle up."

"Don't take that bet, Cornelius." Everyone looked toward the speaker. It was Martial. He walked up and stood arms on hips directly in front of Quintus.

"This scum knows Flamma, the old Secutor, was skewered in the spring. His comrade Delicatus buried him in Sicily before I left Roma."

Quintus stared into the fiery eyes of his Centurion.

"Oh, yeah, I forgot," he said apologetically never taking his eyes off Martial.

"Listen, Cornelius. I'll get you into my uncle's place in Roma or Ostia, no cover charge, free room and meals, and one hundred quadrans–"

Martial shook his head.

"No, I'm sorry, five hundred quadrans credit."

Martial nodded approvingly.

Quintus turned to Cornelius.

"Please accept this with my sincere apologies."

Cornelius looked at his Centurion who winked and nodded.

"All right, I accept your generous offer." He shook a finger at Quintus. "But we go to Ostia immediately after this campaign is over,"

"Sure, sure, friend," Quintus replied and patted him on the back looking at Martial who scowled.

"We go to Ostia first thing!"

Martial was finally satisfied. He whipped his leg with his vitis and addressed his weakest cohort.

"Now that the gambling is settled, get back to work. Everyone's armor looks like you smeared it with merda! Who taught you how to maintain your gear?"

"Uh, no one, sir," offered Marcus.

The Centurion spun around and glared, then softened.

"Spit."

"What?"

"You heard me. Spit."

Aulus looked up from his attempts at polishing.

"How does that work, sir?"

"It's wet. That helps get the scum off of the metal. There is something else in spit. I don't know what it is, but it helps to lift off the grime that gets into the metal. Also, it's gooey. That helps to shine it up. It still takes an afternoon of rubbing, but you will look like Legion Ten when you are done."

They looked at one another with clueless expressions.

"You mean you don't know?"

"No, sir," they all said.

"The Tenth is Caesar's first and finest. He raised the legion in Iberia. They are his most loyal and best trained. If you match them, you will do me proud."

"Thanks, Chief," said Marcus.

Martial got serious again.

"All right, you mules. Work until sundown, then get some rest. You never know when our turn will come." He marched away acknowledging no one.

The group worked as they were told. Within a short time, they saw results from the spit polishing, except they were all running out of spit. Each took a little extra water to replenish their saliva.

The next morning, Martial and the other Centurions had Legion XI in battle formation ahead of the other units. For the first time, they had a standard in front of them. It was on a separate pole capped with an eagle that stood next to, but slightly lower than the Roman standard. The flag underneath had a maroon XI emblazoned in large letters in the center and a staff horizontally across the middle with a trident at either end.

"Our Legatus chose Neptune as our protector," Martial whispered over his shoulder. "We are under his sign."

Marcus was filled with pride. They now had their own standard. When the order came to stand at attention, he gladly did so, but halfway through the morning, still at attention, they all began to fatigue.

Orders to march came at midday. They moved into a standard column and marched double time for ten miles. They crossed a small stream in formation and halted within one hundred feet of the stream. After reforming battle positions and standing at attention for half the evening, they were dismissed. The group went back to tending their gear. Some sharpened their swords and knives while others sweated over their tarnished armor.

"When are we going to attack?" Marcus moaned. "All we do is march around and wait."

"You sound like the troops under Marius at the battle of Aquae Sextiae," said Memmius.

Cornelius rolled his eyes. "What are you talking about?"

"While I was studying in Roma, I had an opportunity to read a manuscript written by Plutarch. He chronicled the feats of Gaius Marius, the great Consul of our fathers. Marius was elected Consul seven times, a feat not seen before or since. He was the great Consul who rewrote the military laws and allowed non-citizens like Appius to join." Memmius grabbed Appius' head and ruffled his hair. Appius threw ineffective punches back at him.

"Yeah, Marius finally tamed Cisalpine Gaul at that battle. The Cimbri were attacking one area and the Teutones and Ambrones moved south against Marius. He kept his forces behind the fortifications and waited for the right time to attack. The troops complained and bellyached that they were not allowed to fight. They insulted their commander saying that he must think they were girls, incapable and unworthy of fighting. Marius led them to believe that he was afraid of what Plutarch called the enemy's unsupported insolence. However, when the enemy finally tired of plundering the countryside and turned to head home, Marius divided his troops and ambushed the Cimbri, killing over one hundred thousand. They took so much booty, that the soldiers gave all the extra to Marius. So, don't question our general. He is a lot wiser than you."

Chagrinned, Marcus kept his mouth shut and sharpened his sword waiting for his turn to fight. His only consolation was that the pus and burning from his night of debauchery had finally vanished and he was urinating freely again.

*   *   *

That evening in the Medical section, Taurinus paced in circles. It had been three days since he and Publicus had a feast. He was jittery and talked to himself more than usual. Lucius noticed that the old man had a new tremor. Just before sundown, he summoned Lucius.

"Listen here, son. I am going to spend the night with Publicus, even if we don't have food for a feast. I miss his company and I don't think I can go another day without some of his delicious wine. You're in charge. Don't do anything crazy or stupid. I will be back at dawn."

He turned and scurried away leaving Lucius standing by the wagon. He turned to face the back doors of the wagon. Aia lay inside. He had not been able to get close to her in days under the stern gaze of the old curmudgeon. He wondered what she thought of him now. At least, he would be able to share his evening meal with her without Taurinus glowering at him.

Aia was suspicious when Lucius motioned for her to join him. He had ignored her completely since the argument with the old surgeon. She knew that he had other duties, but even when Taurinus was asleep, Lucius refused to acknowledge her. Now, he wanted her to sit next to him. He was quite animated in motioning with his hand and holding up his rations. She slowly inched her way toward him. He was saying something to her, but she still understood very little Latin. The only words she had picked up were *asine, stulte* and *merda.* The first two seemed to be some sort of greeting and the last described any kind of mess. The rest was still gibberish. Eventually, she got up and sat an arm's length away.

Lucius broke his hardtack in half and offered her a piece. She took it and nibbled watching him the entire time.

Lucius was disconcerted by Aia's cautiousness. Their meal reminded him of the first night when they met under the worst of circumstances. He tried smiling to show kindness, but he got only a chilly response. He resolved to have a talk with her through Magnus.

Aia still felt nauseated. She decided she did not like riding in Roman wagons. She felt every rut and rock they hit. She longed for the relatively comfortable ride of her family's wagon, but she knew that would never happen again. She accepted a portion of Lucius' bacon. She would take a small nibble followed by a bite of hardtack. Still, she refused the vinegary water.

When they finished, Lucius motioned for her to follow him out the back of the wagon. She emerged to the early evening. Lucius took her by the hand and led her to the center of the Medical section where the trainees were just finishing their meal. Lucius motioned to Magnus who waved. Lucius, began to feel quite agitated and motioned more forcefully until Magnus came to join them.

"What's up, Vigoratus?" Magnus said in a mocking tone.

"Magnus, I need your help again. *Decimus* seems to distrust me."

"I believe *he* should have reason to be distrustful," Magnus said with a wink.

"Yeah, I get it, but not being able to have a conversation makes this stressful. Can you tell *him* I want to help and I am not the enemy – well I am, but not really..." His voice trailed off.

"You're a piece of work, Lucius. You're the luckiest man in Caesar's Army and you act like you're the prisoner," Magnus laughed.

"Okay, I admit it, but you must agree this is a strange situation. Please have a talk with *him* and tell *him* what I said." Lucius grabbed Aia by the waist and pushed her toward Magnus. She took halting steps in the direction of Magnus offering considerable resistance against Lucius.

Magnus put his arm around Aia and they walked toward the stream. They were gone a long time. The sky turned black and the stars shone bright under a new moon. Lucius wondered what was taking so long. He began to pace the way Taurinus had earlier.

"Maybe this was all a terrible idea. Maybe Priscus was right. Maybe we should have turned her over to the Centurion. She might have been killed on the spot or released to the wilderness to be at the mercy of the Sequani, but at least I would not be dealing with this deception, which has only gotten more complicated

with each passing day."

While he was absorbed in his thoughts, Magnus and Aia approached him from the rear. Magnus tapped Lucius on the shoulder. He jumped and spun around to face Aia directly. She was as startled as he. They stood wide eyed, chest to chest with heads pulled back. Magnus laughed.

"You two make quite a pair."

"Did you tell her, I mean *him*? Does *he* understand?"

"Well, yes, but *his* response was not what I expected."

"How so?" Lucius turned to look at Magnus.

Magnus looked around first to make sure no one was near, then leaned close to Lucius.

"She wants to help us."

"She wants to do what?"

"Remember, she is a Druid. The Druids are the scholars of their people, and she was the tribe's High Priestess. She thinks we could use her skills."

"How could that be possible? We have the most modern medicine and surgery in the world. She's nothing but a lowly barbarian!" Lucius looked back at Aia who was watching Magnus plead her case.

"So you don't think you can learn anything from barbarians?" Magnus was turning red. His family had become Roman citizens, but his heritage certainly was not Roman.

Lucius stood in front of Aia but totally ignored her.

"No, it's not that," Lucius said. "First, she's a girl. Second, she shouldn't even be here. Third, we are in deep merda for creating and perpetrating this situation!"

"There was that word again," Aia thought to herself. *"I wonder what mess they are talking about now?"*

Magnus raised an eyebrow.

"What do you mean we? This was all your idea."

"Yeah. Well, the only reason it has worked so far is that you speak her language. I could not have done this without you."

The two men stood nose to nose breathing into each other's face for what seemed to Aia to be an eternity. Finally, Lucius took a deep breath and composed himself.

"How would this work?"

"The Druids use medicines, charms, and incantations to focus the healing powers of the earth," Magnus explained. He shrugged his shoulders. "How can that be bad?"

"I'm sure something bad will happen to us if we blow our story. Let me think."

Lucius paced up and down as he had done earlier. He could think of no good reason why it was bad, other than possibly getting caught and being crucified, but likewise, he could think of no evil coming from another form of medicine.

"If she is a High Priestess," Lucius reasoned, *"she must be well schooled in her arts. Maybe she knows things we don't. Maybe that could be the edge for us in healing these young soldiers."*

He turned and hurried back to the two who were now engaged in quiet conversation.

"Okay, what exactly does she want to do?" he asked Magnus.

"She says first, she must survey our medication supplies. She wants you to show her tonight.   Then, if we do not have what she needs, she will collect the materials to make her own medicines.   She says she can do that tomorrow while Taurinus whips us again.   Then, she will tag along with you since she is supposed to be your assistant.   She will apply what she thinks is appropriate after you perform your treatments."

Aia, who had been watching Magnus plead her case, now turned to Lucius with a supplicant look awaiting his response.

Lucius looked at her face shinning under the light of the Medical torches. She had not looked that enthusiastic before.   She exuded hope and faith in him.   He could almost feel his heart melting.   He tightened his lips.

"All right, yes.   As long as it doesn't hurt, maybe it will help."

Aia turned to Magnus to interpret the answer.   He nodded.   She clasped her hands and jumped up and down, then grabbed Lucius and planted a kiss on his lips.   Lucius was stunned, but tried to enjoy it.   She pulled away before he could reciprocate.

"We need to make a note for her to carry," Magnus was saying.   "She may be approached by guards or members of our medical team.   Since we weaved a story that she can't talk and no longer understands Latin, she needs something that tells others what she is doing and to leave her alone."

Lucius thought for a moment then brightened.

"How about, 'I am gathering herbs for Vigoratus.   Get away, you ass."

"That will work!" laughed Magnus.

They found a piece of parchment and wrote,

Pro Vigorati, chirurgus de Legio XI herbas lego.
Nunc, asine, apagete vah!

They showed it to Aia.   Magnus translated the words for her.   She giggled, then rolled up the parchment and waited for the next move.

Magnus bid them good night and Lucius led her to the medication chest. She surveyed the drawers, feeling and smelling the contents.   After she was satisfied, she nodded her head.   She was ready.   They went back to the wagon and climbed in. As they stood inside, Aia put her arms around Lucius' neck, gave him a tight hug, and tenderly kissed his cheek, then pushed him away.   She went back to her side of the wagon and settled in looking very content.

Lucius stood transfixed to the spot.

"At least she touches me again," he thought.   His loins were aching. *"Maybe we'll get back to the way we were before Taurinus began sleeping with us. Let's call it A.M. – Ante-Manius Fabricius Taurinus."*

A smirk crossed to his face.   He lay down hoping the two of them, with the help of Magnus, would be able to pull it off.

Chapter 24: On the Edge

Aia was up before sunrise. As usual, Lucius was asleep and Taurinus was still with Publicus. She managed to slip out of the wagon without waking Lucius. She relieved herself and splashed her face with water from the stream. When she returned, she put on her armor and woke him. At first he was grumpy, but after a kiss on the cheek, he was willing to get up. As he sat up, they were both startled by a knock at the door and a shout.

"Salve!"

They looked at one another, then opened the door. Standing in front of them was Taurinus holding up a legionnaire's sack.

"Decimus, look what I've got!"

Aia stared blankly at the pack, then at Lucius who shrugged. She looked back at Taurinus with a quizzical expression.

"It's your pack, you melon head!"

Lucius finally understood and quickly covered for her.

"Uh sir, remember. *He* seems to have forgotten nearly all of *his* Latin. I'll take it for *him*." He reached out and accepted the nearly empty sack from Taurinus.

Taurinus squinted at faux Decimus. Lucius's heart began to thump wildly.

"Have we been discovered?"

"That dressing looks filthy," complained Taurinus. "You may do passable work in practice sessions, Vigoratus, but you don't take care of your patients very well. Come down here and let me show you how to do it right."

"This is it," Lucius thought. *"We're headed to the cross."*

They got down from the wagon while Taurinus went to the front and rummaged in his personal medical chest. He came back with scissors and some fresh bandages. Meanwhile, Lucius grabbed Aia by the shoulders and turned her to look at him. He made hand signals for her to remain calm which she found curious and did not understand.

"Okay, let's cut this filth off," Taurinus said as he came at faux Decimus with scissors raised. Aia's eye got wide. Lucius, still holding her shoulders, turned her around to present her back to Taurinus.

"I think it is best to start in the back, sir," pleaded Lucius. "There is less damage there."

Taurinus munched his way through the bulky dressing throwing bits of gauze and lint on the ground. Finally, he cut through everything and started to remove the dressing. Aia winced and gave an involuntary raspy cry.

"This is stuck," declared Taurinus. "Get some water to loosen the dressing."

Lucius grabbed his wineskin and sprinted to the stream. He dipped the wineskin under water. His hands trembled with the slow pace of refilling the skin. He hoped Taurinus would not discover the truth while he was away. Finally, he could stand it no longer and sprinted back to see Taurinus standing directly in front of faux Decimus staring into *his* face.

"This boy is still pale and thin," he said as Lucius pulled up breathless with the water.

"Yes, sir. We have little food to supplement *his* diet," Lucius got out between gasps.

"Tell me about it!" replied Taurinus. "Publicus had no treats. Vinegar water and bacon was our dismal feast last night." He slowly poured the water on the dressing, tugging the edges until it broke free from the inflamed flesh of Aia's neck.

Taurinus inspected the red weeping wounds created by Lucius in his attempt to make the ruse seem believable. Aia's neck was inflamed from her jaw to her clavicles. The area from the front of her neck around the right nearly to her spine sported multiple ulcers, all weeping with small areas of bleeding and patches of slimy yellow scabs. Fortunately, there was minimal odor.

After inspecting the mess, Taurinus shook his head.

"What have you been using on this wound?" Lucius immediately knew he was in trouble.

"I used the plaster of–"

"You did what?" Taurinus was exasperated. "Have you forgotten your lessons on plasters? They are wet and irritating! Many are designed to eat away flesh, not heal it! Idiot! Scumbag! By Jupiter, sometimes you are such an ass!" Taurinus' insults trailed off as he shook his head.

Lucius felt the sting of the words. He had to accept the criticism, even though the mistake was intentional.

"Sorry, sir."

"You should tell Decimus you're sorry! He could have healed quicker if you had used the pastil of Polyides! Go compound it immediately!"

"Yes, sir!" Lucius called as he sprinted to the ingredient chest.

While Lucius worked feverishly to compound the pastil, Taurinus examined faux Decimus up and down.

Aia stood rigidly at attention as Taurinus inspected her. She was glad she had gotten up early. It had allowed her time to fully dress in the dead man's armor.

Taurinus ended his exam back on Aia's face. He narrowed his eyes as he examined her features. Aia knew he suspected something, but hoped he had not figured out she was a fake. Taurinus gave no clue in his stare.

Lucius returned with the plaster. Taurinus applied it in silence and placed a light dressing over it.

"There, that should heal in two or three days now." He turned to Lucius. "Don't be such an idiot again!"

"Yes, sir!"

"Eat fast. It's time for practice."

Taurinus kicked dirt on Lucius and left to prepare for another day of haranguing his trainees.

Lucius turned to Aia and gave her a weak smile. He helped her back into the wagon and offered her breakfast. She refused and pointed to the sack. Since she was impersonating the dead Decimus, she decided to collect her herbs and flowers in his sack. Lucius handed it to her. She immediately grabbed it and jumped out of the wagon leaving him to stew.

*   *   *

"Hey you mushrooms!" Martial's voice could be heard before he was seen. "We have an assignment. Ninth and tenth centuries, assemble!"

Marcus had slept in his armor like his mates. They were ready to move out at a moment's notice. He scrambled into position for a quick inspection. Martial inspected his troops, then stood in front of them.

"We are to accompany the quartermaster into town. Today is the day the natives promised to resupply us. This is an important assignment. Don't make me and Protus look bad! Ready, March!"

As they moved out, Quintus whispered to Marcus.

"At least we get to do something other than spit on our armor."

Marcus nodded his head, but kept quiet.

They approached the narrow road where the quartermaster's empty wagons waited.

The centuries formed up on either side of the wagon train and began a slow march into the center of the village. Since they were the closest legion to town, the trip was mercifully short. The sun was halfway up to its zenith when they arrived. A delegation of Aedui officials decked out in their ornaments of office were waiting there.

Publicus came to the front of the column. He was accompanied by a quartermaster's assistant who was fluent in Gaulish. Martial called out of the ranks Marcus, Quintus and Cornelius to be the honor guard. Protus joined them with an equal number of legionnaires from his century. The mini parade began with Publicus and the quartermaster's assistant flanked by the Centurions. The six legionnaires followed in two short columns.

The entourage marched up to the dignitaries. By now, there was a huge crowd of villagers gathered around the meeting. Marcus noted that there were no warriors among the them. Introductions in Latin and Gaulish were exchanged first, then the quartermaster's assistant read a short proclamation of cooperation and collaboration from Caesar – first in Latin, then in Gaulish. The mayor of the small town read a similar proclamation, then directly addressed the quartermaster's assistant who translated for Publicus.

Almost immediately, Marcus sensed it was not going well. He was too far away from the officials to hear the conversation, but the body language was wrong. Publicus had an expression of disbelief.   Questions were asked and answered. Publicus was not happy with the responses. Soon he was shouting and the Aedui were holding up their hands and pleading.

Publicus looked like he would annihilate the village by himself. Martial and Protus had to restrain him. He spat and shouted insults and gestured with his arms, then turned and bolted back toward the wagons. Marcus understood the gestures and cringed. He hoped the dignitaries did not understand Roman sign language.

Publicus was restrained by the Centurions who grabbed him and slowed him down so the contingent could reassemble around him. They tried to exit honorably. When they returned to camp, Marcus could not control himself.

"Chief, what was all that about?"

Usually, Martial would berate Marcus, then punish him, but he just gave a brief explanation.

"They refused to resupply us. They made some lame excuse that the crops were just being harvested and had not yet made it to the town. The quartermaster had to be restrained from making further trouble."

"We're getting very low on our rations, chief," Marcus commented.

"Yes," Martial agreed. "We've been told we are out of grain. After today, we only have four day's rations."

*   *   *

Aia did not know where to begin. The banks of the little stream were packed with every imaginable flower and herb she needed and more. She decided first to take generous amounts of bark from willow and birch trees. These pieces would be heavy and might crush the delicate flowers she wished to collect. She knelt down under a large birch tree and pulled out the dagger that had belonged to Decimus. She carefully whittled at the bark and removed several large pieces from the southern side of the tree. When she opened the sack to place her harvest at the bottom, something in the sack flashed in the sunlight.

She rummaged in the nearly empty sack and pulled out a necklace of leather with a solitary blue egg-shaped charm attached. Her heart began to race. It was a Druid serpent egg. She turned it over and over examining the deeply cut spiral lines on the dark blue crystal. It was similar to the green one she inherited from her grandmother. She had placed her heirloom on her dying father and left it with him as protection. Now, she had a replacement charm.

That charm was different from the ones she knew. All the ones in her tribe were cut from green stone that was abundant in the beautiful valley of her homeland. What a distant memory that was now. The charm she held was a blue crystal etched with more intricate designs than any she had ever seen. She assumed it was made by an artisan of a costal tribe. The blue represented the water of his homeland.

She clutched the charm to her bosom, closed her eyes, and said a silent prayer of thanks to Father Sky, Mother Earth, and to the dead man whose identity she stole. Maybe he was a distant cousin. She prayed that he was happy in the otherworld. She hoped someday to meet him and return the beautiful gift from beyond the grave. She slipped it over her head. The strap was a little long, but that made it easier to fit over the neck dressing. She allowed the stone's energy to course through her. Father Sky and Mother Earth would be there to protect her now.

Emboldened by her new strength, she began to collect in earnest. She needed the birch bark and leaves for an astringent. She found some lady's mantle that would work for the same purpose. She collected cowslip for its calming effect on fevers and general afflictions of the body. She collected marigolds for their effect on diseases of the skin, particularly the feet and toes. She found lungwort and comfrey root to use as emollients. She collected the leaves of the comfrey for fevers as well. She collected agrimony leaves to heal wounds. She thought, maybe she would slip some on her own wounds. She collected hawthorn and foxglove, both of which worked as a tonic for the heart. Hawthorn also could be used as a sedative. She collected borage flowers and cat's paw to make stimulants if they needed it.

She was about to stop when she noticed some ragwort. Although she knew none of the men in the Army would ever need it, she could use it to bring on menses. She thought she might be late, but had lost track of time. She picked some anyway. Underneath were several mature bonetă frigiană mushrooms. She had been taught to be very cautious in choosing them because some were poisonous. These looked like perfect specimens and she could not pass them up.

She carefully packed everything in the sack, which had a surprising amount of room. There was still a little room left in a side pocket, so she decided to collect more willow bark. She enjoyed the shade of the large weeping willow as she whittled away at the trunk.

"Salve!" she heard someone call from the road. She looked up. It was a group of young Aedui tribesmen who were returning to their homes after the debacle in the town. She looked in their direction as they approached. They waved at her. She raised her hand slightly hoping she would not have to speak. They talked among themselves and laughed pointing at her. She became self-conscious. She wondered if they were laughing at her or who she was pretending to be.

As they came closer along the road, she could hear the Gaulish banter. It was a dialect she did not fully understand, but she got the gist of the conversation.

"What a job! That fool gets sent to pick flowers while the other soldiers make war," said one.

"Some guys get all the fun jobs," said another.

"Hey, Iccauos, that was quite a line of bull crap the mayor laid on the Romans, no?"

"Yeah," he answered as they all laughed. "He is such a tool. Chief Ategnatos pulls his strings and he just opens and closes his mouth. The words that come out belong to Ategnatos."

"It was hilarious to see the surprise on their faces when he told them the grain is still delayed. All the while, it is stored at Bibracte. What fun it is to tweak their dicks." They all laughed again.

"It's amazing that the stupid Romans have not figured out that our spies know their every move before they make it," said the one called Iccauos. "We get the run of their camps and they run their mouths and spill all their secrets."

Aia sat widemouthed. These Aedui walked right by dropping their strategy, never dreaming she understood them. She waited until they were a safe distance away, then ran back to camp.

Before she rounded the Medical wagons she could hear Taurinus exploding at someone. She peered around the edge of the nearest wagon to see Taurinus in the face of Petrus. The others were milling around looking everywhere but at the scene. Magnus and Lucius stood together. She snuck up behind them and pulled on their tunics simultaneously. They both turned around to see Aia bent down using them as a shield from the others. She grabbed Magnus who bent a little. She strained up to his ear and whispered raspy words to him. He turned to Lucius with eyes of surprise.

"Lucius, your *little assistant* has some strange news. Cover for me while we go behind the wagon."

Lucius shrugged and looked away. The two scurried behind the nearest wagon, but returned quickly.

"We have some important information on supplies that needs to be reported to our command right away," Magnus whispered. "We can't send her because she doesn't speak Latin. Can you make up some excuse for me while I will run to the headquarters tent to deliver the message? I promise to be swift."

"It's the least I can do for you, brother." Lucius whispered back without hesitation, "You have saved my culus so many times."

Magnus sprinted away. Lucius looked at Aia. She to was still wide eyed. He wondered what was so important.

"Vigoratus!"

Lucius snapped to attention and pulled Aia close to him.

"Where in the name of Jupiter is Magnus?" Taurinus bellowed.

"Uh, sir," Lucius searched for an excuse. "He had an unstoppable urge to defecate," he said with a wince.

Taurinus screwed up his mouth and shook his head.

"Merda accidi!" "Shit happens!" He turned to face all the trainees.

"Here is another important lesson. There will be times when one or more of your assistants is incapacitated or unable to help. It may be for a few moments or it may be for days. You must continue with the help you have, no matter how good or bad. Injuries like the ones in the field require fast work. What is the most important quality of a surgeon?"

"Speed!" everyone answered in unison.

"Right!" exclaimed Taurinus throwing his right hand in the air, index finger pointed to the sky. He spun around and pointed to Lucius.

"Perform an amputation!" he commanded.

Lucius stood paralyzed, mouth agape.

"Move it, man!" Taurinus shouted. "Make Decimus your instrument assistant!" He came over, grabbed faux Decimus and physically moved *him* to Lucius' right side next to the instrument trays.

"Let's go! Your patient is bleeding to death!"

Lucius snapped to attention. He held out his right hand toward Aia, palm up and said,

"Scalpel!" Nothing happened. He turned to her. She looked at him with blank eyes and shrugged.

"See," said Taurinus teaching everyone. "This is what may happen." He looked at Lucius. "Find a way to make him understand."

Lucius thought a moment, then held out his right index finger making a cutting motion, then opened his palm and repeated his request.

"Scalpel!"

Aia looked at the array of instruments. Her eyes lit on the blades. She picked up the scalpel minimus and looked hopefully at Lucius.

Lucius realized he had to be more specific. He raised both hands and spread them apart then made the scalpel motion.

"Amputation knife!"

Aia put the small scalpel down. She spied the long knife, picked it up and looked back at Lucius who nodded his head. She advanced the blade toward him. Lucius jumped back.

"Here, boy," interrupted Taurinus. He grabbed the knife from *Decimus* and demonstrated passing the handle into the open palm of Lucius.

"Like this," he demonstrated again, then had *him* hand it to Lucius.

"Good!" Then to Lucius, "Keep going!"

Lucius turned and made an incision on his imaginary patient then put it down. He held out his palm and made his next request.

"Forceps!"

He turned to Aia who had the same blank expression as before. He thought for a moment. He turned his hand slightly so his thumb was up and made a pinching motion with his thumb and first two fingers.

"Forceps!"

He figured that might not be enough so he pointed in the direction of the forceps.

Aia surveyed the array and figured the forceps were appropriate because they could open and close. She handed them to Lucius with the points up. He looked at her. He turned the forceps over so the points were away from his thumb and closed his palm.

"Okay?"

Aia watched and nodded her head.

Lucius transferred the forceps to his left hand and picked up the knife again making imaginary cuts. Then he put both down. He wanted clamps. He had to think how to distinguish them from the forceps. He made the sign he created for the forceps and put the forceps in his hand as he said the name again. Then he put them down, turned his palm down and put his first two fingers together with his thumb, pointed to the table, and called for the instrument.

"Clamp!"

Aia looked next to the forceps and noticed something that looked like it could be what he wanted. She put her hand on the clamp and looked at Lucius. He nodded. She picked it up and held it by the points. She held it in front of his palm and looked for approval. He nodded. She placed it gently in his hand. He took it out with his left hand and slapped it into his palm then handed it back to Aia and held his palm out. She slapped it in his palm the way he had done.

"Excellent!" Lucius told her and asked for another one. He pretended to clamp a blood vessel. Now he needed a tie. He was clueless about how he would signal that to Aia. He pointed at the precut threads to the side of the table. He put his hand up by his shoulder and opened it.

"Ligo!"

Aia picked up a fist full of the threads.

"No, no, no! One thread!" Lucius gave the sign for one, then opened his palm again. Aia pulled one thread and dangled it.

Taurinus grabbed it and addressed faux Decimus.

"Like this."

He positioned her hand, then held both ends of the thread and firmly put the belly of the suture into her hand. Aia nodded that she had the idea. She duplicated the suture pass of Taurinus.

Lucius accepted it and pretended to tie one end of the vessel then asked for another. Aia obliged. He completed his imaginary knot. Now, he needed a scissors to cut. That one was easy. He made a cutting motion with his index and middle finger.

"Forfex!" he called.

Aia knew that sign and easily passed the scissors in the same manner as the clamps. Lucius made his cut. Now he needed to expose the bone. First he would need a hook. He put out his hand palm down and crooked his first two fingers.

"Hook!"

Aia got the message and handed him the double hook. He transferred it into his left hand and asked for the small knife by making a small sign with his thumb and forefinger then the cutting motion.

"Scalpel minimus!"

Aia was getting the hang of it. She picked up the knife she had tried to hand him the first time. Lucius made motions like he was exposing the bone.

Now, it was time to cut the bone. Lucius held his hand out with his fingers straight and his thumb up making a sawing motion.

"Bone saw!"

Aia handed him the ugly saw. Lucius took it and made his motions. Lastly, he needed a rasp. There was no way to explain that one, so he reached over and touched the rasp and called for it. Aia felt a little slighted that he did not even try to sign for the rasp. She picked it up and slapped it in Lucius' palm. He winced but got the message. He would work out a sign later.

Now they were done. Lucius called for dressings. Aia knew that word from her own neck dressings. She looked but the dressings were not out. She looked at Taurinus who ended the exercise.

"Well done, you two. I like those hand signals. I think I will use those the next time I have to train mushrooms." He laughed.

Magnus had returned toward the end of the exercise. He was impressed that Aia was able to take his place and keep up.

"How about it, Magnus. Did it all come out in the end?" Taurinus chuckled.

Magnus turned to Lucius.

"I told him you needed to take a crap."

Magnus smiled. "Nice cover."

"All right, that's it for today, gentlemen. Medics, clean up! The rest of you dismissed!"

Lucius grabbed Magnus.

"What was so important that you left us hanging?"

"Aia overheard the villagers talking. They have been hiding the grain in the town of Bibracte. Also, they have spies everywhere relaying our military plans to the enemy."

"Wow!" Lucius shook his head. "That's amazing!" He turned to Aia and patted her on the back.

"You are one of us now!"

Aia turned to Magnus who translated for her. She smirked. She knew her family would not have approved. She hoped they might understand, at least under these circumstances.

*   *   *

"Wake up you mushrooms!" Marcus rolled over directly into the foot of Martial. He looked around. It was still dark.

"What time is it chief?" he asked Martial.

"Time for you to get up, ass!" Martial kicked him in the stomach knocking the wind out of him. He got up holding his stomach waiting for his diaphragms to work again. He looked at Martial with anticipation.

"It's the beginning of the fourth watch. Legions Eleven and Twelve are to move out under the command of lieutenant Titus Labienus. It's like being led by Caesar himself! Now move!" Marcus stumbled toward his position slowly catching his breath.

Everyone fell into perfect ranks despite the blackness of the moonless night. They barely had time to dress the ranks before the order came to move out at double time. Marcus was grateful for the troops ahead of him. He only had to watch the heals of the legionnaire directly in front of him. They marched all day between hills reaching the base of a large hill as the sun was setting. Orders now were given in hushed voices. They camped in place until the fourth watch, reformed ranks, and ascended the hill.

By the time they reached the summit, dawn was breaking. Titus Labienus lined the legions in battle formation side by side. That put Legion XI to the right of

Legion XII. Since Marcus' cohort was on the left of his legion, they were in the middle of the formation nearly at the top of the summit. As the light of day illuminated the valley, they could see the entire camp of the Helvetian nation stretched out before them. They had heard estimates of a half million people in the migration. No one could fathom such a number. Now Marcus was able to gauge the size. The valley was a teeming sea of humanity.

Chapter 25: No More Waiting

Lucius woke to shouting outside his wagon. It seemed more frenetic than the usual morning hubbub. He opened the front doors. It was still dark. The military column was marching by at double time. He wondered why, after days of inactivity, the sudden rush before sunrise. He jumped down and stretched. The entire support train including the baggage, medical, and quartermaster wagons were still in place. A rotund figure was headed toward him. He recognized Taurinus.

"Salve, Vigoratus!" Taurinus called. "Our troops just moved out on new orders. We are to follow Legion Seven at sunrise. Prepare the wagons to move out."

Lucius jumped back into the wagon. He had to get Aia dressed before Taurinus got there. She was curled up sleeping quietly. Her military tunic was rolled up exposing her bottom. He quickly pulled it down and shook her. She just brushed him off and settled again. Frustrated he shook her shoulder and called in her ear. She woke abruptly and spun around shooting him the evil eye.

"Aia, wake up, get dressed quickly!" he said gesticulating wildly. Aia found Lucius comical and giggled. He lost control. He grabbed the armor and pushed it against her chest. She grunted and pulled it on, all the time letting him know by her expression that she disapproved of his methods. As she slipped on the sandals, Taurinus was climbing onto the front of the wagon. Then, she realized why Lucius was so animated.

Lucius and Aia climbed out of the back and walked toward the stream where they each quickly refreshed and returned to the wagon. Lucius pulled his pack out and they sat on the ground to share the morning meal. Aia felt hungry but the sight of the rations turned her stomach. She only nibbled on her portion. Lucius put away the leftovers and walked past the other medical wagons. Everyone had received the message and had secured their supplies.

After assuring that the medical team was prepared, he climbed back in the wagon and indicated to Taurinus that they were ready to travel. As the first rays of the morning sun illuminated the inside of their tiny space, the baggage train of Legion VII rolled past. They pulled in behind and were underway before the sun was completely up. The column moved slowly with six baggage trains. A few miles to the Northwest, they traveled past a line of small hills. They continued the slow pace into the afternoon, then stopped. The order came down to stay in place and to be ready to move at a moment's notice.

"I'm out of here," Taurinus called into the wagon at Lucius and the faux Decimus. "I'll be back when it's time to move out." He partially closed the doors and jumped down.

Aia immediately took off the armor. For some reason it really hurt her breasts, even though she wore it for less time than usual. She threw the armor down and sat in a heap brooding in the semidarkness. Here she was, amidst thousands of criminals who had killed her family and her countrymen. As far as she knew, she was the last survivor of her tribe. She had cooperated with the enemy. She felt like a traitor to her kin. Although it turned out well so far, she remained a prisoner. To resist now would be suicide. Maybe it was time to resign herself to becoming one of them, but was impossible. A woman could not be a Roman legionnaire. She sighed. She needed insight.

She opened the sack of herbs and flowers she had collected the day before. She reached in and pulled out a bonetă frigiană mushroom. Her father had reminded her during their herbal review that it was to be used only when the Druids needed clarity. Some warriors took it before battle to keep them focused, even though the practice was strictly forbidden. They could be severely disciplined for using such a sacred and dangerous ingredient. After a moment of hesitation, she nibbled at the edges of its cap. She felt nothing. She decided to eat the entire mushroom, then pulled out her wineskin and took a drink of the sour Roman water. She offered Lucius a mushroom. He took it and ate a small bite to be polite, then settled back. He found his eyes getting heavy. He took another bite and tried to hand the rest it to Aia, but she was already asleep. After another nibble, he was asleep as well.

Aia walked along the shore of a clear blue lake. She was holding hands with a young boy and girl. They were clearly Tigurini, but she had never seen them before. Both walked in silence at her side. The girl occasionally picked wild flowers while the boy collected flat stones and skipped them across the calm water. She followed one of the stones as it bounced along the surface of the lake. Not more than a kilometer out she saw a dew drenched island that shone like an emerald in the morning sunlight. They continued to walk toward a short pier. Tied at the end of the pier was a magnificent water craft. It was five meters long. The gunwale stood one meter above the waterline amidships and curved gently upward to more than two meters above the water fore and aft. It was painted a deep cerulean blue and was covered with Druidic symbols of protection. An eagle with its wings fully extended in flight sprung out of the bow of the vessel as if it were transformed from the wood itself. Standing at the rear was a single oarsman who bore a strong resemblance to her twin brother, Toutios. She and the children walked out on the pier to admire the craftsmanship. The oarsman gestured for Aia to board. She released the children's hands and took the hand of the oarsman. He guided her onto the craft and assisted her to a seat. Then he cast off and began to row away. She turned to look at the pier. The children still stood there. She begged the oarsman to return to the pier for the children, but he silently shook his head. When she looked back at the pier, the children were holding the hands of a handsome man dressed in the tunic of a Roman citizen. They enthusiastically waved good bye and blew kisses to her. As she watched them, the boat came about. The oarsman in the stern of the boat blocked her view of the pier and she turned to look toward the island. She could make out shapes of people waving to her from the emerald shore. As the vessel approached, she recognized their faces. She gasped as she realized they were her family. There was Oueni and Sina and her parents. Behind them was Lugurix in his shirt and leather pants.

She woke with a start in the arms of Lucius. Her eyes filled with joyful tears. She looked around. It was sometime in the middle of the night. She nuzzled into Lucius' chest and fell asleep again. Aia's motion awakened Lucius. Initially, he was a little groggy, and surprised to feel Aia in his arms. He squeezed her to his chest and laid back again. The squeeze woke Aia. She moved her right hand down his chest rubbing his belly. She allowed her hand to drift to the edge of his tunic. Grabbing the edge, she gradually lifted it grazing his inner thigh. Instantly his cock stood at attention. Aia passed her hand over his leg to his erect penis. She gently held it and pulled him toward her as she eased down on her back. He pulled up her tunic and was on top of her in an instant. They made love effortlessly. When Lucius finished, he noticed that Aia had passed out. He rolled off and lay beside her drifting off to sleep himself.

When Aia woke again, it was still dark. She looked to her left to see Lucius asleep next to her. His tunic was still up exposing his genitals. She gently passed her hand over his penis. As she caressed it, he became rigid again. She gently tugged on it. The throbbing in Lucius' groin awoke him. He rolled back on top of her and made love again then rolled back. They both passed out quickly.

Twice more, Aia massaged Lucius to attention and twice more they made love. The last time, they both fell asleep in the act. When Lucius felt himself disengage, he rolled off Aia. They both lay motionless until rays of light penetrated the wagon. Lucius woke with a start, pulled down his tunic and shook Aia awake. As she sat up, a ray of sunlight flashed in her eyes. She squinted trying to orient herself.

As consciousness crept in, she realized she was incredibly nauseated. She crawled to the rear of the wagon, opened the door and vomited out the back. She looked around. There was barely any activity, so she quickly hopped down, spotted a small stand of trees, and made her way there to relieve herself. She felt some burning in her bottom which cleared as she finished, but the nausea remained. She vomited twice more before she made her way back to the wagon and climbed in. After a while, she noticed her nausea had abated, but it was replaced by a throbbing global headache. She struggled to put on her armor.

She watched Lucius rapidly consume his breakfast and felt her nausea return. She reached in her bag and located a small piece of willow bark. She borrowed an acetabulum from the medicine chest and left the wagon. She obtained some hot water from the medics and dropped the willow into the water. By the time she returned, the tea was drinkable. She sipped the weak brew slowly sitting opposite Lucius. She remained silent trying to reconstruct the previous night. They both jumped when Taurinus knocked on the side of the wagon.

"We're moving out." He saluted the faux legionnaire who acknowledged it with an ever so slight movement of the head.

The wagon started with a jerk. Aia nearly spilled her brew. Lucius went up to join Taurinus on the front seat. Aia closed her eyes and put her head back against the wagon wall. They traveled for some time. The sun finally rose sufficiently so it was no longer shining through the wagon doors. That helped Aia, who was now beginning to feel as though she would survive. All of a sudden, she felt the wagon change directions, and slow down. Orientation changed inside. She sensed that they were climbing a hill. When she felt they were straight again, the wagon stopped. She peered out of the back door. They were with their legion again on the crest of a hill. Even though it was morning, she figured they were done traveling. She slumped back and fell asleep in full armor.

*   *   *

Legions XI and XII stood on the hill crest at parade rest watching the undulating mass of barbarians in the valley below. Marcus allowed his imagination to wonder.

"Why are we positioned here on top of the hill in the sun? Why are we not getting ready to attack? Standing here, we will just get hot, sweaty, and thirsty."

He wanted to break his solemn promise and ask Martial for relief, but he knew his Centurion would give them no break.

He watched the Helvetian camp. Out of the undulating mass, he could see the enemy warriors form loose lines and move out of camp to his left. He followed the line toward the East where his eye caught movement in the distance. He turned his head slightly to get a better view. He hoped Martial would not notice. It was the Roman cavalry riding to engage the enemy as the barbarian foot soldiers were organizing to march up the hill.

Soon, the whole spectacle was in front of him. The four veteran legions moved in from the left forming a battle line in front of them. Orders were shouted and the four legions attacked. Near the bottom of the hill, the barbarian warriors began to charge. On orders, the Roman front lines threw their spears repulsing the attack. Then, the first two lines of the infantry moved forward, advancing directly into the face of the enemy.

Marcus perceived yelling before he saw anything. It came from the left side of the barbarian camp. He turned his attention towards the tree line on his right between two small hills. He could see fierce warriors coming out of the woods. They were going to attack the legions' flank. As they approached, he saw no response from the legions ahead of him. *"Are these warriors going to crush the experienced legions?"* Marcus thought. *"Why aren't the legions preparing for a counter attack?"* His heart raced in anticipation.

Legions XI and XII were ordered to attention. Marcus stood ready to fight, but no further orders were issued for them. In front of him, he saw the commander ride toward the right yelling orders to the Hastatus Posterior of the four veteran legions. They broke ranks, reformed into battle lines, and engaged the enemy flankers. Battles raged on in front of Eleventh all day and well into the night. Although the Eleventh returned to parade rest, they were given no breaks and no relief.

As night wore on, the clang of sword against shield and sword against sword diminished until it became sporadic. A lone officer rode up to their Legatus and conferred briefly. The legatus turned to the troops and ordered them to attention. He rode up to the front line. Marcus waited with anticipation.

His commander looked at them.

"We control the field!" he shouted. "Victory is ours!"

A spontaneous cheer arose from the entire legion.

"The enemy has been driven from their camp and they are running away. They have left their wagons and supplies. In the morning, our job is to collect the spoils for Caesar. We will move out at dawn!"

Immediately, the order was given to stand down. They were allowed to sit and eat. Everyone was ravenous. They ate and lay down for a quick nap before sunrise and their first real assignment in the war.

       *   *   *

Lucius stood by the wagon with the other trainees next to Taurinus watching the battle. Before he left the wagon, he had tried to wake up Aia to witness the battle, but she just slapped at him and turned over. The spectacle was amazing. Seeing four legions cover the field was awesome. However, the flanking maneuver scared him. Taurinus assured him that Caesar was a great commander and the tide would turn in their favor. Although it took well into the night, the old surgeon was right.

As the battle raged on, Taurinus directed them to set up the medical tents and tables and to lay out all the instruments well before the sun went down. They placed barrels of vinegar and piles of dressings at each station. Before he left to see his friend Publicus, he warned Lucius that the battlefield would be a frightful sight in the morning. He encouraged all of them to get a good night's sleep. It might be days before they got another chance.

Before first light, Taurinus was pounding on the wagons waking up his team and getting them ready for the incoming disasters. Aia woke up with the noise. She felt better than she had expected. She got up, still dressed and climbed down. She slipped away to relieve herself. She was glad she took the opportunity after sleeping for nearly a day and a half. The burning sensation she had the day before was gone and her nausea was under control. She rejoined Lucius in the first medical station.

Soldiers were lining up for sick call. Taurinus deployed two medics to send away anyone who did not have a serious injury. Lucius watched countless soldiers line up only to be turned away. Taurinus retained a few of the soldiers with minor injuries to assist the medics in hauling the wounded off the field. Several legionnaires whose injuries were serious were directed to the front of the triage line.

As the rays of the morning sun lit the battlefield, Lucius' heart sank. It was littered with legionnaires and barbarians alike. Aia had missed the entire battle and was stunned to see the devastation. She saw the Helvetian camp. Tears filled her eyes for her dead brethren. Even though they were to blame for uprooting so many happy families, even though their camps were disgusting, even though they trespassed on Roman soil, they had met an undeserved fate.

*   *   *

At dawn, Legions XI and XII marched down the hill in battle formation. As they approached the area of the fiercest fighting, the bodies were too dense to march around. Legion XII was ordered to collect the dead from the battlefield. They were to bury the legionnaires and burn the barbarians. The barbarians left their dead warriors on the battlefield to be eaten by vultures. They believed that vultures would carry them directly up to the otherworld and glory. Burning their bodies was a desecration in the eyes of the Druids. It stomped on their spiritual traditions and denied the warriors the glory they sought from an honorable death in battle.

Legion XI was ordered to make a left turn and march around the dead to the far side of the enemy camp. The mild morning winds swept off the mountain and into the valley. Up to that point, they had been upwind of any odors. As they moved to the other side of the battlefield, the winds blew the smell of death at them. Marcus felt fortunate that he was furthest from the smell on the left side of the formation. They crossed the small stream that was the northern camp boundary and moved to the back side of the camp. There, the legion fanned out into a thin line. The three thousand legionnaires stretched across the extent of the camp. Each man was separated by one body length. Their first mission of the campaign was to go through the camp and kill any remaining barbarians.

Chapter 26: Graduation Day

"What an awesome sight," exclaimed Taurinus as he surveyed the battlefield. "I have not seen this many casualties in one place since the Sulla's battle at the Porta Collina." He turned to Lucius and faux Decimus.

"There will be more than enough injured soldiers to keep the medical staffs of all the legions busy for days. We will be inundated."

Lucius took stock of the forward team. It consisted of himself, Magnus, four medics, and Aia. The two rear teams were Priscus with Atticus and Petrus with Modestus. Each were assigned six medics. Taurinus positioned himself at the entrance to the medical area as he said he would. First, he screened the walking injured who managed to drag themselves up the hill in the darkness. He deemed most of the injuries serious enough for attention, but he sent them all to the rear teams.

Lucius wondered what sort of injuries they would see. He watched the medics on the battlefield approach the victims at the bottom of the hill near the stream. These soldiers fell early in the conflict, sometime in the afternoon before the battle was turned. Anyone in that group with a survivable injury would already have complications. The excessive delay before the initiation of treatment would make management of their injuries much tougher. The medics picked up two soldiers and lugged them back up the hill to Taurinus. After a brief exam, both were sent to team one. The medics deposited them on the tables and left to gather more wounded.

Lucius and Aia approached the first victim. He had an arrow sticking out of his abdomen. It had penetrated his armor. Aia felt her own armor. It was the same type as the soldier's armor. She realized it was not so protective.

Lucius broke the arrow near the armor. With Aia's assistance, he lifted the heavy chain mail off. The missile penetrated the abdomen near the left side. Stool was oozing out around the arrow. The soldier was lucid and showed no signs of delirium. He complained of pain around the injury site, but nothing else. Because he survived nearly a whole day without showing signs of illness elsewhere, Lucius assumed the injury was special. Maybe the body had walled off the bowel injury from the rest of the abdominal cavity.

They turned the patient and noted the point had partially penetrated the back. It must have been shot at very close range to penetrate so deeply. He motioned for the medics to hold the man while he pushed the arrow through. He dressed the wound and ordered him moved to a cot in the second hospital tent for the less critically injured to be reexamined the following day. Before he was transported, Aia laid a hand on the dressing. With her other hand, she touched the blue charm attached to the leather chain around her neck and silently said a prayer.

No harm nor mishap can befall you
No sprite shall slay you, no arrow shall kill you,
No fay nor dun water-nymph shall tear you.

Patient two was worse off. He had received a sword wound through his armor that ripped open his abdomen. He lay on the battlefield until the fighting line moved across the stream, then he tried to get up only to have his intestines gush out of the wound. His buddy rolled him back over and pushed the intestines back. He placed a field dressing soaked in stream water over the wound. Each time the soldier raised his head, a loop of bowel would squirt out, so his buddy wrapped the dressing around him. He lay on his back motionless during the raging battle until he passed out.

Lucius noted the legionnaire's lips and tongue were dry and cracked. His dressing was soaked with blood and serous fluid. The bleeding had long since stopped. He was semiconscious and talking nonsense. Periodically, he would call out to no one in particular. Each time he did, his dressing bulged. Without the bandage, his intestines would have escaped his abdomen. Magnus removed the dressing poured vinegar on the wound which caused the soldier to scream. That pushed out the intestines. Lucius tried to reinsert them without much success. The exposed bowel was swollen and dry with bits of grass and mud stuck to them. However, the sword had not penetrated the bowels.

With the help of wine fed to the soldier, they were able to control him. Lucius used more vinegar to wash off the debris while Magnus attempted to keep the intestines inside. As the patient was prepared, Lucius showed Aia how to thread the suture material onto the needles. Magnus used hooks to hold the edges of the wound straight up to make a sort of well for the intestines. Lucius sewed up the abdomen the way they had practiced on the sheep. A medic held up the soldier's hips and Lucius and Magnus wrapped a tight dressing around him like a girdle, then they moved him to a cot in the first hospital tent. When they turned around, two more soldiers replaced their initial patients.

The patient Magnus received was a very young soldier who had been felled by an axe. It caught him in the left knee and shattered his bones. They were sticking through the skin at odd angles. His ankle was frozen and he could neither feel nor move his foot. Below the knee, the extremity was cold and black with the toes pointed downward. Magnus showed it to Lucius. They both agreed the leg required amputation. Magnus instructed the medics to have the young man drink a large dose of poppy tea and whispered to Aia to prepare the instruments. She set them out the way she had seen when she was conscripted to work as Lucius' assistant.

While preparations were underway, Magnus performed the secondary survey. Meanwhile, Lucius examined the next man who was the victim of an axe to the helmet. The left side of the helmet was split and he was covered in blood. He was somnolent but arousable and could not hear out of his left ear. Lucius tried to remove the helmet, but it was stuck to the skull. He had to use warm water and vinegar to release the mangled leather and metal cap. Using scissors, he cut the hair and the helmet leaving only a small portion attached to the area of axe penetration. Throughout the ordeal, the patient barely complained. Gradually, Lucius was able to remove the remaining leather and metal. As he did, brisk bleeding started from the scalp edge just above and in front of the ear. Lucius held pressure for a while then released it, but bleeding began in one spot, then spread to the entire edge of the ruptured scalp. He again held pressure releasing only the bottom area of the wound. He noted a single large vessel which he clamped. That controlled most of the hemorrhage. He placed a dressing of vinegar and rose oil over the wound, wrapped the head, and went to assist Magnus.

The young soldier was now fully prepared for the amputation. Everyone was in position. Lucius stepped into the assistant's spot. Using the hand signals

Lucius had devised, Magnus asked Aia for the instruments.   Magnus worked at a
deliberate pace without wasting time.   Lucius held back each layer of the leg as
Magnus cut them. They identified the vessels before cutting into them and clamped
and ligated them swiftly.   They whisked through the above knee amputation
smoothly as though they had done hundreds together.   There was so little oozing
from the surfaces that they were able to place the dressing immediately after cutting
the bone and letting the amputated lower leg drop to the ground. As they finished
the dressing, Aia placed her hand on the soldier's thigh and said a silent prayer.

Nantosuelta went out
In the morning early,
With a pair of horses;
One broke his leg,
With much ado,
She put bone to bone,
She put flesh to flesh,
She put sinew to sinew,
She put vein to vein.
As she healed that,
May we heal this.

They all embraced across the table for a job well done, then allowed the
medics to clean up and transfer the patient to the second hospital tent.

The three of them moved back to the patient with the head wound. He
required no sedation and little immobilization from the medics. Aia assumed her
position at the instruments. Lucius assumed the surgeon's position with Magnus as
his assistant. They removed the temporary dressing and washed the wound with
vinegar. Lucius pulled back the flap of scalp to expose a depressed cruciate skull
fracture. He asked for a single pronged hook and winnowed it into a small space at
the center where a chip of the skull was missing. The first piece flipped out and fell
on the ground. A medic immediately picked it up and placed it in a basin of
vinegar. Lucius explored the other pieces noting that they were attached to the
underlying membrane. He needed a chisel and a flat retractor to protect the brain
and its membrane. He had no idea what hand signals to use so he looked at Magnus
who had never used medical terms in his native tongue. He took a deep breath as
he thought then turned to Aia.

"Fa uschè bain, gilb e placaid."

Aia screwed up her face and gave Magnus a strange look. He knew he
must have said something weird, but did not know what else to say, so he pointed
to the chisel and a narrow flat piece of metal. Aia raised her eyebrows and picked
them up. Her voice was weak and raspy.

"Cugn e plat." She handed them to him with authority.

"Taing." Magnus replied with a bow. He handed them to Lucius.

"I don't know what I said, but I hope it wasn't rude."

Lucius barely acknowledged Magnus as he concentrated on the exposed
brain. He had eaten brains of cows and sheep before. He had even harvested and
cleaned cow and sheep brains, but he had never seen the functioning brain with
blood flowing through vessels on the surface. He was surprised to see that the
brain was the same white color alive or dead. He whittled out the bone fragments
and washed the surface with vinegar. The patient moaned and his right leg shook.

He poked the brain a little higher up with his retractor. The patient's right arm moved violently. That was enough to make Lucius stop his curious experiment. He turned to Magnus and asked,

"How are we going to cover up this hole?"

The gap was the size of Magnus' fist. They both pondered the problem. The skull fragments could be placed on the brain again after they filed the sharp edges, but it would leave a large gap.

"What about part of the metal from the helmet?" suggested Magnus.

They picked up the mangled cap. A section of the center of the helmet where the pieces crossed could work. Using the chisel and mallet, Lucius fashioned a crude metal plate. He placed the bone fragments back after filing off the spiked edges and covered the area with the metal plate. He pulled the scalp flap over the area. It would be a tight fit, even if they sutured carefully. They both took a suture from Aia and sewed from the ends of the cut toward the middle. That advanced the scalp nicely and they tied their suture ends together, then they bandaged the soldier and sent him to the first hospital tent.

For the better part of the morning, both Lucius and Magnus sutured innumerable deep muscular lacerations in nearly all parts of the body. They felt like they were doing well and working smoothly until a new patient was placed in front of Lucius. The soldier lifted his tunic to reveal his penis. It had nearly been severed off. Lucius called Magnus over. The two looked at the injury. Aia peered over Lucius' shoulder to see the injury. She was immediately disgusted and looked away. After a prolonged examination and discussion with the owner of the damaged part, they decided to complete the amputation. It left the man with half an organ, but at least he still could urinate. Aia would not look or touch the amputated penis, but silently recited the prayer of the red wave.

Great wave, red wave,
Strength of sea, strength of ocean,
The nine wells of Acionna
Help on you to pour,
Put stop to your blood.
Put flood to your urine.

The next patient brought to Magnus seemed to have a simple injury. He had received a blow to the upper left arm, which fractured it. The ends of bone were overlapping. Magnus was able to position them, but each time he did so, the patient lost feeling and use of his hand. They decided it would be necessary to open the arm and explore the area of the fracture to see if they could prevent the problem. The medics laid out the bone instruments and Aia stood in front of the tray. The two surgeons explored the wound. They found the sinews intact and the muscles responding well. They distracted the ends of the bone as gently as they could. With that, the patient could move his hand. They held the bones in place and closed the wound. They never discovered the source of the temporary paralysis. With the medics holding the arm in place, they made an extra generous plaster dressing. While they worked, Aia said the fracture prayer again.

Feeling good about the last soldier's potential for successful healing, they turned to the next patient. They were surprised to see Taurinus sitting on the table. His eyes were wide and he could not speak. His color was purple. He was gasping for air, clutching his chest and spitting out foamy pink sputum.

"What's wrong, chief?" they asked in unison.

Taurinus just shook his head vigorously clutching first at Lucius, then at Magnus. Magnus tried to get Taurinus to lie down, but he refused continuing to clutch at anyone's clothing if they got too near. Lucius quickly examined him. His pulse was very weak and very fast. Lucius could not perceive heart sounds because of the bubbling in Taurinus' chest. Lucius could only think of dropsy and turned to the medics to order a massive dose of parnassus seeds mixed in the smallest amount of wine possible. A medic ran off to compound it.

"Pain," Taurinus blurted out. "Chest pain... Terrible..."

He gasped for air again. His color turned from purple to ashen, then grayish black. Lucius ordered quadruple strength poppy tea which he personally administered. Eventually, the pain seemed to ease. Lucius felt his mentor's pulse. It was still rapid and thready. Lucius looked around for assistance. He noticed Aia was missing. He wondered where she had gone.

"I can't believe she would choose this moment to escape. Maybe she just got hungry, or maybe she is relieving herself."

Before he could ask a medic her whereabouts, she reappeared with her herb filled sack and two acetabula. One acetabulum contained hot water, the other, wine. To the hot water, she added crushed willow bark. She plucked foxglove leaves from her sack, tore them into small bits, and added them to the wine. Aia handed Lucius the wine concoction encouraging him to give it to the old man. Lucius stood beside Taurinus and cajoled him into taking the elixir. Then, Aia removed the willow bark from the second acetabulum and gave it to Lucius. Even though it smelled awful, He got Taurinus to drink it. The medic who made the parnassus seed elixir finally returned. Lucius administered that as well.

For a while, Taurinus continued to spit pink foam. He was taking short breaths in and wheezing out long breaths. Then, he soiled himself. A great puddle of urine formed at his feet. His breathing eased a little, then he soiled himself again. He stopped making frothy sputum. His color turned from grayish black to purple. His breathing became more regular, although he continued to take short breaths in and exhale out three times as long. A medic got a pile of dressings to use as a pillow. Taurinus laid back and closed his eyes.

"That's better," he murmured.

Lucius ordered the medics to take him to a cot in the second hospital tent. As he turned back toward the working tables, Aia was in his way. She made motions that she wanted to join Taurinus and care for him. Lucius called Magnus over who spoke with Aia. He told Lucius that she felt her place was not with the injured soldiers at that moment. She knew how to bring back Taurinus' health and was willing to sit with him if she could have access to wine and the parnassus and poppy seeds. The decision was an easy one for Lucius. He agreed. Aia left for the tent. Lucius assumed the position of triage officer. He had to rearrange the teams. He moved Modestus to Team One and consolidated the second two teams.

The teams worked well into the night without a break. Lucius would occasionally survey the teams to be sure no one was overburdened. The stream of wounded finally abated after the start of the fourth watch. He headed back to check on Taurinus and his personal assistant. He found them to the right as he walked into the tent. Taurinus was on his back asleep with only a small pile of dressings behind his head. Aia was sitting in a chair facing him and away from the entrance with her sack of herbs at her side. Lucius came up beside Aia and put his hand on her shoulder. She turned to see him and gave a big smile. She gestured that

Taurinus was okay.

Lucius walked up beside Taurinus and reached down to feel his pulse. It was slow, but irregular. Taurinus woke up at the pressure on his wrist.

"Your assistant is good, Lucius," Taurinus said. "I don't know where he learned his medicine, but he is better than half the physicians in Rome."

"Take it easy, chief," Lucius said trying to calm him down. "You scared us half to death."

"Well, I scared myself nearly to death," he chuckled. Then he got serious. "Listen, this incident tells me I am no longer the man for this job."

Lucius tried to object.

"No, really. I see now that I am too ill to go galavanting around the world like I was twenty again. Life has a way of stopping you."

Lucius tried to be hopeful.

"I'm sure you will be fine again."

"This is serious responsibility and Caesar will not tolerate anyone who is less than great. My days at doing this job are numbered. It is time for you to take over."

"Please, you will recover," Lucius protested.

"No, I have made my decision. When the army moves on, I will remain behind with the Aedui. If I survive, I will be their physician. If not, they will bury me with Caesar's finest who lost the final battle on this mountain of death." He stopped for a moment and pondered what he had just said.

"That seems to be an appropriate name – Montis Mortis." Then he humphed. "I am sure they will bastardize the name into some Gaulish idiom."

Taurinus shifted his elbow to lift himself and looked skyward.

"I swear by Jupiter and all the gods that is my destiny now." Then, he lay back and turned to Lucius.

"I have one more lesson for you, son. We talked about being a leader of the team, but we never discussed what it means to be a leader in the Roman legions. You know about the daily report, but it goes beyond that. You need to represent two very distinct groups to the high command. You are not only a healer of patients, but also, you are protector of your team's welfare. You must ask Command for the supplies and tools necessary to do your job." Taurinus paused to catch his breath.

"You have no experience in the military, so you must take this from my experience. Supplies and tools are only a part of your resource. The most important resource is your team. Without a well trained team, the supplies are useless. Command doesn't care how you do your job as long as you do it well. So you must be sensitive to your team's needs. Do not push them to the limit without cause. Be sure they are well provided for and never feel that you are above them. You are a working stiff like the rest of them. Rank brings few privileges in the legion's medical corps."

Taurinus lay back exhausted. He took a moment to regain his breath.

"I'll give you advice as long as we are here in camp, then you will be on your own. There will be a meeting of the legion's chief surgeons in the morning. You must convince them that we are not ready to move on. Not just yet. From my own experience, we need at least two more days. Don't let them move out any sooner." He grabbed Lucius by the forearm. "This is your command now. Lead it well." He lay back and closed his eyes.

Aia looked at Lucius. Although she was grasping more Latin, she hoped he

would explain. He only looked at her, smiled, and squeezed her shoulders.
"Taing," he whispered to her and left for the triage tent.

Chapter 27: Revelations

The East end of the Helvetian camp looked normal, except there were no people. Pots filled with stew sat over smoldering embers. Wagons covered with curious symbols and spiky letters contained neatly folded linen and unmade beds. Oxen, still hitched to their wagons, munched what little grass remained at their hooves. Steady breezes whipped clothing still hanging on lines strung between wagons. Throughout the camp, silence was broken only by the occasional caw of a crow.

Legionnaires of the Eleventh banged on wagon doors and searched undercarriages. They crawled into the migration ships and tossed around contents as they searched for stragglers. Most searches came up empty. Occasionally, Marcus could hear scuffling near the center of the camp followed by silence. A fellow legionnaire would report that he had found and eliminated a barbarian threat. He and the members of the ninth cohort were so far out on the edge of camp, he figured they would be lucky if they found a live rat.

Marcus was frustrated. He joined the military to kill barbarians. He wanted to bring glory to his family name and avenge his brother's untimely death. So far, all he had done was incur the wrath of his Centurion, dig latrines, get dragged into schemes by a thug from a seamy port city, and contract a whopping case of morbus indecens trying to prove he was a man. Now, on his first real assignment, the cursed barbarians eluded him and their empty wagons tormented him. He kicked the wheels and slapped the oxen with the flat of his sword. After searching another empty wagon, he rocked it from side to side.

"Tip that wagon over, and I will have you whipped in front of the centuria," Martial bellowed.

"Chief, there's no one in this part of camp," Marcus whined.

"Keep looking until there are no more wagons to search," came the response.

He walked to the next one and kicked the nearest wheel. There was a scuffling noise inside. Marcus jumped back. He called out to Quintus.

"Hey, Quint, I think I have a live one!" He held his up his sword and shield at the ready, then circled around to the back of the wagon while Quintus quietly climbed onto the front side. Marcus slowly opened the back door. Two pairs of eyes blinked at him from the darkness. His heart pounded like thundering horses. He shouted to Quintus.

"Now!"

Both soldiers threw open the doors and jumped into the wagon. Two very frightened children no older than six clutched each other and cringed.

Marcus poked his head out of the door.

"Hey, chief," he yelled, "it's two kids – one boy and one girl."

"Well, take them out and kill them," Martial yelled back striding in their direction.

Marcus' jaw dropped.

"But, Chief, they're children."

"Our orders did not specify age, ass! Take them out and kill them!"

Marcus trembled. He wanted to kill warriors who fought against Rome. Where was the glory in killing children? He looked at his Centurion who stood next to the wagon.

"I can't, chief."

"What?" Martial bellowed. "Are you disobeying a direct order?"

Marcus hung his head.

"Yes, sir."

"Give me your sword and shield, you worthless scum!"

Marcus looked at his tormentor of the last two months.

"Are you serious?"

Martial narrowed his eyes.

"Dead serious! Now!"

He removed the shield from his left forearm and turned his sword around. He passed the handle to Martial who yanked the sword and shield away from the dejected youth.

"Quintus, kill him, then kill the kids."

"What?" squawked Quintus in total surprise.

"This scum won't carry out the orders of our General. He deserves to die with the filthy barbarian scum here and now."

Quintus climbed off the wagon and walked in a daze to face Marcus. He turned to Martial. The rest of the century had stopped searching and gathered around the spectacle.

"Do it!" commanded Martial.

Marcus, now defenseless felt like a cornered Retarius. He was an easy kill for an armed Secutor. He watched as Quintus raised his sword and swung. He hid behind his forearm expecting to lose his hand. The flat of the blade fell on his forearm armor without making a dent. He looked up at Quintus.

"Come on, brother, change your mind." Quintus begged raising his sword again.

"Never," replied Marcus wincing even before the next blow fell. He felt a thud on his head. Quintus hit him again with the flat of the blade.

"He could have easily split my skull open, but he spared me. Why?" Marcus was confused.

Quintus thrust his blade at Marcus' chest glancing off the side of his armor. The move brought the two into a clinch.

"Say yes and I'll help you," Quintus whispered in Marcus' ear.

Marcus pushed him away. Quintus brought the blade down on his left shoulder directly on the leather strap connecting front and back parts of the torso armor. Marcus felt a sharp pain shoot down his arm. He staggered back. Quintus took his opportunity. He jumped on Marcus knocking him down. They rolled over on the dusty dung covered ground by the oxen.

"Listen to me! I have a plan!" Quintus whispered.

"Screw your plan! I'd rather face fuck you!"

"Yeah? Well, you have to be alive to do that, mushroom!"

That made Marcus mad. He threw Quintus off, then jumped up and rushed his surprised buddy. They fell to the ground rolling toward the oxen of another wagon.

"Marcus, please say you'll kill the kids. I'll get us out of this!"

"Yeah, how?"

"I'll explain later." Quintus rolled off Marcus and quickly stood over him. He raised his sword and swung knocking Marcus' helmet to the ground where it bounced away from them. Marcus looked briefly at it and sprang up toward

Quintus, but he was ready for Marcus and pressed the point of his sword into the center of the chest armor. It dented the chain metal but did not penetrate.

"Say you'll kill the kids, or I run you through right now."

Marcus looked at the blade in his chest and looked at Quintus who winked with his left eye so Martial could not see. The two men stood in that position breathing hard and staring at one another. Finally Marcus nodded his head.

"I'll do it chief."

Everyone waited with bated breath for the decorated Centurion to say something. He let the two catch their breath, then called to Marcus.

"This is your last chance, ass. Next time, no mercy. You will be sent to the rear to be scourged and crucified!" He threw the shield at Marcus hitting him on his exposed head. Marcus stumbled toward the wagon, bounced off the nearest ox, and sat with a thud in a pile of dung. The ox did not even look up from his grass. Marcus pulled himself up, retrieved his helmet, and went back to kneel in front of Martial.

"I am truly sorry. I don't know what got into me. I have let my fellow legionnaires down. It will never happen again."

Martial handed Marcus his sword.

"It better not!"

Marcus took the sword. He was covered in dust and dung.

Martial turned to the rest of his team.

"Let's go. This ass has wasted enough of our time." He stood with his arms on his hips while the remainder of the century returned to the search. Marcus and Quintus climbed into the wagon to retrieve the children.

"Okay, mister chief of crimes, what is your plan?" Marcus asked Quintus.

"We each grab a child and throw them down on the ground. We make noise and rattle our swords. They will start to run away. We chase them past the edge of the camp and into the woods. On the far side of these trees, I saw some grazing sheep. We kill a lamb leaving the blood on our swords and return claiming we caught them in the woods and killed them."

"Not bad for a criminal," Marcus admitted.

"I've used this trick before when I got assigned to kill my best friend."

"Wow, you are a criminal!" commented Marcus.

"No, not really. It was just family business."

They rousted the kids out and threw them down a few yards from Martial, then they circled their captives.

"Death to the pagans!" they screamed.

The children did not understand, so Quintus raised his sword. The boy grabbed his sister's hand and they began to run.

Quintus and Marcus followed them acting like shepherds, goading and directing the children into the cover of the trees. The girl stumbled on a tree stump. Her brother could not get her to stand and they both crouched and covered their heads. Quintus and Marcus ran right past them yelling and screaming even louder. After they went past, the boy was able to get his sister up. They ran behind a large oak and hid.

Quintus and Marcus emerged on the other side of the woods and immediately fell silent. Quintus pointed out several sheep. Marcus circled around while Quintus approached a ewe with her lamb. He raised his sword and spooked the mother. She ran a few feet away leaving the vulnerable lamb. Marcus pounced and whacked the animal in the head. It fell to the ground. Before the surprised lamb could bleat, Quintus slashed its throat. They both got spattered with blood as the little animal squirmed its brief death dance. The young soldiers wiped their blades in the blood and headed back to the legion line. As they hurried through the forest, they ignored the trembling children who were hiding within easy striking distance.

When the boys emerged, they held their swords high for Martial to see.

"The deed is done, Chief!" Marcus called. Martial waved his Vitis in acknowledgement and gave orders for the camp sweep to continue.

Marcus and Quintus rejoined the line. To Marcus' relief, no one made any further discoveries that day. When they returned to base camp, Marcus was in no mood for the usual evening conversations. Instead, he skipped supper and lay down in his assigned spot where he passed out from exhaustion.

*   *   *

With the dawning of the day following the admission of all the major casualties, Lucius made a tour of Legion XI's medical area. He talked to each of the staff and got a count of the wounded. The two tents set up to house the seriously wounded were inadequate and were overflowing. They had an equal number of seriously wounded lying under the sky. Up to that point, the hospitalized patients all had potentially correctable injuries. No one had contracted a medical disease.

In all, he counted four hundred and seventy-nine, not including Taurinus. Of that number, two hundred and forty-two would be able to travel in another day and would be able to return to the ranks of their legion in under a week. The remaining two hundred and thirty-seven would require extended care. From the looks of some of the injuries, maybe as many as one-third of the worst would die during recovery and the others might never again be fit for duty. He went to Taurinus to get approval for his report.

"Why in Jupiter's name are you asking me? This is your unit now. You set the rules and you make the report."

"Sir, I don't even know where to go."

"We always meet at the headquarters of the Tenth legion. Since they are Caesar's most trusted unit, their surgeon is the de facto chief for this campaign. Some say he is Caesar's personal surgeon, but that is just a rumor. After the reports are coordinated, there will be a discussion of recommendations to the High Command. Then, everyone traipses over to the command tent. You probably won't see the General himself. Staff meetings are usually conducted by Titus Labienus, his most trusted lieutenant. He will decide what the plan will be. Then, you come back and execute it."

"Sounds simple," said Lucius.

"Sometimes, not so much, especially if you don't agree with the decision. Just remember, you are the most junior surgeon representing the greenest surgical staff. No one will respect your opinion. You must agree with the plan and carry it out exactly as you are told."

"Got it," said Lucius. It sounded exactly like what they had been doing for the last two months.

"Get going, son. Don't be late for your first meeting."

"Right, I'm going." As Lucius turned to leave, he gave Aia a pat and a squeeze on the shoulder.

Aia had spent the night with Taurinus tending to his every need. Although the old surgeon complained bitterly of hunger and thirst, she only allowed him to have one-third of his rations. She gave him alternating doses of willow bark tea, parnassus tea, and extract of foxglove throughout the night. Several times during the night, she had to assist him to the latrine where he emptied his bladder. Between trips, he mostly napped. Aia sat dutifully at his side until he awakened, then she gave him his next dose of appropriate medication.

After his careful, attentive treatment, Taurinus felt stronger. Now, he wanted to know more about his savior. He wondered how such a young man could know and use such strange and unfamiliar medications. He stared intently at faux Decimus. The soldier would not look directly at him, except for occasional glances to assess his condition.

The more Taurinus looked at his volunteer medic, the more he suspected something was not right. The armor and tunic fit oddly on *his* body. *His* features were soft and *his* skin still pale when it should have returned to a more healthy color. *His* neck dressing was gone and *he* was sporting excoriations over most of the neck. Yet, *his* neck seemed unusually long and slender with no lump in front like the other young men. *His* cheek bones were high and *he* had no beard. Taurinus had to confirm his suspicions. After Lucius left to give his report, he asked for help to get to the latrine again.

Aia assisted Taurinus out of bed and supported him on the journey away from the hospital. When they got to the latrine, Taurinus refused to stop. He pointed to a small stand of trees on the back side of the mountain. The pair moved into the trees and Taurinus let go a prolonged stream of dilute urine. Aia looked away while he concluded his business. When done, Taurinus turned to his helper.

"Take off your armor," he said gesticulating with his hands.

Aia immediately flushed. She knew what he was asking, but shrugged her shoulders and gave a weak smile pretending not to understand.

"You know what I am saying, soldier, take off your armor."

Aia had nowhere to run and no one to intercede for her. She was trapped. She was being forced to expose the truth she and Lucius had concealed for more than two weeks. She undid the straps of the chest plate and let it fall.

"Keep going. I want to see it all," demanded Taurinus.

Aia dawdled with the chain metal vest until Taurinus threatened to rip it off. She removed it allowing it to drop in a heap. Her breasts showed slightly through the underlying tunic, but Taurinus wanted full proof.

"Let's go, all of it." He made a motion like he was lifting the tunic off.

Blood rushed to Aia's face. She felt as though she would burn up. She turned away from Taurinus, and removed the tunic and looked down. She had not been out of the tunic since the ruse began. The early morning summer breeze blew on her exposed flesh and gave her goose bumps. Her breasts became firm and her nipples stood at attention. She shuddered, then closed her eyes, took a deep breath, and turned around to face her fate.

"I knew it!" boomed Taurinus. "How could I have been so blind?" He looked at the tall slender Tigurini woman who had pulled off the deception of a lifetime. He waved the back of his hand at her and turned around.

"Get dressed."

He muttered to himself while she quickly redressed. When she was decent, she tapped him on the back. He turned around and placed his hand on her shoulder.

"Take me back," he ordered.

Aia, still blushing, led Taurinus back in silence. She wondered what would happen now. Her fate was entirely in the hands of the fiery old curmudgeon. She imagined she would be crucified or maybe burned at the stake before nightfall. She tried to use her Druidic powers to read Taurinus' thoughts, but the old man just muttered to himself, alternately scoffing and chuckling.

*   *   *

Lucius entered the medical area of Legion X. He spied a tall asthenic man with silver hair at the temples moving from bed to bed giving orders to medics who scurried everywhere.

"He must be the chief surgeon," Lucius thought. He approached trying to look authoritative.

"Excuse me, are you the chief surgeon?"

"Who in Tartarus are you?" came back the answer.

"I'm Lucius Calidius of Legion eleven, sir. I am the chief surgeon."

The surgeon gave him a stern look up and down.

"You don't look like Taurinus!"

"Sorry, sir. He is gravely ill. He put me in charge."

The surgeon smiled broadly and extended his hand.

"So you're the one Taurinus has been calling Vigoratus. I'm Pontius Matius Gracilus, chief of this sorry outfit!" He turned to the medics around him as he growled the last words out. They scurried away to perform their duties.

"We've all been waiting for the old man to turn up his toes. What's ailing him?"

"He has a severe case of dropsy."

"Too bad it's not apoplexy! We would all be better off if his mouth was paralyzed," he chuckled.

Lucius had to smile himself.

"Welcome to the Tenth," Gracilus said proudly. "I'd take you on a tour, but it probably looks just like your unit right now, overrun with casualties."

"Yes, sir. We worked all night."

"Welcome to Caesar's legions, son. Let's go to my tent for this meeting."

The senior surgeon filled the entire walk to the tent with conversation.

"I hate these meetings. We know we are stretched to our limit. We know what we need. We tell the mules at headquarters, but they never listen. Someone has to convince them, but the process is boring and takes me away from doing what I enjoy. I love taking care of trauma victims. Stimulates my humors. Gets me out of my cot in the morning. I hope this war goes on for years. I could operate every hour of the day and night."

They arrived at the chief's tent.

"Ah, here we are. Looks like we're the first ones. Want a bite of breakfast? We have some honey from our medical supplies for the hardtack."

Lucius thanked him and received a two pieces of biscuit with sweet honey. The taste was divine. Other than cinnamon, it was his first luxury since that morning meal near the shores of Montalto di Castro.

One by one, the chief surgeons from the other four legions wandered in. Gracilus introduced Lucius to them by their cognomens.

"Gentlemen, Taurinus may be about to visit Pluto. Vigoratus is the new chief of the Eleventh. Vigoratus, meet Crispinus of the Seventh, Scipius of the

Eighth, Mauritius of the Ninth and Clodanus of the Twelfth."

They all greeted Lucius warmly. As they sat down, Gracilus leaned toward Lucius.

"Watch out for Clodanus," he whispered. "He was appointed by Taurinus to command the Twelfth. He is a real asshole!"

Lucius smiled. He hoped he would not have to interact with anyone else who had a personality like Taurinus.

"Okay, first order of business. How many seriously wounded do we have? Seventh?"

"Four hundred twenty-seven."

"Eighth?"

"Five hundred eleven."

"Ninth?"

"Four hundred ninety-one"

Gracilus looked at his medic who whispered in his ear.

"In the Tenth, we have five hundred twenty-three," Gracilus announced.

"Eleventh?"

"Four hundred seventy-nine."

"Twelfth?"

"Seven hundred sixty-four."

Every one looked at Clodanus.

"How many?" asked Gracilus again.

"Well, three hundred and ninety-seven, if we're just talking about the seriously wounded."

"That's all we are talking about, Clodanus," Gracilus said.

"Moron!" he added under his breath.

He turned to his medic.

"What is the total?"

"That's two thousand eight hundred and twenty-eight, sir."

"We will hear in this morning's report the body count of our dead. This was a costly battle." He paused for a minute to make a mental note to himself.

"Next, how many will not be able to return to fighting shape? Seventh?"

"One hundred ninety-four."

"Eighth?"

"One hundred sixty-three."

"Ninth?"

"One hundred eighty-eight."

Again, Gracilus turned to his medic for the number.

"We have one hundred sixty." His medic nodded in agreement.

"Eleventh?"

"Two hundred thirty-seven."

"Twelfth?"

"None."

"That's impossible!" shouted Gracilus.

"Okay, all of them."

"Come on, Clodanus, be realistic for once!"

Clodanus turned to have a discussion with his assistant while everyone glowered.

"We think one hundred forty-eight."

"Idiot," whispered Gracilus. He turned to his medic.

"How many is that?"

"That's one thousand and ninety, sir."

"That means how many can we promise to return to duty?"

"One thousand seven hundred and thirty-eight, sir"

"Okay, last order of business. How many days should we ask command to give us in camp to accomplish this?"

Clodanus stood up.

"We have accomplished our duty. We decisively defeated the barbarians. We should stay here until all are well, then return home." He sat down with a plop snapping his chair and falling to the ground. The assembled surgeons snorted with pleasure.

"I doubt that will happen with Caesar as our leader. Maybe with Marius or some other general, but not Caesar. So, other suggestions?"

Mauritius stood up.

"As you know, gentlemen, we have numerous fractures. The earliest ones heal in two weeks. The serious ones take six weeks. We know the High Command will not give us six weeks, but a good compromise would be three weeks. We in the Ninth feel we can get most of the fighting force back by then."

Lucius saw most surgeons nodding at the number. He wanted more time, but on the advice of Taurinus, he kept to himself.

"Thank you," said Gracilus. "Is everyone good with that?" Everyone nodded.

"If we can't get three weeks, what is the lowest we will accept?"

"Two weeks," volunteered Crispinus of the Seventh.

"All agreed?" Gracilus looked around. There were no objections.

"It's settled then. As for those soldiers who are not ready, Taurinus is hereby volunteered to run the rear hospital. Each legion, except for the Eleventh, which is already down a man, will donate one surgeon and two medics to remain with him. I will ask for one seasoned century to remain behind as guards. As soldiers get healthy, they can join the hospital guard. Any questions? No? All right, let's go to headquarters!"

They all got up and moved as a group to the top of the mountain and the High Command tents. They had to stand and wait as the meeting of Legatii ended. They were invited into the tent, but everyone stayed together at the entrance. The tent was as large as one of the hospital tents. Three long tables were arranged in a U with the open end facing the entrance. Gracilus strode into the center of the U with his aide.

"Salve, Lieutenant Labienus. We are here to present the Medical report."

The lieutenant leaned on his left arm.

"Salve, Gracilus. Proceed."

"All medical staffs received injured and worked through the night to repair the men. In total, there are two thousand eight hundred and twenty-eight men occupying the Army's hospital beds. Of that number, one thousand and ninety will not be able to fight again."

Labienus conferred with his adjutant.

"With the dead, that makes three thousand two hundred and sixty-two who are lost to us. Of those legions who fought, they have lost nearly a fifth of their strength. Of our total strength, including auxiliaries, that is around a tenth of our force. Of the remaining, how soon can we expect them back with their units?"

"We have one thousand seven hundred and thirty-eight who can be ready in three weeks."

"Three weeks? We don't have three weeks! What is the absolute best you can do?"

"Sir, anything less than three weeks may jeopardize many of the wounded."

"Not happening. Give me another suggestion."

"Sir, we feel we can get most back to you in two weeks."

"You have two days. I will entertain any reasonable plan for a rear hospital to get the rest healed. Do you have one?"

"Yes, sir. We do."

"Very well. Present it to the adjutant. Please convey many thanks from Caesar to all the legions' surgical staffs for their hard work."

"Thank you, sir!" Gracilus turned to the assembled surgeons.

"I have to stay to give the plans to the adjutant. The rest of you are more valuable back at your hospitals. See you tomorrow." He smiled broadly at Lucius.

"That's life in Caesar's Army." He gave him a pat on the back and moved around the U to see the adjutant.

Lucius headed back to his unit wondering what they could accomplish in just two days. He entered Legion XI's first medical tent and asked the medic to summon the surgeons. Once they all gathered, he told them the bad news.

"Gentlemen, we have been given an impossible task. Command is only giving us the rest of today and two more days in camp."

"Are they out of their minds?" asked Priscus.

"It's the way of the Roman Army," said Modestus. "Caesar waits for no one and expects an all out effort."

"Taurinus warned me it might be like this," continued Lucius. "We need to do the best we can. Let's move into the tents those patients we think we can make ready to fight. Once we have moved everyone, we still have hundreds of dressings to change. In two mornings, we need to strike our tents and move out. All remaining wounded will be moved up here to a new rear hospital. The other legions are sending immunes to assist Taurinus, who has been tapped to direct the new facility. I have been asked to tell the old man of his assignment. Once I do that, I will join you to complete rounds."

Everyone left, except Magnus, who had a grim expression on his face.

"Lucius, he knows."

"He knows what?"

Magnus opened his eyes wider.

"He *knows*."

Suddenly, it hit Lucius. He felt trapped and helpless.

"He does? How?"

"He, uh, checked. You know, under there."

Lucius felt the blood drain from his face.

"Am I a dead man?"

"I can't tell, but you need to talk to him immediately. He has been asking incessantly when you would be back."

"Thanks brother."

Lucius could feel his heart slow down and thump harder. Immediately he was nauseous and breathless. His hands and feet began to sweat profusely. As he walked to the second tent, his vision narrowed, blanking out his peripheral vision. All he could see was the entrance to the tent. His ears rung and his legs buzzed as he put one foot in front of another. When he reached the second tent, Taurinus was sitting on the edge of his cot. Aia stood next to him still dressed in the armor of the dead legionnaire.

"Salve, Lucius," Aia said in her raspy voice.

Taurinus looked at Lucius and raised his eyebrows.

Lucius looked back and forth between his mentor and his faux patient. He closed his eyes and bowed his head.

"Salve," he croaked.

Chapter 28: Resolution

At sunrise, legions XI and XII marched down the mountain. All the dead and wounded had been cleared away leaving assorted body parts lying on a mixture of blood and mud. Flies were everywhere. The entire hillside smelled of death. They continued past the gruesome scene into the Helvetian camp. If anything, the camp was even more desolate than the day before when Marcus nearly got himself killed. The sea of empty wagons stood like tombstones of the once proud nation, now utterly vanquished. The legions halted just before reaching the first wagons. Their Legatus rode to the front of the formation.

"Today, the Seventh and Eighth legions have the task of policing the battlefield, salvaging all the armor and weapons," he told them. "Our job is to round up all the usable wagons and oxen. They will be taken to the top of the mountain. Some will be used to collect supplies from Aedui's stores in Bibracte. Some will be used by our medical teams, who will be setting up the rear hospital. The remainder will be destroyed. Your task is to drive these wagons to the top of the hill. The quartermaster will inspect them and determine where they should go. Once you have deposited your wagon in the appropriate location, return and drive another one up the mountain until none are left. We must be finished by sundown. Move out!"

"Where do we start?" Marcus asked no one in particular.

"Take any one and move!" came the reply from Martial. "Command tells us each of you needs to drive ten or more wagons up the mountain. There is no time for discussion!"

"Yes, sir!" the entire century answered in unison.

Marcus moved straight ahead and climbed into the first available wagon. It stood out from the others because it was painted bright blue and was covered with symbols. There were spirals squares and complex circles. The spaces in between were filled with carvings of intertwined rope. The doors were closed. Marcus knew every wagon had been searched the day before and all living creatures had been destroyed. He did not bother to look inside. He hitched the oxen to the yoke and climbed on board. He had never driven a wagon of that size before. He found a whip and snapped it over the oxen. As they pulled and strained, the wagon began to move slowly. Regardless of how loud he yelled at the oxen or how hard he whipped them, they seemed to have only one speed – slow.

He joined the long line of wagons and made his way slowly up the mountain. Although he was near the front of the line, he had to stop every twenty feet or so while the quartermaster briefly inspected each wagon's contents to determine where it was to go. After more than an hour, he finally arrived at the inspection station. The quartermaster opened the back doors and whistled.

"This wagon is packed with strange paraphernalia and chests of fragrant herbs. Maybe the hospital can use some of this."

"Hey, soldier, take this to the hospital," he instructed Marcus.

Marcus whipped at the oxen. He realized now why his wagon went so slowly. It was packed full. His wagon was the first one chosen for the medical area, so he parked it next to the rear tent of his own legion, unhooked the yoke, and marched quickly down the hill hoping to find a lighter load to make up time. He still had nine wagons to go and the sun was already high in the sky.

       *   *   *

"You're good," said Taurinus.

Lucius looked up from his abject position of contrition feeling disoriented.

"Yes, you're good."

"What do you mean, sir?"

"You duped me. Not only did you dupe me, you duped the entire medical team. You even duped the dead soldier's Centurion."

"Yes, sir," Lucius answered not knowing where the conversation was going.

"But, you are still quite the criminal."

Lucius hung his head again.

"I should report you immediately. The two of you deserve to be crucified in front of the army and any pagan within one hundred miles of here!"

Lucius examined his toes.

"Yes, sir."

Taurinus watched the young surgeon's responses. He had gotten the reaction he wanted.

"I would report you, except I know I wouldn't be here if you had not pulled off this deception. First you deceive me into thinking you pulled off the miracle of miracles – saving a dead legionnaire with a fatal airway injury. Next, you keep this woman hidden among all these men for over two weeks. Then, when I nearly die, she is the one who saves me with strange and wondrous herbs. Oh, and I almost forgot. She finds out about the spies in our midst plotting against the Army and the grain they were hiding from us. Yes, we all are lucky you deceived me." He patted Aia on the back. She smiled at Lucius.

"How did you find out, sir?"

"Aia told her entire story while Magnus interpreted for us. I got to know this woman quite well in the brief time since I discovered this ruse. Frankly, she knows a lot more Latin than you two thought." He nudged Aia.

"Say something in Latin."

Aia turned to Lucius with a wry smile.

"Get fucked, you mentula!"

Lucius was stunned. Except for the raspy voice, she had the accent and inflection just right.

"She knows every insult I ever used and then some," Taurinus said.

While Taurinus was talking, Aia noticed Marcus parking the blue wagon next to the hospital tent and became excited. She poked Taurinus and pointed at the unusually colored wagon.

"What?" both men said in unison.

"La, la!" Aia said excitedly and started to run toward the wagon. Lucius helped Taurinus up and they followed some distance behind her. She threw open the doors and climbed in. By the time they arrived at the back door, Aia had a black cloak around her with the hood pulled up.

"Il è cairbhist di Draoidh!" she exclaimed.

She looked at them. They obviously did not understand the importance of the wagon, so she translated, "Wagon of the Druids!"

Slowly, in halting Latin, and a great deal of Gaulish, she described the Druids and her role in her tribe. She showed them the stores of medicinal herbs and the tools of her discipline. She tried to express how she could be an adjunct to the surgeons. As she spoke, Taurinus observed Lucius.

"Vigoratus has been smitten by this mysterious barbarian. He hangs on every word. Certainly, he has committed a serious transgression, yet he is still my best trainee. By far, he is the most intelligent and studied. His acumen as a physician is solid and he has gained in surgical skill every day. I have no one better to take over as chief."

Taurinus formulated a scheme to make Lucius the chief surgeon and spare his honor while at the same time allowing Aia to stay with him.

"We will do things this way," Taurinus told them. He called for a medic to bring Magnus to them.

"I want to be sure the Helvetian understands our plan."

With the help of Magnus, Taurinus laid out his scheme. From now on, Aia was to wear her cloak with the hood over her head until her hair grew out. She would be presented as a missed stowaway aboard the Druid wagon. He would order her to stay with the medical team so they could learn about the barbarians' beliefs and medical practices. She would be assigned personally to Lucius, the new chief, who would be responsible for briefing Command through Gracilus. He was to report immediately any significant medical information. Since Magnus could act as translator, they did not need any other assistance from Command.

"Lucius, I will write a letter for Gracilus, which is for his eyes only. You will deliver it to Gracilus when you make your morning report. Aia may stay with her wagon today. I know my medication routine, now. You and Magnus must return to work."

Aia immediately began an inventory of her supplies.

"Sir, what about Decimus?" asked Lucius. "How do we handle that?"

Taurinus pondered the dilemma for a moment, then concocted his own ruse.

"Let us just say he deserted yesterday while we were busy with the wounded."

"Do you think that will work?"

"No, but unless you come up with a better excuse, let's go with that."

Lucius and Magnus went back to the hospital. It was a beehive of activity. Medics were moving patients in and out of the tents as fast as they could. Magnus returned to help the other surgeons who were changing dressings on the most severely injured. Since they had less than two days to get the less seriously injured back to their units, Lucius decided they needed to concentrate on that group first. He pulled the staff together and they began their evaluations with the patients in the tents.

The medics had grouped the injuries and prepared the dressings for them. The first injuries they evaluated were the joint dislocations. Most of these were upper extremities. They instructed the soldier to swing the affected arm, then try to hold a sword or a shield. All but one legionnaire with an elbow dislocation was able to perform the tasks. They were immediately released back to their units.

Next were the lower extremity dislocations. These were more serious. They instructed the soldiers to attempt standing, then walking, then running. All but one of the patients with a hip dislocation were able to perform the maneuvers. They examined the one who could not. His dislocation had recurred. Modestus could feel the hip dislocated posteriorly. With the help of everyone, they relocated the hip quickly, but when the soldier tried to put weight on the leg, the hip dislocated again. They tried twice more, but the hip dislocated each time. He was transferred to the seriously injured group, probably never to serve Caesar again. At the end of that group, Lucius asked a medic how many they had seen.

"That was sixty-two, sir. We sent all but three back to their units. One stays here for reevaluation tomorrow and two were sent back to the rear."

"That means we still have one hundred eighty to evaluate," declared Lucius. "Let's forge ahead."

Next, they saw fifteen knee dislocations. None of these were stable. They all had significant pain. Some could stand. None could walk. One legionnaire who had a posterior knee dislocation could not feel his leg. They examined him in more detail. His knee had been relocated and was still in the plaster. However, his foot was grayish-blue and cold. He was in constant pain.

"This one will need an amputation," said Priscus.

They all examined the knee and leg separately and came to the same conclusion.

"Send him to the rear," said Lucius. "We will amputate that leg tomorrow. We need to keep moving."

"Wait," said Petrus. "I did not get the disposition on the others."

"None can return to their units," replied Lucius.

Next were thirty-one ankle severe sprains and dislocations. That group could not walk well and none could run. They were held for reevaluation in the morning.

"We're going to have a busy morning tomorrow," said Modestus. "How many are we holding now?"

"Forty-six," answered the medic.

"You are right," said Lucius. "We need to make more definitive decisions, otherwise we will be too burdened tomorrow." He turned to his five colleagues. "What do you think?"

"Send the dislocations back to the rear," said Modestus. "One more day will not be enough to heal them."

"Yes, but some of them will be good fighters in a few more days," countered Priscus.

Lucius shook his head.

"We don't have more time."

"Okay, keep only the sprains," said Magnus.

"Is everyone agreed?" asked Lucius of the group. There was silence, but no objections.

"Okay, keep the sprains. How many do we have?"

"Seven sprains, sir."

"So, we are down to eight for reevaluation tomorrow. Let's move on."

Most of the remaining were lacerations and head injuries. Nearly all the lacerations had developed a scab under the dressing. Two wounds had continued to bleed and had developed huge crusts. These required fomentation with warm water and vinegar to clean out the crusts. Once the crusts were removed, the bleeding was more brisk again. After holding firm pressure, they redressed the wounds with alum and lint to try to staunch the hemorrhage. Five had thin clear yellow sanies still oozing from under the scabs. The drainage was not foul smelling. The wounds were dressed in the same manner as the bleeding ones. Nine had foul smelling pus issuing from under the scab. They were cleaned and the sutures removed. The ones with pus and open wounds were sent to the rear and the remaining were left for reevaluation in the morning.

The head injuries were all serious, except for a few simple lacerations. Out of the forty-three head injuries, only ten were simple and would remain for reevaluation.

"Let's total up the patients."

The medic worked feverishly to get the numbers straight.

"Sir, we sent fifty-nine back to their units today. We sent ninety-nine patients to the rear hospital. We have one dislocation, seven sprains, sixty-six simple extremity lacerations, and ten scalp lacerations for a total of eighty-four for reevaluation tomorrow."

Lucius shook his head.

"We will need to begin work early. We will only have time to remove the dressings before I need to make the morning report. When I return, I will help you finish redressing everyone. Remember, tomorrow is day three of treatment, so all dressings need to be changed, including those in the rear tents."

Everyone groaned.

"I know, we will need to squeeze all that in before we move out. Hopefully, the donated surgeons from the other legions will be here to help." Lucius looked outside the tent.

"Gentlemen, it is late afternoon. Rest up. We will be up early tomorrow."

He watched his colleagues drift away. He thought how strange it was to have reached such a position of responsibility in less than three months. He decided to visit Taurinus and pick up the promised letter.

"He left, sir," one of the medics told Lucius after he had searched the hospital.

"Did he say where he was going?"

"No, sir."

"You talking about that fat old surgeon?" asked a nearby patient.

"Yes, did you see him?"

"Yeah, he got out of his cot, turned it over and went down the mountain toward the East. Oh, look, I think that's him coming back."

Lucius looked in the direction the legionnaire was pointing. There was Taurinus hobbling his way back up the mountain taking a break every five steps or so. Lucius grabbed a medic and they met Taurinus about one hundred feet from their hospital tent.

"Let us help you," they said when they reached him. He waved them off, but allowed them to grab him under the arm.

"I'm fine. Just a little winded."

"You're not recovered yet."

"I'm much better, thank you," he snorted. "Besides, I thought it would be a good idea to visit Gracilus in person to settle the details for the rear hospital."

They eased Taurinus back to the cot he had turned over. He waved away the medic and asked Lucius to stay. He looked around to see who was nearby before he talked.

"The details are worked out for the Druid. She can stay with the Eleventh. You can learn quite a few things about herbs from that priestess, my boy. She seems to have returned much of my strength." He threw down a handful of parnassus seeds and chased it with some water, then he turned to Lucius and ordered him to have a seat next to him.

Lucius sat next to the senior surgeon in the chair that Aia had used to keep vigil. Taurinus spent the evening hours telling his life story again and going over the lessons he had taught Lucius.

"Remember, my boy. Vide, Cura, Exige! See it, Treat it, Street it! The diagnosis is clear. The fixes are limited. Surgery is easy. These soldiers will be forever grateful. If they die after your treatment, it is due to their injuries, not your lack of skill. Anyone you save is a bonus for the legion."

"I don't feel very comfortable yet with fractures."

"You will, my boy. You will improve as you continue to see more cases. Repetition will help you in surgery more than in any other area of medicine. You will be fine. Also, learn what you can from that girl. She knows things even Hippocrates didn't. Without her help, I know I would not be alive."

"Yes, sir." Lucius already planned to spend as much time with her as he could.

"Now, I am going to spend possibly my last evening with Publicus," huffed the old surgeon as he stood up again.

Lucius stood as the old curmudgeon hobbled toward the quartermaster's wagon, then he ran to the bright blue wagon.

Aia was asleep on the floor of the wagon. She had found some women's clothing in the wagon. The dresses were a little snug around her hips, but fit better than the tunic she had to endure for the past several weeks. Lucius sat down beside her. As he did, Aia stirred and awakened. She smiled when she saw him.

"Salve," she said.

They spoke in hushed tones as though they were still hiding their great secret. Aia's voice was improving. Lucius told her he was sorry for scarring her neck, but it may have saved both of them. While he was apologizing, she kissed him.

"I am fine," she said in Latin.

Lucius kissed her passionately, then delivered his disappointing news.

"I must go to my wagon."

"Me, I go to wagon too," Aia said assertively.

"No, no! You must stay here," he protested.

"Why?"

"Because..." He had no good reason.

"Okay, we go to wagon," he said smiling. "Just be sure to wear your cloak."

On the way, he instructed one of the medics to assure that he and all the surgeons were awakened at the start of the fourth watch so they could begin their evaluations in time for morning report.

Lucius and Aia climbed into the first medical wagon, closed the doors, and made love. When they were finally spent, they shared the evening meal. When they were finished, they made love again. Afterwards, they fell asleep.

A knock announcing the start of the fourth watch brought them back to reality. They got up and walked back to the Druid wagon. Lucius asked Aia to stay there another day. She protested. Eventually, Lucius acquiesced and allowed her to come. She put her cloak on and pulled the hood tightly over her head.

Lucius and Aia joined the team, which had already begun working. Dressings were flying off all the wounds. Lucius introduced Aia as the priestess found the day before in the wagon. Taurinus had championed her cause and they would have her as part of their unit. She was to be allowed to observe and give prayers. She would not be allowed to use any medicines unless approved by Lucius.

They all paid respects, then went back to work. They evaluated each wound and made quick decisions. The dislocations and sprains were evaluated with standing, walking, and running. Aia placed a hand on each wound and each affected joint saying a short prayer. After completion of rounds, Lucius decided to release all the less injured, even if they were not completely healed. He instructed Aia to return to her wagon and he went to morning report.

Report was brief. Each chief surgeon gave his number of patients released back to duty. All units had done a similar job as the Eleventh. Between a third and a half of the less severely injured were returned to their legions. The total was six hundred and ninety-five returned to duty. The new population of the rear hospital was going to be two thousand one hundred and thirty-three. That meant they had returned to duty only one-fifth of the total. Of the total casualties numbering four thousand three hundred and five, half had died and half were not going to be fit for duty. Many of those still might die in the next few days.

Gracilus took the information and told the others to return to duty. He stopped on the way out to pat Lucius on the back.

"Remember, if you need advice, you can always come to me. Oh, and give me regular reports about that Druid priestess." He smiled and winked. "You truly are the lucky one."

Lucius slowly made his way back up the mountain. All that hard work and they only saved one-fifth of the soldiers. He knew how severe war injuries were. He expected as many as half of them would not survive. He figured three-fifths would die, one-fifth would be permanently maimed, and one-fifth would make it to fight another day. What he hated the most was not being there to see these seriously injured men through to the resolution of their injuries. He knew he served at the pleasure of Caesar and the goal was to move fast and win battles, not to stay and save every man.

"Was it always this way in war?" he thought. *"It is extremely frustrating, but it is my duty to patch up soldiers. I will do my duty while trying to learn from every soldier's injury. Maybe with my growing experience and Aia's help, I can change the odds."*

Chapter 29: Last Lesson

"New assignment!" yelled Martial as his charges rose at first light of day.

"Yesterday all of you had easy jobs. You plopped your culi on sellae and rode around in the Gauls' carri all day. Today, we get back to real work. Today, you will load those carri! We are going to empty the Bibracte storage facilities! About one thousand wagons were driven up there last night. Our job is to load them."

"More work and no fighting," complained Marcus.

"Even after what you saw in the last two days, you still want to fight?" asked Quintus.

"It's why I joined up," retorted Marcus.

"I'll take a day of loading supplies over a chance at getting killed." Quintus said shaking his head. Just about everyone nodded their approval.

"Hey, ever notice that sella is the same word for wagon seat and for toilet seat?" asked Appius.

"I think that's what the chief was getting at, dumb ass," replied Cornelius.

"Well, it may be a shitty job, but someone's got to do it," quipped Quintus getting a couple of sniggers.

"Just don't load a sack of merda," chuckled Memmius.

"Whatever they've got, we're taking," boomed Martial over the idle conversation. "The cursed Gauls had our grain all along, but were holding out. They had worked a deal with the Helvetians to hold out at all costs, but we get the last laugh. We beat the merda out of those barbarians! Now the Aedui are falling all over themselves to give us what we want, just as long as we don't slaughter them!"

"Any word on how many barbarians we killed, Chief?" asked Marcus.

"Command says we killed over one hundred thousand and only lost about five thousand," replied Martial. "For those of you who are weak in the head, that's twenty of them for one of us."

Everyone was impressed and started congratulating themselves.

"Silence, you gas bags!" admonished Martial. "We still lost five thousand of our finest troops. Have some respect for those who gave their lives. Next time, it will be you on the front lines."

That shut everyone up as the legion marched double time to the storage site.

       *   *   *

When Lucius arrived back at the hospital, the team was just finishing the last dressings on the less severely injured. They took a short break and headed to the larger group of severely injured. They had neglected them in favor of getting the few less injured patients back to duty. Dressings were at least three days old. All were in desperate need of changing.

Over three hundred and thirty awaited their ministrations. Medics had circulated through the patients while the surgeons were occupied with the soldiers who would be released to their units. One of medics approached Lucius and the other surgeons.

"Sir, we found some of the patients died since yesterday."

"How many?" asked Lucius, although he really did not want to know.

"Eighty-seven, sir."

Everyone was shocked.

"That's nothing."

They turned toward the owner of the voice. It was Taurinus hobbling back from the quartermaster area, which was now deserted. He had the Druid priestess in tow.

"What's with you people? You look like you saw a ghost! Well, I'm not a ghost. I'm still very much alive. You asses are leaving me with your mess to clean up, so I thought I'd better see it first hand. That way I can give each of you one last kick in the cula. Besides, the quartermaster left to get resupplied and I've got nothing better to do today."

They parted and allowed Taurinus to move through the group as he talked. He assumed the lead position as though he had never left. Lucius quietly and gladly acquiesced. Aia took her place behind Taurinus and next to Lucius.

"So how many live patients does that leave us, medic?"

"A little over two hundred and fifty, sir," he replied stiffly. Lucius noticed that the medic was more formal with Taurinus than he had been with him.

"Lost less than a third in a day and a half. Not bad, gentlemen, but there will still be much to do today. I have brought along the Druid priestess to observe. You have met her, yes?" He looked around as they acknowledged that they had.

"Then, let's begin!"

Taurinus led them around from cot to cot relating stories of similar wounds he had seen during his tours of duty. The medics would remove the dressings and he would inspect the wound commenting on the method of management and criticizing every stitch. After inspecting a long gash on the left arm of one soldier, Taurinus spun around to his coterie and stared at Petrus.

"Petrus, you sutured this one, am I right?"

"Yes, sir. I did," Petrus admitted.

"And how did I know that?"

Petrus looked at the wound and grimaced.

"The uneven edges, sir."

"Right, you moron! Every incision you close looks like this! You take too little of the wound edge on the first side, and you take too big a bite on the opposite side."

By that point, Petrus was hanging his head and the others were looking around at the sky, the ground, another patient, or at Aia. They were all hoping they would not be the next to incur the wrath of Taurinus. It was always comical for the onlookers, but humiliating for the receiver of the excoriating diatribe.

"Sir, his bones were set well and the wound is still clean. He should have full use of his arm once it heals," Petrus protested.

"While that may be true, this incision looks like a cliff – the Cliffs of Petrus!" Taurinus spat. "By Jupiter, you might as well have tattooed 'Petrus did this' on his arm. It is going to leave a nasty scar, when it eventually heals."

Taurinus turned to the wide eyed soldier and patted him on the shoulder.

"You will be fine, soldier," he told him. "Your surgeon may be an idiot, but the goddess Fortuna is smiling down on you. She tells me you will fight another day."

The legionnaire smiled weakly, thankful for the encouragement.

A few patients later, the medics removed a very loose dressing from an above-the-knee amputation. Inside was an undulating mass of small whitish yellow objects.

"Ah, maggots!" exclaimed Taurinus. "You won't see this often in your cushy medical practices back home."

Everyone peered in. Up close, they could make out individual yellow creatures about as long as the width of an index finger. They were randomly moving around, but stayed clumped in a mass in the deepest part of the wound.

"Gentlemen, these maggots are wonderful and terrible all at the same time. They grow from almost invisible, to half an inch in a matter of days. From the looks of these little ones, they have been in the wound for maybe two days. At this stage, they are great consumers of dead flesh and pus. They can clean a nasty wound in less than a day. Unfortunately, they have a tendency to go spelunking. If they get onto the ear, they burrow directly into the brain. If they do, the patient dies. Also, if you let them transform into the next phase, they start crawling all over the body and patients swoon."

Taurinus took a small stick and poked around in the gaping amputation hole. Medics had to hold the patient down and gag him so he would not scream.

"They are still this soldier's friends," he declared. "The bone looks as clean as it did when it was fresh cut, but we need to get them out of here now. Bring me some pounded white veratrum or hellebore mixed in vinegar. That usually kills them."

One of the medics ran off to make the concoction. Taurinus continued his pontifications.

"Some say these creatures come from flies. Some say they become flies. Others say both beliefs are true. Personally, I have no opinion. Wherever they come from or whatever they become, I am grateful for their presence in dirty wounds. They clean better than anything we can create. Then, after letting them do the dirty work for a day or two, it's time to get rid of the little buggers. Ah, here comes the magic concoction!" He took it from the medic and winked at Aia.

"Watch this!"

Everyone leaned in for a closer look, except Lucius. His memory of the erupting empyema was still imprinted on his brain. He held Aia back. She was annoyed because she wanted to observe everything, but she was willing to obey the man who seemed to have a knack for doing the right thing at the right time.

Taurinus ceremoniously decanted the yellowish liquid into the legionnaire's stump. Immediately, some of the little bodies exploded spewing juice onto the faces of Atticus and Priscus. Some of the maggots floated out of the wound. Some of the larger ones seemed to move like worms and crawled out of the wound scattering in all directions. They crawled up the legionnaire's leg and crossed the feet of the observers. Two of the younger medics turned away and vomited. Everyone pulled back, brushing their tunics and stomping their feet. Taurinus gave a great belly laugh.

"That was spectacular! None of you will ever forget my lessons!" He examined the wound. The maggots were gone and the wound was clean.

"Let's rinse this out with some plain vinegar and dress it."

The medics scurried to comply.

The entourage moved on to the head injury patients. The first patient was the one Lucius and Magnus repaired with the piece of helmet. He was asleep and difficult to arouse. Taurinus yelled at him. He slowly opened his eyes. It took a long time for him to focus on the old surgeon. When he did, he seemed to be surprised that someone was there.

"What's your name, soldier!" Taurinus yelled.

"Don't yell. I can hear you," he whined.

Taurinus cleared his throat and lowered his voice.

"What is your name?"

"What is my name?"

"Yes, what is your name," Taurinus persisted.

"My name... What did you ask me?"

"Your name! Your name! What is your name?" Taurinus raised his voice again.

"Don't yell. I can hear you," he whined again. After he spoke, he closed his eyes and fell asleep. Taurinus shook him.

"What is your name, boy! What... Oh, merda. Forget it." He turned to the gathering.

"He has lived three days with his injury, but it is hard to tell if he will survive or not. What was his exam like yesterday?"

No one spoke up.

"Did anyone see him yesterday?"

"No, sir," said Lucius. "We spent our time with the troops who would most likely return to their units."

Taurinus raised his eyebrows but kept his thoughts to himself. He removed the head bandage and examined the wound. It was crusted over with some blood, but looked intact and free of pus. He pushed at the edges of the wound. It did not cause the patient any significant pain. He felt the firmness under the scalp. He could not push it in against the brain tissue as he should have been able to do with skull fragments. He turned to Lucius again.

"How was this wound managed?"

"Sir, we opened and cleaned off the membrane over the brain. The scalp fragments were shattered and would not cover the brain so we used a piece of his broken helmet in place of the bone."

Taurinus listened and nodded his head.

"Very ingenious, Vigoratus. Unorthodox, but ingenious. Let's move on."

The next patient could not be aroused. When Taurinus shook him, the soldier pulled in his arms and groaned.

"This man will die. Move him to the back of the hospital area."

They went quickly through the remaining head injury patients. Most injuries were not very significant, but they required watching due to the nature of their wounds. Even if they had no complications, the soonest they could be released for duty was four weeks.

The next group were the fractures, the second largest type of injuries. Nearly every femur fracture required resetting because the dressings had loosened allowing the fracture to shift. The lower leg fractures were only a little better. Half of them required resetting. One had a cold gray foot.

"This man needs an amputation," declared Taurinus. "Set him up for surgery. It should be done immediately after we finish examining all the legionnaires." The medics took him away.

The next patient was the man with the knee dislocation whose lower leg was gray the day before. Now, he was in obvious pain. His foot was black and had the all too familiar death smell. Taurinus shook his head.

"This man needed an amputation yesterday." He put his hand on the legionnaire's shoulder.

"Son, we will do what we need to help you survive. Say your prayers to Aesculapius for a successful outcome."

Taurinus walked away shaking his head, but said no more.

The final group was the abdominal injuries. The first patient was dead.

"Get this man out of here," Taurinus ordered continuing to shake his head.

He moved to the next cot. It was the man who had his intestines hanging out for nearly a day. Lucius had repaired the abdominal wall. The soldier was in obvious pain and afraid to move. He was sweating and shaking. Taurinus placed his hand on the man's abdomen near the umbilicus. He jumped in pain. Taurinus shook his head and spoke into the soldier's ear.

"Son, soon you will visit Pluto."

The man grimaced and began to cry. Taurinus walked on to the next patient. Lucius whispered to one of the medics to bring the man strong poppy tea.

Mercifully, the remainder of the patients brought no more disappointments. Taurinus assigned Magnus and Priscus to perform the two amputations. He stopped Lucius from joining the operative teams.

"Let's talk. This may be the last time."

They were about to go when Aia grabbed Lucius.

"Is it okay if she comes along?" asked Lucius.

"Sure, bring her. I have one more lesson for you. She might as well hear it."

They walked through the remaining cots past the tents where the teams were gathering for the two amputations. They continued to the wagon line.

"Let's go into the Druid's wagon," suggested Taurinus. "The others will think I am making a visit to examine the barbarian's medicines and ritual paraphernalia."

They climbed in through the back of the wagon. Taurinus allowed Aia to enter first, then he pulled himself aboard. Lucius climbed in last. Taurinus motioned for him to close the doors. He now faced Lucius with Aia behind him.

"What were you thinking?"

"What do you mean?" Lucius was unclear how he had made an error.

"You did not examine the seriously wounded patients for over a day!"

Lucius thought for a moment. He did not feel he had done anything wrong.

"Sir, we were overwhelmed with injured legionnaires. We had a duty to return as many legionnaires as we could to their units. We concentrated–"

"Your duty is to all the legionnaires, not just the less injured ones!" Taurinus was smoking mad.

Lucius gave an incredulous look toward Aia.

"We worked hard for those men."

"You did not work hard enough. You cannot ignore your patients!"

Lucius tried to defend himself.

"I made a decision to spend all our time on the salvageable soldiers."

"You work twice as hard on them, but you do not ignore patients!"

"We had to get some rest. We had to–"

"Now I understand," Taurinus interrupted raising his eyebrows.

"Listen, son. You must learn the lessons of war. You watched the battle, right?"

"Yes, sir."

"The battle went all day and into the night, no?"

"Yes, sir."

"Why?"

"Because the battle was not finished, sir"

"What would have happened if Caesar decided to sleep instead of continuing to fight?"

"We would have lost, sir."

"Right! Soldiers have to fight on, even if they are tired. They have to fight to the end. Rest comes only when the battle is over."

"Yes, sir." Lucius bowed his head, but Taurinus was not done.

"Although they were born of the darkness and the night, Mors, the god of death and Miseria, the goddess of suffering do not sleep. They do not take a holiday. They do not take breaks. The horrific immortal siblings are forever watchful. They seek the smallest opportunity to jump in to the body. They prey on the weak and the damaged until they win." Taurinus got into Lucius' face.

"You let those legionnaires down!" Lucius bowed his head.

"Yes, sir."

"You must work all day and all night and through the next day and the next night and so on, and so on if you need to. You work on those men constantly until they are sent for care elsewhere, return to their unit, or die. You will have plenty of time to rest when it is over."

"I understand. I apologize." Lucius hoped Taurinus would relent, but he kept on.

"You can't get off that easy! Apologizing to me does not help! You need to apologize to the men who did not make it. You will never know if your negligence led to their death."

"Yes, sir."

"A physician tries to manage conditions beyond his control. He treats the symptoms and prays for a good outcome. A surgeon can cure a man by his intervention, but only if he is swift and persistently vigilant for problems or complications. Correction of a postoperative problem may mean the difference between not just a good result and a bad result, not just a functioning individual and an invalid, but a live human and a dead piece of meat!"

"Yes, sir."

Taurinus began poking Lucius in the chest.

"I put you in charge because you are the most intelligent and you have the most talent. It's up to you, the surgeon to create the best results, but in wartime, there are more patients than any one surgeon can handle. It requires a team of surgeons. You are the chief surgeon. You must lead them to the best results. If you slack, they will slack. If you accept less than the best, they will too. They take their signals from you. You must be strong. You must be fearless. You must be at your best all the time. You must be tireless. You must accept nothing less than a perfect result."

As he was harangued, Lucius finally began to understand the old curmudgeon. He understood his passion. He understood why he yelled at his trainees and why he became so upset at poor technique. It dawned on him what enormous confidence Taurinus had in him and how big the sandals were that he had to fill. He thought about the dedication of Theodosius. He realized that Theodosius often was powerless to alter the course of disease. His profession was to be there for the patient, to be the friend the patient never had, to be the comforter and the kind ear, to be the rock for the patient and his family. He thought that was an all consuming profession, but he knew the surgeon had a higher duty, one that was even more awesome. The surgeon controls with his hands the patient's fate. He must recognize the problem and correct it. Then, he must guide the patient back to health and fend off all assaults that might steal his health or his life. Now Lucius understood his responsibility, not just to his own patients, but to his fellow surgeons. He understood, and he was ready.

"I understand, sir. I will not let you down."

Aia watched the spectacle. Taurinus, the old dying surgeon, was the last of his breed. He was ominous yet perceptive, viscous yet instructive, irascible yet caring. She watched as he destroyed and rebuilt the man she admired, the man with such compassion, the man with great intelligence and skill, the man who provided her with hope in the face of the darkest times.

She observed Lucius as he went from surprised and incredulous, to depressed and disheartened, to calm and resolute. Although she only understood less than a third of what was said, she admired Taurinus for his ability to change a man. No one, not even her father or her dear Lugurix could have done such a masterful job. She admired Lucius, not only for his ability withstand the barrage, but also for his ability to absorb it and grow before her eyes. She became resolute in wanting to stay with the Roman surgeon, to share in his triumphs and to be there to console him in his failures.

When Taurinus finished, he was huffing and puffing. He reached into his pouch, pulled out a handful of parnassus seeds, and downed them with a large swig of water.

"I know they work better if they are brewed into a tea, but I need something now." He embraced Lucius.

"This is your time now. It's your turn to make the Republic great. Serve her well."

"Yes, sir. I will make you proud."

Taurinus hobbled out to spend his last evening with Publicus leaving Lucius and Aia alone. She gave Lucius a knowing hug. She stroked his hair and kissed him tenderly on the cheek. Lucius was stiff, but softened with her caress.

They stepped out of the wagon into the afternoon sun and walked through the tents. The amputations were completed and the patients moved out. Medics were striking the tents in preparation for moving out in the morning. All the able patients had returned to their units. They walked toward the sicker patients. The surgeons who were lent from the other legions had arrived during the "discussion" with Taurinus. They were busy ministering to the patients already. Lucius greeted each of them making sure they had what they needed and orienting them to the area. He talked briefly with his surgical group and made sure that everything was ready for breaking camp in the morning.

Their conversation was cut short by commotion on the mountain top. Legionnaires were cheering and running toward a train of Gaulish wagons escorted by a small contingent of Roman soldiers. The train made a wide turn and, like a parade, passed by the field hospital of the Eleventh. As the wagons drew close, Lucius and Aia could see they were driven by quartermasters' assistants. They were waving wildly at the ever growing crowd of legionnaires. The small contingent of the Eleventh guarding the flanks of the wagon train were easily overwhelmed. The wagons stopped as each was surrounded by swarms of cheering legionnaires.

From further down the hill came sounds of trumpeting Cornicens followed by shouted orders. Initially they were drowned out by the enthusiastic troops, but eventually the Signifiers made themselves heard.

"Attention! Attention!   Silence!   Return to your posts immediately!" Centurions circled around the outside of the mob, each using their vitis to strike at stragglers as they herded the crowd away from the wagons. The scene reminded Aia of her brother-in-law Frontú herding his sheep. The scene was comical and brought a smile to her face and a tear to her eye for her departed family.

Slowly, order was restored and the small beleaguered convoy guard reorganized. After a few shouted orders from the officers of the guard, the wagons broke up into six groups and headed toward their respective legions. Word spread through the hospital that the wagon train brought the promised, but delayed supplies from Bibracte. Everyone began to talk about what culinary delights might be in store that night.

Chapter 30: Celebration

"Dismissed," Martial yelled over the din of the receding mass of soldiers. Marcus collapsed on the spot.

"I don't know about the rest of you, but loading supplies in Bibracte wore me out. My arms are shaking, my legs feel like squid tentacles and my feet are numb," he complained.

"Then I guess you don't want to share the gift the quartermaster set aside for us," boomed Martial.

"I'm fine," piped up Quintus. "I could load supplies for another ten days."

"Me too," said Memmius. "I could do twenty."

"Same here," agreed Appius and Cornelius.

Marcus spat as he tried to catch his breath.

"All of you can just get whipped. You were complaining as much as I on the way back."

"I'm not saying I didn't complain," said Quintus, "but you are stupid enough to say it in front of the chief."

Everyone laughed.

"What say you?" asked Martial. "Should we let this stinking little gas bag share our treat?"

"What is it, chief?" asked Appius.

"No, no," admonished Martial. "You have to decide before I tell you,"

No one said a word.

"Come on, you melons," whined Marcus. "Give me a chance. I would if I were in your sandals."

More silence.

Finally, Cornelius spoke up. "Okay, chief. Let him share, but he has to go last after we have all we want."

"Yeah, let him go last," agreed Memmius. Everyone else grumbled in agreement.

Martial whipped his thigh with his vitis and spat.

"You're all catamites." He turned toward the quartermaster wagon.

"All right, bring it out!"

Three quartermaster's assistants hauled the gift out of the wagon and brought it over. Marcus immediately wished he could learn to keep his mouth shut. Two were carrying a boar roasted the day before by the Aedui and a third was rolling a barrel of wine. Everyone was salivating before they got their hands on the prize.

"Eat wisely, you asses. You have been eating only field rations for weeks. This is very rich." He carved a slice the size of his hand from the loin area. "This is more than enough."

The first four to scramble over to the carcass grabbed legs. Quintus carved the cheek meat off of the head. The rest attacked the loins and the buttocks. Marcus was left with what meat he could carve from the ribs. The meat was sweet and so tender it fell off the bone. He was grateful his buddies let him enjoy anything, but he was just as happy with the rib meat.

The quartermaster's assistants poured each man a small cup of wine. They toasted Caesar and his victory then drained their cups.

"By Jupiter, this wine is delicious," exclaimed Memmius. "It's far better than our vinegar water."

"Be careful," cautioned Martial. "This Gaulish wine has a great taste, but it packs a mean punch. You should dilute it even more than you do Roman wine. Remember, we move out in the morning."

No one heeded his warnings. They all ate roast boar and drank undiluted Gaulish wine until they passed out.

        *   *   *

As Lucius and Aia walked toward Legion XI's quartermaster wagons, they saw Taurinus calling to them and waving his hands.

"We have been invited to a formal dinner with the other medical units."

"A formal dinner?" asked Lucius.

"It's something new," explained Taurinus. "After this most auspicious victory, Caesar wanted to hold a special dinner to honor the valor of his officers and commanders, but we had no provisions. Now that we have all the stores from Bibracte, our general is holding his feast tonight. He has allowed the immunes to hold their own smaller version."

"Are we all invited?" asked Lucius.

"Only the surgeons," replied Taurinus. "It should be a formal affair, so if you have it, wear your striped tunic and toga."

"Sorry, my Pater did not pack that for me."

"Okay, then just wear a clean tunic."

"What about Aia?" Lucius asked.

Taurinus looked at the woman who saved his life. She stood next to Lucius costumed in her black hooded cloak.

"Of course!" he exclaimed. "She will be my special guest!"

After Lucius changed, they walked together at a slow pace so Taurinus could keep up. The ceremonial dinner was to be held in the empty Legion X hospital tent. Tables set in a U shape were already prepared. Medics acted as the servants. The base of the U was for the presiding officers and the honored guests. Gracilus as chief surgeon was the presiding officer. Taurinus and Aia took their place as honored guests on the right side of the head table. Crispinus, chief surgeon of the Seventh sat just to the left of Gracilus as the Under-Chief Surgeon. Also seated at the head table to the left were the other chief surgeons - Scipius of the Eighth, Mauritius of the Ninth and Clodanus of the Twelfth. As the most junior chief surgeon, Lucius sat at the far left end. The thirty-five junior surgeons took what places they could find.

The medics brought out the first course – a fragrant salad consisting of mint, cilantro, thyme, parsley and leeks mixed with oil and vinegar and sprinkled with cheese. As it was being passed, Gracilus stood causing everyone else to stand. He picked up his full wine goblet and held it high.

"Caesar has asked that we salute all who made our fateful war successful. I begin by proposing a toast to the Senate Consul Major, Lucius Calpurnius Piso Caesoninus."

"To the Consul Major!" everyone answered. They each emptied their goblet. Lucius noted the wine was quite tasty and uncut. The medics scurried to fill the goblets again.

"Now, I propose a toast to the Senate Consul Minor, Aulus Gabinius!"

"To the Consul Minor!" everyone said in unison followed by downing of the second goblet of wine. Aia drank the first toast and felt tipsy immediately. She decided to drink only a sip of wine for the next toasts and discretely pour the rest on the ground next to her.

They were about to sit when Crispinus held up his third goblet.

"I propose a toast to the Senate of this great Republic!"

Everyone saluted the senate and downed their third goblet, then they sat and devoured the salad. The plates were whisked away and replaced by platters of roast wild boar and lentils with coriander. As they were about to dig in, Gracilus stood again.

"I propose a toast to our great General Gaius Julius Caesar!"

"To General Caesar!" everyone shouted in unison draining their fourth goblet. Gracilus quickly got a refill and raised his goblet.

"I propose a toast to Titus Labienus, Caesar's lieutenant and right hand man!"

"To Labienus!" called everyone as they downed number five. Before they could sit, Crispinus waved his goblet.

"I propose a toast to our Legatii! The commanders of the battle!"

"To our Legatii!" The cheer was less in unison than before. Once the toast was completed, everyone sat quickly to dig in to the boar. Conversations broke out around the tables. Gracilus turned to Taurinus.

"Tell us about your guest here."

Aia pulled her hood down a little further over her face, but Taurinus beamed. He stood to introduce Aia to the assembled surgeons.

"This is Aia. She is the Druid High Priestess of the Tigurini clan."

Aia stood and bowed stiffly, then immediately sat down before anyone could get a good look at her. Taurinus continued.

"She was hiding in a chest inside the Druid's wagon when our troops commandeered the camp spoils and deposited her wagon at our hospital. I made her acquaintance and found out that she speaks some Latin. I do not know where she learned it, but she has agreed to share her knowledge if she can travel with our legion. Lucius has agreed to take her with him. She already taught me about the use of foxglove for the treatment of dropsy. She will be an important addition to our unit."

Even before he finished, the dinner participants went back to consuming food and drink.

Once the platters were empty, the medics cleared them and replaced them with bowls of crushed almonds, walnuts and pine nuts baked with eggs, milk and honey. While the dessert was being passed, Gracilus stood again.

"I propose a toast to Manius Fabricius Taurinus, chief surgeon of the Eleventh and now chief surgeon of the Caesar's rear legion hospital!"

Everyone stood slowly.

"To Taurinus!" They downed their goblets which were immediately refilled. Gracilus turned toward Aia.

"I propose a toast to the guest of Taurinus – the High Priestess of the Druids who will share her medical knowledge with us!"

"To the guest of Taurinus!" Many of the young surgeons craned their necks to get a glimpse of the lone woman in their midst, but all they could see was a shapeless hooded figure.

Gracilus already had his goblet filled and raised it again.

"I propose a toast to the Army Medical units!"

"To the Medical units!" everyone shouted enthusiastically and downed another goblet. They sat and enjoyed the warm nut dessert. While they ate, Crispinus stood and raised his goblet.

"I propose a toast to Gracilus, Caesar's Legion Medical Chief!"

Everyone stood and raised their goblets.

"To the Chief!" While they completed that toast, Gracilus was already beginning the next toast.

"I propose a toast to the chiefs of the legions' medical units!"

"To our Chiefs!" The junior surgeons all shouted. After downing their goblets, they cheered again and sat to finish dessert.

After the dessert plates were cleared, Gracilus, who now was quite unsteady, rose and raised his goblet.

"I propose a toast to our surgeons! Without your dedication we could not have done our job!"

All cheered loudly and downed their goblets.

Crispinus raised his refilled goblet.

"I propose a toast to our staff! Not only can they take care of patients, they are outstanding servers!"

Again everyone cheered and upended their goblets.

By now, everyone was woozy. Lucius felt emboldened and decided to offer a toast. He raised his goblet.

"I propose a toast to our patients dead and alive! We salute their bravery!"

Everyone stayed silent but raised their goblet and then downed it. Aia admired Lucius for the thought, but felt sorry that he brought the party's spirit down.

"We can't let the dining end on that toast," said Gracilus trying to save the moment. "I propose a toast to the Republic! May Roma remain strong and powerful forever!"

"To Roma!" everyone cheered suddenly feeling better. They upended their goblets.

At that point, the official dinner was over, but small groups of young surgeons continued to drink and toast everything and anything from the food and drink to the gods. Lucius lost track of the number of goblets he had consumed. People and objects were spinning before his eyes.

Taurinus felt himself getting short of breath and decided to have a few more goblets of wine hoping the medicinal properties would help him.

Aia, who had drunk the equivalent of only two goblets, collected her two men and pushed them in the direction of the hospital of the Eleventh legion. She herded her wayward sheep as they stumbled toward the tents. Taurinus had to stop several times to catch his breath. On the third stop, Lucius felt a revolt in his stomach and vomited. From then on, every time Taurinus stopped to catch his breath, Lucius vomited until he was bringing up nothing but green bile. His head buzzed and he could not keep objects from spinning. Aia stood back from her two charges until they were ready to travel again, then she poked them toward their goal.

Finally, they all arrived back at the hospital area. Taurinus was still short of breath, but Lucius was beginning to get a grip on his head. His stomach, which had roiled all the way back, was just making him nauseated. He put out his hands and propped himself against the wagon.

Taurinus knew he was at his limit. He did not feel that he was responding as well to the medicine regime. He needed to be bled, but he did not trust Lucius or his other charges that night. He was afraid their inebriation would impair their surgical skills. Through his wine fog, he remembered the leeches. He poked Lucius, which caused the young surgeon to vomit bile again.

"Lucius, what happened to those leeches we gathered? Do we still have them?"

Lucius tried to focus. He wiped his forehead, which was steaming hot and covered in freezing cold sweat. With the moisture on his hands, he stroked his neck to keep himself from vomiting again.

"If they are still alive," he panted trying to keep himself together, "they should be in the medicine chest."

"Don't just stand there, man. Get them! It may be the last thing you can do for me!"

Steadying himself on the wagon, Lucius pawed his way around to the back where the medicine chest was stored for travel. He carefully climbed the rear steps and hung on the doors trying to get the wagon to stop spinning. When it slowed down, he opened the doors and grabbed the railing. He crawled inside and placed his hands on the chest. After a few deep breaths, he was able to suppress his nausea. He opened the drawer and found the container. Clutching it to his chest, he reversed his trip slowly padding his way back to Taurinus. His deep breathing made his lips go numb. He changed to panting with better results. It decreased the pressure on his abdomen and his nausea became tolerable.

"Here is the container," he announced. He leaned against the wagon for support. Taurinus hobbled over with Aia at his side. Lucius opened the container. In the fading light, it was hard to see much inside the container. Lucius gently shook it. There was almost no motion. Taurinus stuck his finger into the blackness.

"It's full. I can't get my finger to the bottom." He pulled it out. Three leeches were already attached.

"They must have reproduced," he said examining the creatures.

Lucius reached in and allowed them to attach, then removed them and placed them on Taurinus' legs. He had never seen the old man's legs so swollen. They looked and felt like tree stumps. Lucius eventually placed nearly fifty black creatures over his lower legs.

"I don't feel a thing," Taurinus said looking at his legs. They all watched the little black worms slowly swell. Aia was fascinated. She had never seen animals like these before. She reached out and tentatively touched one. It did not move. She touched it again feeling the ridges down its back. She could see them increasing to two then three times their original size.

By that point, Taurinus was considerably more comfortable.

"I am breathing better already!" He took a deep breath without difficulty.

"Leave these creatures with me," he told Lucius. "You will have little use for them and they seem to like me." Then he became more serious.

"Well, son, we best make this our good bye. The legions will move out early in the morning. The commanders will be itching for more glory and they don't care about the fallen anymore. You have all my knowledge and all my teachings to guide you. Serve Caesar well and one day, you too will have a great surgical practice."

The old man embraced Lucius. Lucius hugged back, mainly to keep his balance as the wagons began to spin again.

Next, Taurinus embraced Aia.

"Thank you for saving my life." He jerked a thumb in Lucius' direction. "Watch out for this one. Keep him out of trouble."

Aia gave Taurinus a kiss on the cheek, then stood by Lucius to hold him up. They slowly walked toward the Druid's wagon leaving Taurinus to tend to his leeches. Aia helped Lucius into the Druid wagon. He plopped down feeling his nausea return. She had seen the Tigurini warriors get that way after returning from a successful fight or hunt. When Toutios was just a young warrior in training, he developed a violent hangover. Their mother had cured him with willow bark and chamomile tea. She had not collected any chamomile and suspected the Romans had none. Then, an idea came to her. The Druid wagon should have supplies. She rummaged through their collection of herbs and flowers and discovered some chamomile. She left Lucius, who was in no condition to move, and wandered around until she found medics boiling a pot of water to clean instruments. She borrowed two acetabula and made willow bark and chamomile tea. She brought the brews back to Lucius.

He was in the same position on the floor of the wagon where she left him. He was wiping his forehead with ice cold hands trying to make the fire in his brain go away. She gave him the willow tea first and watched him drink. It seemed to take him forever to finish. She added some mint to the chamomile and served that next. When he was done, she covered him with a blanket and let him sleep it off.

She worked her way to the back of the wagon and sat on the stairs. She was facing east. She could see the tiny waxing crescent moon rising in the last blush of twilight. All of a sudden, she realized that she could not remember when she had her last period. So much had happened to her, she had paid no attention to her own body. She concentrated for a moment. She reckoned two full moons and three new moons had passed since her last flow. That was better than two weeks before Beltane and her introduction to the joys of intimacy between a man and a woman. So much had happened to her since that wonderful night with Lugurix. She reasoned the stress had held back her flow.

She dug in her sack and found the ragwort she had picked. She took one of the acetabula and borrowed more boiling water from the medics. She dropped in the leaves and stems allowing them to steep as she walked slowly back to the wagon. There, she sat to sip her tea and watch the stars. When she was done, she felt quite warm and sleepy. She climbed into the wagon and made her bed far away from Lucius who was snoring loudly and drooling. She was asleep the moment she lay down.

*   *   *

Marcus wiped his mouth. It was the fourteenth time he vomited. Initially, he was on his hands and knees, but collapsed to his elbows and used his hands to support his head. The rest of the cohort was as bad or worse.

Only Quintus had managed to hold down his boar. He had built up some tolerance to wine during the time he worked for his uncle. He used a technique that was successful for him in the past. He continued drinking, but switched to diluted wine. It seemed to work except for his queazy stomach. His belches were foul and hot. Every fourth or fifth belch brought partially digested meat to his mouth. He swallowed as much as he could, but occasionally spit out the foul tasting mush.

Marcus saw the sky was getting lighter. Soon, it would be sunrise and they would hear Martial's bark to assemble. He wondered how far they would march. If everyone was like his cohort, it would not be far, but every step would be torture. He pulled himself to a standing position. His dizziness had passed, but the nausea came in rolling waves. He opened his pack and pulled out a hardtack biscuit. Between waves, he nibbled at the edges of his biscuit. He found that it made him feel a little better. He continued to nibble away until he had eaten it all. By then, the first rays of sunlight were breaking.

"Here it comes," he thought.

"Get up you filthy stinking heaps of manure!" Martial clanked into the century area trying to avoid the piles of vomitus.

"I told you to be moderate, but you didn't listen. Now you are going to pay!"

Everyone groaned and tried to stand. The puking continued, except for Quintus and Marcus, who was finally coming out the other side of the sickness. The two picked up their armor and helmets. After dressing, they were fragile, but ready to line up. The rest were still crawling.

"We don't have time for this!" shouted Martial. "If you are not up and ready now, I will have Marcus and Quintus whip your culi!"

That got the rest moving. They supported one another slipping through the slime. They dressed with difficulty and stumbled into line. Once they got there, they saw the rest of the legion was no better. Marcus passed the word that a biscuit seemed to help. While they waited for the other legions to muster, they nibbled at their biscuits and thanked Marcus as they stabilized.

All legions were ready by late morning. They moved down the hill and retraced their path toward their previous camp site.

Chapter 31: New Enemies

Aia woke first. To her surprise, she felt rested. Also, she was quite hungry. She quietly left of the wagon and slipped into the tree line to relieve herself. There was no sign of her period. The ragwort had not done its job. She would try again in the evening. She climbed back in the wagon and looked at Lucius. His hair was matted and his tunic filthy from the fallout of the evening's debauchery. She shook him.

Lucius woke with a start. He sat up ignoring Aia completely. His mouth was dry and his breath foul, even to him. He was dizzy, but at least everything had stopped spinning. His stomach rumbled and he felt a hint of hunger pangs, but twinges of nausea told him he should not tempt fate. He worked his way to the back of the wagon and eased himself to the ground. After relieving himself, he found the energy to go to the first wagon and change into a clean tunic. As he did so, he realized that he and Aia would be traveling in separate wagons. He decided to remedy the situation by asking Magnus to ride in the first medical wagon.

Taking slow deep breaths, he was able to gain some composure. He made his way to the second wagon. It was shuttered and locked from the inside. He banged on the door and listened. He heard stirring, then a groan. The shuffling and groaning got louder and closer. Suddenly, the back doors flung open and a stream of vomitus spewed from Priscus who shared the wagon with Magnus. When he was finished, he hung his head over the side and moaned. Magnus appeared shortly after with his hair tousled and his tunic torn. He squinted into the early morning sun and climbed down heading for the latrines.

Lucius waited patiently for Magnus to return. He straightened out his tunic and ran his fingers through his hair to look a little more like himself. When Magnus reappeared, Lucius tried to act cheery.

"Salve, Magnus. How do you feel?"

"I have had better days, but not too bad."

"You are not as bad as poor Priscus."

"I only drank a little of the wine last night. It was green. It's an old trick of the Gauls – keep the best and unload the rest. Just be glad we don't have to work today and our troops don't have to fight. How about you?"

"I regret that I drank far too much wine," Lucius replied. "At first, I was afraid I was going to die, but now I am afraid I might survive."

Magnus hrumpfed. Lucius cleared his throat.

"I want to ask you another favor."

"What now?"

"Would you drive the first wagon? I want to learn what I can from Aia. I believe traveling with her would help."

Magnus shook his head.

"I wasn't born yesterday, Fortunatus. You are sly, but not too subtile. I'll do it if Priscus recovers enough to drive our wagon."

They looked at Priscus. He was now sitting in the doorway holding his head. He looked green.

"Are you feeling any better?" asked Lucius.

"Every time I vomit I feel better for a while, then the nausea returns and I don't feel so well." He leaned out of the wagon and heaved, but nothing came out.

"I swear by all the gods I will never get drunk again."

"Until the next time," laughed Magnus. "Do you think you can drive the wagon today?"

"I think the fresh air will help. If I have to vomit, I can just lean over the side."

Before Magnus could say a word, Lucius grabbed his shoulder.

"Thank you again," he said and walked away supporting himself on the side of the wagon every few steps.

Lucius returned to the bright blue Druid wagon to find Aia already seated in the driver's seat. He climbed on and sat next to her. He began the conversation with an apology.

"Sorry about the dinner."

Aia readjusted herself, but said nothing.

"Did you give me something last night?"

She looked at him. Color had returned to his face but his eyes were still bloodshot.

"Yes, Màthair's teas for wine sickness."

"Thank you. I must have been very bad last night. I barely remember it."

"No again do," Aia admonished.

"You have my word. I will never get drunk again." He smiled weakly and took a deep breath.

"Soon we will be off to who knows where."

Aia did not acknowledge his last comment. They traveled in silence for the rest of the day. By the time they stopped for the night, Lucius felt more like himself.

Over the next few days, the pace of travel was slower with no enemy to pursue. The scenery was mostly flat with occasional rolling hills. Lucius taught Aia more Latin during the day. She caught on quite rapidly. Her vocabulary was larger than Lucius realized.

After a shared meal, Aia showed Lucius some of the herbs she collected and tried to explain their usage. Her Latin was improving, but it was not good enough to help him understand. He would nod his head studiously as though he understood, but he did not gain any real insight.

After two nights of fractured Latin, Lucius decided to restart his herbal education by asking Aia to show him the medicine for wine sickness. She pulled out the willow and chamomile. He recognized the willow bark.

"You gave this to Taurinus, right?"

"Yes, for pain."

"I see," Lucius nodded, "and the chamomile?"

"To calm." She put them away. "Very strong. You no need now." She pulled out the ragwort.

"What's that for?" he asked.

She clutched it to her bosom.

"For woman. No for man." She turned away. "Lesson over."

Lucius raised his hands.

"Okay, I understand."

Aia got up and left the wagon. She returned with an acetabulum of hot ragwort tea. She sat across from Lucius with her legs crossed and, without a word, slowly consumed the liquid. When she finished, she lay down and went to sleep. Lucius did not understand, but left her alone. He figured she was punishing him for his night of debauchery and his horrific hangover.

The next two days were repeats. Aia was always first to rise, fretting that her period would not start. Then, she would settle in for traveling. The days were filled with Latin lessons and the evenings with medicine lessons. First, Aia would show Lucius a Druidic herb and describe its use and preparation, then Lucius would do the same with the Roman herbs.

Occasionally, they found that they used some herb for the same purpose. They discovered that parsley was for digestion. Lucius explained that Romans also used it for their breath. The discussion reminded him of the cinnamon. He hesitated for a moment, then decided to share some with Aia.

She was fascinated as he produced from his sack two sticks of the spice. She accepted a piece and rubbed her fingers over the rough surface. She sniffed the bark, then licked it. It was too bitter for her. She showed her displeasure and returned it to Lucius.

He had to coax her into trying a piece. He demonstrated how to suck on the bark. She mimicked him, but she looked comical with the stick hanging out of her mouth trying not to cough or sputter on her spittle. He tried to stifle a laugh. Aia saw his amusement and giggled. Soon, they both were laughing out loud.

The tension of the past few days broke and they sat face to face looking into each others' eyes. Slowly, tentatively, they came closer touching cheek to cheek, a light kiss, then deep passion. Their romp wore them out and they slept until daybreak.

The following day, Aia was moody. She was distracted as Lucius tried to teach her the nuances of the subjunctive. After multiple failures, he decided to take a break. He concentrated on driving, allowing Aia to be with her thoughts.

A week of ragwort tea still had not stimulated Aia's period. She could come to only one conclusion. She was pregnant.

"That would explain my tender breasts, my moodiness, my hunger, and my morning nausea." Aia looked down at her belly and rubbed it lovingly. *"When did it happen? Who is the father?"*

She carefully traced back through the past months of exhilaration and devastation. From the start of her womanhood, she had always been regular. She could time herself with the phases of the moon until this past Beltane. Since, Beltane, she had no flow. That meant she had missed two periods and Lugurix was the father.

She was at once filled with joy and sadness. She was thrilled that she was not the only Tigurini any more. She carried the next generation. She was sad that her offspring would never know their father. They would never feel his gentle touch or sense his deep passion. They would never experience his magnanimous character. Now that Aia knew she was pregnant, she felt fortunate to have been saved by Lucius. She believed that it was the Mother Goddess's design that she should be saved. It was the only way to keep her tribe alive.

Most of all, she was saddened that she could not share her thoughts and feelings with her mother and her two sisters. She only resolved her tumultuous relationship with her mother at the end of Adiega's life. Now she yearned for her màthair's loving caresses and longed to benefit from her wisdom gathered while raising four children. She wished she could have seen Sina's joy at the news. She wanted Oueni to share her experiences of pregnancy and to compare their feelings. Tears flowed. She could not stop them.

Lucius, unsure of what was going on, felt helpless. He decided it was best to ignore her. He could not imagine what she felt, having lost her entire family, then being forced to hide in an army of assassins. He kept his eyes on the haunches of the oxen in front of him. Not too long afterward, he felt her nuzzle his arm. He put his arm around her, squeezed her arm, and patted her back to let her know he was there for her.

By the time they reached Cabillonum, a small Aeduan town on the Arar River, Aia's tears had stopped and she was calm. They made camp outside the town. In the distance, they could see a contingent of Gauls heading toward the Roman Army. By the flags that surrounded the warriors, Lucius surmised they were dignitaries of high rank. He watched them make their way to the command tent of the Roman Army. Lucius assumed they were meeting with Caesar to pledge their allegiance. He turned his attention back to his team. Eventually, word would filter down about what transpired.

Aia busied herself with straightening up the wagon, which had become quite a mess during the night of the debauchery. She took Lucius' soiled clothes along with hers and went to the river's edge to wash them. It was late afternoon and the river was filled with barges plying the center of the river, carrying goods to and from the little hamlet. Nearer to the banks, men in smaller vessels fished for catfish, carp, and eel. Aia was close enough to them to hear their conversations. Although their accent was strange and the language filled with idioms, she understood much of their Gaulish dialect.

"Look, over there. What is a Helvetian woman doing in the camp of the Roman Army?"

"I heard they killed the Helvetian men but kept the women as personal slaves."

"Who told you that tall tale, Toutissos?"

"Potitos."

"You fool," spat Biracos, his boat mate. "Everyone calls that guy 'Chef Menteur' – the chief liar. He's always talking about that giant catfish that got away." He turned to another boat.

"Hey Doiros, how much did he say it weighed?"

"Seventy-five kilograms!" yelled back Doiros.

"See? You can't trust him," declared Biracos

"All right, Signur Je sais tout – mister know-it-all," Toutissos said with his hands on his hips. "What have you heard?"

"I heard they killed nearly everyone," replied Biracos. "They even went through the camp and slaughtered little children."

"I don't believe you."

"Okay, I'll ask her." He cupped his hands around his mouth and called to Aia.

"Hey, little brionnach. My name is Biracos. Come join us in our fine vessel so we can get to know you better."

Aia ignored him.

"You clumsy idiot, you insulted her," said Toutissos. "She must be frightened and traumatized by the Romans." He turned to her.

"Please forgive my clumsy friend," he called. "Ma geneta daga uimpi – my good and pretty girl, would you kindly tell us your name?"

She decided to answer the kinder man.

"If it please you, sir, I am called Aia," she called back.

"Aia. What a beautiful name!" Toutissos replied. "Where are you from,

Aia?"

"I am Tigurini. I lived near the tall mountains called the Alps. My whole clan was killed by the Romans."

"You poor young thing," Toutissos said in a consoling voice.

"See, I told you," he whispered to Biracos. Then, he turned back to Aia.

"Why are you with the Romans now?"

"As you say, I am a slave."

"How many slaves are there?" asked Toutissos.

"I am the only one."

"Well, we can rescue you from your captors," called Biracos. "Come join me in our boat and I will take you home."

"He just wants to take you from the Romans so you can be his slave," called Doiros. "Come with me instead."

"Hey, don't butt in, Doiros. We saw her first," yelled Biracos.

"Quit!" said Toutissos. "You're frightening her." He turned to Aia.

"My dear Aia, we can liberate you if you wish. Just climb in with us."

Aia was tempted for a brief moment, but understood her situation and felt she was much better off with Lucius.

"Thank you kind sir, but no. I wish to stay with my captor."

"No!" exclaimed Doiros. "You would stay with the ones who killed your family?"

"I know my master and he is kind. I do not know your intentions, sir."

"See, you ruined it!" yelled Toutissos. He began to fight with Biracos. The tussle got over zealous and they capsized their boat losing their catch. Doiros started laughing.

"You lecherous idiots! Now you have no food for your families." He slapped his knee as he laughed, losing his balance and overturning his own craft. The three held on to their upside down skiffs and called to Aia for assistance.

"No, you men have been foolish!" she called, shaking a finger at them. "You got what you deserve!" With that, she got out of the water, grabbed the clothes, and started back to her wagon. As she left, she could hear Toutissos talking to Biracos.

"You really don't want that dirty little plac'h. Not only do the Romans have her body, but they also have turned her mind. She is the enemy now."

She arrived back at the wagon red faced and angry. She threw the clothing down on the front of the wagon surprising Lucius, then stormed around back and up the steps. Once inside, she started flinging contents around. She roughly rearranged everything that she had just sorted. She slapped objects down and flung other items across the narrow wagon. Lucius tried to be solicitous.

"What's wrong? May I help?"

"Futue te vestrum!" she snapped.

Lucius threw up his hands and decided it was best to stay away. He left to join his staff for the evening meal. When he returned, Aia was on the floor of the wagon covered over with her blanket. He approached carefully and knelt beside her. She appeared to be sleeping. He gently touched her hair.

Aia abruptly sat up and threw her arms around his neck sobbing. Lucius was pinned by her grip. He sat on his legs and held her. Gradually her sobbing slowed. She closed her eyes kissing Lucius all over his face ending on his lips. She quickly pulled up her dress and his tunic then reestablished a stranglehold around his neck. She pulled him on top of her and ground her hips against his until he surged with passion. When he was done she still would not let go. Holding his neck with her left arm, she worked him up again and directed his penis into her.

After the second time, she again tried to arouse his passion, but he was spent. She rolled him onto his back and threw her leg over him. She used his chest as her pillow. Pinned down, Lucius finally gave up and fell asleep.

Aia slept intermittently. Every time she woke up, she rubbed Lucius' torso and caressed his penis. When she felt Lucius become tumescent, she would pull him over and invite him in. She lost track of how many times he was in and out of her.

Exhausted, they both passed out until a medic knocked on the side of the wagon for morning sick call. Aia held him tight, but he finally pushed her away and stumbled out of the wagon.

Sick call was mercifully small. Lucius was lightheaded and spent the entire time trying to rehydrate. By the end of sick call, he felt in reasonable shape. He received the legion report and walked over to the Tenth medical area where he was greeted by an enthusiastic Gracilus. When all the chief surgeons were assembled, he began the meeting with an announcement.

"We have a new enemy. His name is Ariovistus. He is the ruler of the Suevi, a German tribe who invaded this part of Gaul and conquered the peoples on the left bank of the Arar."

Lucius was surprised.

"I thought our campaign was to send the Helvetians packing and go home," he said

"Well, Caesar has been overwhelmed with requests from the Gauls to get rid of this tyrant. The German is a cruel master and he is turning the country into his personal slave camp. Now that the Gauls see how powerful Rome is, they want us to defend them against all threats."

"So what's next?" asked Mauritius.

"We cross the Arar above the Dubis River. The right side of that river is said to be relatively easy going all the way to Vesontio."

Lucius brought the news back to the Eleventh. No one was happy that the campaign would continue. He climbed into the wagon and found Aia asleep. He decided not to wake the lioness. She had become unpredictable and he was in no mood for romping. He sat down and waited to move out.

*　　　　　　　*　　　　　　　*

The legions lined up as usual for the day's march, but they were ordered into battle formation for inspection. The entire six legion formation stretched out as far as one could see. Shortly, the command contingent trotted by on horseback and then galloped to the North. The troops were allowed to go to parade rest while they waited. As the Legatii returned to their commands, the order was given to return to attention. Marcus had no idea what was happening. The Centurions were called to the side of the commander. After a brief conversation, they ran back to their positions. The next order was to form a travel column and wait.

"Hey, chief," shouted Marcus, again forgetting his promise to keep his mouth shut. "What's up?"

Martial took his cue to belt out a tirade at his favorite target. He reminded Marcus of his brash behavior in the past and all of his punishments. He assigned Marcus to permanent latrine duty for the rest of the campaign, then he addressed everyone.

"Our jobs for this year are not done. We have new orders. We are going to fight the Germans!" He slapped his vitis against his leg and surveyed his troops.

"I guarantee that because you melon heads did not get to fight last time, you will get to fight this time! I don't want to hear any bellyaching out of any of you! Now, stay in line and keep your swords sharp!"

They moved out at double time. Martial ordered Quintus to call cadence. Marching to bawdy songs helped keep their minds off the future fighting.

Chapter 32: Change of Scenery

Aia woke with a start as the wagon lurched forward to pull into traveling formation. She was groggy and felt cold, even though it was a warm summer morning. Her nausea returned as it had every morning for the past four weeks. She threw her cloak on and pulled the hood over her head. She was in no mood for conversation. She crawled up to the front of the wagon and silently took her seat next to Lucius. She bent down and put her head in her hands. Lucius glanced in her direction waiting for her to say something. When she did not, he sighed and turned his attention back to driving.

Aia remained within herself. She did not notice they were going through the village of Cabillonum. She did not see the villagers pointing at her and whispering. She stayed lost in her thoughts as the column moved through the narrow muddy streets.

Eventually, they reached the end of the village and prepared to cross the small bridge over the Arar River. The Aedui tribe's tiny fleet of fishing vessels were moored near the bridge. Still lost in her thoughts, Aia stared idly in the general direction of the fishermen beginning their daily routine. One of the fishermen, Toutissos, watched the hooded figure as he repaired his net. When he caught a glimpse of her face, he could not contain his excitement. He poked Biracos and pointed at Aia, then he called out.

"Demat Aia, ma geneta daga uimpi! – Good morning Aia, my good and pretty girl! We did not expect to see you so soon!"

Aia snapped to attention and focused on the two Aedui fishermen waving at her.

"Yes," echoed Biracos. "There's still time to join us. Just jump down. We will catch you in our net!"

Aia immediately flushed.

"Digarezit ac'hanonon? – Excuse me?"

"Just jump on me!" called Biracos

"Never!"

"Please don't be that way, Aia. Do not be our enemy! We love you!"

Aia was seething now. She raised her arm preparing to cast a curse.

"Paouez! – Stop! If you do not stop, I will be forced to place a malloc'h on you!"

They raised their hands in supplication.

"Please don't curse us! We mean you no harm."

"That is not true!" she retorted. "Only yesterday you wanted to violate me." She stood up trying to keep her balance as the wagon bounced onto the rickety bridge.

"You deserve a malloc'h for your intentions."

Aia, now breathing fire, pointed her outstretched arm at the two inept fishermen, and gave them the evil eye. They threw up their hands.

"We're sorry! Please do not curse us. We are just poor fishermen."

"Tascha! – Shut up, then! If you do not, I will be forced to write my curse. Once I do, my brictom will last for eternity!" She folded her arms, turned abruptly, and sat with a plop.

As the wagon rolled by, the men turned to one another. Biracos stuck his tongue out in a mocking manner, then stifled a laugh. Toutissos slapped him and they began fighting. Aia ignored them.

After crossing the bridge, Lucius drove for some distance before attempting conversation.

"Who are those men?" he asked.

"They are no one," Aia said trying to act normally, but she was shaking.

"How do you know them?"

"I saw them yesterday when I was at the river. They have evil intentions."

What did you tell them?

"I told them to stop or I would curse them."

"My, my. They must have very bad intentions for you to curse your own people."

"They are not my people!" she snapped. She took a few deep breaths trying to calm down. She gritted her teeth.

"We may speak the same language, but they mean nothing to me. I belong to you."

Lucius was surprised by her words.

"Does she think she is my slave? I know I have sent mixed messages about her being a slave, but I don't want her to feel that way."

He thought about the number of times they made love.

"Maybe she thinks she belongs to me, because we made love."

In Rome, men and women, married or not, made love with many different partners all the time. It was acceptable, even encouraged among citizens. He thought about Acca's aunt Livia. Her parties were famous in the region. Once a month, she would open her house to all the young men of Canino. She would have sex with them until all were satisfied. He knew his own Pater had been to see her. He had been with many other women around town as well.

"Maybe in her culture, having sex is different," he mused.

He turned to his tempestuous wagon mate. Aia sat stone-faced with her arms folded. Now was not the time for a cross-cultural discussion. He would save his questions for another time.

They rode in silence for the rest of the day following the eastern tributary of the Arar they called the Dubis. To the local tribes it was the Doubs. Along the right bank of the Dubis, the land was mostly flat.

Aia started to work her way out of her funk. For the first time in weeks, she began to appreciate the scenery again. She observed the lazy river curving back and forth. The trees that lined the banks were full and green. Birds were everywhere. She saw wrens flying in small groups with their young. There were hawks circling high above on the warm air currents. Eagles perched majestically in the tops of the tallest oaks and surveyed the ground for small rodents. On the tree trunks, she caught glimpses of shy woodpeckers digging for grubs. On the branches, she could make out brightly colored thrushes and several families of the distinctive hoopoe. On the ground were robins and lapwings with their long skinny black crests. In the fields were bee-eaters and little humming birds sucking nectar from colorful wildflowers. Near the water's edge were terns and pipits and a great white egret hunting for unsuspecting minnows. Bird songs filled the air with sweet music. Aia could make out the song of the cuckoo, the warbler, the lark, and the diminutive finch.

The sights and sounds of summer warmed Aia's heart. She sat back and sighed. The countryside was beginning to look more like her home. Warm breezes carried the sweet smell of the growing grains and grasses. Even the odors reminded her of her homeland. She hoped it would be the land she could call home. She put her head in Lucius' lap and closed her eyes still hoping her terrible experience was only a dream.

She dearly missed her former life snuffed out by greedy tyrants who were not satisfied with their beautiful rich homeland. They forced her and her family into these strange lands where her mother died a horrible death and the Romans obliterated her tribe. Now, her only hope of a future was to survive with the enemy in a foreign land. As far as she knew, she was the sole Tigurini survivor. She was alone and pregnant, sitting next to a man who was part of the army that destroyed everything she knew. He was her enemy, yet he was also her protector. He could make love her or have her killed at any time. Her future already had been destroyed twice. She wondered if she even had a future at all.

Lucius was confused. The Tigurini woman had been an enigma from the day he met her. She made a suicide run into her enemy's camp to get supplies for her father, who obviously was dying. Although the Romans brutally murdered her entire tribe, she was willing to hide in the enemy camp disguised as a soldier. She spied for her enemy and helped to heal an old man with medicines and prayers unknown to him. She taught him her strange medicine. She had been given an opportunity to escape into a Gaulish tribe, yet chose to stay with the Romans. As for their relationship, she lured him into ecstasy, then spurned him, then wore him out, then ignored him. Her mood swings seemed to be worse than ever. He prayed to Juno Fluonia. He hoped the goddess might mellow out the barbarian woman of harsh extremes.

They camped by the river that evening. After their meager dinner, Aia seemed calm and receptive to conversation. Lucius got up the courage to talk.

"Aia, are you feeling well?"

She looked at him quizzically.

"Yes, why do you ask?"

"Did those men hurt you?"

"No! Why do you bring up those creatures?"

"Because they are Gaulish like you. I mean they speak your language..."

"That is all we have in common."

"Well, they sure made you very angry and moody."

"They think because I am a woman and I speak their language that I would sleep with them."

"You sleep with me and we don't speak the same language."

Aia looked at Lucius.

"I sleep with you because I choose to."

"Yes, but I am a Roman. We killed your entire tribe. You should hate me."

"You did what you could for my Athair. You saved me. You were kind to me and you still protect me. You recognize that I have skills, skills that may help your patients. You permit me to care for your injured. It makes me want to be with you."

Lucius shifted. He needed to know.

"This morning, you said you belonged to me. Do you think you are my slave, because you are not..." He allowed his voice to trail off.

She frowned at him, then it dawned on her.

"Oh, I meant I belong *with* you. My Latin still is not very good." She gazed into the distance.

"My family is gone. The Gauls and the few filthy Helvetians who survived mean nothing to me. I spit on them!" She spit into the grass, then turned back to him with tears in her eyes.

"You have shown me only kindness. You treat me with respect, not as a loathsome barbarian. You make me feel that I am worth something. There is no one else with whom I wish to be. You are my family now." She leaned over and kissed him tenderly on the cheek.

That night as Aia lay in his arms, Lucius thought about his first dog Patricus. He was five years old when Patricus came into his life. He was playing by the top of the cataract near the villa when a black short haired dog came loping along the stream. He was playing with the water. Periodically, he would stop and watch it cautiously. He would crouch with his haunches close to the ground, then he would spring toward the water stopping short of it, barking furiously. Then, as though it had never happened, he would trot a few feet further downstream and repeat the process. Sometimes, he would take a drink. Once, he slipped and fell in as he darted towards the stream. It surprised the animal and it took him some time to get oriented. He paddled toward the shore struggling in the swift water. It took several tries before he could climb out.

As he came closer to Lucius, he sniffed the ground and trotted up to him. Lucius noted that the dog was about two feet high at the shoulders and that he weighed as much as him. He had small pointed ears that stood on end. The dog surveyed the little human. Lucius stood quietly as the dog sniffed his shoes, his legs, and his crotch. The dog's sniffing tickled him and he giggled pulling away. The dog leapt on Lucius knocking him down. They rolled on the ground until the dog was on top of him licking his face.

They played together for a while until Lucius got tired and hungry. He headed back to the villa to get something from Basilius. The dog followed him. When he shooed the animal away, the dog would stop, but he never took his eyes off of his new playmate. Lucius, thinking he had successfully separated from the dog, would start out again, but the dog followed him all the way to the kitchen. Basilius came out and helped Lucius shoo the animal away. The dog circled around moving about twenty-five feet away and sat down. Lucius got his snack and ate it in the kitchen. When he went back out, the dog was still there. Basilius told him to ignore the animal and he would soon lose interest.

Lucius went about his play trying not to acknowledge the dog. The animal stayed a good distance away playing his own games. When evening came, Lucius started home. The dog followed, but no closer than twenty feet. Everyone tried to shoo the dog away, but he stuck near the villa.

The next day, when Lucius went out to play, the dog was waiting for him. They played together and that evening, he asked his mother if they could keep the dog. After some discussion about his responsibility for the animal, his mother agreed. They decided to name him Patricus because he had chosen to live with a noble family. He remained loyal and faithful to Lucius until his death ten years later. He persuaded his parents to commission a mosaic of Patricus in the peristylum. He wanted it installed in the vestibule, but because the dog was dead, they placed it with the other memorials.

Now, another had chosen to stay with him. She was not a dog, and shooing her away was improper. He had no one to ask if he could keep her. He remembered his discussion with his mother, though. Caring for a dog was a big responsibility for a five year old, but it was nothing compared to the responsibility he faced now. He was not sure he was ready to take on the role. For now, he had little choice, but when the campaign ended, he would face a much tougher decision.

It took another two days to reach Vesontio. Traveling was easy because the land was flat with only a few rolling hills. Lucius returned to teaching Latin to Aia. She practiced while enjoying the scenery. In the evening when they stopped, she gathered more flowers and herbs. She shared their medicinal secrets with Lucius. The days were warm and the nights chilly. They kept warm under the same blanket, but Aia did not invite Lucius to romp with her.

*   *   *

On the final day of travel, the land on the left bank of the Dubis rose up to form long hills that paralleled the Army's travel direction. The river, which had taken many lazy turns, became even more tortuous. The troop column moved away from its banks following a straight path heading almost due east.

At the crest of a small rise, they could see several small mountains clustered together ahead to the right. As they approached, they made out the silhouette of the town of Vesontio. It was laid out in a horseshoe-shaped bend in the river. At the closed end of the horseshoe was a mountain. The total amount of land for the town could not have been more than three thousand by six thousand feet. Except for the mountain, it bore a striking resemblance to the Tigurini camp where the tribe had been massacred.

The legions stopped short of the town while the commanders and a small contingent of troops marched across the bridge. After a very brief time, the villagers welcomed the Romans and the legions resumed their march. The Army entered the town by the southwest bridge, skirted the edge of the village by traveling along the river, and ascended the mountain. There, they established a large camp with the two newer legions as the forward guard overlooking the city. The remaining four legions camped on the highest point of the mountain. The river protected the rear and their flanks. The vista from the mountaintop commanded the entire valley. No army could approach within ten miles without being detected.

Shortly after the order for dismissal, Marcus and his cohort were called out for first watch. By now, the routine was all too familiar. Martial separated Marcus and Quintus placing Memmius between them. The view was stunning and it distracted the three from their watch. Soon, all three were talking among themselves.

"I wonder what our new enemy is like," wondered Memmius.

"What do you mean?" Marcus asked.

"You remember our discussion the day we crossed the Rhodanus River into enemy territory?"

"Yeah," said Quintus. "We thought the Helvetians were going to be giants, but Decimus helped set us straight."

"Right," continued Memmius. "We know nothing of the Germans. I wonder what they are like."

"They are giants."

The three turned back to see a contingent of Sequani carrying supplies to headquarters escorted by a detail from Legion XII.

"Yeah, how do you know?" quipped Marcus.

"The Germans are not far from here. Maybe one hundred forty kilometers,

I mean seventy-five of your miles northeast of here. They attacked some of our kinsmen and captured our villages. Some who escaped sought refuge with us."

"Well, spill it scum!" Memmius was anxious. "What are they like?"

As the Sequani passed close by, he spat at Memmius' feet.

"Be afraid," he whispered.

"What's that supposed to mean, pagan?" Marcus yelled at them.

"He means they are fierce giants," said another Sequani near the end of the procession.

"How would you know?" Quintus asked.

"I am from a small village called Pouxeux along a beautiful little river called the Moselle. One day without warning, the Germans swarmed out of the mountains and killed my family and most of the villagers. I alone escaped without harm. After three weeks of running and hiding from them, I made it to the safety of this town. The Germans are immense. They have a horrific appearance. Just to look at them struck fear in my heart. I still have nightmares of their faces. They have super human strength. Even when you strike a fatal bow, they do not die. They keep fighting. Oh, yes. Be very afraid."

The three guards stood in silence as the detail continued up to headquarters. Finally, Quintus spoke.

"That's it. I am done with this army stuff!" He ripped his armor off. "I am going back to Neapolis. I don't care whether my family has forgiven me or not. I would rather die at their hand than face monsters."

It took the combined efforts of the cohort to calm Quintus down and persuade him to stay. He was better off in the army than trying to navigate his way back across Gaul. He agreed, but spent a sleepless night thinking about their new foe.

By the next day, word of the ferocious new enemy had spread through the entire Roman camp. Everyone was agitated and wished for an end to the campaign. Many senior staff who had come up from Rome with Caesar were ready to leave. The camp was placed on lock down. Guard duty was reassigned to members of Legion X. No one was allowed to leave their tent area. Martial was furious. He stormed into the tents of his century uprooting the poles and collapsing tents as he went.

"All right, you scumbags, out! Form up!"

The ninth cohort scrambled out of the collapsed tent with some difficulty and lined up with the other cohorts in the sixth centuria under Martial's command. He slowly paced up and down the line scowling at each of them as he passed. Each time he reached the end of the line, he spit and spun around. After a dozen passes in silence, he stood in front of them.

"I hear rumors that we are afraid of the Germans. I wonder how that got started?" He began to pace again breathing in their faces.

"I'm certainly not afraid of the Germans, and I'm sure no one in my centuria is afraid."

He scowled at his troops.

"Who's afraid of the Germans?"

There was silence. Martial stormed down the line. He stopped in front of Marcus and glared down at him.

"Are you afraid of the Germans?"

Marcus stiffened up and looked straight ahead.

"No, sir!" he shouted.

Martial moved to stand in front of Memmius.

"Are you afraid of the Germans?"

Memmius reacted the same way.

"No, sir!"

Martial spun in front of Quintus.

"Is it you, scum bucket?"

Quintus was sweating. He could taste Martial's breath he was so close. He continued to look at the horizon trying to avoid the gaze of the Centurion.

"No, sir!"

"You're not afraid of the Germans?"

"No, sir!"

"Then I guess no one is scared of the Germans, is that right?"

There was no response. Martial was frustrated. He rephrased his question.

"Are we afraid of the Germans?"

"No, sir!"

"I can't hear you!"

"No, sir!"

"Our job is to kill Germans. Is that clear?"

"Yes, sir," came the response.

"I can't hear you!"

"Yes, sir!" they shouted.

Seeming a little more satisfied, Martial paced up and down.

"Legion Ten will lead us into battle. Are we with the Tenth?"

"Yes, sir!" they responded.

"Will we fight with the Tenth?"

"Yes, sir!"

"Will we kill Germans with the Tenth?"

"Yes, sir!"

"If we must, will we die with the Tenth?"

"Yes, sir!" was the response.

"Wonderful! I'm glad that's clear!" Martial stood at attention in front of his centuria.

"Meus caparum Romanus..."

"Ad Victoria!" the centuria shouted.

"Meus caparum Romanus..."

"Ad Victoria!"

"Meus caparum Romanus..."

"Ad Victoria!"

"Dimitto!"

With that, Martial marched directly to headquarters.

"What just happened?" asked Memmius.

"I think we just got new battle orders!" mused Marcus.

*   *   *

The next day after report, Gracilus detained Lucius.

"We have new orders. We are moving out tomorrow."

"Yes, sir, I understand," said Lucius.

"We are fighting a fierce enemy and your legion definitely will be involved."

        "We are prepared," Lucius replied with confidence. "You can count on us."

        "Thank you, Vigoratus," Gracilus said, "but there is one more thing."

        "Anything," replied Lucius.

        "The Druid has to stay."

Chapter 33: New Trials

Lucius exhaled.

"Headquarters orders," said Gracilus.   "We can't have any extraneous baggage when we go against the Germans."

Lucius knew the day would come. He hoped it would never happen, but deep down he understood. Aia wasn't just a barbarian, she was a barbarian woman. Even though she had been a strangely wonderful companion, an able medial assistant, a resourceful herbalist, and a vital spy in the Roman cause, Lucius knew that her time with him was both improbable and inappropriate.

Gracilus watched the young surgeon try to absorb the news, then put his hand on Lucius' shoulder.

"I know you were getting attached to her, chap, but we just can't afford any distractions in the coming battle against Ariovistus and his hordes."

Lucius took in a deep breath trying to compose himself.

"I understand," he whispered.

"Everything already has been arranged.   There is a Druid colony here. They have agreed to take her in. I secured permission for you to accompany her there today."

"Thanks."

The two clasped arms briefly, then Gracilus left to attend to his unit.

Lucius' mind was blank. He trudged back to his legion's medical station. The center of camp was full of activity. Lucius walked through it in a fog. Without knowing how, he found himself in front of the bright blue Druid wagon. He stared at the back doors. He had no idea how he would tell her. He thought about the way Theodosius broke bad news to patients and their families when he expected a negative outcome. Lucius always hated to give bad news. When Aia's father lay dying, he left that job to Magnus. With no better option, he decided just to tell her.

"What?"

"We are leaving tomorrow and our orders are that you should—"

"I heard you!" Aia broke in, her fists clenched. "Why?"

"The Germans are much more fierce than your tribe." Lucius winced as the words came out. "I mean more fierce than the cursed Helvetians. Command simply will not allow it."

"Then I will dress as Decimus again."

"No, no!" Lucius pleaded. "We were lucky you were not discovered, and even more fortunate that it was Taurinus who found out. The disguise will not work a second time."

Aia spun around folding her arms. Lucius gently placed his hands on her shoulders. She immediately shook him off. Almost instantly, tears flowed without stopping. Lucius watched helplessly as she sobbed. After a long embarrassing silence, she spun around and jumped into his arms hugging his neck and sobbing into his tunic. Lucius froze to the spot, stunned by her sudden action. After he recovered, he put comforting arms around her.

Aia sobbed until no more tears would come. She continued to cling to Lucius with her head buried in his tunic breathing huge shuddering sighs. Suddenly she pulled back, wiped her eyes, stood up stiffly, and spoke in a detached voice.

"Allons."

With that, she moved to the front of the wagon, pulled her hood over her head, and sat waiting to be driven away.

Chagrined, Lucius looked down at his tunic. It felt wet and heavy. He was drenched in Aia's tears. The wet spot covered nearly his entire chest. He looked out the back of the wagon and saw Magnus. He waved him over and briefly told him the situation. He left Magnus in charge while he completed his distasteful duty. After taking time to change his tunic and compose himself, he climbed in next to the sulking Aia and directed the oxen toward the winding path off the mountain. As he did so, he realized he had no idea where he was going.

"I don't know where to find this family of Druids," he whispered to Aia. She just humphed and stared off in the distance.

They went down the mountain in silence. At that hour, almost no one was on the road to disturb the icy aura surrounding the pair. In the village, houses of wood and mortar were crammed together lining both sides of the street. Each new street they reached looked the same. Lucius was lost in a foreign land. He tried asking for directions, but got only curious expressions. No one spoke Latin. Finally he pleaded with Aia to help him. She humphed again, but called out to a villager who spoke rapidly pointing in several directions.

"He said we are almost there," Aia told Lucius. "Turn left at the next street."

Lucius obliged. The street was not quite as narrow as the one that led off the mountain. It was all dirt and led to a wooded area in the middle of the village. The Druid's building was in the middle of the dense stand of oak and ash trees extending for an entire village block. In the middle of the block was a small, but well traveled path. Lucius carefully guided the wagon down the dusty trail to the building at the back of the woods. It was a two story structure constructed of bricks and covered with mortar. Lucius could see it stretched the length of the block. The entrance to the building was in the center at the end of the trail. The massive wooden double doors extended more than halfway up the building.

Lucius and Aia got down from the wagon. Together they knocked on the massive door. Someone looked out of a portal above the door and then disappeared. Shortly after, a small door within the door opened a crack. A figure peered around the edge and looked at Aia. She bent down and held a brief conversation with the doorman in hushed tones. The small door closed and they stood looking at the massive wooden structure in silence. Lucius noted that the door was carved with whorls that looked very similar to the drawings on the wagon. As he reached out to touch the carving, the two large doors slowly began to open. Two men opened the doors and motioned for them to bring the wagon inside.

Lucius and Aia climbed back into the wagon and he negotiated the doorway with little room to spare on either side. They entered a large courtyard. Lucius saw that the building was square and ran the perimeter of another block enclosing a large open space nearly as big as the stand of trees through which they had just come. There was a continuous covered walkway around the entire inside for each floor. In the center of the courtyard stood a family of six – four adults and two children.

Lucius and Aia climbed down. Lucius let her lead the way. He stood behind her as she spoke at length to a woman who looked only a little older than Aia. Eventually, the woman hugged her. She introduced Aia to each member of the family. Each gave her a gentle hug. Once Aia was introduced to the two children, the boy began to chase the girl around the courtyard. They were both giggling and screaming. Then, Aia walked back to Lucius, put her arm around his and pulled him in front of the woman.

"This is Severa and her husband Vrittakos. They are the High Priestess and High Priest of this village. Their family has been here for many generations. They are kind enough to take me in since you will not take me with you." She looked daggers into his eyes and poked him in the side.

Lucius grunted from the blow, then greeted them with as much dignity as he could muster.

Next, Aia introduced him to the two older individuals.

"This is Severa's mother and father, Eskenga and Vlatiú." Lucius bowed stiffly.

Severa called to the children and they immediately returned to their mother's side.

"And this is Potita and Vectitos," Aia said as she tousled their hair. Lucius bent over and extended his hand, but they both backed up and ran away.

"They tell me there is one more member of the family, Eskenga's mother," Aia continued. "She is very old. When the children heard there were visitors coming, they ran around the home causing her to lose her balance. She fell and broke her wrist. She is in the house in a great deal of pain."

Lucius sensed an opportunity.

"Aia, you have given me so much help with our patients and you even cured Taurinus. Might I be permitted to help the old woman?"

Aia was surprised and touched by the Roman's kindness. She could not stay mad at him.

"I will ask."

She had a prolonged conversation with Severa and Vrittakos. Aia began to gesture with her hands. Severa and Vrittakos paid careful attention to Aia as she spoke. Every time she pointed at Lucius, they would look at him. First the looks were curious, then wary, then curious again, then approving. Finally, Aia came back.

"Yes, they will permit you to see her."

The group crossed the courtyard to the apartment opposite the entrance. It was dark inside and Lucius had to wait for his eyes to accommodate. Once they did, he could see an old woman in a rocking chair near a small fireplace. Her eyes were closed and she was holding her wrist and singing softly to herself while she rocked.

"This is my grandmother," said Severa. "Her name is Banona."

Aia turned to Lucius.

"Can you help her?"

"I will try. Please stay with me. You will need to talk to her for me."

The two approached.

"I am most honored to meet you," Lucius said. "I would like to help you." He looked at Aia who translated. The old woman looked with suspicion at the two of them, then at her granddaughter. Severa had to reassure her that they felt it was best that Lucius be allowed an opportunity to examine her.

Lucius asked Aia to talk with the woman as he examined her. He asked her to find out about her general health and about any current problems. He held the old woman's hands and gently took away her good hand. She limply held out her hand without moving her fingers. There was a lump on the back side of the wrist.

Lucius had Aia ask her to move each finger, then asked her about pain. After his exam, he decided her wrist broke when she tried to brace herself against the ground as she fell. He spoke with Aia who announced the findings to the family.

Lucius asked for a number of supplies. As Aia was relaying the information, he remembered pain medicine and gently touched her arm.

"Ask if they have any poppies to make some tea."

Aia asked Severa who told her no. Lucius frowned.

"That is unfortunate." He thought for a minute, then he spoke to Aia.

"You made a tea with willow bark that relieved pain for Taurinus and for me. Can they make some willow bark tea?" Aia turned to Severa. After a brief conversation, Severa left.

"She will make some willow tea," said Aia. She was still curious about the poppies.

"You like this poppy tea. It works well for pain, no?"

"Yes," said Lucius. "It is very powerful. You crush the whole flower together with the seeds and mix it with a little water or wine."

"I will ask Severa if the children can gather some."

"If the willow tea works, you will not need it, but if not, you will be grateful that the children collected the poppies."

When the materials he needed were gathered, he prepared his dressings. He asked for two small planks of wood. These he fashioned with the help of Vrittakos. Aia acted as translator.

After Banona drank the tea, he instructed Aia to hold a conversation with her. After passing pleasantries, Aia did not know what to discuss, so she decided to relay the story of hiding as Decimus in the Roman Army. She made it amusing and the old woman was enthralled. As the story went on, Lucius got Vrittakos to hold onto the old woman's fingers and to pull gently. As he did so, Lucius turned his back to Banona and held her forearm. With his thumbs, he pressed on the protuberance until it crunched back into position. Banona yelped briefly, but said she was in less pain with the fracture reduced. Holding the reduction in place, he wrapped the wrist and arm with a piece of sheepskin, then he put one plank on the back and one plank on the front of the hand extending onto the forearm.

With Vrittakos still holding the fingers, Lucius did a masterful job of wrapping a bulky dressing over the fracture and onto the hand. He pushed the hand sideways until the thumb was in a direct line with the radius bone. He flexed the fingers downward and wrapped his dressing around the hand and between the fingers making a large ball of her hand. When he was done, only her fingertips stuck out. He left two very long pieces of linen hanging out of each side of the dressing. These could be used to tie her hand into the air above her head to decrease the swelling. They used a rafter to dangle her hand in the air. Both Severa and Vrittakos were impressed. Eskenga asked Lucius to stay for dinner. He weakly protested and easily relented. At least it would give him a few more hours with Aia.

The meal consisted of a stew made of eels caught from the Doubs and served with a crusty bread to soak up the liquid. Afterwards, they shared several pungent cheeses. The tastes were foreign to both Lucius and Aia, but quite delicious. After supper, Lucius checked the old woman's dressing. Banona was very grateful to him. She told him that she could feel her fingers and she could move them around a little in the dressing without difficulty. The willow bark tea had relieved her pain and she was comfortable, except for having her hand dangling in the air. He instructed Aia that the dressing should stay on for at least six weeks. If it had to be removed, it would need to be replaced. He tried to explain how to redo it, but eventually decided the best way was to have her undo it layer by layer and reconstruct it in the same way.

Following the examination and treatment of the matriarch of the family, Lucius and Aia took a walk around the balconies and stared silently into the courtyard. The sun had set and darkness was gathering. Aia was moody. She had lost so much during that year and now she was losing Lucius. She wanted to tell him she was pregnant, but demurred.

"Why should I tell this Roman I am pregnant with Lugurix's child on the day I may never see him again?"

She kept her pregnancy to herself. Instead, she clung tightly to his arm and took frequent deep sighs.

Lucius realized he had to return soon to be ready for the next morning's exit. He could not find the words to express his joy at having known Aia and his sadness at leaving her. They had the most unusual relationship those last few weeks. He was unsure who had benefitted more.

The full moon was high in the sky. Lucius finally decided he must leave. He paused and turned to Aia. They both tried to speak at once. They smiled and tried again starting at the same time, then fell silent. Finally Lucius spoke.

"I have to–"

Aia put her hand on his mouth and shook her head slowly, then she kissed him passionately. When they broke she put her fingers back on his lips.

"Don't speak. Do not say those words." She kissed him again, then pulled back.

"Say a revair – until we meet again."

"A revair," he said. They embraced for a long time. They did not notice that Vrittakos had come out to open the compound door. When they finished, he spoke to Aia.

"He says it is easy to return to the mountain. Go right on the street and right again at the corner. The road goes straight to the mountain." She looked into Lucius' eyes. Her eyes welled up as she embraced him one last time. When she released him, she ran away to the dwelling leaving the two men.

Vrittakos gave Lucius his personal backpack containing his belongings from the wagon, then ushered him out. He bowed and said something in Gaulish repeating it several times. Lucius assumed he was being thanked. He bowed back. Vrittakos grabbed Lucius and the two briefly embraced. Vrittakos returned to the compound and closed the door leaving Lucius alone in the stand of trees outside the compound. He sighed and trudged back to camp.

Although the night was clear and the moon bright, Lucius noticed nothing on his walk through the village and up the mountain. He abruptly came back to reality when he was stopped by the sentry.

"Lucius! What are you doing out of camp?"

He looked up.

"Marcus?"

"Why are you so surprised? I am a legionnaire in Caesar's Army and my duties sometimes involve guard duty, you know."

"Yes, how could I forget? Anyway, it's good to see you."

"Likewise. Now, I have to do my guard duty. Why are you out of camp?"

"I had to run an errand."

"I bet it had something to do with that Druid witch."

Lucius was surprised.

"What do you know about a Druid?"

"Just rumors. We heard there was a witch in our legion's medical wagons. How did you get so lucky to have a woman?"

Lucius was in a little bit of a dilemma. He wanted to tell his brother about Aia, but now was not an appropriate time to confide.

"Uh, it was... She was being forced to share her herbal secrets."

"You mean like her ferns? How about her figs? Did she let you water them?"

"What? No, of course not!" Lucius lied. He was suddenly embarrassed about his sexual escapades.

"It was strictly to enhance our medical knowledge."

"I don't believe you."

"What's all the racket, Marcus?" It was Cornelius who had been appointed temporary watch commander for the night.

"This is my brother, Lucius. We were just having a conversation."

"You know this is not the time. Are you trying to get us all in trouble again?"

"No, we were just catching up."

"Well, do it later."

"Okay." Marcus stiffened up. "Pass, brother."

Lucius was glad to get away. He wished he had seen Marcus under different circumstances, but that would have to wait. He returned to his old wagon. As he opened the door, he realized that Magnus had been using it for the past two weeks. He was in no mood for conversation, but it was too late.

"Fortunatus! Welcome back! Sure took you long enough. Plowing the field one last time?"

"What?" Lucius winced. *"Will it ever end?"* he thought. He was getting irritated.

"No, I didn't. When we got there I had to take care of an old woman who fractured her wrist."

"A surgeon's work is never done, eh? How was Aia? How did she take it?"

"I really don't know. She said nothing."

"Wow." Magnus was skeptical. "How about you?"

"I don't know. My mind is a blank."

"That bad, eh? Well, you won't have too much time to ruminate tonight. We move out at first light."

"I can't deal with that right now. I am exhausted."

"Well, don't think you are going to sleep in here. I'll move back to my wagon in the morning, but I am not going to bother grumpy Priscus tonight. You can just sleep outside for a few hours."

"Okay, I deserve it. I am so indebted to you, my friend."

"And don't you forget it. I plan to collect when this campaign is over."

Lucius climbed down and sat against the rear wagon wheel. He looked into the sky. The moon had set and Venus was already visible over the horizon to the East. Soon Sol would rise and they would be on their way. As he watched, his eyes grew heavy. Maybe he would rest better with Aia gone.

Lucius felt Magnus shaking him and awoke abruptly.

"Wake up, sleepy head," said Magnus. "Time to go back to real work."

Lucius looked up. It was still not light.

"What's up?"

"Orders just came that we leave now."

Lucius pulled himself up and trudged to sick call. He was surprised to find a long line. He hailed Priscus.

"What's all this?"

"You know we're moving out," replied Priscus. "We have a legion of legionnaires who want to stay in the garrison instead of chasing Germans."

Lucius smiled and put his arms around Priscus and Magnus.

"Well, amici, looks like it's time for Operation Taurinus!"

Chapter 34: Refocused

Lucius whispered instructions to a medic who smiled and nodded, then he to the front of the sick call line and announced to the troops the "Taurinus" protocol. Lucius enjoyed the show. Before the medic could finish his announcement, the line vanished. Only two legionnaires remained, both with pneumonia. Lucius gave them oxymel and assigned them to garrison duty. The medical team quickly packed up and joined the growing formation. For reasons unknown to Lucius, the order of the legions had changed drastically. The Tenth led the column followed by the Eleventh, Ninth, Eighth, Twelfth, and finally the Seventh as rear guard. That meant they had to move out much sooner than ever before.

Lucius had forgotten how poorly Roman wagons functioned. Since leaving the battlefield at Bibracte, he had ridden with Aia in the commandeered Helvetian Druid wagon. It was a finely crafted ship. Like all Helvetian wagons, it was built with the best hand-picked aged wood. The metal parts were constructed with precision by the best tribal blacksmiths. Wagons made for the revered Druids received special care during construction. By contrast, the wagons commissioned for the new legions were built rapidly out of uncured wood by disinterested and underpaid craftsmen who were pressed into service. Due to the ultra-short timeline, many flaws went undetected during cursory inspections by legion engineers.

The day before, Lucius was distracted by his mission to deliver Aia to the locals. He did not appreciate the Druid wagon's smooth ride down the mountain. Now, he wished he had that craft back. The hastily built Roman wagon creaked and groaned under the weight of tilted gravity. Driving the rickety craft took his full attention. He had to control the oxen with tight reins to avoid taking bumps and ruts too fast and rupturing an axle. By the time he made it off the mountain, he was exhausted.

As the six legions negotiated the narrow streets of the North side of Vesontio, villagers thronged to watch the spectacle. Lucius hoped to see Aia there, but she was not among the onlookers. He knew he had been inept at breaking the bad news the day before. He had fumbled his way through their goodbye. He figured she blamed him for her continued misfortune. He wondered if he would ever see her again.

The Army coursed through the village, eventually crossing the Northeast bridge onto the open plains and camped within sight of the hamlet. With no distractions from Taurinus or Aia, Lucius joined the other five surgeons for supper. He had to endure intense ribbing from his colleagues. They had fertile imaginations about what Lucius was doing in private with the Druid woman. He allowed them to have their fun hoping they would get it out of their system.

Once they settled down, Lucius began to relay the lessons he had learned from Aia about the Druids' herbal medicines along with something of the rituals that accompanied them. The most significant lessons were about dangerous herbs carefully prepared for proper therapeutic use. These were powerful medicines the Greeks and Romans had never imagined. Many of the plants were poisonous. However, with proper balance and dosing, the Druids could treat diseases in ways the Roman physicians never thought possible. Gradually, the young surgeons' interest in medicines outweighed their desire to skewer Lucius for not sharing the woman with them.

The next morning at report, Lucius found out the reason for the change in order of the legions. In the last days before leaving Vesontio, several commanders, including many centurions of prime companies and decurions of the cavalry, expressed their timidity about facing the Germans. The Tenth, Caesar's first and most loyal legion, was unwavering in support of the campaign. The commanders of the Eleventh were the first to stand with the Tenth to face the new enemy. Thus, Caesar promoted the Eleventh to second position behind the Tenth. That meant their legion would be on the strong side of the battle formation and the surgical team of the Eleventh would have to be prepared for heavy casualties when fighting eventually came.

Lucius was not concerned about his surgical unit. He knew they were proficient after their performance in the aftermath of the battle near Bibracte. He was much more concerned about having the supplies they would need. Each evening when the column stopped, he would send Magnus and Modestus to barter with the Sequani for torches, linen, and thread. The barbarians gladly traded supplies for minor operations such as drainage of abscesses and removal of skin tumors and cysts. The surgeons would work after supper on as many of the locals as they could. The work was tiring, but they were able to pack their wagons with all the supplies they could carry.

*   *   *

To keep the baggage train with the legions, marching speed slowed as they traversed the rugged foothills. Marcus and his cohort were thrilled to get a few days of easy traveling. Every evening, they focused on the coming battle. Before supper, Marcus helped each of his mates get ready by teaching them fighting skills he had learned from his father. Then, they would sharpen their swords. Throughout the travel, they ate well, because they were resupplied by the Sequani tribe almost daily. They benefitted from fresh meat and vegetables. Sometimes, they could bargain for something extra like honey or eggs. Quintus had become reasonably proficient in Gaulish. They appointed him their chief negotiator. He won surprising discounts for them.

After ten days of traveling, hostilities began. Reports filtered down about meetings between the Roman command and the Germans. Daily skirmishes raised everyone's anxieties. Now, they traveled across flatter land where they were more exposed. They went back to double time marching as they followed the diminutive Savoureuse River. Locals named it that because of the bounty of delicious foods growing near its banks, but fancy food was the last thing on anyone's mind as they prepared for their inevitable conflict. That night, the Army set up camp within sight of the Germans.

The next morning the troops mustered into battle formation, then received a curious order. They were ordered to form three massive lines. When done, the Pilus prior stood to the right of the Pilus posterior followed by the Princeps prior and posterior then the Hastatus prior and posterior. The new Roman line stretched over a quarter of a mile. When they were given the "At Ease" order, Marcus leaned forward to view the spectacle. He stood twenty-three men from the extreme left of his legion placing him almost one-third of the way in from the edge of the right flank. Pride surged within him. He now belonged to the strong side of the Army.

He and his rank would be among the first to fight. Maybe now he would get his chance to show his valor.

All morning they stood under the hazy late summer sun. They could not see the German camp from their position. At high noon, a cloud of dust appeared over the nearest hill. Soon, they saw the massive German cavalry unit. As the enemy came closer, Marcus guessed there were hundreds of horse soldiers, each with a single infantry soldier at his side. The Roman cavalry moved forward through the narrow spaces between legions and assembled in front of the line. Once the six cavalry wings were assembled, the combatants were evenly matched. Cautiously, the two lines approached and stood within three hundred feet of one another.

Marcus watched the enemy between men and horses. His view of the battlefield was nearly completely obstructed. Occasionally, he could catch a glimpse of the action. Each army would send ten or twenty horsemen to the center. They would slowly dance in circles around one another, each sizing up the other. Then, one cavalry officer would charge and the others would follow. The encounters were brief, but fierce. Casualties were heavy for both horse and man. The less injured Roman casualties walked or crawled back. The others, along with the felled horses, were left to die. German casualties were handled differently. When an injured cavalry man fell, he would be surrounded by footmen. They would lift him and quickly pull him back to their line.

Skirmishes went on all afternoon until the Germans abruptly pulled out. Marcus figured there were over twenty mini-battles. There was no clear winner and the number of injured for each side seemed to be about the same. As the sun set, the cavalries moved back to their original positions. The men marched back into camp where they were dismissed.

"Well, that was a waste of time," Marcus said as they pulled off their armor and sat down to supper.

"Hey, we're still alive!" exclaimed Quintus. "I'd rather have sore feet than a missing body part!"

"Did you see the size of those Germans?" asked Cornelius.

"Giants," mused Appius. "Did you see how fast they ran?"

"They weren't running," said Memmius. "The foot soldiers held onto the manes of the horses and got pulled along. That's pretty ingenious."

"Do you think we could do that?" asked Appius.

"Never," said Martial. They all looked up. Their Centurion, who was surveying his troops, had stopped to listen in on their conversation. "We are foot soldiers. It worked for our grandfathers, it worked for our fathers, and, by Jupiter, it will work for us."

Marcus was getting rambunctious. He asked, "When do we get to fight?"

"It's OK, chief," The rest protested. "Honestly, we can wait."

"Don't worry. Our time will come. This King Ariovistus has yet to commit his soldiers. When he does, you will fight and you will fight hard."

Marcus jumped up. "I'm ready now!"

Quintus tugged at his tunic to get him to sit down.

"You will get to fight only when I tell you to fight! In the meantime, you will do as I say!" barked Martial.

"Yes, sir!" everyone shouted.

After Martial left, Quintus punched Marcus on the upper arm.

"Shut up and enjoy your life before the Germans take it."

Marcus rubbed his arm, but kept his mouth shut. Next morning, the troops marched out and stood in line as they had done the day before.

*   *   *

Several hours into the morning, the Decurion of the Eleventh cavalry walked into the medical area leading his mount.

"Hey, surgeon," he called to Lucius. "Come fix my horse."

Lucius was with his team as they inventoried their supplies. He wanted to be ready in case that day was the big battle. He gave his tablet to a medic and greeted the leader of the cavalry.

"How can I help, Commander?"

It was unusual for the medics to treat animals. The horses were well cared for by the groomsmen. If an animal did become sick or lame, they simply killed it and appropriated another from the local tribes. However, they were actively engaging the enemy and the locals had disappeared with their livestock leaving the valley devoid of horses.

"This is Polidoxus," the Decurion said patting and rubbing the great animal's neck. "I brought him from Tuscany. His sire is from Sicily and his dam is from Iberia, which makes him smart and swift. He is only three years old. When he is healthy, he can outrun and outperform any steed in our wing. Yesterday, he was spectacular. He did everything I asked of him, but toward the end of the day, he seemed tired. He had more froth than usual and it was pink. This morning, he is sluggish and off his feed. I tried to exercise him. A little exercise usually helps him work out his problems, but he only got worse and he is coughing and frothing worse than ever."

Lucius looked at the tall horse. His black coat was immaculate. The commander must have had him groomed daily. Lucius stood only shoulder high to Polidoxus. The great horse was dripping copious amounts of pink foam from his mouth. Lucius watched him breathe. The muscles between his ribs retracted each time. He coughed about every fourth or fifth breath. His eyes were opened wide exposing bloodshot sclerae. Lucius raised his hand to touch his mouth, but the animal reared back, shook his head, and whinnied. As he did, Lucius saw the horse's gums were blue. It reminded him of Taurinus.

"Can you keep him calm while I listen to his chest?"

"I'll try," said the commander. He held the reins close, petted the beast's long nose, and whispered in his ear.

Lucius got close to Polidoxus' body and put his head against the undulating chest. At first the horse jumped away, but the commander's words calmed him down. Lucius heard wheezing and crackling. They were the same sounds he had heard in Taurinus. As he moved his ear down the chest toward the ground, all sounds gradually disappeared.

"Sir, I think your horse has dropsy," Lucius said. "We can try to give him some medicine, but I do not know if he will cooperate." He ordered parnassus and poppy tea and a small amount of foxglove elixir prepared the way Aia taught him. When they were ready, the commander tried to coax Polidoxus to drink it, but he refused.

"Isn't there some other way to do this?" he asked.

"He must take the medicine, sir. We could let out blood, but then he would not be able to fight for several days until the wounds healed."

"If there is nothing else to do, I will have to kill him and take a steed from one of my men."

"Don't you have any extra horses?" asked Lucius.

"We have a few, but they are from the Sequani. Mostly, they are tolerant of pain, but they are not swift. I am afraid that will not do against the Germans. Plus, the few we have are not the best stock."

"Tell me about the German horses," said Lucius trying again to get the frightened animal to drink the concoction.

"They are ugly, but made for war. They have large heads and strong inflexible necks. Their manes grow down to their knees allowing foot soldiers to hang on when they run. They have large bones and a long body. They are all muscle and no fat. They tolerate deep wounds and keep fighting under their rider's command."

"I see why you want your mount for battle," said Lucius. He was getting frustrated as he chased Polidoxus around with the bowl.

"We are not being very successful here," he declared.

The Decurion withdrew his sword and prepared to slay his horse. He was about to stab him in the chest when a wild thought came to Lucius.

"Wait, commander," he said. "If he is to die, let me try one thing first. If it works, you may ride him today. If not, he will suffer the same fate anyway. I need to assemble my team. Please keep trying to get him to drink the medicine."

Lucius ran back to the medical tent while the commander petted his steed and tried again to feed him the medicine. Lucius grabbed four medics and Magnus. He explained what he wanted to do as they worked to assemble what was needed.

"If this animal was a man, you would be killed," Magnus told him.

"Yes, but he is a horse who will die if we don't do it. If it works, we are heroes."

Lucius asked for a scalpel, a stout suture loaded on two needles, and the largest cannula they had. He took four medics with him, one each to hold the animal's legs. They placed the instrument table near the horse, then removed his saddle.

"Commander, we need to keep Polidoxus as still as you can for this delicate surgical procedure," Lucius explained. "Is there anything you can do?"

"When the horses are spooked, we sometimes blindfold them. It calms them down."

Lucius ordered a medic to bring a thick bandage. With the Decurion's help, they blindfolded the great horse. The commander held the reins and whispered into his ear. Lucius examined the chest, mapping out exactly where the noisy breath sounds disappeared. He chose a spot inside the horse's leg and four ribs from the bottom of the chest. He made an incision three finger breaths long and held pressure with lint until the edges stopped bleeding. He placed his suture through the edges of the wound making a U stitch, then he placed the end of the cannula through the skin incision and had Magnus tie the suture loosely around it. He knew if he went straight in, the chest wall hole would line up with the skin incision and that might allow air into the chest and the lung would collapse. So, he pulled the cannula one rib space up toward the head. He grabbed the cannula one hand's breath away from the chest wall so he would not jamb the cannula into some vital organ.

"Okay, everyone," he announced. "I am going to hurt Polidoxus when I shove this cannula into the chest. Be ready to hold him tight. Ready, one, two, three..."

With all the force he could muster, he jammed the cannula through the chest wall up to his hand. Polidoxus whinnied loudly and reared back his head. The Decurion was yanked off the ground as he tried to hold him. The great animal first reared up on his front legs with the medics hanging on, then dropped back down and kicked with his hind legs sending the medics holding the hindquarters sprawling. He continued bucking fiercely.

Clear yellow fluid gushed from the chest through and around the cannula. Lucius tried to keep the cannula in place during the bucking. He had to run around to stay under the chest. Magnus let go of the suture and tried to grab a hind leg. Polidoxus kicked him in the chest sending him to the ground.

The kicking continued as the animal bucked through the medical area knocking over the medicine chest and scattering the other medics among piles of bandages. Eventually, they were able to grab the legs and, with the commander's soothing words, subdued the great animal. Fluid continued to pour from the chest. Lucius estimated maybe two amphora, about a dozen gallons, had drained.

As the drainage slowed, Polidoxus began breathing easier and his froth was no longer pink. He pawed the ground, but became docile to the commander's words. Magnus got up slowly holding his chest.

"That horse has the strongest kick," he panted.

"I wager if I stuck a cannula in your chest, you would kick like a mule too," said Lucius.

"By, Jupiter, I would rip off your head," Magnus grimaced. "I think he broke my ribs."

"We'll fix you later," said Lucius. "Right now, I need you to get ready to tie this suture."

Magnus, still bent over, avoided the horse's hind legs and walked toward his front. He found the soggy ends of the suture and untangled them.

"Ready," he called.

"Okay, now!" called Lucius as he yanked out the cannula. Magnus tied the knots swiftly. Lucius got a second suture and sewed the entire incision closed. After tying the knots, he listened to the animal's chest. The noisy breathing was almost gone and breath sounds could be heard throughout the chest.

"This treatment may have worked," Lucius declared to the Decurion. He slowly removed the blindfold. Polidoxus was still skittish, but his eyes were not as bloodshot. The Decurion got him to drink the medicine while everyone caught their breath.

When Polidoxus was calm, they replaced the saddle. The broad strap did not cross the incision. To prevent leakage, Lucius placed resin and a thick bandage over the area using a secondary strap to secure it in place. The commander mounted up and walked Polidoxus around the medical area, then took him out of camp and trotted around behind his cavalry wing. When he returned, he was obviously pleased.

"I want to thank you for a fine job. I will not forget you and your team. Ad Victoria!" With that he turned around and galloped back to his wing.

They watched as he galloped away. Lucius turned to Magnus who had lifted his tunic to inspect his injury. They saw a hoof shaped bruise just under his right nipple. Lucius carefully palpated the chest wall. No ribs were broken, but it was very painful. He wrapped Magnus' chest tightly with a long bandage and they sat down to rest.

"Where did you dream up that crazy idea?" Magnus asked.

"I don't know," mused Lucius. "It just came to me. I had an experience draining an empyema and thought releasing the fluid might make him breathe better. At least the fluid didn't stink and I didn't get it all over me."

"You are a piece of work, Fortunatus, but I would rather be with you than with any other surgeon in this Army." They clasped forearms and embraced causing Magnus to wince. The team cleaned up the mess and waited to receive casualties, but none came.

Chapter 35: Anticipation

Each morning before breakfast, Aia would assemble a basket of bread, sheep's milk cheese, hard boiled eggs, and wine. She would quietly leave the Druid compound and carry the basket up the mountain to the Roman garrison. She became a familiar face to the soldiers and a welcome sight to the Tesserarius. She would greet the commander cheerily and present her gift to him.

They would pass pleasantries. The commander obviously enjoyed a little feminine diversion. Even pregnant, Aia easily captivated the lecherous old legionnaire. By discussing different topics each day, she was able to maintain her fluency in Latin. She would deftly guide the conversation around to the construction of the new stone wall and watch tower. With only a little pushing, she would cajole her mark into giving her a tour of the ramparts.

The tour always began at the temporary wooden watch tower. Aia would beg the commander for a view from the top and he would always acquiesce. He would help her up the ladder and allow her to survey the valley. She knew he would stand under her and steal a look up her dress. She did not mind, because she was allowed to stay in the watch tower as long as she wanted. She would scour the horizon for any sign of Caesar's Army, but each day, she saw only Sequani tending to their livestock and their crops.

Over the weeks, she watched from the tower as the fields of wheat turned golden. She watched as the men harvested one crop after another. She watched as they brought the bounty to the town to be sold in the market and shared with the Romans. Throughout her observations, she saw no sign of the legions. There was no word whether the Romans had won or lost. Most of all, there was no sign of Lucius.

Vrittakos and Severa tried to make Aia feel comfortable in her new surroundings. They knew she had lost everything. Besançon, the name the Sequani used for Vesontio, was a wonderful town and they wanted Aia to call it home. Since she was the Tigurini's High Priestess, they asked her to work with them. They gave her the task of instructing the next generation of Druids in the ancient arts. She happily applied herself to the chore. She enjoyed working with children. Also, it kept her occupied and left little time to think of her own plight.

The little Sequani Druids of Besançon excelled under Aia's tutelage. She got along well with all the children. She made lessons playful and they found learning fun. They did their morning chores efficiently so they could spend more time with their wonderful new teacher. They begged her to tell stories of her homeland and the Roman Army. She would oblige them, but only after they could recite their lessons flawlessly.

While she played with Vectitos and Potita and the other Druid children, she imagined what it would be like when she had a child of her own. By that point, her abdomen was bulging and she felt life. She allowed the children to feel the little kicking feet. Potita, the same age as Aia's poor dead sister Sina, was particularly interested in the pregnancy and constantly asked questions. She looked forward to being mother's helper when the new baby came.

As summer wore on, Aia found her pregnancy more difficult than she expected. She had gained considerable weight. Severa, whom she called her

Sequani sister, lent Aia her old maternity clothes. She was the same age as Aia's older sister, Oueni, and was about her same height and weight. The clothes should have fit, but as Aia continued to grow, even they were tight around her massive belly. She had to stop climbing the precarious guard tower ladder. She became easily exhausted in the late summer heat and eventually had to stop going up the hill altogether. She still made the baskets, though. She would send Vectitos up to the commander of the guard. She would slip in little notes in Latin for the commander bestowing blessings and wishing him well. One afternoon, she was particularly uncomfortable and had difficulty breathing. Severa examined her.

"Girl! But, your belly is so large! How far along do you think you are again?"

"By my recollection, I have not had a period for four cycles of the moon."

"Are you sure?" Severa was wary. Aia nodded her head.

"I had my last visitation two weeks before Beltane."

"Then you are too big. Maybe you have twins."

"Twins?"

"Yes, twins. You said you were a twin, yourself. Often twins are born to families with a history of twins."

Aia leaned back to better catch her breath. "So this is what my Màthair went through with Toutios and me."

"I am sure she did. Now, you stay inside with us so we can take proper care of you."

"Thank you my Sequani Sora. I am blessed that you are so kind to me."

Severa returned to folding the wash, but glanced at Aia.

"By the way, have you thought of names?"

Aia admitted she had not.

"You better have some names in mind for both boys and girls. They should be named before they come. It is our tradition that you call them by name and talk to them while they are growing inside of you."

As she began to think of names, she remembered her dream. She held the hands of two children. She felt certain she would have a boy and a girl, but the dream did not reveal their faces. She remembered the Roman standing on the dock and her family waiting for her on the island.

"I will name them Lugurix and Lucia. If they are both boys, I will name them Lugurix and Lucius. If they are both girls, I will name them Lugas and Lucia."

"Lucius, Lucia... Those are not Gaulish names, no?"

Aia turned her head to look out the window and sighed.

"No, but they will grow up in a Roman world."

"I see. Isn't that Roman who brought you here named Lucius?"

"Yes," Aia said. She sighed again trying to catch her breath. "Yes, he is."

"I see..." Severa kept quiet and busied herself by straightening the linen.

Aia thought about trying to explain herself to Severa, but she knew it would be pointless. Severa would not understand how much Lucius had sacrificed to save her and how much in love she was with him. Aia did not even realize it herself until he was gone. She longed to be in his arms now, but all she could do was dream of his return, if he would return.

She stayed in bed the rest of the day. Eskenga brought her some soup. Aia thanked her profusely and apologized for not being able to help with the chores. Eskenga shushed her and left to make supper. Aia sipped the rich broth but she was not hungry. She lay back and slept until the next morning when the children woke her at daybreak. She straightened herself up and joined the family for what they called petit-déjeuner. She knew it as pitschen ensolver.

Severa had gotten up early to bake bread. It was hot and crusty and filled the room with a wonderful aroma. Aia broke off the heel of one of the loaves and placed some soft cheese in it. She allowed the cheese to melt as she sipped some camomile tea that Eskenga made for everyone. She nibbled at her bread and cheese. The smells and the sounds reminded her of her home nestled in the shadow of the Alps. She closed her eyes and savored the memory.

After breakfast, the men went out to chop firewood. The children cleaned up the table and presented themselves to Aia, ready for their lessons. They grabbed Aia's hand and pulled at her eager to start their day of schooling, but Banona shooed them away.

"Aia is still tired this morning, children. She needs some rest. Your Màthair will give you your lessons today."

The children both pouted. Potita gave Aia a big hug, then she and her brother trudged off anticipating a boring day.

Aia protested, but Banona, now fully healed from her wrist fracture, patted her arm.

"Take the day to rest, my dear."

Severa left with the children. Eskenga brought three cups of dandelion root tea and sat opposite Aia.

"This is our daily routine," she told Aia. "Now that we are old women, we need a little diuretic in the morning." She acknowledged Banona. "Màthair and I share our tea while we sit and reminisce about our ancestors," said Eskenga as she patted Banona's arm. "We keep their memory fresh in our minds so we may pass our history to Severa and Potita. One day, they will sit here and do the same. We want you to become part of our family, so it is only natural that we share our history with you."

Aia took a sip of the tea and made a face.

"My Màthair never made dandelion tea and I can see why. It is so bitter. Is there any way to make it taste better?"

Eskenga chuckled.

"We are used to it after so many years, but you may add a little honey." She pushed the honey pot in front of her.

Aia poured some of the thick golden clover honey into her brew and stirred it in silence thinking of her own history and ancestors. At length, she acquiesced.

"I would love to hear about your family history." Eskenga was pleased and patted Aia's hand.

"That's a good girl."

Banona began as though she were a crone telling a mythical tale.

"Our clan is very, very, very ancient. Some say we are distant relatives of the Trojan tribe of Greece. We traveled from those lands many, many, many generations ago and settled west of the River Saône. We lived peacefully there for many, many years. All the peoples of the land were very friendly and eventually we married into each other's clans. Because of that, we are related to the Aedui, the Ambarri, the Aulerci, the Carnuti, the Lingones, the Senones and the Turoni tribes." She counted the seven tribes on her fingers then took a sip of tea.

"Our collective strength was our ability to work and live together because we each brought special skills and talents to make our lives better. We were known for raising and trading horses with the other tribes. Our horses were the finest in the land. Our men used them to herd sheep and cattle because these horses were especially good in small spaces. They could stop and change direction as swiftly as a dog or cat. Still to this day, the men perform a riding dance with their steeds at festivals and hold competitions to see who can herd a bull the fastest."

Eskenga took over the story.

"One day, many years ago, an aggressive tribe known as the Mandubii wanted our lands. Fierce battles were fought and many of our warriors died. Eventually, our tribe was too weak to defeat the Mandubii, so we crossed the Saône to these lands and found this beautiful area to make our own. The few people who lived here allowed us to share their land and we settled with them. We brought our horses and raised even stronger stock. Our peoples lived peacefully for many, many years."

Eskenga took a break and prepared a midday snack. Banona took up the story.

"My great grand Màthair told me that her great, great grand Màthair was the first to fall in love with one of the local people. She met him one spring day while she was gathering medicinal flowers by the river. He was a fisherman from the East. He was quite young and fishing alone for the first time. Because of his inexperience, he got too close to the swift white water currents. They dragged him down and away from shore. He could not fight the strong current. The waters took him far from home all the way to our village. The river flows slowly around Besançon so he was finally able to swim ashore. He climbed out right where she was collecting herbs. He was a handsome young man. He was very tall and spoke a strange dialect. Although she should have been frightened, she was moved by his story and asked him to stay with her family until he could return home. To show his gratitude, he caught fish and cooked them for the family. He told stories that kept the family amused and he taught the men the best way to fish. Before the spring was over, they were in love. Their marriage brought our clans together. Now, we are one clan."

Eskenga brought back grapes, freshly cut pears, some cheese and cups of milk. She distributed the snack and took up the story.

"About the time Severa was to have her coming of age ceremony, we were brutally attacked by the Aedui. It stunned us since they are our relatives. We had no choice but to beg King Ariovistus and the Germans to help us fight them. He was successful, but after he restored peace, he did not go home. He and his people loved this land better than their own and they stayed. They began to take our fields and our cattle. We all grumbled, but we could do very little about it."

Both women became teary eyed as Eskenga continued.

"When Ariovistus began to take our young men and women as slaves, we became terrified and angry. We had to turn to the Romans to chase him away. When they entered our city, we thought of them as liberators. Then you came with your stories of the slaughter of your tribe and your brethren. They sounded as bad as the Germans. Now we are learning first hand for how cruel they can be."

Aia wanted to protest. She harbored her own conflicted feelings about the Romans. Yes, they had killed her family, but they were no worse than Bimmos with his outrageous aspirations. He was the tyrant who burned her village and was responsible for the eventual destruction of her tribe. The Roman surgeon, Lucius, saved her and protected her. Without him, she would have died alone in foreign lands.

Banona stood up and moved close to the hearth.

"These Romans may drive away King Ariovistus and his people, but they themselves are cruel masters." Banona was so angry that she was shaking. "They demand we change our ways and they take our harvest with little more than a thank you. They do not pay us what it is worth. They take the best and leave us with the almost nothing."

"I had no idea you felt that way about them," Aia said, apologetically.

Eskenga sensed Aia's uneasiness and patted her hand.

"That's enough history for now. Let's go for a walk. There is someone I want you to meet." They went out arm-in-arm leaving Banona muttering to herself.

When they were in the courtyard, Eskenga apologized for her mother.

"Lately, Màthair has changed. Sometimes she gets angry and lashes out at the littlest things. She remembers her youth as if it were yesterday, but she forgets what I made her for breakfast. Why, this spring at Beltane, before you and the Romans arrived, she sat with Oclos, one of the elders. He had been her childhood sweetheart before she met my Athair. During the ceremony, they started kissing and before long, they began to strip! In front of everyone! It was most embarrassing for us. That evening, she remembered nothing of it." Eskenga shuddered and said a prayer.

They came to a pair of large oak doors near the West end of the building.

"Ah, we are here," Eskenga told Aia. They stood and admired the massive doors for a moment. They were carved with whorls and complex squares more intricate than the carvings on the doors of the main entrance. Some circular whorls blended into other whorls to form a triple pattern. Both doors had a bronze plaque. The center of the plaque was raised to form the face of a Sequani warrior. His arms were raised and held a sword and an arrow. Aia noted that the arms were joined below the chin to form a knocker.

Eskenga picked up the heavy bronze arms of the one on the right door and slowly knocked three times. At length, the door opened slowly. An old thin Druid in a white cloak sporting a long beard stood at the door. He recognized Eskenga and gave her a big hug. They held a brief conversation, then Eskenga introduced him to Aia.

"This is my uncle Silus. He is my Athair's older brother. He was selected to be the High Priest, but chose to spend his life becoming a celestial scholar instead. I am very proud of him." She rubbed his arm. "He is considered the greatest scholar of the Sequani."

"That is not true," he said shaking a finger at her.

"It most certainly is," she retorted. "You dedicated your life to the study of the heavens. You never leave the Great Study Hall except at night to look in the sky. You never married because the stars are your mistress."

"Yes, you are right, but for being a scholar, I did get this ring." He showed it to Aia. It was carved from a black stone and had whorls like the ones on her necklace. Eskenga playfully pushed her shoulder into his.

"That's enough bragging. Now share some of your knowledge with Aia. She is the Tigurini High Priestess and I am sure she will be very interested in your research."

Silus bowed deeply to Eskenga.

"As you wish, my dear." He smiled at Aia.

"She is my favorite niece. I would do anything for her." He turned and they followed behind him as he guided them into the cavernous space. As they walked, he began his detailed tour.

"When our fathers came to this beautiful land, they were delighted because of the terrain. The mountain, one of the tallest in the area, made it easy to defend. It was not long before they realized that it also provided a perfect spot to observe the heavens. The elders established the Druid colony at the base of the mountain for protection from the elements and to preserve a grove of trees for our rituals. They built this compound to be self sufficient except for the food, which is grown outside of the village." He waved his hand toward the great open space of the hall.

"They also established this great hall for us to store our celestial observations and to study and learn from one another. As we walk through, you will see five other scholars, each about ten years apart in age. I am the oldest. The youngest just had his coming of age ceremony. They each have their own desk for studying past writings and for making new observations and correcting previous calculations. Our goal is to better predict how the stars, the sun, and the moon will interact with the earth."

Aia marveled at what she saw. The hall was quite large. There was no second floor, so the space rose over ten meters to the pitched wooden roof. There were tall narrow windows every three meters allowing in plenty of light and offering places for observations of the heavens. She could make out carvings on every rafter. Some of the symbols she did not recognize.

"I see strange symbols on the rafters," she commented.

"Ah, yes. Those are symbols for the sun, the moon, and the planets. We have devised a unique symbol for each. When we make an observation, we do not have to write out the whole name."

"You write these observations?" Aia was astonished.

"Yes, my dear. It allows us to make better predictions. Many, many, many years ago, our forebears deciphered the heavens and passed it to us by word of mouth. I assume it is so in your clan as well," he asked Aia.

Aia nodded. "We spend many years in the study of our ancestors's knowledge."

"Wonderful. I am glad we have so much in common," Silus replied, then continued his discussion.

"There is a relationship between earth, sun, and moon. They are in a delicate dance with Mother Goddess and Father Sky. This dance repeats, but it is a long dance – too long for any one of us to comprehend. Our crops live by the cycle of the sun, but we live by the cycle of the moon. The moon cycle is not just from full moon to full moon, but we did not know how long the dance really was until we began to write down our observations." He showed her a sheet of parchment with symbols denoting the path of the sun and moon.

"You see, the cycle lasts many, many years. I personally have witnessed only three cycles, and I am an old man. My Athair showed me the beginning of a cycle when I was very young. It is marked by a change in the height of the moon as it courses across the sky. In one half cycle from full to new moon, it can vary halfway up or down the sky. Nine sun years later, it only moves the width of your hand." He demonstrated with his outstretched hand.

"Yes, I saw some of those changes, but paid them no mind," mused Aia.

"Well, my child, you are too young to remember even one cycle. It takes nearly nineteen sun years. That is why each of us is so different in age. We make our observations and pass them to the next generation so we can become even more accurate in predicting what will happen next in the dance of the heavens. Come, let me show you what I have been working on." He directed them to his desk.

They walked past a giant fireplace on the outer building wall. Aia estimated that it was three meters high and six meters wide.

"Why such a large fireplace?" she asked.

"It is the home of the fire we light at Beltane. We keep it going until our next Beltane. Villagers often come here to relight their home fires. In the winter, we can grow the fire to heat the entire hall warmly. When the weather is foul, we can hold our sacrificial rituals here. A few years ago, we held the beginning of the mistletoe harvest ceremony here. It was large enough to immolate a large white bull."

Aia was impressed that the Sequani Druids had learned to live almost entirely indoors. She was not sure she could ever leave the forest and the meadows to live in such a way. She certainly hoped her children would experience the outdoor world the way she had. Thoughts of her clan's valley began to play before her eyes and she had to hold back a few tears.

They reached Silus' desk. It was messier than the other scholars. He rummaged through scraps of parchment until he unearthed what he was looking for.

"Here it is," he announced.

The women stood by his side to see. It was a large sheepskin stretched out on a frame. On it was drawn a large rectangle broken into sixty-four squares. Names of months were written across two squares each.

"We have agreed on a theory," he told them. "This entire rectangle represents five sun years. Each square represents half of a moon cycle, so two squares represents a month. You see on the right side, we have the month of Samonios - Summer's End. Then, you see each of our twelve months as we count them for a full five years. Unfortunately, that falls short of five sun years. So, we have added two Ciallos festivals, each of five days. Those festivals have become our most solemn mistletoe harvests. We hold one at the start of our calendar just before Summer's end, one two and a half years later at Winter's End, then in two and a half years, just before the Summer Ciallos, the five year cycle is complete!"

Aia passed her hand over the sheepskin counting the months. She marveled at the simplicity of the idea. She knew how the scholars of her clan struggled to make the seasons coincide with the moon. They frequently made adjustments to the calendar to keep the sun and the moon phases in balance.

"Of course, this is still just theory," he said. "We have agreed to observe several cycles. One cycle began two years ago." He pointed to the space in the middle of the calendar.

"We plan our next Ciallos ceremony after this year's winter. Once we are sure of the accuracy, we will commission our blacksmiths to make a leaden tablet and strike the calendar on it. We will display it in the courtyard for everyone to use." He ushered them back to the large doors, where Eskenga gave him a big hug.

"I am so proud of you, uncle. You gave up so much to study the heavens. I wish you and your colleagues success." Aia thanked Silus for the tour. He gently kissed her on the forehead and gave her a blessing. Aia genuflected and kissed his charm ring, then the two women left.

Aia was excited. She knew now that the Druid colony was the place for her. These people were so much like her family. They were kind and welcoming. They pursued the natural arts with a passion. It was as though the Earth Mother herself had guided Aia with her own hand. That night she told her adoptive family she accepted her place as a foster child of Eskenga and sister to Severa. They were overjoyed and celebrated with a special distilled grape wine that Vrittakos was saving for a great occasion.

Next morning, everyone was up early to prepare for the ritual of Lugos. Aia was welcomed into the inner circle of the Druids by Vrittakos and Severa. As the newly adopted member of the family and a former High Priestess, it was only fitting that she represent Lugos's foster mother, Tailtiu.

They gathered into a circle around an altar in an open space in the woods on the Druid complex. In front of the altar stood Vrittakos and Severa with their hoods down. Four elders representing the four winds stood north, south, east and west. A young Sequani warrior chosen to represent Lugos dressed in his finest armor carried a sheaf of wheat and a basket of grapes. He was escorted into the circle by Aia representing Tailtiu. They stood in front of the High Priest and Priestess. Aia guided the warrior in front of her saying,

This is my son, Lugos
He is the Shining One, the Bright One, the Golden One
And he is the Sacrificed One
He was conceived in the depths of Winter
He was Born in the Spring
You and your people lovingly cared for him
He danced all Summer growing in your love
Now, He is straight and mature, strong and robust, sweet and tender,
I give him to you so that
You may live through Winter's long Night.

All the participants put up their hoods. Aia stood with her hands clasped while the warrior presented his gifts to Vrittakos and Severa. Severa picked up a bowl from the altar and Vrittakos shook the grain releasing the seeds into the bowl. The young warrior standing beside the altar extended his arm. He drew his sword and made a long gash in his forearm allowing his blood to mix with the seeds. Severa and Vrittakos held up the bowl together and intoned,

We partake of the first harvest
So that we may continue our quest for wisdom and perfection.
Lady of the Moon and Lord of the Sun
We offer our thanks for the continued fertility of the Mother Goddess.

Severa took the bowl and poured the seeds mixed with the blood into the shallow pit prepared that morning by the young Druids. The Druid elders covered the seeds with dirt, then all together the participants said,

May these grains be buried in Mother's earth
Ensuring Lugos's rebirth this coming Spring.

Young women brought baskets of bread, berries and jugs of wine to the participants. They stood in front of the altar while the congregation lined up to receive the gifts from them.

For the first time, Aia viewed the ritual in a new light. Even though the young warrior was not sacrificed and buried with the grain as the Tigurinis would have done, he still gave his blood, his life force to the seeds. He represented Lugos who made the ultimate sacrifice for those in this world.   Her Lugurix, who was named after Lugos, had sacrificed himself for his people.   Toutios sacrificed himself to give her a chance to save her dying father.   Lucius was willing to sacrifice his career to save her life, which gave her the opportunity to join a vibrant community and where her children would continue in the traditions of her homeland.   In the ritual, she played Tailtiu giving her son away to be sacrificed for a bountiful harvest in the year to come.   She rubbed her belly and wondered what her own real life sacrifice would be for her unborn.

Chapter 36: Fortifications

For five consecutive mornings, the infantry formed up, marched to their designated spot, and stood at parade rest to watch the cavalry skirmishes. Between camp and battle line, they had worn away the grass. The ground had the look of a new highway. The troops nicknamed it Via Germanica. With nothing else to do, Marcus and Quintus worked their sandals into the dirt making impressions where they stood. When they returned to their stations the following day, they found to their bored amusement that they stood in the same location. However, that day they did not stay long.

"To the left – Face!" The entire line turned into a three line marching column.

"March!" came the next order. They marched for a quarter of a mile and stopped.

"To the right – Face!" They turned back into the three line battle formation.

"March!"

All six legions marched in quarter mile wide lines. Marcus observed that the lines did not waver. Because they had marched together for months, their paces measured the same. Now, they were ready to do battle. They marched straight toward the enemy. It looked as though they would march directly into the German camp. When they stopped, they were no more than five hundred yards from the enemy camp, which was situated on a hill above the field. Legatii swung their horses around and galloped behind the lines.

"Third Line, to the rear – Face!" They executed the maneuver.

The legatus of Legio XI trotted to the front, then up and down the line before stopping in the center to address his troops.

"Today, your assignment is to build a second camp. This must be done in one day. All hands are needed. Upon dismissal, report to your Centurion. He has your assignments. Ready, dismissed!"

"What?" cried Marcus.

"Hush!" said Quintus as he grabbed his buddy. "Just do your job and shut up!"

Marcus understood and kept quiet as the centuria gathered around Martial.

"Listen up, you melon heads," boomed Martial. "We must construct this camp in half a day. It needs to be just like the fine camp in Placentia. It will house two legions. Our job is to dig the trench around the perimeter of the camp. We are working with Legions Nine and Ten. Cohorts one and two dig the North ditch, cohorts three, four and five, the East ditch, cohorts six, seven and eight the West ditch, cohorts nine and ten the South ditch."

"That sounds odd," whispered Marcus to Quintus. Quintus elbowed him so hard he lost his breath.

"Our auxiliaries are being pulled in to help. Report to the engineers. Any questions?"

Quintus poked Marcus again.

"No? Move out!"

"Why did you do that?" Marcus gasped once his breath returned.

"Because I don't want any more 'special' assignments."

They walked quickly into the area selected for the new castra. There was a young engineer's assistant directing them to the appropriate mustering area.

"North wall to your right. South wall to your left.   West wall keep marching. East wall stay here."

As they walked to the South area, Marcus saw the reason for the difference in the size of the groups. Engineer's assistants stood at the corners of the planned perimeter. The east and west walls were twice as long as the north and south walls. They gathered around a lean middle aged engineer who stood on a small mound of dirt piled there by two engineer's assistants who had started digging the trench. Standing on the opposite side of the trench were the auxiliaries.   Once everyone was assembled, the engineer addressed them.

"Good morning, gentleman. Our job is to build the south wall trench."

Marcus thought he looked and sounded like a Patrician. His manner was easygoing. Marcus hoped he would be kinder with them than Martial and the legion commanders. He listened to the engineer describe the assignment.

"The trench must be nine feet wide and six feet deep at the middle. Your dirt must be piled toward the camp side to make a rampart.   Each man is responsible for a twenty-five foot section. Line up in two legion columns in your respective cohorts. Auxiliaries, line up between the legions."

That resulted in shuffling and milling around until they heard the voice of Martial.

"Legio Nine, form a column!   Legio Ten, form a column!   Legio Eleven, form a column!"

The legionnaires quickly fell into position.   Martial addressed the auxiliaries next.

"You, in here!" he shouted motioning with his hands where to muster. The groups quickly aligned in proper order. He turned back to the engineer who began positioning them from the East with the first six, then the next, and so on, each about ten paces apart. When the line was complete, Marcus could see the order. One legionnaire of the Tenth, then an auxiliary, then one of the Ninth, then an auxiliary, then one of the Eleventh, then an auxiliary, and so on.   The engineer came back along the line repeating the orders.

"Begin your work facing the castra. Work from right to left until you reach the trench of your neighbor. When the trench is dug, climb out and form your dirt into the highest mound you can make. It should stand nearly six feet high."

As the engineer passed down the line, each man received an entrenching tool from the assistants who distributed them from a cart. Upon receiving their tool, each man began his assignment. Marcus started vigorously, but soon stopped for a breath. As he wiped the sweat from his brow, he heard a whip crack over his head.

"Now is not the time for breaks. Back to work!"

He looked up. It was the engineer. He no longer seemed like a kind and gentle Patrician. He was snarling.

"This rampart usually takes three days to dig. We have a half day. Dig, soldier!"

Marcus went back to digging like a fiend. After he was sure the old man had moved on, he stopped and addressed the legionnaire from the Ninth.

"That guy is a taskmaster, eh?" he said.

The legionnaire ignored him and kept digging. Marcus tried addressing the legionnaire from the Tenth.

"What do you think?"

He got no response. He called out to the auxiliary who shrugged his shoulders.

"No Latin I spoke," he replied.

"Crack!" Marcus ducked. It was an engineer's assistant.

"Great!" Marcus muttered as he began shoveling again. He worked in silence as the sun rose high in the sky.

"Crack! Crack! Crack!"

Marcus ducked into the growing trench he had made.

"Break time!" shouted the Engineer.

Marcus stood up. He was sore already. He looked back. He had dug nearly eight feet of trench but still had at least three times that distance to go. He groaned loudly.

"Quit belly aching." It was the legionnaire from the Tenth.

Marcus sized up the older legionnaire. He figured he was twice his age.

"How have you survived so long in the legion, soldier?"

"Keep your mouth shut, stay in line, follow all orders without question, live long." His accent was very thick.

"Thank you for the advice. Where are you from?"

The older legionnaire spit at him. It sailed through the air and landed near Marcus' feet.

"Why do you care?"

"Sorry, I was just curious. I'm trying to be friendly here."

The legionnaire spit again.

"Don't make small talk." After an awkward silence he said, "Cantabria."

It slowly dawned on Marcus that he had heard the accent mimicked by his uncle Nanius, the merchant. He frequently traveled to that part of Iberia. One night while visiting the Romanus villa in Canino, he got drunk and started mocking the Cantabrian accent by reciting humorous lines from the play "The Ass Merchant" by Plautus. His father and his older sisters were laughing hysterically. He laughed as well, but he was too young to understand the ribald humor of Plautus. The only line he understood was "Is my wife's breath bad? I would rather drink bilge water than kiss her." A crack of the whip brought him back.

"All right, back to work!"

Marcus applied himself and left the Cantabrian alone.

"He might be a wily survivor, but he didn't have to be so prickly," He thought to himself.

They worked into the afternoon when a commotion in front of the castra drew everyone's attention. Marcus could barely see since the action was over a mile in front of him, and he was blocked by his own mound of dirt. He peered around his pile to see Germans engaging the two front lines of the Roman infantry. He could hear the shouted orders and swords clanging, but could make out little else. The battle sounded amazingly close, even though the fighting was more than a half mile away. The whip cracked again and they were forced back to work, but even the engineers paused often to watch the fighting. Soon, a Centurion strode across the growing campsite.

"Ignore the fighting," he told them. "The German forces are engaging us in small fights. Our first and second lines will hold them back. Perform your jobs well and trust your comrades will do their jobs."

Marcus worked through the day with only two more short breaks. By late afternoon, they had finished the trench and were shaping the rampart. When first dug out, the earth was moist and clumpy. By that point, the hot sun had dried it out. As the late afternoon breeze picked up, the air was thick with dust. He was covered in dirt like everyone else. They did the best they could to shape the mound into a rampart. When they were done, it stood less than four feet high, but would still be a good deterrent to any attacking force. Marcus sat down and took a long drink of his water. As he gulped, he heard a familiar voice.

"Form a line!" It was Martial.

He stood up feeling every muscle screaming for rest. He joined the other legionnaires who were already done. Only a handful had finished their assignment. Martial walked up and down inspecting the dirty contingent.

"Congratulations on finishing quickly, gentlemen. For your reward, we will dig the latrines!"

"Jupiter!" Marcus muttered under his breath.

Martial walked over to Marcus and stared into his eyes.

"That's right, gentlemen." He turned away from Marcus and walked down the line of muddy diggers.

"Our troops deserve the best crappers and you are our best diggers. So, to you falls the assignment of creating the best latrines!" Martial reversed directions and walked up the line as he continued.

"It just so happens that the best latrine digger is among us." He stopped in front of Marcus and looked at him as he spoke.

"Marcus Calidius will lead this detail. As other soldiers finish, they will join you until the work is done. Everyone understand? Good! Calidius, lead your diggers!"

Marcus' jaw dropped. He stood in silence for a moment looking at Martial who sported a grin from ear to ear.

"Let's go, son. You don't have much time!"

"Right! Yes, sir!" Marcus felt his heart thumping faster and faster. The job was terrible, but at least he was in charge. He marched his troops to the designated area. He had not forgotten that first time on the beach when Martial spit orders at them. He recited them now for his charges.

"Okay, you filthy scum buckets, spread out ten paces from each other. Each of you, dig a hole two feet wide, three feet long and three feet deep. Pile the mud away from the camp. We don't have all day, so get moving!"

With his instructions, they began to dig. He was about to pick up his entrenching tool when he realized he needed to supervise. Martial had not only given him the honor of command, albeit a scumbag detail, he had given him a chance to rest. He watched with pride as his charges quickly completed the project. He inspected each hole criticizing the depth or the length until they were just the way he had been taught. He thanked them, then formed up the detail and called them to attention. He sent the Cantabrian to fetch Martial who was not far away.

With great pomp, Martial first inspected the latrines from the front, then he circled around kicking at the dirt piles and nodding. He smiled to himself and turned to Marcus.

"Well done, soldier! Dismiss your detail to return to their legions. We are forming up to move out."

"Yes, sir!" Marcus replied. Martial took off for the Southern gate of the camp and disappeared. Marcus turned to his charges.

"Detail! Parade rest!" They snapped into position. Marcus walked up and down his line of grubby muddy men.

"We just passed inspection without criticism from one of the toughest Centurions in Caesar's Army! I'm proud of you!" He stopped front and center of his line and came to attention.

"Detail! Attention!" They snapped to like seasoned legionnaires.

"Caparum Romanus..."

"Ad Victoria!" they replied. Marcus took a moment to enjoy his first opportunity to lead the legionnaires' battle cry.

"Dimitto!" he shouted. Immediately, everyone broke out in a run back to their units. Marcus stood there for a moment enjoying his first taste of command, then he too ran through the castra and out of the Eastern gate to find his position in the nearly reformed legion.

By that point, the fighting was over. Few were injured, but there were a great number of prisoners being marched toward the main camp. Orders were barked and Legions Eight, Nine, Ten and Eleven turned and marched back to the main camp leaving Legions Seven and Twelve behind in the smaller camp.

When they were finally dismissed, they collapsed in their tents, not even attempting to clean up the mud that was in every crack, crevice, and oriface. Even supper was seasoned with a bit of dirt.

The next morning as the four legions formed up, they saw that all the auxiliary troops were forming up with the two legions at the smaller camp. The troops were in the standard battles, but in their new order. Legions Eight and Nine made up the weak side and Eleven was inside of Ten on the strong side. It was the most impressive sight Marcus had ever seen. Then, in unison, the three line army began to march across the open space toward the German camp.

When they were within three hundred yards of the enemy encampment, Marcus saw the German Army pour out of the West side of the camp and form up in front of the Romans. Before each legion was a different tribe. Behind the tribal warriors were their wagons filled with their women and children. He could hear the women screaming and wailing, although he could not understand the strange words.

"This is it," he thought. *"We are about to get the action I have been waiting for."*

"Attention! Listen Closely!" The Legatii and their staff for the Tenth and Eleventh legions rode to the back of the formation.

"Lines one and two, advance!"

Marcus watched as the lines in front of him began to march forward. Almost immediately, the Germans charged the Romans. Marcus could see that there was too little room for the front line to throw their javelins. The gap between adversaries was shrinking quickly.

"There's no time," he said to Martial. "They should lay down their Pila!"

"Pipe down scumbag." snarled Martial. "You're not the commander! Let them do their job."

Marcus clenched his teeth and sucked in a breath.

"Lay down your Pila!" yelled the commander. Marcus exhaled in relief. The order was repeated by the Centurions. At once the front line dropped their javelins.

"Draw your swords!"

"Ready! Charge!"

Both Roman lines ran ahead to engage the Germans, but the enemy was prepared. The barbarians formed a tight phalanx similar to the Testudo they had practiced during their long march into Gaul. Their shields were large and, when held together, covered most of the warriors in the tight formation. They ran ahead like a battering ram.

Marcus watched in amazement as legionnaires from the front line climbed on top of the formation and pulled at the shields hurling them like a discus away from the formations. Others took advantage of the openings, plunging their swords through the gaps. Soon, the German phalanx disintegrated. Open hand-to-hand combat broke out all over the field of battle. He had never been that close to the battle before. He saw swords going into torsos drawing gushes of blood. He watched as a Roman sword swung at the neck of a German warrior delivered a fatal blow. More kill shots were delivered by the Romans than the Germans.

Before the sun was high in the sky, the Romans turned the left flank of the Germans. Some were pressed against the next tribe, but most fled to their wagons and headed off the battlefield to the Northeast. Marcus focused on the commanders' tactics as the first two lines of the Tenth and Eleventh joined the Eighth and Ninth to attack the tribes in front of them. His concentration was broken by the sound of hoofbeats and shouting from his commander behind him.

"Third line! Left Face!"

Marcus followed the command.

"Form Battle line!"

With the precision pounded into them in Placentia his cohort executed the maneuver flawlessly.

"Advance!"

They marched in double time to the West. As they got closer, they could see the Seventh and Twelfth legions locked in a fierce battle with the Germans. They had lost ground and were nearly pressed back to the small camp he helped build the day before. Their line moved to within one hundred feet of the fighting.

"Third line! Draw your swords!"

Marcus whipped out his sword. It caught the sun and flashed in his eyes. He blinked to get his vision back. In front of him was the enemy killing his brothers in arms. His heart was racing. He felt a surge of heat and energy.

"Third line ready! Charge!"

At once, his cohort was screaming and running ahead in a wavy line with swords raised high.

Chapter 37: The Cost of War

Marcus was first to reach the enemy line. He swung his sword at the nearest German. His blow tore through the cuirass at the shoulder cutting deeply into the flesh and knocking the warrior down. He plunged his blade into the chest of the screaming barbarian. Without waiting to see the result, he withdrew his sword and began hacking at anything that was not Roman.

He broke ranks and moved ahead of his line killing or fatally wounding every German he faced. He unleashed his pent up anger. He had not been allowed to join the legion without his brother Lucius. He did not get to be a horse soldier like his brother Faustus. He had no rank. He was forced to enter as a raw recruit like a non-citizen or a farmer to be belittled and berated by one of the Roman Army's most hardboiled centurions. He had seen no action for five months. He had been forced to dig latrines nearly every day. Now, he finally had his opportunity to show his valor. No one would match him. He simply was too swift and powerful for the German warriors. He felt his confidence grow with each blow. He had no idea how many of the enemy he killed.

Martial and the rest of the century tried to catch up to the crazed young Roman who seemed possessed by Mars himself. No one would be able to match him that day. Martial had to smile. Few of his trainees over the years developed such ferocity. He still was able to ingrain the true qualities of a legionnaire in his charges.

Marcus broke through the first wave of Germans and looked around. He was deep in the enemy formation far ahead of his line. Bodies lay all around him. Now, he faced a fresh wave of barbarians. He could see the Roman line still some distance away working toward him. He turned back to the warriors who seemed a little wary of him.

He remembered one of his Pater's lessons of combat. He charged at the biggest warrior bringing down his blade like a hatchet, but the German blocked it with his shield. The giant barbarian swung at Marcus. As Marcus pulled back, he felt the sharp blade cut his cheek. He felt no pain and ignored the blood. They swung and hacked away at one another until the Roman line broke through. The first to arrive was Quintus. When the German looked up to see the Romans rushing into the opening, Marcus seized the moment. He skewered his opponent through the upper abdomen. The big German looked down, surprised at the blow. He looked up at Marcus and vomited blood on the young legionnaire, then collapsed. Marcus used his shield to deflect most of the blood.

By that time, Quintus was at his side. Together, they fought on cutting down warrior after warrior until the German attack was repulsed. As the resistance eroded, the enemy broke formation and ran for their wagons pursued by other legionnaires. Marcus and Quintus stood watching the retreat and catching their breath at the edge of the battlefield. Both were unaware that the giant German, skewered by Marcus, had struggled to his feet and was coming up behind them. He raised his sword with both hands to deal a blow to Marcus, but collapsed as he came forward. When he crashed to the ground, his left hand lost grip on the sword. The right arm swung the sword downward and to the left. The blade hacked into the back of Marcus' right lower leg. Marcus winced at the pain and looked down.

Blood was gushing out of the wound. He fell to his knees.

"Quintus, help me!"

Quintus turned around to see Marcus staring wide eyed at a gaping wound. Blood spurted onto the ground, mixing with the blood of the Germans. He quickly removed his pack and pulled out his field dressings. He stuffed the wad into the bleeding space.

"Here, hold this."

Still kneeling, Marcus reached around and pressed the dressing with his right hand. Quintus placed a long cloth underneath the area and wrapped it around the wadded dressing. He tied it as tight as he could. The gushing stopped, but the dressing soon became saturated with blood.

"We need to get you to the hospital," Quintus yelled over the din of the battle. He helped his buddy to his feet.

Marcus put his hand on Quintus' shoulder and began to walk, but he fell almost immediately. He looked up at Quintus. He was frightened to his core for the first time in his life.

"My foot doesn't work."

"Come on," said Quintus. He helped Marcus up again allowing him to place his arm around his neck. Marcus held his right leg off the ground and hopped as they headed off the battlefield.

The distance back to the major camp was only a mile, but it seemed like ten. They had to step over and around countless bodies. They tried to avoid slipping in the gooey blood and body fluids covering the ground. Marcus slipped twice, one time taking Quintus with him.

"You were a maniac on the battlefield," Quintus told Marcus as they navigated the fallen warriors. "You must have killed over a hundred men by yourself. We could see you moving deeper into the enemy line, but we could not keep up with you. You might have won this battle all by yourself."

"Thanks, but right now, you are the most important person in my life. Thank you for staying to help me."

Quintus shook his head.

"You know I would do anything for you, brother."

They finally made it to the main camp. They headed for their medical area where there was a growing line of walking wounded. Lucius was leading the triage station. They could see him quickly examining the wounded legionnaires and gesturing to the medics. The medics would whisk away the wounded to other stations. By the time they made it to the front of the line, blood was dripping through the dressing and onto the ground.

"Lucius, am I glad to see you!" Marcus told his brother.

"Likewise!" exclaimed Lucius. "I am glad you are alive and out of the battle, but are you injured?"

"Unfortunately, yes," said Quintus. "It's a good thing for the Germans, though. Marcus was a one man army."

"A cursed barbarian sliced my leg. Now my foot doesn't work."

Lucius looked at the blood soaked dressing. Without taking the dressing down, he placed a dressing around the lower thigh and twisted the ends together. He placed a short stick between the ends of the dressing and tied it into place with the loose ends, then he used the stick to twist it until Marcus began to complain.

"Prepare this man for surgery," he told one of the medics. "Possible amputation."

"What?" Marcus was dumbfounded.

"We won't know until we get a look at the wound," Lucius explained. "Right now, hold this." He put Marcus' hand on the tourniquet. "If it begins to bleed again, twist this until it stops."

"But it hurts," Marcus whined.

"Your pains are just beginning, soldier," Lucius told his brother. The only way he could hold back his emotion was to treat Marcus like any other legionnaire. He turned to Quintus.

"You're his buddy. Knock him out if you have to, but keep that tourniquet tight."

"Yes, sir!" a stunned Quintus answered.

Lucius went back to triaging while they were led away.

"That wasn't very compassionate," Quintus said to Marcus and the medic.

"Try doing two or three thousand evaluations and let's see how compassionate you are," the medic told them. "You won't find a better surgeon in Caesar's Army."

Quintus kept his thoughts to himself after that. He tried to pass the time with idle conversation, but Marcus continued to have severe pain in the leg at the site of the tourniquet with numbness below it. He whined and begged Quintus to loosen the tourniquet. Quintus reluctantly obliged.

"It feels like someone just poured hot water on my leg from the knee to the toe," Marcus told him. A few moments later he said, "Now everything feels fiery and tingles except for the sole and the outer part of my foot. I don't feel anything there."

The bleeding started again and Quintus had to tightened the tourniquet. Marcus persuaded Quintus to loosen the tourniquet twice more with the same result. He had just retightened the tourniquet when a medic brought Marcus an acetabulum full of mashed poppy seeds. Before he gave it to him, he spied the blood on the ground. The medic shook his head and glared at Quintus.

"I can tell you loosened the tourniquet, soldier. You disobeyed a direct order. You could be crucified for less."

"I know," said Quintus, "but he was crying—" The medic cut him off.

"I don't care, ass. Not following the directions of the surgeon could jeopardize the surgical result. Then you might have the death of your comrade on your head for the rest of your miserable existence."

"Sorry, sir." Quintus looked at the bloody ground. "It won't happen again."

"Damn straight, it won't!" spit the medic. Then he turned to Marcus. "Take this. Chew the seeds thoroughly and swallow them with your water ration. Take all of it quickly"

Marcus obliged. He took a large mouthful and chewed. The tiny seeds crunched. They were dry and he coughed on the mash. He finally got it down with the help of several swigs of water. After that, he took smaller mouthfuls and chewed more slowly. By the time he finished the whole acetabulum, he felt lightheaded. Shortly afterwards, the medics came to collect him for surgery.

"You can't come with us," the medic told Quintus.

"What am I supposed to do?"

"You did what was necessary to save a legionnaire, now you must report back to your Centurion."

As the medics took Marcus away, Quintus felt lost. He thought about

Decimus lying on the ground gasping for air. It might be the last time he would see his buddy alive.

"That's Okay, brother," Marcus told him. "Do what you have to do. I'll put my trust in Aesculapius and my brother."

"Vigoratus is the best surgeon in the legion," said the medic, "but it won't hurt to pray to all the gods you can think of to guide his hands."

Quintus watched them leave, then exited the tent. It was dark. Night had fallen while he stayed with Marcus. He headed to the tent of the ninth cohort. No one was there. He looked around. Most of the camp was empty. He figured they were still in pursuit of the enemy. He had missed his unit, but he knew his place was with his friend. He prayed to Aesculapius that Lucius would be able to heal Marcus, then he went in search of the watch commander.

*   *   *

Lucius stood at the operating table under the torchlight as Marcus was brought in and thrown face down on the table.

"Hug the table," a medic commanded. Marcus grabbed on as tight as he could.

Magnus joined Lucius at the table. Magnus loosened the tourniquet and Lucius cut and removed the dressing, then he poured vinegar into the wound. The pain was intense. Marcus screamed and shook his legs. A medic held his left leg. Magnus had to hold his right leg because the wound was too close to the heel for a medic to hold it without compromising the operating field. The gaping wound began to hemorrhage again. Lucius put direct pressure on the area.

"Clamp," he called.

A medic responded slapping the clamp into his hand. Lucius slowly pulled his fingers upward toward Marcus' knee while holding pressure on the wound. He exposed the upper part of the wound to show a thick-walled tubular structure about one-third the size of his index finger. As he released pressure on the structure, blood hosed out of it. He applied pressure again and clamped it. That stopped the major hemorrhage. Now, they were able to inspect the wound.

They washed it out again with vinegar and Magnus used hooks to hold the tissue open. Marcus screamed and cried like a baby. The cut went down to the bone through several cord-like structures, some had lumens, some were solid. They clamped the ones with lumens and tied each individually. When they got to the large one that Lucius first clamped, they noted that the clamp included a large solid cord as well. It was interesting because it contained many fascicles similar to a rope. They could not locate the other end of the solid cord in the lower aspect of the wound. After ligating the last structure, the wound was dry. The sword blade must have been very sharp to cut without jagged edges.

Magnus poured more vinegar into the wound and Lucius ordered a medic to bring the torch closer so he could examine in detail the inside of his brother's leg. In the lower end, deep within the wound, he spied a wide, flat ribbon of tissue. He recognized it from helping Basilius dress animals in the kitchen. Some muscles of the extremities ended in these structures. He looked in the upper portion of the wound and located the other end of the structure. He followed it up for a short distance and confirmed that it indeed came from a large lower leg muscle.

"Magnus, look at this," he said to his assistant.

"I can't see it," Magnus replied.

Lucius was reminded of the berating he received over not speaking with frankness. He knew it was his obligation to demonstrate the structure to Magnus. He took a clamp and grasped the structure in the lower leg and pulled it to show the edge. As he did so, Marcus' foot moved down. Lucius was fascinated. He pulled on it a few times to confirm the phenomenon.

"This sinew must pull the foot down," he declared. "We must try to repair it."

"Shouldn't we just pack the wound and allow it to heal in?"

"That would be what Taurinus would have screamed at us, but this patient is my brother, I want to make him whole again."

"We are supposed to treat all legionnaires the same using the Army's time-tested methods."

"I know, but I must try this for my brother. If it doesn't work, we can always just amputate later."

Marcus groaned and gritted his teeth. He could not believe his brother's detached matter-of-fact voice as the two surgeons discussed hacking off his lag.

"What do you propose to do?" Magnus asked.

"We will sew the ends together and cover it with a plaster."

"Suture!" Magnus barked at the instrument assistant. He prepared the suture with needles at both ends and handed it to Lucius.

Lucius transferred the clamp to Magnus who pulled on the structure so Lucius could see it easily in the open wound. Lucius put the needles through the structure near each edge, then crossed the sutures and placed the needles through the upper end of the cut structure in matching places. With a second suture, he reversed the process beginning in the upper end of the cut structure. He took the ends of the suture coming through the bottom end and Magnus took the upper ones. They each placed a single knot in their suture. Gradually, they tightened their knot, watching the ends of the structure come together. Then, they alternated tying. One would hold the structures together while the other tied until they completed their knots and the structure was together again.

Lucius looked at Marcus' foot. It was pointing down.

"Marcus, move your foot," he told his brother.

Although it was painful, Marcus was able to move his foot up and down. He began to sob.

"It works! Merciful Gods, it works! It works! Lucius, a thousand blessings!"

"Thanks, but it is not healed yet. A lot may happen in the next few weeks. You must follow instructions to the letter."

"Yes, sir!" Marcus replied in a mocking tone.

"I mean it!"

"Okay, okay! I'll do what you say."

Lucius and Magnus called for a Polyides pastil to be mixed with resin. They filled the wound with the sticky mess, then covered it with a Barbarum plaster and wrapped it with cloth. Lucius made sure to include the foot in the dressing to prevent Marcus from moving his foot and rupturing the repair. It would have to stay that way, at least until it was secure. That would take a minimum of three weeks.

Lucius whacked his brother on the buttocks. "We're done," he told him.

Marcus turned over.

"Lucius, I am not asking for more pain, but would you look at my cheek?"

Lucius was chagrined. He had missed an injury because he had not done a proper secondary survey. He was so intent on saving his brother's leg that he broke his own rules. He examined the gash. It was a long one extending from his left ear down nearly to the corner of his mouth, but no bone was showing.

"It's long, but not ragged," Lucius told his brother. "We need to sew it up."

"Great!" Marcus moaned. "Go ahead. Let's get it over with."

Lucius and Magnus worked quickly, each starting their stitch at opposite ends and meeting in the middle. They tied the ends together and covered the wound with resin. The medics lifted him off the table and prepared to take him to the infirmary. Marcus stopped them and grabbed his brother's arm.

"Thank you. You did the right thing, not becoming a soldier."

Lucius grabbed him by the arm and hugged him tightly. "Take better care of yourself, Marcus. You're the only brother I've got left." They wept briefly, then separated.

Marcus was led away while another legionnaire was plopped onto the table.

Marcus could not believe how hard his brother worked. Before, he always thought of him as odd. He believed Lucius was not a real man. Now, his opinion was different. Maybe he was the only real man in the family. He was proud of his brother and thankful that Lucius was there for him. He lay down on his cot and allowed Morpheus to visit him.

*   *   *

The next evening, Quintus came to visit with a German woman on each arm.

"Quintus!" exclaimed Marcus.

Quintus was beaming.

"I have some new friends,"

"What are you doing? How did you get them? Isn't this illegal?"

"Slow down, brother. I bring you companionship and all you do is ask questions? I'm brokenhearted."

"Sorry, brother."

"Well, first let me introduce them. This is Boro and her sister Paliz. Boro does all the talking. Paliz means the quiet one in the German language. She says almost nothing."

"Pleasure to meet you," Marcus acknowledged the women. He turned to Quintus.

"I love this, but how did you pull this off? This isn't another Placentia trick, is it?"

Quintus feigned a hurt expression.

"Have a heart, brother!" Then, he related his escapade.

"Yesterday, after I left you, I went to find our unit, but they are all gone. They are pursuing the Germans. There was almost no one left in the camp except the designated guard and the injured legionnaires. So, I reported to the Praefectus of the camp. He was asleep and his assistant was in charge. Within moments I recognized the guy. He is my uncle from Rhegium. The story goes that he got into some sort of bad trouble with several citizens. He was in the family business as the manager of the gambling for the gladiator games. Unfortunately, he screwed up the bets. So, he had to go away. We never knew where he went. I told him my story, which was pretty much like his, only I botched a whack job. He wanted to know why I was not out hunting Germans, so I told him about you. He made all the arrangements and here we are."

"Your family deals have gotten us in so much trouble," Marcus said warily.

"Not this time. Apparently, the girls are of the Harudes tribe. It's the tribe you sliced through and defeated nearly singlehandedly. They watched the whole thing from their wagon. When they were caught, they fought like cats telling the Centurions they would be slaves only to you!"

"What?"

"I told them I was your 'aide' and I could make all the arrangements. They were all too willing to come here this evening!" He winked at Marcus.

"Get yourself out of here! Are you serious?"

"Absolutely, brother!" Quintus had a huge grin. "It's good to be your friend! Now, choose one."

Marcus leered at the two sisters. Their torn and ragged clothing barely covered their assets. They both were tall and slender with long tousled blonde hair nearly down to their knees. Their features were pale. Their blonde eyebrows above their bright blue eyes were nearly invisible. They had tiny noses and long thin lips.

"Taekanan ekan! Taekanan ekan, minaz Kunjnaz," said Boro. Marcus looked at Quintus.

"She wants you. They call you Kunjnaz, their King." Quintus grinned.

A smile finally came to Marcus' face.

"I think the talkative one is cute, but I think I will choose the quiet one," he said pointing to Paliz.

Paliz squealed and jumped up and down. Quintus released her. She whispered something in her sister's ear and the two giggled. She came over to him and climbed into his cot straddling his legs. She put her hands on his chest and started to bend down.

"We're off," said Quintus. "I'll come back later to collect Paliz."

"Habhjanan iuwiz ainaz godaz tidis, swestar!" Boro told her sister.

"Samon, swestar!" replied Paliz smiling and waving to Boro.

Marcus looked at Quintus who shrugged.

"I'll try to find out later what all that meant." Then, he left with Boro clinging to his arm.

Marcus turned his attention back to Paliz who bent down and kissed him. As he reciprocated, he felt her tongue slip into his mouth and lick his teeth. The sensation was strange and he tried to pull back, but he was pinned against the cot. She lifted her tattered dress and pulled up his tunic. He was rock hard.

Paliz began working him over the way the whore had done in Placentia. He cherished the sensation, but this he wanted to participate more in the action. He pushed her over intending to get her underneath him, but the cot tipped over and they fell to the ground with Paliz on the bottom. The landing jarred his foot causing a shock wave of pain to run up his leg. He grimaced and deflated. To regain momentum, he pulled her dress up to expose her breasts. They were round and firm, the nipples hard. He kissed each one in turn and slipped himself back into her. He pounded away enjoying the sensation of her vagina. He exploded with great satisfaction.

They lay breathless for a moment, then he got up slowly. She helped him right the cot and they climbed in together. She rubbed and kissed his chest and abdomen until he was ready again. She climbed on top of him and slipped his penis into her. He wanted to be on top again, but, after the last attempt resulted in jarring his leg, he was willing to let her do the work. They climaxed together. She arched her back and moaned as he released into her. She oozed back onto him breathing into his mouth. These mouth sensations were new for Marcus, but he enjoyed every bit of it. He closed his eyes allowing her to do whatever she wanted.

His revery was interrupted by a tap on the shoulder.

"Time's up, brother." He opened his eyes. It was Quintus and Boro standing over him.

"Was it good for you?" Quintus asked.

"Spectacular!" Marcus exhaled as Paliz climbed off of him.

"Me too," said Quintus, "except Boro, here, talked through the whole thing."

"I think I like the quiet ones better," said Marcus. "So, same time tomorrow?"

"I will make it happen, Kunjnaz!" Quintus winked as Paliz joined him. Marcus watched intently as the girls wiggled into the darkness. He fell back on the cot and into a deep sleep.

*   *   *

Marcus awoke to a tap on his leg. It was Lucius and his medics. Day was just dawning, but the room was bright with the light of three torches. He squinted up at his brother.

"Morning inspection," said Lucius. He looked at the cheek wound which was healing fine.

"Tomorrow, we take off the dressings and look at your leg," he told him, then the entourage moved on.

The day passed slowly as Marcus relived the previous night. He felt sticky and cleaned himself off with vinegar water. He watched the activity in the hospital with medics flitting about. He did not see Lucius again, but he heard screams in the direction of the operating area and assumed he was busy. He took cat naps and recited Greek poetry trying to pass the time. It seemed as though the day would never end. As night fell, he could feel his heart racing with anticipation. Finally, Quintus came through the door with Boro and Paliz on his arms. Marcus sat up on the side of the cot as they came in.

"Salve, Kunjnaz!" Quintus said. He released Paliz. "See you in a little while."

Paliz sat beside him and rubbed his back. When she was done, Marcus turned to look at her. He was much shorter than Paliz. He stared at her collar bones trying to decide whether to kiss her lips or her breasts. She sensed his dilemma and lifted his chin with her hand. They kissed as they had done the evening before. He allowed her total access, then he gently nudged her to lay down on the cot. She did so pulling him on top of her where they expended their passions. They were on their third time when Marcus felt the familiar but unwelcome tap. He finished quickly and raised himself up on his hands and knees. Paliz slithered out from under him and went back to Quintus. Marcus passed another blissful night.

*   *   *

The morning tap came sooner than Marcus expected. He looked around. There was a bigger crowd. All the surgeons were present.

"Today, we look at your wound," Lucius told him. "Everyone wants to see." Marcus lay on his back for the exam. Lucius and Magnus unwrapped just the foot dressing.

"Move your foot up and down," Lucius directed.

Marcus tried to move his foot. The pain in the back of his leg was intense. He took a deep breath and forced it down. It was stiff and weak, but it moved.

"Okay, that's enough," Lucius commanded.

"Should we allow him to exercise it to prevent the sinews from tightening up?" asked Priscus. "You know, the Methodists would have him working it several times a day to keep the sinews loose."

"I am not comfortable with activity right now," Lucius answered. "The sutures may not hold in that thin ribbon. I want more time for it to heal."

Lucius instructed Marcus to roll over. They took down the rest of the dressing and removed the pastil. Magnus used a hook to lift the lower edge of the wound.

"See the repair?" asked Lucius. Each surgeon peeked in as Lucius showed them the repaired sinew asking Marcus each time to move his foot a little.

"This looks good now," said Atticus. "What happens if it develops flesh eating pus deep in the wound?"

"We will be forced to amputate," said Lucius bluntly.

The words shot into Marcus like a pilum through the heart. He put his head in his hands and waited silently while the dressing was reconstructed. When they were done, he sat up and looked plaintively at Lucius.

Lucius shook a finger at his brother.

"Do not walk on that foot, do not exercise that foot, and do not touch the dressing."

"Yes, sir," Marcus answered dejectedly. He watched as the entourage moved on.

That day passed even slower than the previous one. Each time he napped, he dreamt Lucius stood over him with an axe. By the time Quintus arrived with the women, Marcus was agitated and exhausted. Even Paliz could not cheer him up. He went through the motions, but she could sense his uneasiness. When they were done, she kissed him tenderly and whispered in his ear. He had no clue what she said, but the tender moment outside of passion brought him a brief relief from his torture.

*   *   *

Each day was the same. Visits in the morning, boring day-long waits, nights of indescribable passion. On one occasion, a medic lingered after the morning visit to remove the facial sutures. It was painful when the medic dug in Marcus' cheek to deliver the sutures. He cut each stitch with a large knife that made Marcus nervous. When the medic stood up to examine the scar, he shook his head.

"That is one nasty scar."

"That bad?"

"Yeah, that bad."

The news did not help his mood. He had no way of seeing the scar, so he would have to rely on what others thought. That night, Quintus confirmed that it was hideous, but Paliz did not seem to care. She kissed it and muttered some German at it.

The dressing changes demonstrated no deep pus. Marcus was relieved. His spirits gradually improved with each dressing change. The wound began to fill in with pink tissue that had shallow craters. The surface of the tissue was covered with a loose yellow gooey substance that looked like mucus. It washed off easily with vinegar before each new dressing was applied. Lucius called that a healthy sign. The words were sweet music to Marcus' ears. He warmed to Paliz again. Soon, they were exploring new ground.

About four weeks after the battle, troops began to return. Marcus heard the cheering and the commotion from his cot. A few days later, his entire cohort, including Martial, came to visit. They each sported the spoils of war. Some wore bracelets, some wore necklaces, some sported jewel encrusted scabbards and belts.

They told Marcus stories of chasing the Germans day and night. They eventually overtook the wagons at a river the locals called the Rhine, but they knew it as the Rhenum. Since there were no boats or bridges, the Germans were pinned against the riverbank. The legionnaires freely slaughtered countless barbarians. Warriors, women, and children all pleaded for mercy, but the commanders gave them none. When the slaughter was finished, almost none had escaped. The Roman Army collected as much loot as they could hold. They placed the rest in wagons and brought it all back to camp. Marcus admired the loot. He expressed a little jealousy at not getting to slaughter more barbarians. His cohort mates retorted that he had stolen all the fun from them during the battle. Martial interrupted the reunion.

"The Centurions met with the Legatus to report on the battle and the successful chase. I told him of your valor. We were not sure if you survived because you were unaccounted for until we returned. We decided to recommend you for honors, even if you were dead."

Marcus was stunned.

"I am speechless, chief."

"That is the first time," chuckled Martial. Then he said, "We are honored to have you as part of our century. Your ability to fight has become legendary."

Martial ordered all to come to attention. They gave Marcus a salute and Martial presented him with a bronze cuirass, a sword, a scabbard, and leather belt with an engraved golden buckle.

"These came from the chieftain of the Harudes. Since they were defeated primarily at your hand, you deserve his spoils."

Marcus was overwhelmed with emotion.

"Thank you."

He decided to defy his brother's orders. He stood up at attention and saluted his cohort mates. He embraced each of them as they left.

That night when Quintus came by, the girls spied the spoils and immediately began to wail. Quintus let them go. They ran over to the armor. Boro hugged the cuirass and Paliz kissed the scabbard. Finally Boro looked up teary eyed and said,

"Er was os Fader."

Marcus and Quintus looked at each other.

"Fader, Fader." They both beat their chest. "Os Fader!" They started wailing again.

The meaning suddenly dawned on Marcus. "Pater? Fader?"

"Ja, Ja," they sobbed.

"This is awkward," Marcus told Quintus. "They think I killed their father."

"You're right. I don't think any pleasure activities are happening tonight."

"I think we should call it off."

"I agree."

Quintus went over and helped the grief stricken, sobbing girls to their feet and ushered them out leaving Marcus to sift through the events of the day.

Chapter 38: End of Hostilities

"Wake up, sleepy head," Lucius bellowed as he poked his brother. "Today's the day."

Marcus rolled over and stretched.

"The day for what?"

"Today, if your wound still looks good, we let you walk."

Marcus immediately rolled on his stomach and lifted his foot for his brother. Priscus removed the dressing and the team inspected the wound. The pink tissue had completely filled in the defect. The yellow purulent surface scum washed off easily. There was no need for the plaster any more. Lucius smeared pastil of Polyides on the surface and rewrapped the wound with a simple dressing.

"Okay, move your foot up and down."

Marcus moved his foot. It was quite stiff and felt strange. The sole and the side of his foot were still numb.

"Good. Now stand up."

Marcus obliged, but kept his right foot in the air.

"Put your foot down," Lucius ordered.

Marcus gently placed his toes on the ground. He felt pain and pulling in the back of his leg as he tried to push his heel down. Lucius encouraged him.

"It's Okay. Place your heel on the ground."

Finally, he got the heel down and stood up straight. The pain and pulling gradually dissipated.

"Now, keep your soles on the floor and bend your knees."

Marcus started to bend his knees, but stopped as the pain and pulling returned.

"Keep going."

Eventually, he got to a half crouch position.

"Good. Now, stand up and walk to the end of the room and back."

Although the distance was only ten feet, it seemed like a mile to Marcus. He walked normally with his left foot. His right toes touched the ground first and he placed just enough weight to get his heel to touch. His gait was unsteady and he had a decided limp. He held his arms out to maintain his balance. He grabbed his brother as he approached the cot.

"Not bad for your first time."

"Thanks, brother."

"You may walk on both feet to the latrine now. Also, I want you to take short walks around the hospital three times a day."

"Yes, sir," said Marcus smiling broadly. The facial scar made his smile seem larger than life. He hugged his brother.

"Thank you, again."

Lucius left thinking about how lucky he had been. Amputation rates for such injuries were frightfully high and eventual death from the whole ordeal exceeded fifty percent. He repeatedly thanked Aesculapius. He prayed for his brother's continued recovery, but he secretly hoped the injury would be enough to disqualify him from the military. Marcus was a hero. He had every right to retire and tell war stories to his grandchildren. Lucius thought of the image and smirked.

Deep down he knew Marcus would not give up his ideal career as long as there was the slimmest chance he could fight again.

The entourage finished the morning tour quickly. Of the one hundred and ninety-seven who had entered the hospital after the battle, only ten legionnaires remained. The team had been very efficient at triage and admitted no fatal or near fatal injuries. Overall, they still lost a third to infection. The remaining were returned to duty except for the last ten who were on their way to reasonable recovery. Isolated in a satellite tent behind the hospital were an additional dozen with dysentery. Most of them were dying. Under Lucius' orders, the medics kept them drugged with strong poppy tea and wine awaiting the inevitable.

Lucius headed to the Legion X hospital for morning report. It was held a little later than usual, because the surgeons from Legions VII and XII had to come over from the smaller camp. He arrived early and was greeted warmly by Gracilus. He was always happy and upbeat, but he seemed especially ebullient that morning.

"Salve, Vigoratus, old man! A fine morning!"

"Yes, sir. It certainly is."

"How is your brother? Have you let him test your repair?"

"Yes, sir. Thank you for asking. He walked for the first time today. I am cautiously optimistic about his eventual recovery."

"Hush, man. You are too cautious. If he made it this far without an amputation, he will do fine!"

"Thank you for the encouragement and the advice." Lucius decided to probe why Gracilus was so happy.

"Sir, you seem particularly happy today. Is there anything you can share?"

"Yes, yes! Well, Caesar has declared this year's campaign over! He will make a decision in a few days about where the legions will winter. In the meantime, he has ordered us to have another formal dining as we did after the battle at Bibracte! Oh, look. Everyone has arrived. Let's spread the news!"

The meeting was a blur for Lucius. That night of debauchery in Bibracte and its aftermath flashed through his brain. He gave his report at the appropriate time without emotion. He responded mechanically when everyone else cheered. He only came out of his funk when Gracilus patted him on the back. He realized they were looking at him.

"Come on, man. What do you have to say for yourself?"

"What?"

"We voted your medical unit the best and most efficient! You will sit at my right hand tonight!"

Lucius refocused.

"I – I am honored," he stammered.

"Splendid! Splendid! He addressed the assembly of surgeons. "Everyone, be here at sunset!"

Lucius walked back to his hospital in a daze. He was thrilled that they were chosen as the best unit. He had Taurinus to thank for the honor. They were all just raw trainees six months ago. He had whipped all of them into shape, but Lucius felt that the old surgeon had been particularly hard on him. Taurinus believed in him and invested countless days pounding into him the traits of a surgeon. In the meantime, he gave him advice on leading a team. He wished Taurinus was there to share the honors. He wondered if Taurinus was even alive.

When he got back, he assembled the entire staff and broke the news. Everyone cheered and hugged one another. Magnus put his arm around Lucius and shook him.

"It has been an honor to work with you, but I must say you are by far the luckiest surgeon I know."

Lucius finally smiled.

"It has been a pleasure to work with this team, especially you, Magnus." They embraced. Lucius embraced everyone and thanked them personally for their work. Then, as Taurinus would have done, he gave new orders.

"Well, the day is still young and death and suffering do not take a holiday. Back to work, everyone."

He shook his head as they left to continue their duties.

"What a profession," he said to himself. *"How did Taurinus keep it up so long?"*

He thought about the old curmudgeon. Taurinus had given him the answer in so many words every day. It is the satisfaction of helping soldiers return to battle. Their gratitude is boundless. Even the generals depend on the surgeon. He sighed and allowed himself a moment of true pride.

The afternoon passed quickly. All the routine work was completed rapidly. The staff spent the extra time tidying up. By the end of the day, the hospital looked nearly new.

Lucius spent his free time trying to remember the ingredients of the hangover remedies Aia had given him. He hoped he would not need them, but he was not sure how to escape the endless toasting. He remembered that one of them was willow bark tea. He had no bark and even if he had some, he had no idea how strong to brew it. He took a knife and went out the North gate of the camp to find a willow. Unfortunately, his search was fruitless. By this point, the nearby countryside had been deforested. He returned empty handed. He would have to face his anticipated hangover the old Roman way – endure and hope to survive.

Lucius cleaned his face and hands and donned his best tunic, which was in sad shape after months of wear. He joined his surgical staff and walked to the Legion X hospital. On the way, he asked each of them if they planned to stay in the legion.

"Not I," said Priscus. I have been away from my father's practice far too long. I plan to rejoin him once the winter is over and it is safe to travel.

"Nor I," said Modestus. "I believe the political climate has changed, especially with Caesar's victories. I would like to return home and see if I can work my way into the senate. I will start by campaigning to become Magistrate in my home town of Capua. If it doesn't work out, at least I have Medicine and Surgery to fall back on."

"Well, I plan to stay," said Atticus. "This campaign has taught me much. I finally feel confident."

"Me, too," said Petrus. "I think I finally memorized everything. I don't want to have to learn anything new."

"What about you, Magnus?" asked Lucius.

"I have learned a great deal from Taurinus and all of you. I feel I could have a thriving practice back in Milano." He turned to Lucius. "However, I could be persuaded to stay if you plan to stay. What do you plan to do?"

Lucius had not thought seriously about his own future.

"I have not made up my mind, but I will let you know when I do."

They entered the tent that was set up for the banquet. The inside was arranged as before. Lucius wound his way through the crowd to the head table.

Gracilus greeted him warmly and made small talk.   Soon, a bell sounded for everyone to take their seats. The food came out quickly. It was not as lavish as the feast at Bibracte, but inviting nonetheless. The first course was an asparagus salad from the local farmers. Before they started, Gracilus stood.

"Caesar has asked that we salute all who made our most auspicious war successful. I begin by proposing a toast to the Consul Major Lucius Calpurnius Piso Caesoninus." He turned to Lucius. "He is still Consul Major, is he not?" Everyone laughed.

"To the Consul Major!" they shouted and downed their goblet of wine. As the medics scurried to fill the goblets again, Lucius noted the wine was served Roman style. It had been cut with water. He said a silent prayer of thanks to Bacchus.

"Now, I propose a toast to the Consul Minor Aulus Gabinius!"

"To the Consul Minor!" everyone said in unison followed by downing the second goblet of wine.

Toasting went on forever, it seemed.   In between, Lucius managed to consume enough food to buffer the wine. He had never eaten asparagus before and enjoyed the taste. They were pickled with Gaulish wine vinegar. The next course was roast lamb and carrots stewed with cumin. Dessert was quince with honey. The quince came from the local farmers. The fruit was at the peak of ripeness. He was especially glad that the wine had not dulled his palate. Others around him had not been so discrete. Many were slurring their speech. Some had thrown up into their plates, but the toasting went on. Gracilus stood again.

"Now, let us toast the chief surgeon of the best team, Vigoratus!" As he said Lucius' cognomen, he swung around and clunked his goblet into Lucius' head spilling the wine down his back. Lucius stiffened but smiled and acknowledged the toast. Gracilus leaned into him.

"Sorry, old man. Now give us the toast you gave at the last formal dinner."

Lucius looked at him.

"It wasn't so well received the last time."

"I know. That's why I will introduce it." He waved for a fresh goblet and turned to the assembled drunks.

"It is time we have some more wisdom from our best chief." He turned to Lucius.

"Go ahead. They are all yours." Then he plopped down in his seat.

Lucius thought quickly. He stood and raised his goblet.

"I have three toasts. First, I propose a toast to Gracilus, our Army Medical Chief!"

Everyone stood and raised their goblets.

"To the Chief!" While they drank that toast, Lucius started his next.

"Second, I have been asked to repeat a toast from our last formal dining. So here goes. I propose a toast to our patients dead and alive! We salute you. It is because of your sacrifice this campaign has ended in victory!"

Everyone cheered and drank up.

"Finally, I would like to propose a toast to all of us. We stay up night and day fixing broken soldiers. We put up with the stench of death. We cleaned up pus and corruption. We wiped away merda. They made it faster than we could throw it away. Without us, Caesar's Army would be a sorry sight!"

To that, everyone cheered and drank and drank.   Lucius sat down exhausted but satisfied he dodged being a wet blanket on the party. Gracilus tried to hold onto consciousness before he succumbed to using his goblet as the crown of Bacchus. He put his arm around Lucius.

"I love you, man," he slurred. Lucius tried to pry himself free, but he was pinned.

"I...love you too," he managed to get out.

"That's why I want you to serve as Under-Chief Surgeon."

Lucius was unprepared for that.

"I don't know."

"That's okay, my boy," he slurred. "Think about it. The offer stands. I would be proud to have you around for next year's campaign."

"Thanks."

After Gracilus passed out, Lucius twisted his way out of the chief's arm hold and made his exit. The vision of being assistant chief would not leave. It kept him awake most of the night.

Next day at morning report, they learned where each legion would winter. Legions Seven and Twelve would remain at the present camp, but they would be given the opportunity to move to the permanent camp site if the Legatii chose to do so. They would serve as the Eastern guard of the newly expanded province and the first defense against the Germans should they chose to invade again. Legions Eight and Nine would move to the Western territories of the Sequani and winter in the village of Crusuda on the banks of the Dubis. Their job would be to guard the outermost territories and keep the Aedui in line across the Arar. Legions Ten and Eleven would winter in between the two outposts in Vesontio. They would be positioned to reinforce either border if necessary. That village would serve as the command center headed by Lieutenant Labienus. Caesar himself would return immediately to Rome to give a personal accounting to the Senate.

Lucius felt his heart racing. He would have the opportunity to see Aia again. He vowed to study in more detail the medicines of the Druids. He missed her lessons in broken Latin. Most of all, he missed her companionship. He prayed she was well and that she would be willing to see him again.

Preparations began that day but took nearly a week. Wagons left by King Ariovistus and the Germans provided sufficient space not only for the supplies and the spoils, but also for the prisoners – all of whom were to be moved to Vesontio. The terrain and location of the town nestled in the horseshoe bend of the river would make escape nearly impossible. Even if they did, they would have to get by two legions between them and the Rhenum River.

Lucius supervised the packing of the hospital. It had become very routine for them. By now, only three patients remained. Marcus was nearly healed, but his limp made it clear he would not be able to march with his unit. The other two patients had complicated courses and were finally healing their amputation stumps. Lucius recommended that they be assigned to drive the prisoner wagons. Marcus was assigned to one of the women's wagons. When Quintus found out, he finagled his way to be Marcus' guard.

On the final day, morning report was brief. After the meeting concluded, Gracilus approached Lucius.

"At the formal dinner, I know I had made Bacchus my best friend and I apologize."

"It is forgotten," Lucius replied.

"Well, I apologize all the same." He cleared his throat.

"I was wondering if you have given any thought to my proposal."

"I was not sure you were serious. You were in quite an altered state that night."

"I know, but I was serious about the offer."

"Now that I know you are serious, I will carefully consider it."

"Very good! I would be honored to have you as my second." They embraced and left for their wagons. Lucius felt relieved that he had bought some time. He was not ready to make that kind of commitment. Still, it made him proud that he had learned so much so fast.

*   *   *

Quintus drove one of the women's prisoner wagons up to the hospital to pick up Marcus. He stopped by the tent and called out his name. Marcus hobbled out and tried to mount the wagon. Quintus extended his hand and hauled him aboard.

"Welcome Kunjnaz! Your humble assistant Quintus at your service!" He smiled broadly.

"It's good to see you too."

"Allow me to introduce our prisoners." He turned and opened the doors. There were ten women, each one more beautiful than the next.

"Of course, you know Boro and Paliz." They gave a meek wave. Quintus leaned over to whisper to Marcus.

"They're still grieving, but they seem to be coming around." Then he pointed to each of the others.

"There's Agila and Borga and Lamaz and Pirbijaz and Urbaz and Wagigaz and Wiwaz. They all volunteered to be in our wagon!"

Marcus's cock stood at attention. He tried to hide his excitement.

"Thanks, Quintus. You always have a way of brightening my day."

"I have been learning a little German from the girls. Let me point out the name Wiwaz means the consecrated one. She was betrothed from birth, but you killed the warrior she was to marry. Wagigaz next to her means the impetuous one. I can tell you she certainly is!"

"You mean you tested her out?"

"Of course, my brother!" We can't have any ice princesses in our wagon, can we?"

Marcus chuckled.

"I appreciate your thoroughness."

"Also, Urbaz means the one who makes you weak. Don't take her unless you are ready for a wild ride."

"You are something else," Marcus said shaking his head.

"Now, watch this." Quintus turned to the women.

"Magads, sagjanan godaz murginaz Kunjnaz!"

"Godaz murginaz Kunjnaz!" they giggled in unison.

Marcus was still clueless about German.

"What was that all about?"

"They're just telling you good morning!" Quintus was gloating.

"Quintus, my man. You are one piece of work!"

They embraced and settled in for the ride. Marcus eventually got the smile off his face, but he could not hide the staff under his tunic.

*   *   *

Lucius climbed into his wagon.   Suddenly, he was overwhelmed with sadness.   The exciting, whirlwind romp through foreign lands was over.   He was thrown into the furnace of Roman Military Medicine.   He was forged from an inexperienced novice physician into a battle hardened surgeon.   He feared no wound or broken body part.   He could whip up emollients, pastils and plasters in moments.   He could turn a blind eye to the mortally wounded.   He could shut his ears to the screams of veteran soldiers while he dug deep in their bodies.   He could command his nose to ignore putrid rotting flesh, the stench of human waste, and the smell of death.   He was no longer a wide eyed student of medicine at the side of a classically trained Greek physician.   He could be as crusty as his hardboiled teacher.   He had become an iron man.   He grieved for his lost innocence.

As the columns of Legions Ten and Eleven moved out of camp in the crisp autumn air, Lucius pushed aside his feelings of sadness and replaced them with anticipation.   In less than a week he would be back in Vesontio and, hopefully, back the arms of the mysterious and moody barbarian woman he had come to love.

Chapter 39: Rest in Peace

Aia's became more miserable with each passing week of her pregnancy. She was grateful that her nausea and morning sickness were gone, but those problems were replaced with a persistent pounding frontal headache. Her regular herbal diuretics no longer helped. She was short of breath all the time. The smallest tasks winded her, even though she religiously drank her dandelion root tea during her daily talks with Banona and Eskenga.

She examined her legs. They were grotesquely swollen. Large tortuous veins had popped out on her thighs. She kept her legs covered with long dresses. She told no one of her symptoms. She did not wish to burden her wonderful new family. They had selflessly welcomed her into their community, even at a time when the Roman occupation made their lives tough. She chose to suffer in silence.

She no longer slept well. As a girl, she liked to sleep on her stomach. Now, her huge belly made that impossible. Even worse, she found that the only comfortable position was on her left side. Sleeping on her back or right side made her even more short of breath.

One evening while trying to get comfortable, she recalculated her time of conception. There was no doubt it occurred on Beltane. Now, it was time for the festival of Maponos. That meant she was only completing her fifth month. She could not believe she still had four more months to go. Depression added to her misery when she realized she was due on the eve of Imbolc, the beginning of her long downward spiral. Her emotions overwhelmed her. She cried herself to sleep.

Aia awoke to Vectitos and Potita tugging at her. She sat on the side of the bed. Her eyes were puffy and her vision blurry. Her legs were as swollen as ever and her pounding headache immediately returned. Despite her state, the smell of breakfast made her ravenous. The sweet smell of uffizi da paun filled the room. It was a treat made with stale bread soaked in a milk and egg mixture and fried in butter. Here in Besançon, they called it paun perdu and traditionally ate it with honey. The irresistible odor lured her into the kitchen. Eskenga was at the hearth making the delicious treat. Aia went up to her and put her arms around the woman's waist and hugged her.

"You are welcome, my dear," Eskenga replied without looking up. "I heard you crying last night and I wanted you to have something comforting when you woke up."

"Thank you, Madrastra. You are such a kind and wonderful stepmother. Your cooking is even better than my own Màthair."

"Thank you, my dear. The paun perdu is ready. Grab a plate and I'll give you the first piece."

Aia obliged. Eskenga slid the thick fluffy golden slice of "lost bread" out of the pan and onto the plate. Aia took her treat and sat down at the table. She broke off a piece, smothered it in honey, and stuffed it in her mouth. She let the flavors fill her senses. She sat back and sighed. She could feel her headache retreating. She ate the remainder slowly while the rest of the family was served. Eskenga made another small piece for Aia and delivered it to her. Everyone quietly enjoyed their treat. Vrittakos was the first to break the silence.

"I checked our supply of herbs and dried flowers for our rituals. Even though we collected a large amount of mistletoe this summer, we have almost none for the ritual of Maponos.   We need to collect more.   The timing could not be better.   The month of Edrinios has just begun with the full moon.   Our best harvest time is five days later, just a few days from now.   The Ritual of Maponos is only ten days after that."

Mistletoe simultaneously brought joy and dread to Aia.   Her forehead began throbbing.   She thought of the crown of mistletoe she wore on Imbolc just before her village was torched.   She thought of her escapade trying to harvest the last of the mistletoe at the banks of the River Saône.   That foray may have saved her from the tribal massacre, but it had plunged her into a strange existence.   She thought of her sister Sina's headless body clutching her mistletoe amulet.

Aia closed her eyes.   She saw the nighttime scene of her slaughtered family lying there lit only by the flames of the burning camp.   As the gory details played out in her mind, the images grew darker and darker.   She seemed to be floating across the camp site, then floating above her breakfast plate.   She fought the strange sensation.   She opened her eyes and tried to focus on her new family around the table, but her body began to shake violently.   She plunged into blackness.

All was silent in the void.   She lay on nothingness.   She could not move. She could not tell up from down.   Slowly, in the distance directly in front of her, was a faint glow.   It looked like the first rays of dawn.   The fuzzy light grew slowly and spread out in all directions.   As she marveled at the curious light, a sound caught her attention.   It was far away and barely perceptible at first.   She listened intently.   It was someone in the distance calling her name.   The staccato noises were muffled as though she had her hands over her ears.   She willed her hands away.   The calls rattled out of a barrel growing louder and more shrill, then the scene came together all at once.

"Aia, wake up," yelled Severa.   "Oh, merciful Mother Goddess, please save Aia! Aia... Aia!"

Aia tried to focus.   She had no idea who she was.   She did not recognize her surroundings.   There were blobs moving in front of her.   She concentrated hard on the two blobs closest to her.   Eventually, she made out Severa and Eskenga kneeling beside her.   She looked up.   She had fallen from her chair.   She tasted something metallic in her mouth and saw Potita taking away a bloody cloth.   Her tongue throbbed and burned like fire.   Sparkles exploded before her eyes and her right side ached.   She had soiled herself.

Banona shook her head.

"I have seen this before," she told Eskenga and Severa.   "She will need much rest to make it through this pregnancy.   Put her to bed and give her no stimulants."

The women helped Aia sit up.   Vrittakos lifted her and carried her into the bedroom.   The women shooed the curious children out of Aia's small room, then they cleaned her before placing her in bed.   They covered her naked body with heavy blankets and tucked her in.   Vrittakos extinguished the candles and covered the window to block out all light.

Aia spent the next two days drifting in and out of consciousness.   On the third day, she felt much better.   Banona allowed her to sit up in bed.   Aia was not permitted to participate in the mistletoe harvest and she was just as happy to miss it.   The next day she rejoined the family in the kitchen.   She apologized for her problems and begged forgiveness.

"There is nothing to be ashamed of, child," said Eskenga.   "You are part of our family and we will do everything in our power to make you well."

"Thank you." Aia gave her a hug. She felt at ease with these women. They treated her like the daughter of a chieftain and gave her special status and attention, even though she was no relation to them.

Aia stared into her dandelion root tea and fingered the blue charm hanging from the leather chain around her neck. She had given her own precious heirloom to her dying father, but a replacement miraculously came to her. She sincerely believed that the Mother Goddess herself had allowed the dead Roman to reach out to her from beyond the grave. For a short time, she had been Decimus. She wore his clothes. She stood in his sandals. As faux Decimus, she had been an inspiration to his comrades. In return, he passed along the bright blue charm of such intricate beauty and design.

Aia thought of her other dead protectors – her father, her brother, and her first love, Lugurix. Then there was Lucius, her Roman savior. She needed him, now more than ever. She longed for his return. She prayed to the Mother Goddess.

"Protect Lucius. Wherever he is, keep him alive. Oh sweet Mother, please send him to me as quickly as you can."

She was brought back to reality by the voice of Banona who was prescribing her diet. Since the seizure, the family matriarch had taken charge. With the challenges of Aia's illness to focus upon, she was clear-headed and energized.

"Every morning you are to have a large goblet of mint infusion made by my hand the night before. It will calm your nerves. Your breakfast will consist of hemp seeds and sheep's milk to keep you calm, especially when the children get rambunctious. You must drink not just one, but two cups of dandelion root tea by midmorning. For your noonday meal, you will be allowed to eat with the family. At this time of year, we have stews rich with root vegetables and potatoes. They are quite filling and will help you maintain your weight during this critical time in your pregnancy. I will make blackberry leaf tea to relieve cramping. For supper, you will have a salad of hemp and mint leaves to provide the strength of the Mother Goddess."

From her apron pocket, Banona produced a small jar.

"This is lavender oil from my own personal supply. It is very potent, so you need only a small amount. Rub this on your forehead if you feel a headache coming on."

Within a few days on the regimen, Aia felt calmer and was breathing easier. Also, for the first time in months, she was not constipated. Her depression improved and she was able to suppress the thoughts that made her anxious. As she gained strength, she wanted to help with the holiday preparations. She tried to help make some of the candles that the women would carry for the Maponos ritual, but the effort wore her out. She knew she was still too weak, so she contented herself with helping Severa prepare her gown. Severa sewed the dress and Aia added the designs on the neckline and the hem of the skirt.

One afternoon during their work, the chieftain of the tribe and his wife came to visit. They cajoled Aia into telling her tale. The chieftain was so impressed with the foreign priestess that he commissioned his bards to compose a ballad of her life. He ordered the crones to tell her story every year on Imbolc. The next day was filled with interviews by bards and crones who asked her every detail of her ordeal. They wanted to make her life story at once sweet and tender, terrible and ferocious, exciting and triumphant. By evening, Aia was emotionally drained. Finally, Severa stepped in.

"You have more than enough information from this poor girl. Can't you see you are wearing her out? No more interviews! If you need some other detail, come to me."

They apologized and took their leave. Aia patted Severa's hand.

"Thank you again for all your kindness and protection. You are always so kind to me."

"Nonsense, Aia," Severa said as she placed her hand over Aia's. "We are sisters now. I will always protect you."

Banona and Eskenga hovered over her and often sat with her in the afternoons. The conversations were always the same.

"When are you due, child?" Banona would ask.

Aia would recount the story of her Beltane night of bliss with her betrothed. Banona would tell of her pregnancy with Eskenga so many years ago and then dispense advice. Aia would thank her profusely and Eskenga would pat her hand and give her a knowing smile.

One afternoon, Eskenga interrupted the usual routine.

"Màthair dear, don't you have a special request of Aia?" she asked of Banona.

Banona thought for a moment, then brightened up.

"Tonight we will swear a brictom and we want you to join us."

Aia was stunned.

"What are you planning?"

Eskenga explained.

"On the eve of every celebration, we swear a brictom. We have not asked you before because you had been a prisoner of the cursed Romans. We needed to be sure your faith had not been turned. You have proven yourself by educating our youth better than any teacher we can remember. We know your Druid beliefs are strong. We plan to write the curse tablet tonight and bury it on the eve of the Ritual of Maponos. Will you join us?"

Aia's heart was pounding. All she could think about was Lucius. She looked up at Banona.

"Surely we can spare Lucius from this curse, no?"

"Who is this Lucius?" Banona asked. Eskenga patted Banona.

"You remember, Màthair dear. He is the Roman who saved little Aia. He is the one who fixed your wrist." She turned to Aia.

"I have to do this more frequently with Màthair," she whispered. "I am so worried for her."

Banona lifted up her hand and turned it around studying it as though she was seeing it for the first time, then she remembered.

"Oh, yes, yes, yes. Thank you for reminding me." She turned to Aia.

"Of course, young lady. He was very kind and did a marvelous job on my wrist. We will specifically write him out of the curse."

With that assurance, Aia agreed.

Banona prepared the evening meal while Aia kept her company. Banona talked about how much their community had grown since she was a child. The town had become crowded and needed its own government.

The Druids had lost some of their connection to the countryside by being confined to the village. They made up for the loss by maintaining the wooded area in front of their building. The biggest change was the dedication to the serious study of the earth and heavens. She relayed the story of the construction of the

Great Study Hall and the dedication of a segment of the Druid men to the calendar project. Aia told Banona of her tour through the hall and the wondrous calendar Silus had shared with her.

Supper went rapidly as everyone was hungry from preparing for the ritual. After they cleaned up, the women gathered around the candlelit table. Banona fetched a box containing leaden tablets and an iron nail for writing. She gave them to Severa.

"You are High Priestess. You write the curse."

Severa solemnly took the box. She pulled out a large leaden sheet and began to write. As she wrote, she spoke the words.

Inside de bnanom brictom...

Herein a magical incantation of women
Their special magical infernal names
The magical incantation of a
Seeress who fashions this prophecy
The goddess Adasagona maintains
Severa, daughter of Eskenga as their scribe
Their witch of thread and their witch of writing
Below where they shall be impressed
The prophetic curse of these names of theirs is a
Magical incantation of a group of
Practitioners of underworld magic:

Banona daughter of Flatucia
Eskenga daughter of Banona
Severa daughter of Eskenga
Potita daughter of Severa
Aia daughter of Adiega

Aia's heart pounded as Severa scratched her name into the lead. She touched the blue charm as her mother's name was added.

They call upon Maponos Arveriatis
Through the magic of the underworld gods
The oath they will swear

As Severa scratched the curse, the women and little Potita intoned the words.

The small shall become great
The crooked become straight
And, though blind, we will see
With this tablet of incantation
This will be good for us Lugos
Take them Lugos
Take them Lugos
Take them Lugos

Severa sat up. Eskenga bent down and whispered in her ear. Severa raised her eyebrows and looked at Aia, then nodded and wrote,

Every man according to judge
That they would have struck the curse
That she cancels the curse of this man, Lucius

Then she signed it with a flourish.

Severa
Witch by the writing
Witch by the thread

When Severa concluded the tablet, Aia felt better about the curse. The words were sufficiently vague. Even if Lucius was not specifically cancelled from the curse, she interpreted the intent of the curse as protecting him.

Severa then took a knife and sliced her forearm dropping her blood onto the lead tablet. She gave the knife first to Banona, then Eskenga, then little Potita, and finally, Aia. They all stood over the tablet dripping their blood and watching it mingle. When their blood stopped flowing, Severa took the tablet to the hearth and held it close to the fire. They watched the blood turn a dark brownish red as it dried. She rolled up the tablet and placed it in a different box covered with charm designs.

"We go now."

Aia was puzzled.

"Where are we going?"

"We are going to bury the curse tablet in the Abyss. It is a day's journey there and back. If we wish to be back in time for the ritual of Maponos, we must leave now."

Banona took out three baskets filled with food and handed one each to Severa, Eskenga and Potita, then she reached deep into the cupboard and pulled out another basket for Aia.

"I made this especially for you," she said. "It contains the herbs and medicines you need to stay well. The journey is arduous. Do not overexert yourself."

The four headed out of the compound and into the night. Aia noted that Banona did not join them.

"What about Banona?" Aia asked Severa.

"She has made this journey many times," said Severa, "but now she is too old. She is scared ever since she fell and broke her wrist. She does not feel she would be able to make it. Once you have been there, you will understand."

They walked silently to the East side of town. There at the main wharf, a man was waiting for them in a skiff. Aia recognized Vrittakos. Once the women were seated, he cast off and poled the vessel upstream into the cool misty night. They traveled southeast in the shadow of the Roman camp high above them. The river curved around the mountain out of sight of the watchtower. They headed east for a short distance, then stopped on the southern bank. Waiting at the landing with a hay cart was Vlatiú. The women got out of the boat and climbed into the cart.

They rode through the night and into the early morning hours. Mists hung in the valley well into the morning and Aia was chilled to the bone. She pulled clumps of hay around her to stay warm. Eventually the sun warmed the earth enough to dissipate the mists. About midmorning, they stopped beside a nondescript farmhouse nestled in the edge of a stand of tall spreading oaks. They climbed down and knocked on the door. They were greeted by a Sequani warrior. After a brief conversation between Severa and the warrior, they were granted passage.

They entered the sparsely furnished building. It was crowded with warriors who allowed the women to make their way through to the back room. At the rear were steep stairs heading down the mountainside. It was so well hidden by the trees that a traveler would never suspect there was a ravine. Aia negotiated the stairs carefully because her pregnancy had changed her center of gravity. She felt quite unsteady and clung tightly to the railing.

At the bottom of the stairs was the entrance to a large cave in the mountainside. The passage was dimly lit by torches. The descent into the rock was as long as the stairs they had just negotiated. The deeper they went inside, the colder it became. Aia pulled her cloak tighter around her. At length, they entered a vast vaulted cavern. It was over a dozen meters high with a lake of clear dark water in the center. Off the main cavern were several passageways piled high with grain and vegetables.

"This year's harvest was especially bountiful," Severa told Aia. "We have stored what we can here. Neither the Germans nor the Romans know of this."

They moved to the far side of the vaulted space and up a small rise to what looked like a stone altar. It was a natural structure made by lime laden water, which deposited its minerals over many centuries. It was cold, wet, and slippery. They gathered around it and held hands. Severa stepped forward, produced the box, and placed it on the limestone altar calling out,

Mother Goddess,
We come deep within you
To beg for your assistance
Listen to our prayer
Bend to me your ear
Let our supplications and our prayers
Reach your soul

The words reverberated through the cavern. Severa had to pause after every few words to allow the echoes to fade away. To Aia, the echoes sounded more ominous than the spoken words.

Severa opened the box, took out the curse tablet, and hurled it into the pool. They stood silently holding hands watching the trail of bubbles that marked the descent of the tablet through the rich limestone water. When the bubbles finally subsided, they each kissed the altar in turn. It had an acrid taste and left Aia's mouth dry. They retraced their steps back up to the farmhouse where they ate their midday meal. The warriors provided boiling water for Aia to make her blackberry tea. The hot brew warmed and relaxed her.

After thanking the warriors for letting them conduct their ritual, they climbed back into the cart and rode through the late afternoon and into the evening. Eskenga sat next to Aia. She was unusually silent. Aia thought she looked agitated. She reached out and held her Madrastra's hand. Eskenga looked up into

Aia's eyes and began to sob quietly. Aia gently pulled Eskenga's head to her bosom and stroked her.

"Everything will be fine," she whispered.

Eskenga shook her head. Eventually, she stopped crying and raised her head. She dried her face and looked at Aia with sad eyes.

"No, my dear. Everything will not be fine." Her eyes filled with tears again. It took a long time for her to compose herself. When she finally felt stronger, she sat straight up, drew in a deep breath, and whispered, "It's you, my dear Aia. It's you."

"What do you mean, Madrastra? Have I done anything to bring dishonor to the family?"

Eskenga choked back more tears.

"No, child. You have been a wonderful gift to us. It's about your condition. Màthair confided in me yesterday as she prepared your basket. She is the only one alive who has seen this condition in other pregnant women. This illness is rare among women of our tribe. Even in the few who have experienced it, the illness did not happen with every pregnancy."

She went on to tell her about Banona's recollections of several women who had developed Aia's illness. The women who had milder cases of leg swelling and shortness of breath could be treated. They delivered healthy babies and regained their strength. However, two young mothers had seizures like the one Aia experienced. Both women died – one in childbirth and one during labor, taking her baby with her to the grave. Aia rubbed her belly as she began to understand the gravity of her condition.

"*I am going to die,*" she thought, "*but I can't die yet! I have two babies growing in me, maybe the only Tigurini's left in the whole world. I have to be there to raise them, to share with them the traditions of our tribe, to give them the love of an entire nation.*"

Eskenga's words filtered back into her consciousness. She was saying that Banona would do everything in her power to keep her healthy, but the end could come at any time.

Aia resolved to do what she had to do to survive, but knew deep down that she might not. She looked into Eskenga's eyes.

"I will follow Banona's every order so that I can birth these babies into the world, but in case I die, please promise me that you will tell them of their tribal heritage."

Eskenga patted her hand.

"We will do more than that. You are an inspiration to all of us. It is so wonderful that the crones and the bards have your story. We will teach it to all our children. Your babies will be revered."

They hugged for a long time. Eventually, Aia sat back and sighed.

"*I must, I will survive.*"

The wagon arrived at the riverbank in darkness where Vrittakos was waiting. They climbed into the skiff and he took them back to the village. Everyone, especially Aia, was glad to be back home. Banona had a hot meal prepared for them. Aia was exhausted and starving, but she dutifully ate her salad. After her meager meal, she was still hungry. She pleaded with Banona, who acquiesced. She dispensed to Aia a small bowl of lamb stew. Aia devoured it thanking her profusely for all her kindness and help. After dinner, she dove under the covers and fell soundly asleep.

The next morning, all were up early for the celebration of Maponos. The children were excited. They were getting under foot. Aia took them aside and kept them as quiet as she could while everyone else made preparations.   In the excitement, she forgot about her mint infusion and her hemp seeds. They began a procession up the mountain. Vrittakos carried Aia up in a small cart containing the ceremonial supplies.

When the Romans first occupied the village, the elders of the Druids had secured permission from the prefect of the Roman camp to hold their ceremonies on the mountain top. Now, the prefect met them at the gate and his legionnaires escorted them to the open assembly area.

The fortifications had been completed since Aia was there last. The wall of stone was impressive and the wooden watch tower was replaced with an expansive new watch area with stone steps.

Before the ceremony, they shared a meal of roasted lamb, carrots, and mead. By then, Aia was quite hungry and ate a generous serving. She knew she should have her blackberry leaf tea, but the mead tasted so good, she decided to cheat just once.

When the meal was done, they gathered in two lines. Each line consisted of alternating men, women and children.   Once assembled, they began the procession to form a circle. Vrittakos and Severa each led the lines. Vlatiú and Aia were at the rear of the lines. They began in the South and split into two directions to form the circle, ending in the North.   Then, the four Druids moved into the center of the circle. Vrittakos faced east, Severa faced north, Aia faced west and Vlatiú faced south. Together they intoned,

Northlands, Southlands, Eastlands, Westlands –
Come build this sacred circle, so that this will be a suitable place.

Then, the men broke from the circle and brought their sheaves of grain to the center then returned to the circle. Next, Severa spoke.

Oh Great Retiring Sun God
Blessings upon you
As you journey into the lands of winter
Into the loving arms of the Goddess.

Vrittakos spoke next.

Oh Goddess,
As you pull your mantle of earth around you
Leaves fall and the days grow cold
Chill winds blow from the North.

Next was Aia. She raised her arms and sang,

Oh Great Sun God sailing toward the West
You will be wrapped in the coolness of the night.
In the lands of eternal enchantment
Night wins over the day.

Vlatiú raised his arms and sang as well as he had when he was the High Priest.

Oh Blessed Goddess
In this extinction of the Sun God's power
We will wait through the winter
For your gift of life in the spring.

A white bull was led to the altar and tied there. The men placed the sheaves of grain around the animal, then the women with their lighted candles approached the altar. Each used their flame to light the sheaves. Quickly, a conflagration engulfed the bull. Flames and smoke billowed high into the sky. The final chorus belonged to the children. The child chosen to lead them stood in the circle. Aia caught her attention and directed the girl with her eyes.

We give thanks for your bounty
The fertility of the earth and our lives
Now, we face the dark time of the year
We gather your abundance and
Await another fruitful year.

By the end of the song, Aia was crying tears of joy. She finally felt at peace. The circle broke and the participants came up to greet the celebrants. They offered congratulations and compliments, especially to Aia for preparing the children so well. She was so happy doing what she had trained all her life to do.

At that moment they were interrupted by a cheer arising from the Roman guard. Aia wanted to know what the commotion was about, but she knew her place. She stayed until all the villagers were greeted, then hurried over to her friend, the Tesserarius.

She conjured up her best Latin.

"Greetings, commander. How are you today?"

"I am well, my lady," he replied. "I am especially happy seeing you again. I hope you are well."

"Thank you, I am fine." She swallowed hard at her little white lie, then sidled up close to him. "May I ask what everyone was cheering about?"

"A member of the vanguard of the Tenth legion rode in a few moments ago. He announced that we routed the Germans and that legions Ten and Eleven are coming here to winter. They are less than a day's march away."

Aia's heart began to pound.

"Legion Eleven is coming here? Can you see them from your watch tower?"

"We could not before, but we may be able to see the column now."

Aia was breathless.

"May I have a look?"

"Certainly. Let me help—"

Before he could finish, Aia was running up the stairs. She hurled herself into the stone rampart and leaned over straining to see anything. Off in the distant valley to the Northeast was a faint dust cloud. Aia's heart thumped harder in her chest. Her right side began to ache and her forehead and temples throbbed with intense pain. She ignored her body and squinted to see anything in the dust cloud.

As she strained, the familiar darkening began. Shadows came in from all sides. The dust cloud shimmered and began to fade into blackness. Aia knew what was coming. She did not fight it. She turned and sat down against the stone wall allowing the darkness to envelop her.

Epilogue: Letters Home

In the spring of 57BCE, two letters arrived at the estate of Senator Romanus.

        *   *   *

[Address] Deliver at Canino to Titus Claudius Romanus, from his son Marcus Calidius Romanus at the camp of Legio XIII at Ocelum
[Dated] The Kalends of April, in the consulship of P. Cornelius Lentulus Spinther
       Marcus to Titus Claudius Romanus, his father and lord, very many greetings!
       Before all else, I pray for your health and that you may always be well and prosperous, together with my sisters and their families. I am well and I make supplication for you before the gods of this place. Again, I thank you for securing my commission as Senatorial Tribune of Legion XIII. Most important to me is your permission to carry on your cognomen. I am so proud to be Tribunus Laticlavius Romanus. Since my visit with you in Roma to accept my civic crown and my commission from the Senate, I have helped to levy for Caesar two legions in Cisalpine Gaul. I made supplication to my new Legatus that we appoint my Centurion, Tiberius Didius Martial as First Centurion. The other centurions withdrew their appeals and obediently responded to the call for conscription. I have taken my dear friend and cohort colleague Quintus Pompillus of Neapolis as my aide. He agreed with only minor protest. To accept the position, he had to learn to ride a horse. That was almost more difficult than fighting barbarians. We are training the troops very hard and preparing to march into further Gaul soon. Many salutations to my sisters Valeria and Serenilla and their children and to Calidia. Your son salutes you and prays for your continued health and prosperity.

        *   *   *

[Address] Deliver at Canino to Titus Claudius Romanus, from his son Lucius Calidius Vigoratus at Vesontio
[Dated] The Ides of May, in the consulship of P. Cornelius Lentulus Spinther
       Lucius to Titus Claudius Romanus, his father and lord, very many greetings!
       Before all else, I pray for your health and that you may always be well and prosperous, together with my brother and my sisters and their children. I am well and I make supplication for you to the goddesses Salus and Abundantia. Marcus will have visited you by the time you receive my letter. He left immediately when he was called to Roma and has not returned here. I pray for his health and safety. My time with the legions has made me into a better physician and a proper surgeon. It has been my privilege to serve under Caesar. Great surgeons have taught me the craft of battle surgery. Since the end of our campaign, I have used my skills to operate on many Gauls of this place. They never had a surgeon before and they are so grateful. Also, I had the exceptional opportunity to learn about many curious barbarian medications and herbs from a Druid priestess. Unfortunately, during the winter, she died in childbirth. In tribute, I have given my earnings from the winter's

surgeries to the Druid family raising her newborn son and daughter. Pater, this year has been of great benefit to me and I thank you for negotiating my training. With your blessings, I will volunteer for another year of service in the Legion. Many salutations to my brother and my sisters Valeria and Serenilla and their children and to little Calidia. I have sent with this letter the twenty Quadrans I owe her. Your son salutes you and prays for great prosperity and for your continued health.

Source Material

This tale, set during the first year of Caesar's Gallic wars is based upon what we know of daily life, medicine, and surgery in 58 BCE. It is collected from the many sources listed below. A number of books of the era preserve the medical and surgical knowledge of the Greeks and the Romans, and the factual materials in this tale are true to those texts. The practitioners of surgery of that time were quite advanced. It is surprising how long it took modern medicine to rediscover some of those principles.

Few texts detail Celtic life and medicine. The facts concerning the Druids are drawn from many ancient as well as modern texts, current linguistics research, and a little speculation. In the text, the Druid ceremonial prayers are based upon Unitarian and Wiccan ceremonies. Some of the songs, especially the ones related to herbs and flowers, are adapted from the Scottish Gaelic songs chronicled by Carmicheal from a more contemporary time (1900). The curse tablet written by the women of Besançon is madapted from the curse tablet discovered at Larzac, France.

While the chronology follows closely the first year of the Gallic Wars as detailed by Caesar, the characters and their stories are fictional and represent no individuals living or dead.

Thanks to the many who have helped me in this project. Thanks to David MacRae for his encouragement and to Clifford Garstang, Tom Brown and Maryann Lopez for their critiques. Acknowledgement goes to the Historical Collections & Services, Claude Moore Health Sciences Library, University of Virginia for the picture of Roman surgical instrument on the cover.

Gallic Wars
1. Belli gallici liber primus, bellum Ariovisti. Caesar, Julius.(Burns, James Austin translator), Boston, Burns book co. 1901.
2. C. Iuli Caesaris De bello gallico by Julius Caesar Fourth Commentary Holmes, T. Rice. New York : Arno Press, 1979. (Geographical Index)
3. Caesar's conquest of Gaul. Holmes, Thomas Rice. London, Macmillan & Co., 1903.
4. Caesar's Gallic Wars, 58-50 BC. Gilliiver, Kate. Oxford, Osprey Publishing, 2002.

Medicine - Celtic
1. Medicine in ancient Erin: an historical sketch from Celtic to Mediaeval times. Lecture memoranda of the Canadian Medical Association. London, Borroughs Wellcome & Co. 1909.
2. Historical aspects of Celtic medicine. Whittet, Martin M. Proc R Soc Med. 1964; 57 (Sect Hist Med): 429-436.
3. Celtic Medicine in Scotland. Mitchell, Ross. http://www.rcpe.ac.uk/library/read/ scotland/celtic-medicine/celtic-medicine.php.
4. Ancient Celtic Myth, Magic, and Medicine. Klemens, Jonathan. epub Scribd, 2009.

Medicine - Pre-Roman & Roman
1. The Genuine Works of Hippocrates By Hippocrates Edited by: Charles Darwin Adams (translator) New York, Dover 1868.

2. Medicine in the Roman Army. Byrne, Eugene Hugh. The Classical Journal, Vol. 5, No. 6 (Apr., 1910), pp. 267-272, 1910.

3. Outlines of Greek and Roman Medicine. Elliott, James S. New York, William Wood & Co. 1914.

4. Celsus' De Medicina—A Learned and Experienced Practitioner upon what the Art of Medicine could then Accomplish. W. G. Spencer. Proc R Soc Med. 1926; 19 (Sect Hist Med): 129–139, 1926.

5. De Medicina by Celsus. Latin text is that of the Teubner edition by F. Marx, 1915, as reprinted in the Loeb edition, 1935 (Vol. I) and 1938 (Vols. II and III). http://penelope.uchicago.edu/Thayer/E/Roman/Texts/Celsus/home.html

6. Outlines of Greek and Roman Medicine. Elliott, James Sands. New York, William Wood and Company, 1914.

7. The practice of medicine in ancient Rome, Scott, William A. Canad Anaes Soc J, vol. 2, no 8, July, 1955.

8. Botanical Sources of Early Medicines. Keezer, William S. Bios Vol. 34:185-191, 1963.

9. Medicine and the Roman army: a further reconsideration. V Nutton. Med Hist. 1969 July; 13(3): 260–270, 1969.

10. De Medicina by Celsus. Spencer, W.G. (trans.). Cambridge, Massachusetts Harvard University Press, 1971.

11. A History of Medicine. Vol3:. Roman Medicine. Prioreschi, Plinio. Omaha, NE, Horatio. Press, 1998.

12. Aesculapius: a modern tale. Stanton, J. A. JAMA 281(5):476-7, 1999.

13. De Materia Medica: Being an herbal with many other medicinal materials. Dioscordes. Johannesburg South Africa, Ibidis Press, 2000.

14. Surgical Instruments from Ancient Rome. http://www.hsl.virginia.edu/historical/artifacts/roman_surgical/

Medicine - Post-Roman Period

1. The history of prostitution: its extent, causes, and effects throughout the world ; [Being an official report to the Board of alms-house governors of the city of New York]. New York, Harper & Brothers, 1859.

2. Chemistry: general, medical, and pharmaceutical, including the chemistry of the U. S. Pharmacopœia Attfield, John. Philadelphia, Lea Brothers & Co., 1894 (White Poppy - morphine, squill, and oxymel)

3. Gonorrhea in women; its pathology, symptomology, diagnosis, and treatment; together with a review of rare varieties of the disease which occur in men, women, and children. Norris, Charles C. Philadelphia, W. B. Saunders, 1913.

4. Animal Agents and Vectors of Human Disease. Third Edition. Faust, E.C., Beaver, P.C. Jung, R.C. Philadelphia, Lea&Febiger, 1968.

5. Folk medicine; a Vermont doctor's guide to good health. Jarvis, D. C. New York, Holt 1958.

Veterinary Medicine

1. Vegetius Renatus of the distempers of horses, and of the art of curing them : as also of the diseases of oxen, and of the remedies proper for them; and of the best method to preserve them in health, and restore them when sick, and to prevent the spreading and communication of infectious distempers, according to the practice of the ancient Romans London, A Millar, 1748. Digital copy at http://en.scientificcommons.org/46570836http://igitur-archive.library.uu.nl/bijzcoll/

2009-0613-200419/UUindex.html.
2. Opus Agriculturae, De Veterinaria Medicina, De Insitione. Palladius (edited by Robert H. Rodgers). Paris, Comptoir de Fleurus, 1975.
3. The first Latin treatise on horse medicine and its author Pelagonius Saloninus. Fischer, K. D. Medizinhistorisches Journal 16:215-226, 1981.
4. Ancient veterinary medicine. Fischer, K. D. *Medizinhistorisches Journal* 23:191-209, 1988.

Roman Life

1. Roman antiquities: or, An account of the manners and customs of the Romans ... Designed chiefly to illustrate the Latin classics, by explaining words and phrases, from the rites and customs to which they refer. Adams, Alexander. Phidelphia, Mathew Carey, 1807.
2. Popular Antiquities, Volume 3 Illustrating our vulgar customs, ceremonies and superstitions. Brand, John. London, Charles Knight & Co., 1842.
3. A dictionary of Greek and Roman antiquities Smith, William. New York, Harper & Brothers, 1847. (Aster Atticus)
4. The Life of Rome, Rogers, H. L. and Harley, T. R. Oxford, Clarendon Press 1927. (Floor Plan)
5. Around the Roman Table: Food and Feasting in Ancient Rome. Faas, Patrick. Chicago, University of Chicago Press, 2005.
6. Antique Roman Dishes - Collection. http://www.cs.cmu.edu/~mjw/recipes/ethnic/historical/ant-rom-coll.html#1

Linguistics - Latin

1. A dictionary of Latin phrases: comprehending a methodical digest of the various phrases from the best authors, which have been collected in all phraseological works hitherto published, for the more speedy progress of students in Latin composition. Robertson, William. London, A.J. Valpy for Baldwin, Cradock and Joy, 1824
2. A Latin grammar. Hale, William Gardner, Buck, Carl Darling. New York, Atkinson, Mentzer, Grover,1903.
3. The Latin Sexual Vocabulary, Adams, J.N. Baltimore, Johns Hopkins Press, 1983.
4. Classical Swearing: A Vade-Mecum. Baldwin, Barry. Shattercolors Literary Review. http://www.shattercolors.com/nonfiction/baldwin_swearing.htm

Linguistics - Gaulish/Celtic

1. The Carmina Gadelica, volume 1&2. Carmicheal, Alexander. Edinburgh, T & A Constable. 1900.
2. The Cambridge medieval history Bury, John Bagnell. Cambridge, Cambridge University Press, 1911.
3. The Celtic Inscriptions of Cisalpine Gaul (From the Proceedings of the British Academy, Vol. VI). Rhys, John. London, Oxford University Press, 1914.
4. La langue gauloise: grammaire, textes et glossaire By Georges Dottin. Paris, Librairie Klinsksieck, 1920.
5. An etymological dictionary of the Gaelic language. Macbain, Alexander. Glasgow, Gairm Publications. 1982.
6. The Celtic Encyclopedia. Mountain, Harry. http://celtsite.com/, 1997.
7. The Indo-European languages. Ramat, Anna Giacalone, Ramat, Paolo. New York, Routledge, 1998. (Leptonic & Gaulish)

8. The Celtic Languages in Contact: Papers from the Workshop within the Framework of the XIII International Congress of Celtic Studies, Bonn, 26-27 July 2007. Potsdam University Press, 2007.
9. Gaulish Glossary. http://indoeuro.bizland.com/project/glossary/gaul.html.
10. Name Constructions In Gaulish. Tangwystyl verch Morgant Glasvryn (Jones, Heather Rose). http://www.s-gabriel.org/names/tangwystyl/gaulish/.

Linguistics - German
1. Runes and Germanic linguistics By Elmer H. Antonsen.   Berlin, Walter de Gruyter, 2002.

Druids
1. A Brief History of the Druids Ellis, Peter Berresford. New York, Carroll and Graf, 2005.

Gaulish/Celtic Life
1. The Gaulish calendar A reconstruction from the bronze fragments from Coligny with an analysis of its function as a highly accurate lunar-solar predictor of its terminology and development. Olmsted, Garrett S. Bonn, R. Habelt, 1992.
2. Celtic culture: a historical encyclopedia By John T. Koch. Santa Barbara, ABC-CLIO, 2006.

Roman History
1. Consuls of the Roman Republic. Mackay, Christopher S. http://ancienthistory.about.com/gi/dynamic/offsite.htm?site=http://www.ualberta.ca/%7Ecsmackay/Consuls.List.html

Roman Military
1. Roman Era in Britain, Ward, John. London, Methuen & Co. Ltd., 1911.
2. The Roman Soldier Watson, G. R.. Ithaca, Cornell University Press, 1969.
3. Mess Night Manual. United States Department of the Navy, Naval School, Civil Engineer Corps Officers Naval School Civil Engineer Corps Officers Port Hueneme, California August 1986.
4. Roman Military Clothing (Vol 1): 100 BC-AD 200. Sumner, Graham. Oxford, Osprey Publishing, 2002.
5. Roman legionary: 58 BC - AD 69. Cowan, Ross. Oxford, Osprey Publishing, 2003.
6. Legionary: The Roman Soldier's (Unofficial) Manual, Matyszak, Philip. London, Thames and Hudson, Ltd., 2009.

Geography
1. Dictionary of Greek and Roman geography, Volume 2 edited by Sir William Smith. London, Spotswood & Co., 1872.
2. Secret France: Charming Villages & Country Tours edited by Helen Douglas-Cooper, Barbara Mellor. New York, W. W. Norton & Company, 2000.
3. Google Earth
4. Google Maps

Natural Sciences
1. The natural history. Pliny, the Elder. Bostock, John, Riley, Henry T. (translators) London, New York, G. Bell, 1890.

2. Köble, R. and Seufert, G. 2001. Novel maps for forest tree species in Europe. Presented at the Proceedings of the conference "A changing atmosphere" 8th European symposium on the Physico-Chemical Behaviour of Atmosperic Pollutants, 17 – 20 Sept. 2001, Torino.
3. Moon Calendar. http://www.paulcarlisle.net/mooncalendar/   Moon Phase with rise, set & distance (Site requires Java).

Roman Literature

1. Plutarch's lives: translated from the original Greek, with notes critical and historical, and a Life of Plutarch (Vol 1-6). Plutarch, Langhome, John, Langhme, William. London, Edward & Charles Dilly, 1770.
2. Marcus Tullius Cicero, Letters of Marcus Tullius Cicero. Melmoth, William (translator). New York, P F Collier & Son, 1909.
3. The Poems of Catullus - A Bilingual Edition. Catullus, Gaius Valerius (Author), Green, Peter (Translator). Berkeley, University of California Press, 2007.
4. Plautus, Volume 1 Plautus, Titus Maccius, Nixon, Paul (Translator). New York, G.P. Putnam & Sons, 1916.
5. Sportive epigrams on Priapus by divers poets in English verse and prose translation by Leonard C. Smithers and Sir Richard Burton. 1890. Scanned at www.sacred-texts.com, December 2000.
6. Martial's Epigrams: A Selection. Wills, Gary (translator). New York, Viking. 2008.

Miscellaneous

1. Ode to East Tennessee, Haynes, Landon C. http://www.johnsonsdepot.com/southern/landon.pdf.
2. Logging: the principles and general methods of operation in the United States Bryant, Ralph Clement. New York, John Wiley and Sons, 1913.
3. Google Maps and Google Earth.